The Long Shadow

LORETTA PROCTOR

Matador
9 Priory Business Park
Kibworth Beauchamp
Leicestershire LE8 0RX, UK
Tel: (+44) 116 279 2299
Fax: (+44) 116 279 2277
Email: books@troubador.co.uk
Web: www.troubador.co.uk/matador

ISBN 978 1783060 542

British Library Cataloguing in Publication Data.
A catalogue record for this book is available from the British Library.

Typeset in Aldine401 BT Roman by Troubador Publishing Ltd
Printed and bound in the UK by TJ International, Padstow, Cornwall
Front cover design by Bradley Wind www.bradleywind.com
Cover photo courtesy of The Salonika Campaign Society

Matador is an imprint of Troubador Publishing Ltd

Author's Note

The General Hospital in Dorothy's Diary and the village of Mistres are purely fictional and in many ways a composite of the many isolated mountain villages, hospitals and experiences of the people who were on active service in the various V.A.D units and hospitals scattered about Salonika. Most of the General Hospitals were situated around the Kalamaria area, past the main city. Later on as the need grew greater with the influx of malarial cases that was weakening the army, others sprang up on the lower slopes of the Hortiach mountains. Nurses and recruits from The Voluntary Aid Detachments and other medical staff moved from hospital to hospital quite frequently but my characters have had to stay put together a lot longer in the same place in order to fulfil the requirements of the plot.

If there are errors to be found in descriptions of Army life and procedure, rebetika music and Salonika life in general, they are entirely my own and I hope will be overlooked in the interests of allowing the story to proceed and take shape.

Much of my research was amongst the letters, photos, diaries and books written at that time which were kindly loaned to me by the Imperial War Museum, British Red Cross Society, the latter having helped me in my researches since the 1970's when I first became interested in this long forgotten 'sideshow' of the Great War. I am very grateful for all the support and help I received.

PART ONE
DOROTHY'S DIARY

Chapter 1

December 1932

A sudden clanging and banging of car doors. Grandma Clarke's two fat, little Pekes began to set up a furious racket, unused as they were to any disturbance in the quiet and monotonous routine at Downlands. Sara and Rose, scurried about like ants that had just had their neat little anthill broken up by a child with a stick. Panic seemed to pervade them at the dire fact that someone unexpected had arrived at the door and was awaiting attendance.

Sara half ran to the front door but paused and composed herself before opening it. The fact that she had to open the door at all was still a source of deep grievance to her. When she had come to work here as a young kitchen maid, there had been a manservant to open the door and a parlour maid, plus Rose Grant the cook, two gardeners and a coachman. But that had been before the war and all those men had gone to their graves. The parlour maid had married a man who was promoted to an officer and got well above herself ...wanting to be called Madam, can you believe it! ...now only Rose and a gardener remained besides herself. Somehow they managed to keep the place going between them and still maintain the exacting standards of their employer. It was hard work, believe me, it was hard work! Only loyalty and habit kept her there.

'Lord above, it's Miss Agnes!' she exclaimed in great astonishment.

'Yes, of course it's us, my dear woman. Do stop gaping like a fish and go and tell Mother we've arrived,' said Agnes, sweeping into the hallway in her usual dramatic manner.

Though she was now the Hon. Mrs Patterwood, the two old servants still called her Miss Agnes which she rather liked as it made her feel younger. She in turn treated them with little respect. As far as she was concerned, they were part of the Downlands furniture since her birth and would always be there. Following in the magnificent wake of Agnes Patterwood were her husband Henry and their only son, Reginald.

Andrew, attracted by the noise, came to the top of the stairs and leant over the banisters to watch them, a sense of dismay pervading his soul at the thought of his aunt and uncle having arrived so early. He had really looked forward to a few peaceful days alone. Screwing up his face in annoyance, he sat down at the top of the stairs and listened to them, while wishing them a hundred miles away.

During the last two or three years he had spent most of his school holidays at Downlands, the old family home of the Clarke family, preferring it to his mother's home in London. The town house there always seemed so full of children, full of people coming and going. It made sense to come here for his school was in Gloucestershire and nearer to Downlands than to London. But if he was honest with himself – and he was always honest with himself even if not always with other people – he had suddenly become keen to spend his holidays here after the birth of his half-brother Fred. Yes, he had to be honest. That was when he had begun to feel that he was no longer the centre of his mother's love and attention. And that had been painful because Mother had always been the most important part of his universe till then.

Downlands was a quiet, decaying old place set in the soft rolling hills of the Gloucestershire countryside. There was a peaceful emptiness in the house with just the three older women. Grandma Clarke was strict but kind and mainly left Andrew to his own devices. Provided he turned up on time for his meals and behaved quietly and properly, she didn't ask where he went during the day or what he got up to and that suited him very well.

He enjoyed being the centre of all this feminine attention, spoilt by Rose who made him special cakes and titbits to please him. Sara, though cross at times when he came in from the woods and traipsed over her clean kitchen floor in his boots, was generally affectionate and remembered him as a baby, born at Downlands at the end of the war. He often asked her to tell him about this time, trying to piece his own forgotten history together from the fragmented memories of the two old servants. Grandma never spoke of these times and he was afraid to ask her. Sad memories made her unhappy and fretful.

The two servants indulged him, allowed him into the enveloping warmth of their kitchen, let him sit with them near the big black range where things boiled and bubbled in cauldrons, a witches place, yet good to be in, comforting, inviting and entertaining. Andrew loved the old kitchen with its stone-flagged floors, the cool, mysterious pantry with its forbidden interior of shelves on which gleamed jars of jams, chutneys and pickles. Rose had always towered here, a large-breasted, comfortable presence yet at times alarming in her magisterial sway over her domain. Even Grandma Clarke seldom ventured into the kitchen but issued her orders and requests from the parlour, content to leave Rose in charge.

Sara, in contrast, was thin, sharp and gaunt, but in her greying head was a wealth of fascinating local stories which she would begin to tell him as he sat at the huge deal table helping her to shell peas, watching her deft fingers peeling carrots and potatoes, topping and tailing green beans, dicing and chopping away, deeply absorbed in the minutiae of her work. And even as she chopped and sifted and shelled and sorted, she would be talking, speaking out her tales which she knew by heart.

They were gentle tales, sometimes trite, sometimes amusing, never unkind or malicious. Ghost tales, love affairs that had shocked the neighbourhood, war stories, humorous incidents down at Cottersley Farm like the day old Stevens' billy-goat had caught him bending over and butted him hard in the backside. The irate farmer had seized the goat by the horns and stared him angrily in the eye and told him never to try *that* trick again!

And the goat had been terrified out of its wits and highly respectful of old Stevens after that. Andrew loved the story; he could just picture the man and goat, eye to eye, brute strength against brute strength, will of animal against will of human. They were often the same stories over and over again. The repetition soothed him, made him feel a strange sense of peace and order.

If he had but known it, the two women felt sorry for him. They told each other he was a good lad, obliging, polite, a little brusque at times, but then all his family were like that. He was no real trouble. They concluded that he was a lonely, little soul, something dreamy and lost about him, an outsider. He never seemed to have any real friends, was never noisy and tearaway as other lads were. He loved to wander for miles alone or else had his nose buried in books, just like his Grandad, the old Professor. It wasn't that he lacked spirit, he was just withdrawn and thoughtful a good deal of the time.

But then it wasn't surprising, given his history.

For a brief while each summer and winter Andrew would walk about the woods and the gardens and imagine he would one day be master of the house; it would be his very own. He would marry someone rich and beautiful and have lots of children who would walk these paths with him, play in the woods, learn the secret paths he knew. It was a fantasy, of course; Aunt Agnes was the one who would inherit Downlands, not his mother Dorothy. He had once overheard Aunt Agnes say to Uncle Henry that she would sell the wretched place as soon as it was hers; she had always hated the cold, sombre old house stuffed full of unpleasant memories and ghosts from the past. Besides the Patterwoods always needed the money. Henry never seemed to do very well and drank most of any profits he ever made on his shares and investments.

Perhaps it was knowing that this would be the ultimate fate of his beloved Downlands that made Andrew so resent the intrusion of Agnes and her family. He could not have felt as put out as poor Sara though. The Christmas supplies had not yet been delivered and the pantry held only the usual frugal amount for those present in the house.

She announced the guests to an astonished and vastly irritated Mrs Clarke and then hurried off to let Rose know the news.

'Oh, Mama, darling!' said Agnes, sweeping into the parlour and startling the old lady who was seated close by the fire, reading a book and almost lost in a huge, sagging armchair. Mrs Clarke took off her spectacles and frowned at the intruders much in the manner of her grandson, Andrew, who now lurked on the stairs with no anxiety to join his relations yet curious to hear what they had to say.

'You don't look pleased to see us at all,' said Agnes giving Mrs Clarke a huge kiss which the old lady wiped away at once with a pucker of her lips. She hated demonstrations and Agnes was always so demonstrative.

'I didn't expect you till Thursday,' was the frosty reply, 'what d'you mean by descending like this without even a word? Why didn't you telephone? I haven't a thing in the house and it's far too late in the day to call up Simmonds the butcher. It is most uncivil of you Agnes.'

'Mama! And I thought you'd be *so* pleased. Why, Henry has a few extra days off and we felt we'd come down a bit earlier as a surprise, you know. Isn't it a surprise? Isn't it? Don't worry about the food. We've brought plenty of things with us for Christmas.'

Agnes as always had come fully prepared for she knew well the frugality of her mother's table, even at Christmas-tide and Henry, who found it hard to survive in such a tee-total atmosphere, always brought a few bottles of brandy with him. Mrs Clarke had no objection to alcohol. It reminded her of her late husband, Professor Clarke, when she saw Henry settling down after dinner with his brandy and his cigar. It always brought a smile to her lips, pleasant, tender memories.

'There, Mama dear, I knew you'd be glad to see us,' smiled Agnes as she fussed with her mother's shawl, drawing it about her shoulders and making the old lady fidget crossly but feel pleased nonetheless.

'Oh, God, it's so cold in here and you're always sitting in the dark. Mama, honestly …you're not that poor! Do put on the lights before it gets pitch dark.'

For Mrs Clarke always insisted on waiting until it was really dark and impossible to see anything before putting on the electric lights, yet another of her economical measures which came partly from a nature frugal in itself and partly from the deprivations of the war years. As always, Agnes ignored these mandates and turned on all the lamps in the room.

'You'll catch a death of cold, Mama, you really do need looking after …Henry, put some more logs on the fire and get a blaze up.'

'Nonsense!' said Mrs Clarke. 'It isn't cold at all. It's you who need looking after. You've hardly got on any clothes, no wonder you're cold. Really, you young women wear so little on nowadays.'

Henry Patterwood who had followed Agnes into the room now shook hands dutifully with his mother-in-law. He complied with his wife's request and poked the fire into a blaze then stood before it blocking the warmth from everyone in the room, hands clasped behind his back, nodding and smiling benignly on all and sundry. He was a tall, beefy man with a reddish complexion and an unhealthy look about him due to his fondness for drink. His face had the puffed up look of someone whose veins ran with brandy instead of blood.

'And where is my dear boy …where is Reginald?' asked Grandma Clarke.

Andrew from his hiding place at the top of the stairs suddenly felt his heart rise up in him like some black monster that threatened to choke him. Grandma never spoke to *him* in that tender tone, the voice wheedling and flattering. He was glad she didn't but at the same time felt jealous of her preference for his fair cousin. Reggie *was* beautiful, there was no denying it, a fair Apollo, soft tender blue eyes like a woman's, blonde hair that fell in locks across his forehead despite the careful brushing and parting, figure tall, slender, graceful. He was everything Andrew was not.

'Grandma!' said Reggie as if in echo of his mother and he came over to the old lady taking her hand and kissing it with an air of gallantry many would have felt to be ridiculous but which pleased the old lady mightily as he had known it would.

She looked upon the young man with a fond eye. He was so like her Richard; yes …so like dear, dear Richard! In this young man was an incarnation of her eternally handsome and youthful son, lost in his bloom, lost in that terrible war. The down of a blonde moustache now forming on the upper lip completed the likeness and she almost caught her breath and looked at the boy with awe for the likeness was so similar. Andrew had understood long ago just why Grandma loved Reggie. Yet surely she failed to see that despite the uncanny similarity there was something missing in the look of Reggie's eyes and that mouth as soft as a girl's. Uncle Richard's face had shown character and strength.

'Are you expecting Dot and her husband this year?' asked Agnes who, having shooed off Henry, seated herself as near to the fire as she could without setting herself ablaze.

'They are coming Thursday. Andrew is already here …where can he be, I wonder? He *must* have heard the commotion …'

Andrew sank deeper into the shadows of the hallway for he had no wish to join the company. His Aunt and Uncle were always civil but cold and treated him as if he was an inferior.

'He comes from a country of brigands, for goodness sakes!' Agnes would say in a loud, disparaging whisper and he knew she meant him to hear her. ' We only have Dot's word for it that his father was an officer and a gentleman. That boy is so wilful and passionate! It just doesn't matter what school you send him to, he'll never be an English gentleman!'

Chapter 2

Having no desire to meet his relations and feeling their early arrival to be a dire intrusion on his privacy, Andrew took himself off via the kitchen, where a flustered looking Rose was beginning to peel a mound of potatoes. Thrusting a cap on his head and hands in pockets he whistled for Joe, his little mongrel friend, but the dog was nowhere to be seen, out on some expedition of his own. He set off with speed into the grounds for a solitary and thoughtful walk. He wasn't quick enough however and Reggie, spying him from the drawing room window, set off after him. When Andrew heard the light step on the gravel he knew who it was without turning and turn he would not but quickened his pace, hoping to put a distance between them. Reggie, though, was persistent and called him over and over again. Andrew pretended not to hear but the older boy managed to catch up so that he was obliged to turn and acknowledge him.

'Andrew, how jolly nice to see you!' said Reggie, shaking his cousin's reluctant hand. 'Didn't you know we were here? Rather a surprise, eh? Nearly gave poor old Grandma a heart attack.'

'Why the hell did you come so early?' was the less than welcoming reply, 'I thought you didn't like it here and swore never to come again?'

'No more do I, I hate the place. It's so deadly dull to have to spend Christmas here when I could go down to London with friends and have a lark. But Ma likes the family get-together. Boring though, isn't it? Thank God, she's brought some food with her at least, or we'd be lucky to get a slice of ham each.'

Andrew looked across the steel grey lake with its ancient willows bending over it. There was a beauty in the severe starkness that stretched to the horizon, framed with the soft auburn mistiness of birch trees that had shed their abundance of leaves and now stood delicate, shivering and naked in the wind. The morning's promise of sunshine had clouded over and a deep heavy feeling was in the air, lowering almost down to the waters of the lake. The air was full of drops of moisture that clung to one's face, not a day for 'creaky old bones' as Rose would say ruefully. Heavy and grey, cold and damp, yet the sloping gardens and the little lake of Downlands, the woodland and bare fields of Cottersley Farm that lay beyond were beautiful in his eyes. Beautiful, perhaps, because they had an air of impermanence for him.

'How can't you like it here?' Andrew mused. 'It's a glorious place to be.'

Reggie's eye followed his gaze and he looked at the scene as if for the first time but nothing kindled in him.

'It's nice enough, Drew, old chap, don't get me wrong,' he said in his earnest, conciliatory way, 'as houses go it's perfectly all right. A touch of paint would smarten it up in no time. It's the company ...not you, of course!' he added hastily, 'I didn't mean you; don't know what I'd do without you. It's the old uns. It's always the same isn't it? Year in, year out. Next year, I'm rebelling and going to accept the Murdoch's invitation to go to their place. Haven't you got a pal *you* can go and stay with?'

'Don't mind about me,' Andrew smiled. 'I like my own company.'

'Wish I could say the same for myself,' said Reggie, 'I like people about me ...but you were always a loner, Drew. I remember you used to wander off for hours as a kid and Grandma Clark used to go mad when you were late for tea.'

'She still does.'

'Oh well, she never changes, does she? Bless her and all that but she's like an army sergeant. Bet you were glad when you were sent off to school. I know I was and Mother isn't anything like Grandma. She lets me do pretty well anything, though she has got this thing about family reunions and duty and all that stuff, but she's decent most of the time. So I feel I have to conform a bit.'

'I love it here, Reg, I suppose I'm a country type, not a townee.'

'God, I prefer the town anytime. The country's dead as a doornail. Don't you think you'll like parties and theatres and all that when you go to University? I mean what's life without some fun?'

'I don't think so. Ma says I take after Grandpa Clarke. He was a great reader and I am too. Much prefer books for company.'

'Sooner you than me.'

Reggie fished a small packet of Gold Flake cigarettes from his pocket and offered one to Andrew.

'Oh, go on, take two ...it's Christmas!'

Andrew wanted to say no but he couldn't resist. Reggie had started him off on cigarettes about a year ago and it was now a habit, hard to break. They had to be very careful not to let Grandma know about it or there'd be hell to pay. But breaking rules was what life was all about at fourteen. Reggie wasn't such a bad old thing, he decided. He seemed so worldly and full of that gooey charm people seemed to like while Andrew felt himself to be very naïve and socially stupid. He just didn't seem to have that smooth charm, couldn't do it at all. He knew he was too blunt and outspoken. People took offence at that. It seemed unfair that being truthful was offensive

The two young men lit the cigarettes and walked along in silence together.

'I managed to matriculate, thank God,' Reggie said after while, 'got through all the subjects just about and now they want me to cram again and get into Sandhurst. I'm not sure that's what I want anyway. To be a soldier, you know.'

'I once thought I'd like to be a soldier,' said Andrew. 'I suppose most boys do. It seemed romantic. I know that's stupid, but it did. I think it was when Ma first showed me Uncle Richard's room. You've seen it, haven't you?'

'I have and think it's morbid. He's been dead years now and Grandma keeps it as a bloody shrine. '

Andrew looked sad. 'Oh, Reg! Poor old Gran, she really loved him, you know. I don't think it's morbid. He looked so smart in his uniform, so noble somehow.'

'Noble to die? Not my idea of fun,' said Reggie with a shudder.

'I do feel it was noble, Reggie. I do. He died to save our country. I just feel all those men were so great …my father was a soldier, he died to save his country too.' Andrew felt overcome for a few moments as he thought of his father. The father he would never know. He tried not to let the little break creep in his voice but Reggie heard it and looked away, embarrassed.

'Anyway,' Andrew went on, 'when I mentioned it to Ma, she nearly had a fit. She really doesn't want me to be a soldier. She wants me to go in the Civil Service.'

'Oh, God, how boring!'

'Well, that's what I think. I don't know *what* I want to do. Sometimes I feel I have no real future.' The boy looked unhappy and flung stones into the bushes aimlessly as if at some unknown assailant.

'Don't be stupid,' said Reggie. 'Everyone knows you're the swot of the family. You'll do well. I'm the one who hasn't a clue.'

'So, why don't you want to go in the army?'

'Well, what's the point? There'll never be another war, will there? They've got the League of Nations and all that now. Of course, there *are* some amusing compensations. The uniform would look awfully smart and the girls always go for a uniform. I don't fancy all that training though. It sounds absolutely ghastly from what I've heard and just suppose one had to go off and fight somewhere? …some colonial rebellion or other may crop up. They're always up to something, these darkies, they can never be at peace. Be just my luck to end up on the North West Frontier or something.'

'Yes, just suppose you were shot at …it might spoil your uniform!'

Reggie just laughed in his easy pleasant way and refused to take offence at this piece of irony.

Andrew whistled again for Joe. This time there was a response and the dog came rushing forth from the undergrowth to greet his master and jumped up with energetic enthusiasm at both the boys.

Reggie fended the dog off with a look of disgust. 'Good heavens, whose is this scruffy mongrel?'

'Mine.'

'Where on earth did he turn up from? I don't recall you having him last year.'

'I found him in the woods with a dead litter. Some beast had left them in the woods to die.'

'God, I'm surprised at Grandma letting you keep him. I mean he might have anything wrong with him and pass it on to her dear doggy-woggies.'

'I would say the opposite is more likely,' said Andrew with a shrug. 'He's far healthier than those fancy little Pekes that can hardly breathe properly. Anyone knows a mongrel is far healthier. I don't like pedigree dogs of any kind.'

Reggie laughed. He could have taken this comment personally too as his father might be reckoned as 'a pedigree' but he was used to Andrew's candid comments and, anyway, had to agree with him. Henry Patterwood was by no means a healthy man and it was no one's fault but his own.

Reggie looked curiously at his cousin every now and then as they walked in silence through the woods, Joe darting in and out of the bushes before them.

Andrew was a handsome enough chap, wiry and strong. Reggie had heard that he wasn't that bad at cricket either. But he was a bit of an odd fish. Something about his cousin didn't really fit in with the family. His hair was quite black, though tinged with auburn at times when the sun caught it, his eyes a liquid, dark brown. The Clarkes were a fair or red headed family. Dorothy, Andrew's mother still had beautiful auburn hair, almost coppery and her eyes were a deep blue. Reggie had always thought his Aunt Dorothy an attractive person.

He had heard something of the scandal, of course, but only vague rumours. His mother, Agnes, didn't like to speak of it but little things slipped out now and then. Reggie was not of a curious or critical disposition but he gathered that Dorothy had come back from Greece during the war in disgrace. She wasn't married and she was expecting Andrew. Awful Disgrace. Fancy Aunt Dot being such a tearaway.

Still, he reflected, it was hard on poor old Andrew. Didn't know his father; born a bastard. No wonder he was such an odd fish.

Chapter 3

The two young men had been sent forth by Agnes with clippers and a barrow to fetch holly and mistletoe from the woods. The job appealed to Andrew who hated to be cooped up indoors for too long. They walked down to the woods, Reggie shivering and complaining of the cold air all the way.

Andrew clipped away, loading the little barrow with boughs while Reggie looked round aimlessly for branches within easy reach. Andrew always felt at home in the woods and it rather amused him to lead his city cousin in deeper and deeper, knowing full well this made Reggie uneasy.

'God, it's getting dark in here,' said Reggie, looking about him, 'you're sure you know the way out again, Drew, old chap?'

Andrew looked at him with some contempt. Here in the woods, the fields and lanes he was in command of the situation, unlike Reggie, and this made him feel less inferior. He couldn't help but savour the situation.

'A baby could find its way out, Reg.'

'Bloody baby wouldn't be in here, it would have more sense!' muttered his cousin. Then Reggie emitted a very unchristian curse as an enraged holly bush seized his hand. 'Damn this stuff, this is no fun! Haven't we got enough yet?'

'Look, you cut off somewhere and leave me to do the job; you're just wrecking the trees.'

'Couldn't leave you to do this beastly job alone.'

'Really don't mind a bit.'

Reggie looked relieved but then, like his father, he was never fond of any kind of work and getting out of 'beastly jobs' was always his intention.

'In that case, I'll pop down to the village for a bit of a constitutional …if I can find my way out of this wretched place. There's a rather nice little creature I saw down there the other day …what did you say her name was?'

'Heaven knows, you spoke to so many.'

'The one with the fair hair, who else? The little lass in the Post Office.'

'Oh, Molly Cox,' said Andrew in the tone of one as yet relatively indifferent to the pleasure of pretty girls.

'Ah, that was it! Well, off to see Molly Cox …you're absolutely sure you don't mind?'

At last the partly reluctant, partly eager Reggie slipped off to the village, quipping cheerfully, 'and send the search parties out if I'm not back for tea!' leaving Andrew in peace with his own thoughts.

On the walk back to the house, Andrew began to feel a shift in the atmosphere. A mild wind bent the trees towards him caressingly, touching his face with their twiggy hands and the evensong of the birds sounded like an ancient melody sung specially for him. Something in the thrilling liquid whistles and trills always made him shiver strangely inside as if it beckoned him to a pure and more luminous world that he could neither enter nor understand. Even the house as he approached it looked less grey and cold. The indefatigable Agnes had lit up all the lamps and yellow light streamed out onto the lawn giving a friendly, welcoming look, a cheering sense of warmth and companionship.

Andrew left his barrow load of green stuff by the kitchen door. As soon as he entered the hallway, he knew that his mother, her husband Ethan and their two young children had arrived. A doll had been dropped on the rug by a small hand; an abandoned shoe followed on hard after that. He smiled to himself and a feeling of tenderness stirred his heart for his little half-sister May. She was a charming mite who worshipped him.

Agnes had by now installed the Christmas tree in the hallway and was busy decorating it, eagerly assisted by the elder of his mother's children, Fred Willoughby. Andrew ruffled up his brother's ginger poll in greeting and received a mock punch in return. A sense of bustling festivity now pervaded the air with the new arrivals.

He went into the drawing room. Dorothy was seated in an armchair with little May on her lap, the Pekes sitting on her skirts and Ethan bending assiduously over her. She was looking up at Ethan with that gentle, tender look she always had for her husband. They seemed to be in a special world of their own when they looked at one another like this. Andrew, ever jealous, burned with the discomfort he always felt when he saw them together.

It was not that he disliked Ethan. He was a very good man; no one could fault him. He had been a brilliant surgeon in his day, forced against his will to retire early due to ill health. He was thin now and almost emaciated, his face hollowed in the cheeks, his hair receding and grey. There was always a look of suffering about him though he never complained about a thing. Towards Andrew he had always been kind and considerate, thinking nothing of paying his school fees and doing his best to set the boy up in life.

Dorothy looked after Ethan with immense tenderness. Her nursing skills helped to keep this man alive, of that there was no doubt. That he loved Dorothy with a deep devotion was evident to all. He never tried to hide the fact yet was not a demonstrative man. It shone out of him, the urgent love he bore for his wife. People were often genuinely moved by this couple who seemed to live for one another despite the very obvious difference in their ages.

Although Dorothy was not pretty as Agnes was pretty, she had a beauty that was quite different. There couldn't be more of a contrast in their appearance. Agnes was slender, fair and elegant in a patrician style. Dorothy who was now almost forty had become just a little plump and was never too bothered about fashionable clothes as long as she looked neat and clean. Her beauty lay in the fine mass of chestnut brown hair, now slightly greying at the temples, which fluffed around her face in an artless, natural manner, constantly escaping from a soft bun at the nape of her neck. All the family were blue-eyed but Dot's were the most vivid blue, the iris ringed with a black circle that made them all the more startling and lovely.

'Andrew, my *dear* boy!' she said as her eldest son entered the room and came up to her, kissing her upturned face.

'Dwoo!' cried little May holding out her arms and chuckling as her brother swept her up into the air.

'Glad to see you, sir!' said Andrew returning his sister to her mother's arms and shaking hands warmly with Ethan.

Now he was happy. His own people were here. He felt their welcome; he knew they belonged to him. It struck him then that he was foolish to isolate himself from this warm and happy family. Why did he do so? He knew why. Foolish as it was, he was jealous of Ethan's love for his mother and her love for him. It excluded him in some way and he felt no part of it as he might have done if Ethan had been his father. If only Ethan *was* his father. How different things might have been!

However, none of this should be dwelt upon now. It was Christmas time and peace and goodwill were meant to reign and unpleasant thoughts turned aside.

They had just listened to the first Christmas day broadcast given by King George. It was such a historic moment. Listening to the King and his words made them all fall quiet, even the little ones seemed subdued, silenced by the adult emotions.

Dinner had been plentiful enough, the frugal provisions of Grandma Clarke enhanced by the bounty of both the Patterwoods and the Willoughby's. Everyone now felt replete and came into the drawing room to relax by the roaring fire and to open their presents as it was the custom to do this after dinner rather than first thing in the morning.

Ethan was delighted with a copy of '*Brave New World*' by Aldous Huxley and began to read it at once. Henry yawned considerably, dosed himself with brandy and fell fast asleep in his armchair. Grandma soon joined him in slumber and Agnes began to flick her way through the pages of the latest Vogue, having delighted herself over her presents, which were mainly jewellery. Reggie had set off for what he called 'an after dinner walk' but Andrew suspected was more likely an assignation with Molly Cox from the village. Reggie had smuggled a piece of mistletoe into his pocket and Andrew had spotted this and laughed to himself. What a silly idiot!

'I'll take the little ones to their room for a nap,' Dorothy whispered to her son.

'Are *you* going to have a nap, Ma?'

'I think I shall go to my room and rest a little. You do the same, my dear. You have plenty of new books to read now. I thought you'd be pleased with the new Agatha Christie …you love mysteries, don't you?'

'Life is a mystery,' said Andrew, looking at his mother strangely, 'something I am always trying to solve.'

His mother looked at him for a moment. A little frown crossed her face but she made no comment. She gathered up the two sleepy youngsters and took them upstairs with her to the old nursery at the top of the house.

After a while Andrew looked over at Ethan. The book had now dropped from his fingers and he too was asleep and Agnes looked likely to follow suit fairly soon. He rose quietly and left the room carrying his books under his arm.

It had been such a marvel to hear the King speak as he did. The miracles of the modern world thrilled Andrew and he contemplated the idea of a career in telegraph or wireless communications of some kind. Recently he had tried to make himself his own set following the instructions in an old copy of *Practical Wireless* that Ethan had given him ages ago. He was almost there. It would be marvellous to tune into other people all over the world. So far his set was a huge thing that took up half the table in his room and had six valves, several switches and coils everywhere but he hadn't yet figured out how to make a loudspeaker, nor had he persuaded his grandma to let him set up a pole to pick up signals on the shed roof. She might be more affable about the idea now for she too had been delighted when she heard the King speak.

'I have never, ever before heard his Majesty's voice,' she had said, deeply moved.

As Andrew tiptoed up the stairs with their huge, polished balustrades and rails, he felt a different mood come upon him, one that was mellow and romantic. This large hallway always had a sense of the past about it. The dark panelling was so well polished by Sara that he could see his ghostly reflection in it, wavering over the shining panels and gliding along with him mysteriously.

Leaning over the banisters, he looked down into the hall below with its decorated Christmas tree on which little candles glimmered here and there. There were old chairs in worn red velvet and the dull gleam of framed pictures on the walls. Vague disjointed memories of characters in novels floated through his mind, noble heroes from his favourite books or beautiful, tragic heroines whose lives were filled with love and passion and excitement. All these phantom images crowded and flickered and danced in quick succession through his mind.

Perhaps it was the effect of the wine he had been allowed and the brandy he had tasted afterwards. He felt disembodied for a moment, floating in the past, and a strange sense of unreality came over him. For a brief moment, he seemed to live a thousand lives; it was as if there were ghosts in the house who wanted him to know and understand them and bring them to life again, bridge the time lapse and be present in their own era. Then the feeling ebbed away, the visions and fantasies were gone.

As he went to his room, which was near the back of the house, he passed his mother's room and saw the door was ajar. He glanced through the crack as he went by and saw her seated at her little desk. She seemed to be looking in a small box and holding a photo up before the light to see it better. It was difficult for Andrew to see who the person was but he felt sure it was a dark haired man in uniform, a soldier. But who?

The answer burst upon him like a lightening bolt. His first feeling was to fling open the door and challenge his mother but sensing his presence she hastily put the photograph back in the box and replaced the lid.

Turning she said, 'Is it you, Drew?'

She looked a little flushed. The wine perhaps? Or her sudden sense of guilt?

Andrew stood at the door and looked at her speechlessly.

'What is it, dear?'

She shrank back before his compelling gaze and looked so forlorn suddenly, so vulnerable. Andrew couldn't bear it. Thick, stony castle walls had been built about her over the years; for a brief moment he sensed he had spied a chink that he might break through. Yet he also felt that if he did so he would regret it, destroy her in some way; lose her love.

He did not dare. He had to tell a lie this time.

'Nothing, Mother, I just saw the door open and came to say hello.'

Her shoulders settled down as if with relief. She smiled and blew him a kiss.

'I'm going to lie down a little now,' she said, 'close the door after you, there's a dear.'

He did so and went on to his own room. As he shut the door softly behind him he came to a decision that was to alter his life forever.

Chapter 4

Another of these sudden flashes of memory. As a child of four or five he had passed that half-open door and seen his mother in there. She hadn't noticed him come into the room on that occasion and he had seen her putting that very box back into a cupboard, right at the very back, covering it with a cloth. Then she had moved to her desk …and what was this vague flash of a memory …had she opened a little drawer into which she put something shiny, perhaps a little key? …the key to that box!

She had turned then and seen him. He had held out his arms and asked to be picked up and she had done so, hugging him very hard. There had been tears in her eyes and even then he had wondered why. The tears soon went and she was as she always was. Mother obviously supposed that he'd forgotten this little incident and so he had – but it now returned to his mind, fresh and vivid. He even recalled that her dress was blue, the exact colour of her lovely eyes. She was the most beautiful person in the world to him then and now.

The significance of her actions had meant nothing to him at the time but now he knew that this enigmatic box contained all her secrets and that those secrets underpinned her life, fed and nourished her very being and that he too was captured in that deep dark web. Struggle as he might his mother would not free him and he could not free himself.

Andrew had formed a plan in his head and was determined to carry it out. He knew what he planned was wrong but felt that he too had a right in this matter. He had caught that glimpse of his father. There *was* a photograph of him and his mother refused to let him see it. Nobody in the family had ever really mentioned his background, his father and mother's past. In that unspoken way in which children skirt around adult sensitivities and feel the undertow of secret happenings moving beneath the family life like some great dark, underground river, he had never dared to ask. Almost never dared to wonder.

He knew that in some way his birth was not quite right; that it was to be glossed over, not mentioned, pushed away into some secret space he was not allowed to know about. His heart hurt thinking of this unknown father. Andrew knew only that he had been a Greek Officer who had died bravely in battle. There was comfort in that. It sounded glorious and brave and heroic. He could be proud of that at least.

When mother spoke of his father, which was very seldom, her face would change. It would soften, retreat into some deep place where no-one could reach her. There had been many times she had shut herself up in her room alone and asked not to be disturbed. In those lone moments she had been looking in that wooden box and he felt certain it held all the answers to her past and to his own beginnings. There had been many, many such moments with a sadness about her at those times that he had never really understood and vaguely felt had something to do with him. He had felt guilty but had no idea why he should.

He had to look in that box. He had to know and understand.

Mother loved Ethan Willoughby, he was sure of that. His mother was not an insincere person but deep feeling and loving. It was not in her to pretend to love. Yet, something else held her heart beyond the present and her happy, comfortable, respectable life with Willoughby. It was that early, unspoken love for his father and his sudden end that held her. Young as Andrew was, he understood that much.

There was nothing he could do while all the family were there but in a few days time they would all return to their London homes and he would be alone once more. There was a brief respite before he returned to school and in those few days Andrew was determined to find a way of opening that box.

The last wave and the last goodbye had been uttered by his grandmother and himself. The cars turned out of the gates and into the main road. Andrew ran to the gates and with a clang, shut them after his departing relations.

'Well!' said his grandmother looking at him in astonishment. 'You seem mighty glad to see them all off, young man.'

If you only knew how much, he thought, his heart fluttering with strange excitement.

'To be honest, I'm not so sorry either,' sighed the old lady, drawing her coat about her shoulders, 'these festivities are beginning to tire me more and more each year. We shall have some peace and quiet now, won't we Andrew?'

'We will, Grandma.'

She smiled and leant a little on his shoulder and he helped her back to the house, holding an umbrella over her head for it had begun to rain again. She did look tired and seemed glad to sit herself down.

'I like routine and all these visitors do so confuse me at times. They all have their own ways and patterns. It's a shame to admit but when we get older we do want predictable patterns in our lives, not shocks and surprises. I've had far too many of those.'

'Poor Grandma.'

'Oh, poor nothing! Everyone had them …it was the war, my dear, and not a family went unscathed but didn't lose a relation. The first few years were so sad after the war. Everyone wore mourning and everyone was grieving. And then all those silly young people just forgot the whole thing in five minutes and were dancing and jigging about and singing such ridiculous songs and acting as if nothing had happened.'

'Did Mother do that?'

'Oh, no. Dorothy was always a serious person. She wasn't the jigging sort, that's why I was so surprised when …'Grandma veered away from the fascinating but dangerous topic of Dorothy's misdemeanours, not wishing to rouse her grandson's interest. It had been hard to fend of his questions when he was very young and she was relieved that he no longer seemed to bother. She went on, 'but Agnes loved to dance and she just carried on having all her fun and her brother scarcely in his grave.'

'We have to stop mourning the dead sometime, Grandma.'

'Well, yes …but at least a decent interval should elapse, don't you think? You young folk are all the same. All you want is a good time and to be amused.'

'I'm not like that, Grandma.'

'No, dear, you're serious like your mother. Too serious, maybe. You're a strange child, Andrew. But you are a good hearted boy and never any trouble to have around. Will you read to me now? I want to rest my eyes a little but it would be nice to hear something read.'

'Can I read you my Agatha Christie? *The Mysterious Affair at Styles*?'

'I'd rather have Dickens, dear.'

She smiled at his crestfallen expression, 'Oh, all right …go get your book and read me a page or two. Then we shall have some lunch and you can amuse yourself while I rest a little.'

Andrew duly read some of his book and then on the dot of one, Sara came in with some duck soup and thin buttered bread, which they ate at a little table near the fire. Andrew smiled. Life was back to normal and Grandma looked more rested and happy than she had for a while. It occurred to him as he watched her sipping slowly at her soup that she didn't enjoy these visits half as much as Agnes liked to think. Perhaps too he was mistaken in thinking she valued Reggie so much. He reminded her of Richard that was all. It was he, Andrew, who was her true companion.

Andrew waited till Grandma closed her eyes and was snoring gently before going upstairs. The Christmas tree candles had burnt out, the presents and sweeties were all gone and the poor little tree, now swiftly shedding its needles, looked bare and dismal. Andrew was not interested anyway. He had but one idea and one purpose that carried him forward up the stairs.

An atmosphere of gloom pervaded everything. The house was dark even on bright days. Today with the rain running in fine lines down the window-panes and nothing but a view of grey, sad skies laden with yet more rain, the whole place was cold and dreary. The two servants went about their duties with a slow stiff air as if the damp had got into their joints. Andrew knew that they too would retire to their warm kitchen and have a nap. He was surrounded by the old and ageing. In his heart he felt as old as they did themselves, not a young boy at all.

He made his way slowly to his mother's room and paused for a moment. Was it right what he wanted to do? He opened the door and entered her inner sanctum. The remains of yesterday's fire still lay in the grate. Sara had not yet got around to clearing it, not supposing anyone would come in here now. An odd ember still glowed when he raked the ashes.

The boy looked around at the room. It was a place that had been so familiar when he was small. Then he would come and sit on his mother's bed while she sewed or read aloud to him. Now that he was older he knew he had to wait to be invited to enter, making it feel all the more strange to walk in like this when she was not here. It felt an ill-mannered invasion of her domain and territory.

Nothing much had changed. The white lacy coverlet, the brass bedstead, the old-fashioned jug and basin on the washstand were all still there as he remembered them. By the bed was a picture of Ethan and the two small children. Next to them a photograph of himself looking rather stiff in a new school suit. On the washstand was a photo of an unknown woman. Mother always had this photograph there but he had never asked who she was, thinking it was some unknown relation. Now he looked at it more curiously. It was a woman with short, blonde, permed hair and a face that must once have been very pretty but now looked slightly pinched and tired. She looked about the same age as his mother, which to him was middle aged. It was signed 'To dear Dot, love May.'

Had his sister been named after this lady? Who could she be? He had no recollection of her at all. Well, it was of no interest.

He went to the wall cupboard and opened it, feeling about in the back. There beneath the pile of clothes his mother had heaped on it was the wooden box. Andrew brought it out and laid it on the bed his heart beating wildly. It was locked. Damn, he had forgotten about that!

Going over to Mother's little writing desk, he began to open the drawers beneath. The top one held little besides paper for writing letters, envelopes, blotting and a small box with remnants of a pencil and a pen holder without a nib. Another little box full of fine nibs. An elastic band. A tin full of Victorian pennies. Some postcards for birthdays and a few old brown photographs of no one he knew at all. The other drawer had a broken necklace of crystal beads that had lain awaiting its reincarnation all these years and a couple of books. There was little else, no revelation of any kind.

However, the top of the desk was locked. This was a most unexpected annoyance. Suppose Mother had taken this key away with her. To be so close and yet so far! He eyed the box on the bed with a feeling akin to fury. He wanted to pummel the desk and wrench it open. Andrew bit his lip and considered his next move. He went over to her dressing table, debated using a hair-pin to try and pick the lock but he wasn't at all sure that would be a wise move either.

On the table was a very small silver box. He looked inside and amidst an assortment of safety pins was a little brass key … was it the key to the wooden box?

It was not.

Perhaps the desk?

Yes, it fitted the keyhole at the top and at last he could open up the lid. He pulled it down, bringing out the supports as he did so. Inside the desk was another small drawer amongst the pigeon-holes and places for letters and other bits and pieces. He opened this and in there found a small silvery key wrapped in a handkerchief. He held it and smiled to himself. It was like one of those fairy tale stories where one went from copper to silver and then to gold but in reverse.

This must be it. This must have been what he saw glint in his mother's hand when he was a small child. This then was the key to Pandora's box.

He now turned the lock of the wooden box and opened it. Inside he saw two books, a red one and a black one that looked like diaries. Opening the first page of the red one, which lay on top, he saw the date January 1916. Beneath the diaries were several photos, yellowing slightly and curling at the edges. There was a Christmas Day menu with various pencilled signatures all over it, dated December 25th 1916. There was also a thick yellow-gold wedding ring. He took out the photos and found several of his mother, dressed in the long skirts which now seemed so old-fashioned, a long white apron over an ankle length dress with a Red Cross on the bib, white tents behind her, bleak hills in the background. In some pictures she was with other nurses, in others by herself, looking so young, gentle and dignified with that sweet smile of hers on her face. Another was with Ethan in what looked like an operating theatre. In many of these pictures was a pretty blonde nurse, arm affectionately linked with his mother's, whom he now recognised as the mysterious May whose photo was on the washstand.

At the very bottom was another picture; a man in full military uniform, his peaked and braided cap shading his eyes a little. Andrew took it out with trembling hands. A lean, hawk-like face looked back at him. They were not kindly features but full of stern character. The likeness to himself took his breath away.

For the first time in his fourteen years, Andrew looked upon his father's face.

Andrew looked at the photograph for a long, long time. He fancied he heard a noise and pricked his ears, poised like an animal about to take flight. He tiptoed to the door and listened but all was still downstairs and the rain pattered away at the windows. All the same, he felt unsafe. Grandma might wake up soon and it would never do to be caught in Mother's room. What would the old lady think?

'I *want* to read these diaries, Grandma,' he could hear himself saying. The disapproval on her face would be alarming. 'I *need* to know about my father, my past, where I come from!'

But no amount of protestation would prevail. His act of

invasion would be sinful in her eyes. And she would lecture him on his curiosity and take the diaries away and his mother would hate him for his wicked curiosity and never forgive him. Yet what else could he do? Maybe he *was* wicked. Maybe he was.

'Am I being wicked, God?' he murmured looking upwards as if expecting some fearful visitation to assuage his guilt. But there was no sign from a jealous and angry Jehovah and meanwhile he had the diaries there in his hand and he had to read on.

Quietly, he put the box and the photos back in the wardrobe, covering them over with care. Taking the two diaries, he returned to his room. As he did so, he heard the sounds of Sara emerging from the kitchen rattling tea cups and taking in the 4.00 pm tray to Grandma. He hastily put the books into the back of his own small cupboard and answered the summons of a little bell tinkling faintly in the parlour calling him down to the mundanities of tea, sliced Dundee cake and meaningless chit-chat.

Later that evening, he asked if he could go early to bed. His head ached a bit, he explained.

'I hope you're not sickening for something?' said Mrs Clarke, alarmed. 'Let me see your tongue.'

'No, I'm fine, honestly. Just been reading too much.'

'Well you're just like your Grandad, aren't you, you silly boy? Off you go, then …but no more reading!'

'No, Grandma,' he promised, feeling his ears going pink, feeling a heel. For read was what he meant to do, all night if need be. At any rate he was going to get through those diaries by the time he went back to school and maybe then he might know who and what he really was. He quivered with subdued excitement and also a strange sense of fear. Suppose he didn't like what he learnt about his mother and father?

Andrew got himself ready, washed his teeth and debated locking the door so as not to be caught unawares but felt it wiser not to do that. It would be a good deal more likely to rouse his grandmother's suspicions if he forgot to unlock it again and

Sara tried to come in early next morning and mentioned the fact to her. Nobody was likely to disturb him till the morning. It should be quite safe; he had read forbidden books from the library many a time in bed and no one any the wiser. He climbed into bed, clutching the red leather bound diary, and switched on a powerful camping torch. Then he turned off the bedside lamp and wriggled down under the sheets. He opened the first page which read January 1st 1916, then paused for a moment, almost afraid to go on.

Today was January 4th 1933. He knew he would never forget this date. It would be engraved on his memory for the rest of his life. Momentous happenings carve themselves upon the human psyche; frozen in time and laden with an almost mythical meaning. It would be like the dates of famous battles, terrible catastrophes that were said to be acts of God, achievements in history or scientific endeavour. Except that in his case it would not be a date to be proud of but one to shudder over. He was about to commit a tremendous act of violation.

He began to read. Time stood still.

Chapter 5

The Red Diary

January 1ˢᵗ 1916

A New Year and a new life. I am about to embark on a great adventure. When I chose nursing as a career I never dreamt that in a very short while I would be needed to serve not only my own country but one far away. This suits my spirit far better for it widens the whole vision that I have of caring for others not just in some county hospital near home ...I want to serve Mankind.

I was in London, training at St. Thomas's near Waterloo when they announced the terrible news that we were at war with Germany. There was such a deathly hush after the announcement outside Buckingham Palace, a strange stillness never known before in such a vast crowd then suddenly people began to cheer, shout and sing patriotic songs. It was all quite mad and frightening, yet, if it wasn't for this strange state of affairs, I would never have dreamt of leaving England's shores to go abroad and nurse as I am now about to do.

The very idea of my longing to be a nurse horrified Mother at first. It's not that she doesn't believe in hard work, if anything she is a regular tartar for discipline. She certainly believes in a Spartan existence and no frills and fuss. It was the idea of my dealing with bodies, men's bodies in particular, that appalled her. I seriously believe she has never looked properly at either my father's genitals or her own. As far as she is concerned they oughtn't to exist. Her own mother, she once told me, had thought babies were born from a woman's navel. I don't suppose that she was any the wiser herself until she had Agnes.

I don't know where I get my curiosity from but even as a child I would sneak down the lane to Cottersley Farm and watched the mating, lambing, calving, ask questions and be fascinated by the whole thing. The workings of the body, animal or human are very interesting. They are wonderful pieces of machinery and one should understand and care for them. I tried to explain all this to Mother.

'But it is a disgusting idea, Dorothy,' Mother exclaimed, looking at me as if I was an unnatural being, 'mixing with men who will be in all states of undress, seeing horrific sights that surely are far too harsh and unpleasant for a young gentlewoman? Why would you want to do such a thing? It's beyond belief, beyond my understanding.'

I think she considers me a callous and insensitive creature without realising that I am exactly the opposite.

However, enough of all that. These family trivialities – and trivial they do seem now – have no place in this diary. I have aired all these discontents before. Luckily, I have always been Father's favourite and he is very radical in his views, quite, quite different to Mama who is like Lot's wife, always looking backwards. He believes that girls should have as good an education as the boys and take their place as equals. It was Father who told me bedtime stories but they were never the silly nonsense of fairy tales and all that stuff. Like Schliemann's father, he filled my heart with the romantic allure of giant Homeric epics and tales of Gods and Goddesses. These thrilled my soul with passion. Huge beings, huge adventures and imaginations!

Mother yearns for me to settle down like Agnes, who's now married and has a sweet, little baby son. But I really haven't time for the young men who come mooning around. They were always keen enough to meet Agnes with her red-gold curls and pert nose but think me a bit of a blue stocking and give me a wide berth. That's fine by me as most of them have a brain the size of a pea. It suited Agnes no doubt, as all she ever wanted was their admiring glances, inane comments and sheep eyes. Her husband may be second cousin to a Lord Somebody but, I hate to say, is a complete idiot. Men! If there is one good man to restore my faith in the male sex it is my father …and of course my brother Richard.

I will never forget the day that the Reverend Tandy preached his wonderful sermon urging us to help our country against God's enemies in any way we could. Richard stood up there and then, his cheeks burning with feeling.

He said aloud, 'I shall be off to join our brave men this very afternoon, sir, and all you young fellows here today should follow me and be ashamed, as I am, to be idling at home, when our country is being threatened by the kind of fiends who hang up priests as living clappers, ravage the countryside over which their feet pass, destroy, for the sake of destroying, men, women, children without care, feeling or discrimination. These are not men but the Devil's own fiends! It is our Christian duty to annihilate them as they seek to annihilate us!'

Every man and woman in that church had stood up and cheered at my brother who just as suddenly sank back into his seat as if astonished at his own oration. The Reverend said he should have put him in the pulpit for he said better than anyone what was to be done. And go and enlist Richard did, that very afternoon, followed by all the young men in the village who were of serviceable age. How proud we all are of them, these brave boys of ours! And what a marvellous regiment they have turned out to be.

I wanted to apply immediately for service abroad as I heard they desperately needed nurses in Serbia where people are dying by the hundreds of typhus. However, I was told that I must serve some time in a hospital here in England first of all.

Mother waved a newspaper at me one day and said, 'It says here that young women should never be allowed to go to Serbia. The conditions are appalling. Why don't you just carry on working here at home? There are plenty of hospitals here for goodness sake!'

'It says young or untrained nurses, mother,' I retorted, snatching the paper away from her and perusing the passage, 'I *am* trained and I was twenty three in December and mean to apply as soon as possible.'

Mother looked at me resignedly. She knew I was as stubborn and pig headed as herself.

Sadly, by the time I was ready to apply, the poor Serbians had already been driven back by the Austrians and Bulgarians and begun their terrible retreat across Albania. It was too late to help those brave, gallant men who had fought so fiercely for their homeland. We all felt it was the fault of the Allies who had taken so long making up their minds whether to help or not and when they did it was too late. It made me all the more determined to go to Greece. I heard through varied channels that a new front was now opened up in Salonika and that there was a real need for both voluntary helpers and trained nurses, so I applied to go to there. Here, I thought, was a chance to combine what I loved to do – nursing – with the chance to see a country that had obsessed me since my childhood.

February 2ⁿᵈ

My knowledge of Ancient Greek and of Greece which I picked up from my father, scant as it may be, was certainly a point in my favour when I applied to the Red Cross though the main requirement is to speak fluent French, the *lingua franca* over there. I was told that Salonika is a cosmopolitan city, mostly full of Jews and Turks and things are always in a state of flux and danger. Father told me it's likely to be very Oriental still in customs and attitudes.

I'm determined to see as much as I can of the country and all the sights I can manage to fit in. Hopefully, things won't flare up in Athens and make sightseeing impossible; that would be so annoying. At present Athens is in the hands of the pro-German King Constantine who has fallen out with his Prime Minister, Eleftherios Venizelos. The country is divided North and South between these two leaders with bitter hostility reigning everywhere.

I was asked to go and see the Matron-in Chief at Pall Mall and she has advised me on all I might have to encounter on the Eastern Front. It's not a cheerful picture.

'It is rather a dirty city, I'm afraid,' Dame Sarah explained, 'and we are just setting things up at present so you will have to expect difficulties and certainly none of the comforts of home. A few hospitals are up and running but we intend to open up a new one and you might be asked to go there. You will be under canvas at first until some of the huts are ready. Are you prepared for all this?'

I assured her I was ready for anything. She smiled and seemed pleased with my enthusiasm.

'You are not obliged to sign a contract as your work is being given voluntarily. However, if you decide to sign a six month contract you will be expected to do night duty. You wish to do that? Very well. You are to provide your own uniform, we provide all else. Your kit bag will be delivered to you at Waterloo. It will contain a sleeping bag, canvas bath, basin, bucket, and folding chair. Apart from this you may take with you a suitcase and a holdall for more personal belongings. Inoculations for typhoid and enteric will have to be done as soon as possible. It may well be very useful that you have some knowledge of Greek. I shall inform the M.O who will be sailing out with you.'

'It's really just a knowledge of the alphabet and some words that may not be all that useful,' I said diffidently.

'Well, it's a basis, at least, which with effort you may be able to improve upon. Who knows when this might be useful …try and study a little more while you are waiting for your papers.'

I promised that I would and asked the name of the M.O.

'Willoughby is his name, Captain Ethan Willoughby.'

I like the sound of his name and wonder what he will be like?

Chapter 6

March 15ᵗʰ 1916

There we all were standing on the platform at Waterloo ready to catch the boat train for Southampton, dressed in our dark coats and our neat, navy hats, brassards pinned inside our coats, looking like a row of little Quakers. The girls seem a jolly crowd, all cheerful and smiling. Father accompanied me to London and came to wave us goodbye; Mother wasn't well, I'm afraid and stayed at Downlands. She takes it rather badly that I should be going off just now when, as she says, 'her health is poor.' She's simply sulking.

Well, for the present away from the confinements of home life. I can't believe my luck and feel so glad to be going. London is grey, dark and dreary just now, everyone looking troubled, not a smile to be seen on any face. And yet, despite my sense of excitement, when I looked out of the carriage window and saw Father standing there on the platform, his stocky, comfortable figure, his genial, cheerful face smiling at me and waving goodbye with all his might, a sudden little tremor of fear ran through me and I wanted to fling out my arms and say, 'Oh, Papa, take me home!'

The feeling passed, perforce; I was committed now.

I sat down with the other nursing sisters in the carriage and they were as full of enthusiasm and gaiety as myself. There were only five of us travelling on that occasion but at Southampton we were joined by another two girls from the General Service Voluntary Aid Detachment, who were going to Malta to set up a Red Cross Invalid Kitchen.

One of the nursing VAD's was called May Spannock, a jolly, pretty sort of girl with soft, wavy fair hair and a round little face full of liveliness and fun.

'I mean to cheer up all the soldiers,' she declared.

I was sure she could hardly fail such a task, equipped as she was with prettiness, gaiety and a light hearted, irreverent manner that I secretly found amusing though the other two sisters disapproved. (They *were* a rather starchy pair).

'Really' I heard one of them remark in a loud whisper, 'some people join only to amuse themselves. One would suppose this horrible war provided wounded simply for the purpose of being nursed by scatterbrained girls!'

'Yes, it really *is* bad form,' agreed her snooty companion.

Well, I'd sooner have been with May than those two any day. And their criticism seemed very unfair for May was only being high spirited and after all there isn't any need to go about the business of nursing with long faces. A pleasant smile will do far more for the poor Tommies than a miserable severe countenance.

I was soon made aware there existed a vast gulf between the trained nurses who count as officers and the untrained, often lesser-educated girls who form the General Service Units and do the more domestic work. I think the latter are rather looked down upon. Someone has to cook and clean but some of these nicely-bred, dainty dears consider themselves above all that. May, however, is not to be a cook or an orderly but is going to help with nursing and informed me that she had obtained her Home Nursing and First Aid Certificates and been to all the Red Cross Lectures. I like May. She is like a breath of fresh air. I have never known anyone quite like her before.

'I couldn't bear to think of my poor Bill, all cold and miserable in the trenches, while I sit in the comfort of my home with a fire in the grate,' she said when I asked her why she had volunteered, 'so I thought I'd do a bit of work too and might even get a chance to see him for he's with the Wiltshires and did some fighting in France. Now they've pulled out the Division and sent them on to Salonika and they've been stuck there since November. I had a short letter from him the other day; they can't say that much, I suppose, with all this censoring business, anyway he never was much of a letter-writer. He just says he's well and they seem to be doing more digging roads and putting up barbed wire than fighting. He says it's been very cold during the winter though things are warming up now. Apparently there's a horrible wind that blows their tents down as soon as they're up. He says it's nothing to wake up and find your tent sailing away down the hillside. I always thought it would be boiling hot over there.'

It seems that she's engaged to be married to Bill and feel her wish to share his lot very sporting. Her father is a General Practitioner in Salisbury and her mother was a vicar's daughter and had once been a governess. She told me all about her younger brothers, sisters and other members of the family and whiled away the journey amusingly for she has a saucy sense of humour that appeals to me.

'Coming out as a nurse seemed a better idea than slaving away in some boring old munitions factory …can you imagine anything so horrid? I suppose I might have turned my hand to ploughing as my sister is doing, but then she'll try anything and she loves being outdoors. She always wanted to be a boy and wished she could have been a farmer she says, so now is her chance. Isn't the war an odd affair that we women should be doing these things?'

'But isn't it also really freeing?' I countered.

'Rather!' May agreed. 'Why, by now Bill and I would have married and be living down the road from Mum and Dad. We had decided on the date and everything but Dad said it would be better to wait until the war was over before we married. I thought the war would be over in a year, didn't you? Will it go on for ever do you think?'

'I should hope not,' I said gravely, 'or there will be no men left to fight it.'

'So long as my Bill is spared!' said May, clasping her hands and casting her eyes heavenwards in a somewhat dramatic manner.

She saw the look on my face and hastily added, 'Oh, that sounds so selfish, doesn't it? Are *you* engaged, Sister Clarke?'

'No, and I have no wish to be.' I replied.

'Why ever not?'

'Well, there are several reasons,' I smiled, 'but the main one is ...' I intended to say that I hadn't yet met anyone worthy enough to love but that sounded awfully vain and pompous. Instead I said, 'the main one is I don't care for anyone just yet. The only men I have ever loved and admired have been my father and my brother, Richard. Frankly all the others have been such shallow, stupid fools.'

'My goodness! I've met a host of nice young men in my time,' said May with a laugh, 'what an old sober-sides you are! It's your kind that fall the hardest in the end ...oh, yes, I know. Let's see what will happen in Salonika with all those handsome officers milling about!'

I smiled complacently at her banter for I felt myself to be quite invulnerable.

March 17th

We arrived at Le Havre today after a long journey. There is still a long way to go before we reach our destination and I know some of the girls are beginning to feel apprehensive at being so far from home and travelling to what seems such a distant theatre of war. We all expect that it will be fairly easy going ... well, easy in comparison to being stuck on the Western Front. Every one at home keeps chaffing us and saying we are off to do some gardening as all the men sent to the Balkans seem to be spending their time digging roads. They say the Salonika offensive is just a sideshow to keep the Greeks from falling to the Huns and it will be all over in no time. I wonder.

The journey over to Le Havre was not too pleasant for the Channel at this time of year is decidedly choppy. The air is bracing but I shall feel glad, so glad, when our feet are on dry land again at last and this eternal pitching and rolling stops. The little ship is racing along just now for there is a report of a submarine about and all engines are thumping loudly. We heard the news in January of the hospital ship *Marguette* being torpedoed in Salonika Bay. Many of the New Zealand nursing sisters were drowned. It's hardly encouraging but one just has to put it out of one's mind and carry on.

I was more than glad when we reached Le Havre. From there we journeyed on to Paris where we were met by a Red Cross official who was most kind and charming. Much to our delight we were told we could have a day there. A couple of open carriages were hired and off we went to see the sights of that romantic city. It seemed to be bustling and crowded with French soldiers. Some of the older ones were still in the dark blue uniforms with those red trousers that could be spotted by the enemy a mile away but the younger men had the *bleu horizone* and this paler blue was far less conspicuous. There is no two ways about it, they all looked very handsome and dashing as only Frenchmen can. The officers and men saluted us as we drove past in our carriage, our Red Crosses resplendent upon our arm-bands. It made us feel very special and certainly very welcome.

We had a wonderful meal, a luxurious hot bath and a rest; much needed after all those dull hours of travelling. Then the next day we took a train to Marseilles and boarded a larger ship there. The customs officials asked if we were carrying any gold with us as it is forbidden to take anything valuable out of the country. That made us laugh; we none of us had even a gold wedding ring between us! May had her little engagement ring and that was all. Ship's Matron took us off for boat drill, allocated us to our cabins and at last we set off on the next leg of the journey.

I felt quite seasick the first day for the cabin was so hot and stuffy. I share it with another girl who hasn't risen from her bed yet, poor thing, and groans and moans all night. I have to stuff my head under the pillow; it's enough to drive anyone mad. I'm sure she could make a little less noise if she tried; it seems unladylike and silly to me to make all that fuss. The more you lie about and give in to it, the worse you feel so I soon dragged myself up onto the deck and there in the fresh air, with a fine drizzle blowing in my face, felt better in no time. Most people prefer to sleep on deck for fear of being scuttled by a U-boat and I decided to join them and leave Winnie to groan alone.

It's strange to stare over the sea that stretches from horizon to horizon without a break in the monotony of its expanse. I watched the water foaming away from the ship's bows but it made me giddy after a while so stopped that pastime. I hate being at sea; it frightens me the loneliness and the vulnerability of this isolated ship on the middle of a vast and never ending stretch of ocean. All the same, I'm a good swimmer if the worst should come to the worst.

May seems to love the sea and stares out at the water for hours lost in thought, which certainly makes a change for her. It's actually a very nice, large ship and once I found my sailor's legs, I began to enjoy it all. We have now met our Medical Officer, Captain Ethan Willoughby. He joined us at Marseilles and has already seen service in France but is now *en route* to the Salonika Front. Someone told us it was because his health wasn't that good and they could only spare doctors like him for the Eastern Front just now. All the younger and fitter men are being kept for the French offensive. No one seems too sure what is happening in Salonika or where we are to be posted. We do know that malaria, influenza and typhus have become a big problem with soldiers and civilians alike.

Willoughby is a tall, very serious looking sort of chap with strong, severe, aquiline features. His hair is fine and dark and slightly thinning though he can't be more than early forty something and he has a nice trim little moustache. He has a commanding air about him and they say he is a very fine surgeon. Everyone treats him with cautious respect, even Matron. I'm not sure whether I am going to like him or not. He seems so cold, reserved and formal. Maybe he will thaw out. May is working on him already. And she could thaw the North Pole.

Chapter 7

March 21ˢᵗ 1916

It seems that Captain Willoughby doesn't much approve of ladies being involved in the war effort. What an old-fashioned being he is!

'I utterly dislike the idea of well-bred young women being exposed to all this horror,' he said rather stiffly one day in answer to a question of May's.

'Oh, but sir, we couldn't all sit at home while our boys are suffering out there,' she exclaimed opening wide her blue eyes. 'My Bill is already in Salonika and I so want to see him. I hope he'll be able to visit the camp on leave sometimes. Matron says NCO's won't be allowed to take us out and I feel frightfully dashed by that. But he *is* my fiancé.'

Willoughby looked down at her, she is such a wee little thing, and smiled. He actually smiled. My goodness, May is a regular charmer.

'Army rules are army rules, I'm afraid. So, I don't know that you'll have much luck. Well, it's all very commendable, my dear, but my view is that there is a great deal more you nice young ladies can do nursing our fellows at home. You are more worry to your parents, sweethearts and the soldiers, if you are roaming about all over the place like this.'

He must have heard my little snort of irritation for he gave me a quizzical look. I generally remain silent in these conversations. I like to just sit and listen and watch and take everything in; a detached observer one might call it.

'And you, Sister Clarke, is that your opinion too? Are *you* hoping to meet up with a fiancé, or some such thing?'

His question and slightly ironic tone annoyed me. He made it sound as if our desire to help out overseas was a trivial thing, a desire for silly female flirtation or pointless adventure.

'No sir, I have no fiancé and if you really want my opinion it is that this is going to be a far longer tussle than any of us expect. We thought it was all going to be over by now but it doesn't show much sign of that, does it? I think you'll find that women are going to be needed *more* than ever, not less. We are already running the trams and helping in factories and on the land back home. The men, as you well know, are all gone to war and being ...being decimated.'

I thought of my brave brother who had set off with such merry enthusiasm in 1914, now holed up in the trenches of France, many of the men from Cottersley village already dead and gone, and looked away to hide a little tear. I am so troubled about the situation over there. It sounds horrendous and I know the papers back home are not telling us the half of it all. All they worry about is the price of bread and oysters and the nonsensical wranglings of the House of Commons. There is such tight security and secrecy and gags put on any sort of real and honest information. No wonder so many mad rumours abound and people are frightened out of their wits half the time.

Willoughby looked at me for a long time but I refused to meet his eye. I was ashamed of my sudden tears and felt angry with him. He said no more and turned back to stare moodily over the waters.

We made a brief stop at Valetta harbour in Malta, an interesting, rather barren place. The ladies wear the strangest hats of stiff black silk, which were introduced when Napoleon's soldiers came rattling through. They were meant to preserve their modesty and hide their beauty but the custom has remained and the hats are now part of the national costume. I like the manner in which they get their milk supplies. The goats are brought to the door and milked there and then for each customer. Another memory of Malta I shall always have is the sweet, trilling, liquid sounds of little canaries everywhere. The people seemed very kind and pleasant.

From Malta we went on through the Corinth Canal with its high walls, so narrow one can touch the sides, then on to Piraeus, a surprisingly modern looking town with great wide streets and some fine new buildings. It wasn't exactly the Greece I had pictured in my mind but I knew I was being silly. Did I expect to see men in the *hlamis* or something? Well, if so, I was to be disappointed. There were sailors in baggy trousers, as swarthy and weather-beaten as pirates, but most of the townspeople were dressed in European costume and looked very ordinary to me.

Naturally our first thoughts on landing there was whether we had time to visit Athens and the Acropolis. Matron gave us leave and we went in a little party accompanied by Captain Ethan Willoughby, Captain Henry Dunning who is another of the doctors and dear Canon Tudor Jones who is a really amiable and kindly man. Everybody likes him; he is so sincere and such a gentleman. Plus he is very learned about Greek history and able to regale us with all kinds of fascinating facts and figures that make it all the more absorbing.

I was by no means disappointed with my first view of the Acropolis although it seemed so small. Yet it lost none of its awe-inspiring quality for that and was all I had imagined it might be. The atmosphere was incredible, tangible with the ghosts of the ancients who had worshipped and walked on those hills. It was sad to think that the Elgin Marbles now resided in Bloomsbury and were no longer here where they belonged. Yet at the same time, it was wonderful to know that in England we could savour a little of this ancient beauty whenever we looked upon those marbles and that it might make us yearn all the more to visit their source. Hard to believe that that was just what I was doing. I was here in Athens, ancient Athens, standing on the site of the glorious Acropolis.

I stood and looked down from the ruins of the Parthenon onto the little city spread below, and felt a rush of deep feeling.

It was almost as if I had once been a part of it, part of this country and countryside. The group had moved on but I wanted a few moments alone to savour it all. So I stood there and looked over to Mount Hymettus letting my eye travel slowly about the vast terrain below, the straight dark cypresses and olive trees, the rolling plains, the soft blue of the mountains and the distant sweep of the sparkling sea. A sense of exhilaration and freedom came over me. I wanted to hold the scene in my heart forever, never to leave the spot I stood on. I realised in that moment that it wasn't the people who made a country but the landscape and its past that shaped those who came and settled there.

Much to my annoyance my intense reverie was cut into by the slow, flat, unemotional tones of Captain Willoughby.

'Pity the Turks used the place as an arsenal, isn't it?' he said referring to the fact that the Acropolis had its roof blown off in the struggle for Independence. It was true; the Turks had indeed kept their arsenal in there. It was one of life's great sacrileges.

'This place was just a village in the old days,' he added.

'What do you mean?' I said with great indignation, turning to stare at him.

'Well, Padre tells us it was a place of no consequence to the Turks. Salonika was their second city after Constantinople. Athens became a mere village, the Greeks a crowd of superstitious and ignorant peasants. It's not much better now, in my opinion. They're a load of vagabonds and brigands. Don't bother buying anything in Athens, I warn you. The shop girl gave me the wrong change today and hoped I wouldn't notice. They're full of such tricks.'

I made no comment. I wanted to be rid of him so that I could carry on musing. Athens had been great and would be great again. He was one of those people who always saw the blight on the rose. But despite turning my back on him, the horrid man just stayed beside me and rambled on about all sorts of stupid things. I hardly listened to him or replied. I wished he would go away. Eventually, he did seem to get the idea and moved off.

'You had better come on; I came to let you know that we are having a little repast and then going back to the ship quite soon, but it's up to you if you don't want to join us,' was his parting comment and with great reluctance, I tore myself away from the glorious scene and followed him back to the others who had by now produced a little picnic of milk, fruit, goat's cheese and bread which we all enjoyed out in the open air.

March 27th

The journey from Athens to Salonika took us on a long, slow, cautious trip amongst the rocky little islands of the Aegean in order to avoid being torpedoed. The ship's captain seemed to be nervous of the least flock of raucous sea birds for he was afraid that they might mark out where a sub might be. However we managed to avoid danger and at last came sailing into Salonika harbour. It was indeed a splendid sight, shrouded in the soft, misty pink and grey of dawn.

The city lay in a beautiful horseshoe shaped bay with steep hills forming a backdrop like an ancient amphitheatre. As the sun rose in the sky and the ship sailed closer we began to see the sprawl of little Turkish houses clambering the steep slopes, painted in all sorts of cheerful colours, rosy pink, mauve, white, yellow, blue. In between the houses the cypresses made little needle points of solemn green-black that were a counterpoint to the dozens of white minarets that rose up from the trees like tapers or candles lit in a High Church service. The white domes of the Greek churches glistened in the fresh morning sunshine and the whole scene was entrancing.

A long promenade faced the sea lined with grand looking hotels and shops and a large round white painted tower at the other end. This, I assumed, must be the famous Tour Blanche. The calm, tideless waters of the Mediterranean ran deep into the quay. Ships were moored alongside with their prows sticking over onto the broad street on which the trams went clattering by. It was such a noisy, cheerful, colourful scene. The fruit boats with their dusky sails drew up alongside and the swarthy, piratical owners called up to us, fighting to take us ashore. They were waved on their way to my regret and instead a little tug came out to fetch us. We landed at the Marble steps and our luggage was piled high into the waiting transport lorries and off we went to our various destinations.

March 28th

It appears that May and I will be working at a new General Hospital which is being set up on the lower slopes of a hillside a short distance from the city. I am glad we are to be together having by now formed such a pleasant friendship. May is a bit scatterbrained at times but such a kind and loveable girl. Part of the hospital is already laid out in rows of huts and there are some very large tents pitched. A couple of orderlies came along and hauled our kit off to one of the smaller bell tents that had been put up for us earlier that day. Then Matron came to greet us and she seems a nice person. Not half as terrifying as some of the Matrons I have encountered in my training years! She took us to the Sister's Mess tent and we were given a very welcome cup of tea.

We were introduced to our sleeping quarters, a small tent which at present is bare and dreary looking. At first Matron wanted me to share a larger tent with three other sisters but we begged and pleaded to be allowed to be together. Matron looked surprised and considered the matter but looking at our woeful faces, she smiled and relented.

'Well, you can start off together and we'll see how things go,' she said, 'hopefully we may be able to put up some huts in time and then Sister Clarke can move in there with the other sisters.'

I made up my mind then and there that this tent would do fine for me and I wasn't going to be parted from my little friend. Despite the fact that we are as different as chalk and cheese, we feel very much at ease together and I being a very private, prickly individual need to feel comfortable with someone in such enforced intimacy.

May and I have begun to put up our photos of loved ones and set up the canvas wash basins on their little tripod stands and opened out the folding canvas chairs on which to lay our clothes as the ground is rather muddy underfoot due to the Spring rains. The beds look most uncomfortable and the pillows are made of canvas, which is terribly rough to the cheek. I mean to make a pillowcase as soon as I can get my hands on some material. There are two dark army blankets and a large mosquito net attached to a ring for the summertime invasions of these nasty creatures. Generally not the most thrilling of interiors but the little personal items already make it feel more homely and cheerful.

May who has the charm of a siren has managed to cadge some things from the Quartermaster already and we use empty Ideal Milk boxes and other bits and pieces to create ourselves tables, seats and so on. We even procured a looking glass from Heaven knows where.

Female vanity has to be catered to even in war!

Chapter 8

April 5th 1916

May is such a cheerful girl and very willing. Many of the V.A.D's resent the fact that they may be called on to do anything from cleaning the lockers to emptying bedpans, as if it isn't what any junior nurse is called upon to do at first. After all, those of us who are trained nurses are more useful in other areas. I could understand the annoyance that the senior nurses felt over this cavalier attitude and the annoying lack of discipline in some of the new recruits who, it has to be confessed seem more interested in having picnics with the officers than buckling down to hard work.

'But we came here to nurse, not to be treated like maids of all work,' I overheard a young girl say to May.

'I came here to do anything I can to help,' May replied cheerfully, 'I *have* had some nursing training but little experience. I can hardly expect to be trusted with the patients just yet.'

'Well, I have had more than *some* training,' said the grumbler, 'and I'm sick and tired of being bullied and treated like an inferior and made to sweep, dust, polish and make beds like any skivvy. Why can't they get the orderlies to do all that? My father will send for me to return home if he gets to hear of it.'

'Go home then, no-one is forcing you to stay!' was the spirited reply. 'We can only learn by what we do and hope to proceed higher as we go along. We came to be useful, not heroines. I mean to do all I can to help. Surely we can do that best by not grumbling and by showing the regular sisters that we're willing, cheerful and ready to learn.'

'Bravo, May,' thought I and to reward her a little, I went up to her and asked her if she would take the temperature of a patient who was under surveillance, while I attended to something else.

She started at my request and looking very pleased, set off to do as I had asked.

'Did you take the temperature?' I asked a little later on.

'Of course.'

'Well, what was it?'

'Oh …a 130.'

'A 130! …then he must be dead by now!'

'Oh, don't tease me,' said May looking sheepish. 'I meant a 103.'

'May, May! …how will you ever learn to nurse if you're such a scatterbrain!'

Poor May was often in trouble. We were going across to the Mess tent one afternoon for a cup of tea when we met the Matron and she looked us over with a chilly eye.

'Young lady,' she said, addressing May with severity, 'take off that jewellery at once.'

For May liked to wear a pretty brooch that had been given to her by her fiancé, thinking it livened up the dark blue of her uniform a little. I had told her it wasn't allowed but she had not listened. Now she blushed, quickly unpinned the brooch and slipped it in her pocket where I felt sure she would forget all about it till it was sent to the laundry and more than likely lost in some Grecian wash tub.

April 8th

There is not much fighting here at present. There have been some air-raids in January and March which gutted the Banque d'Athenes and the French Stores and always the threat of more. No one seems too bothered. What we can do? We can't abandon the hospital or our patients.

Apparently we have just missed a bad winter with deluges of rain and bitter Vardar winds. I would never have believed how cold it can be in Northern Greece. Even now that spring is here with the most beautiful little wild flowers appearing on the hills, the weather is still bitter, cold and damp and I feel that there is something unhealthy about the climate. We have a stove but don't always have any paraffin to light it or else it blows out in the wind and is impossible to relight. The major wards are in large marquees, big and cold with just a stove at the end to heat them. Some of the more mobile patients crowd by the fire warming themselves and selfishly blocking the heat from those poor souls who cannot come so close, cannot even get out of bed. Supplies of stoves and paraffin are coming soon, our Stores assure us, but we don't hold out much hope.

The war we are waging here in Salonika is not so much against the enemy as the ever-present dysentery, fatigue and exhaustion of the men. At present things are at a stalemate; the Anglo-French troops are still stuck in an entrenched position within the confines of the 'Birdcage' as they wittily call the miles of barbed wire that surround the city. The Bulgars hold their positions on Doiran and from there they have a marvellous vantage point, at present unassailable. The main problem is the terrible terrain out there in the mountains. It is like a wilderness and the low-lying parts are marshy swamps that in the summer breed mosquitoes and malaria. There are scarcely any roads and the army is mainly occupied in building them as they move along, like the Romans used to do.

'It's such a bad business,' said one of the officers to me, 'this place could be cleared of these swamps and mosquitoes but no-one has bothered, no-one has wanted to put any capital into this god-forsaken place because the people are forever at war. It saddens me, it could be such a marvellous country, lush, fertile, instead of this howling wilderness. There could be flocks of cattle and sheep instead of scraggy and miserable goats and oxen with unshod feet pulling wagons along dirt-tracks that have been used for centuries.'

'Perhaps it will be improved after this war is over,' I said.

He looked at me and sighed. 'It would be nice to think so. At least we're making them some really good roads but one can't help wondering if they will just be allowed to grow over and fall into disrepair. The roads just disappear from sight in the winter into the deep mud of this place. We keep on having to re-build them time and again ourselves."

'That sounds positively dispiriting!' I said in sympathy.

'Dispiriting isn't the word for it!' he replied with feeling. 'It's just building it up all the time, over and again with heavy stone bases. We even have the local women and girls working at stone-breaking, keeping up a constant supply for the roads. It's a tough, full time occupation but they are used to hard work these women. They're pretty glad of the money, believe me. I hate to see the women work like navvies but roads we must have. No army can function without them; the Romans could have told you that. And think of all the lorries and transport vehicles that these roads have thundering over them nowadays.'

'But why haven't roads like this been built before? Other cities in Europe have good roads.'

'It's the peasants,' he replied sadly, 'they are used to the poverty and apathetic lifestyle of their forebears. The villagers are sullen and suspicious of us. All they have ever known is a life of turmoil and constant warfare and reprisals. To them there is no sense in major plans. Not a lot of point, I suppose, when you might be invaded, your stuff stolen from you and home burnt down any moment. But it's made the peasants lazy; they do as little as they can. They simply eke out their lives in the small circumference of their tumbledown villages. Their ignorance and superstition is horrifying and as for hygiene ...'

Words evidently failed the man.

'It does sound frightful. We can only hope we shall help to bring peace and prosperity to them.'

'It would be marvellous to be rid of the poisonous swamps,' said the officer, 'malaria will be on the increase again now spring is here, you mark my words. The men will be falling like flies.'

And so they are. Both the men and the flies come flooding into the camp in droves. Those dreadful flies! They come in black swarms and drive us all mad. Any sort of food has to be kept under cover till the moment you want it and even then has to be eaten swiftly along with the odd fly that might have dropped into it! Teaspoons are more busily employed in fishing out the creatures from every cup of tea than stirring in the milk and sugar. Ants too are another plague and if a crumb is left out they come marching up in their serried ranks, scaling heights with an ease that our armies, alas, are unable to emulate. The tea tastes of onions half the time for the Army cook, who was a market gardener in his English life, is absolutely hopeless and uses the same dixie for the stew as for boiling up water for the tea. His efforts with bully beef (which we nickname Army Camel) is mixed with over-cooked and half-dissolved vegetables most of the time. If only we could have brought that VAD cook who was on her way to Malta!

It seems then that we are not fighting the Huns here at all … the real enemy is Mother Nature herself and like the natives she is hostile and unfriendly.

Chapter 9

April 12ᵗʰ 1916

'I don't feel it is a good idea for you girls to go into the city, just now,' Matron stated today. 'Captain Dunning tells me that some of our girls have been spat on by the filthy local beggars. Really, some of the people in the city are just too disgusting.'

We were busily cleaning up the operating theatre at this point; some poor fellow had just been through to have his appendix out of all things and had been taken off back to his bed. Captain Willoughby who was scrubbing down his hands and arms looked up when he heard Matron's cool, authoritative voice and nodded in agreement.

'Oh. Matron, please let us go. I want to visit the marketplace so much. Corporal Willis says it's full of marvellous things,' said May plaintively for she really did chafe if we were obliged to stay in camp.

'Well, Spannock, you shouldn't go at all in my opinion for you're so fair, people might mistake you for an Austrian,' said Matron severely. I looked at her in some surprise. One could never be sure if Matron was pulling one's leg or really serious. However, she looked solemn enough and May took her words to heart.

'I'll make sure all my hair is hidden under my hat, Matron. Nobody could possibly see.'

Seeing Matron had on her inflexible look, May turned to Willoughby and appealed to him instead. 'Please, sir, I am so sick of being cooped up here, please, may I go into town? No-one would think I was a horrid German or Austrian, would they?'

Willoughby looked at her and that gentle little smile came to his lips as it always did when May asked for anything. He seemed to enjoy her artlessness but I don't feel he ever mocked it.

'Surely no-one could mistake you for anything but an English Rose,' he said in his earnest, quiet voice and May blushed very sweetly and prettily while Matron looked exceeding frosty. I rather wonder if he is beginning to get fond of May. All the men seem to dote upon her and she has more picnics out and cups of tea in various officers' tents than ought to be allowed.

'I mean to go into town myself Monday afternoon,' the Captain went on, as he dried his hands with that extreme thoroughness that characterised everything he did. 'We seem a mite less inundated right now, so if Matron is agreeable, perhaps both you young ladies might want to accompany me. I shall take care of them, never fear,' he added turning to Matron who shrugged a little and said that that would be fine, then, if it was no trouble to him.

'No trouble at all, but a delight,' he said with that slightly pompous air that always made me want to giggle. 'Maybe, we could have some tea and French pastries at Floca's. I doubt there'll be any cars available but we can take a lift in the Tin Lizzie.'

I was a bit taken aback but felt he had probably included me because it would have been rude not to. My life, I concluded, would be spent in the role of chaperone or duenna to all the flighty young things. I'm sure he would have loved to have pretty little May all to himself. However, I was quite pleased at the offer. It sounded a real treat. Tea and pastries! What a lovely thought.

April 16th

Whenever one is in the city, crowds of little Turkish children seem to appear from nowhere and surround one with outstretched hands, singing 'Inglees Johnny, Inglees Johnny!'

which is the extent of their vocabulary whether one is male or female. Willoughby shooed them away impatiently but I found them rather lovely with their huge, liquid black eyes, and happy smiles though they all seemed so painfully thin, their faces so yellow.

'No, Sister, don't encourage them,' Willoughby said when I gave them a few *lepta*. He was right for another crowd of really evil looking beggars and children then descended on us like a swarm of locusts, pushing and shoving us so unceremoniously that we began to feel rather threatened. Willoughby shouted angrily at them in French and they retreated in some alarm for he did have rather a severe and fierce way about him. I must say he makes a very good protector and May and I were glad that he was with us. However, as far as company goes, he is *such* a crushing bore. At least, I think so. May isn't as judgemental as I am about men. That's probably why they like her so much.

Canon Tudor Jones who is a mine of information has told us a good deal about the city. He says he has always been interested in Greece and in this he reminds me of Papa.

'The city looks better from the sea than it does once you are walking about in it. It's such a noisy, smelly place,' one of the nurses said grumpily.

'That's true, but you have to remember that it has only just become a Greek City,'said the padre, 'it's been rather neglected for years. Yet you know, it is pretty up to date in some ways too.'

He then told us how Crown Prince Constantine of Greece had ridden into the erstwhile Turkish city with his victorious troops in November 1912 to the weeping, cheering, dancing and wild joy of the crowds who gathered to greet him. Church bells had rung again and the muezzin in the minaret had ceased his ululating call to prayers and fallen into the silence of a long Moslem night. Ancient Thessaloniki belonged once more to Greece.

It is a fascinating place despite the ill-paved, often dirty streets and the seething population of Turks, Jews, Armenians, Serbians, French, English and Greeks (the latter seeming to me to be decidedly in the minority). This city has had so many conquerors and absorbed a little of them all. Captain Willoughby pointed out to us the crumbling Roman arch of Galerius as we passed beneath it in the tram going down the Via Egnatia, the only really well paved road in the city. He told us that it was the road that ran all the way to Constantinople, the ancient trade route of the Byzantine days. The Romans had left that much behind them at least, just as our troops were now leaving their well-built roads along the impassable mountain ranges.

We took the tram back again and eventually arrived at the sea front where next to the harbour stands the so-called White Tower …the Tour Blanche …part of the quaint old city walls. Like all such towers, like our own Tower of London, it harbours a cruel past. Here the Janissaries were massacred for an uprising against their Ottoman masters and the Greeks imprisoned there during the War of Independence so that it has also been called the Bloody Tower. The British Navy then whitewashed it and cleaned it up for their use and now it is called the White Tower and one can climb it and view the city and order tea and ices there. What an odd world!

'Yes, it has a certain beauty, this strange, conglomerate city,' I murmured, half aloud as we stood at the walls of the acropolis or citadel whither we had clambered despite the afternoon heat. It is so unlike the lovely pale Acropolis of Athens. There is no architectural splendour in this buff coloured stone edifice with its thick battlemented walls, wide enough to drive a motor-car along. Yet it commands the eye, perched high up over the city like a watching eagle, and from its walls one may see a most splendid sight, a broad panorama. Below us, on the dark slopes of Mount Hortiatis, sprawl the domes and minarets and little colourful wooden and stone houses carrying one's eye over the vast sweep of the city and harbour to the Thermaic Gulf, glittering a deep, dark blue in the afternoon sun …Homer's *'wine dark seas'*. From this height one can look down and see the French aerodrome and the Canadian hospitals beneath and the white tents of the British and French hospitals dotted about all round the slopes. In the harbour the hospital ships lie moored. They look bright and cheerful, painted white with an emerald green stripe all around them and huge Red Cross on the funnel and sides of the ship.

'How pretty the ships look, don't they?' said May as we gazed down at the scene below.

'That is hardly the term, I would use,' said Captain Willoughby rather sarcastically, 'they are full of wounded men, remember, and it is becoming more and more dangerous to take the men home to Blighty or even to Marseilles or Malta with all the threat of German U-boats in the Adriatic and these wretched air raids.'

'I know,' said May chastened, 'they are quite frightening, aren't they?'

'They take absolutely no notice of the Red Crosses on the ships or on top of the hospital camps,' Willoughby went on angrily, 'there is no honour in these men, none at all. The hospital ship *Egypt* was sunk scarcely a month ago in the recent raids. Do you realise that those poor wounded men never made it home after all? Think how they must have been looking forward to it, relieved of the horrors of war just for a brief while, at least. Think how their families have now had their hopes cruelly dashed, never to see their loved ones again.'

He was right, of course. May and I felt a sense of sadness that blighted our selfish pleasures. The Germans take no notice of the huge red crosses at all; recently yet another bomber flew in again and created havoc. We keep expecting them to come over and drop their bombs on our own hospital …they seem to like crushing the weak and helpless …but so far so good. Canon Jones' fervent prayers are obviously being heard.

Chapter 10

April 18th 1916

It is hard to imagine how cold the winters must have been now Spring is on its way and it is getting hotter and hotter by the day. The hillsides bloom with glorious fields of scarlet poppies and white and blue anemones, and May and I love to take a ramble over them when we have any free time. Sometimes some of the officers come with us and we have marvellous little picnics on the cliffs overlooking the sea and occasionally parties of us go bathing; it certainly helps to cool us after the intense heat of the day that is already becoming unbearable.

Captain Dunning loves to tell us funny jokes and read us hilarious things from the old *Punch* magazines that he brought with him. He is a big florid man with a marvellous twirly moustache who chain-smokes incessantly and coughs all the time. It seems ridiculous that he keeps up this rather nasty habit but he swears it keeps the mosquitoes away and they have begun to come and haunt us with a vengeance now that the weather is warming up. 'Drains' Dunning has the job of looking after the sanitation and testing our water supply in the lab, even though it is brought over to us in carts guarded by soldiers and already chlorinated. If he isn't happy he insists on re-dosing everything with the foul tasting chlorine that even sugar fails to disguise. It is so horrible a taste and seems to get in everything.

I am most humbled when it comes to speaking Greek for, alas, the little I have learnt has nothing in common with the harsh, Oriental sounding language spoken here. Some few words are familiar but I begin to realise how ignorant I really am about Greece and Greek people generally. Were the glorious Ancient Greeks of my imagination anything to do with these lice ridden, poverty stricken people who stare at us sullenly from their doors? Are these rough villages with their open sewers buzzing with flies, with their oxen and goats lumbering through the swirling clouds of dust, their chickens and fierce, yapping dogs, any relation to the fine, paved marble streets of old Athens?

Yet little things catch my eye now and then and renew my faith in the human spirit. Many a home has an old can, painted bright blue and full of geraniums growing somewhere on the veranda, perhaps a blossoming lemon tree or a fig tree shading the doorway, while the children come to one clutching handfuls of wild flowers ...*agria loulouthia* ...as they call them, and they thrust the bunches into my hand as I pass.

I persevere with learning Greek to the amusement of some of the local peasants who laugh at me yet seem rather pleased that I make the effort at all. They bring their children and old folk to us to look after when they are ill and seem to have a touching faith in our ability to cure everything. Their gratitude is overwhelming and almost embarrassing at times. They bring us tomatoes, ducks, geese and hens or fresh milk from their goats and pots of strange sticky jam that tastes like quince or gooseberry.

At first the villagers were highly suspicious of us. They can't be blamed for that, this part of the world has been at war for such a long time. But once one gets to know them they are a simple, courteous and grateful people. The men tend to look on the nurses as something rather astonishing and marvellous, a race apart from the kind of women they know. And little wonder when one sees some of the drab, black- draped, wizened creatures that their women become so soon. They have faces as wrinkled as a piece of leather, real old hags some of them.

In contrast the young girls are so beautiful, they are astonishingly beautiful, with their thick, lustrous tresses and their large, warm, dark eyes ...yet they become fearfully haggard so soon. Is it the life they lead or the climate or both? Their lives do seem hard and I don't believe the women live very long. One of the young girls who comes to help with cleaning and scrubbing is, I am told, no more than fifteen but her dark, solemn eyes seem that of a woman of twenty at least. She says nothing but works like a skivvy from dawn to dusk, seemingly tireless. Her name is Eleni and she is such a beautiful creature, her skin as smooth as ivory and her hair so black and thick that I envy her ...but in a few years what will become of her lovely face, her lithe and healthy limbs?

The women are very small and undernourished and seem to be beasts of burden on a par with the mules and often not so valued. The Turks are especially awful to their women whom they drape in black from head to foot with only their eyes showing. The man rides the mule and the women, wives from his harem, I imagine, follow on behind carrying enormous loads. One of the Tommies told us how they had forced one such fat old Turk to get off his mule by pointing a bayonet at his stomach and prodding him. Then they put one of the wives on the mule and made him pick up her bundle and carry it! But once out of sight, I am sure he would have swiftly reversed this humiliating state of affairs and probably beaten the poor woman into the bargain. So ...much good that will have done! We cannot expect to teach these ignorant people our ways. Their attitudes and customs are just so different.

April 30th

On the whole things are really hectic now Spring is here. The cases are mainly malarial or else men dropping from heat and exhaustion who need a long rest. The authorities back home simply didn't have a clue what sort of place they were sending these poor men to and they have suffered the winter with scarcely enough warm clothing and now that the summer is coming, there are no solar topees or spine protectors and few enough mosquito nets and I heard Matron say she was going to send a strongly worded letter to the Directors in Alexandria who are supposed to be in charge of this sort of thing.

One really does wonder what idiots *are* in charge and if they ever think these things through properly before sending men off on ridiculous and often pointless long campaigns. I'm really not a bit sure that we are doing any good here. But I suppose we *are* preventing Salonika from falling to the enemy even by simply being dug in and making the solid defences around the city.

They call the defences *The Birdcage* because of the amounts of barbed wire they have had to use, which is a bit of a joke really. May tells me that her fiancé, Bill, says the men are getting sick to death of digging roads and putting up miles of barbed wire and view the arrival of any new officer on the scene with consternation. Every 'New Broom' would get it into his head to tear everything up and move to another position and off they would go again.

The people in the city just seem to carry on as if nothing is happening and they are making a good deal of money out of this sudden influx of new visitors. The British are their favourites for our men have no understanding at all about the Oriental love of bargaining and take everything at face value. Somehow we just can't seem to get used to their paper money which seems worthless to us. I think the natives must be open-eyed with astonishment at our apparent stupidity. They don't take long to profit from it, I can tell you.

When the men arrive at the hospital they are always in a terrible state and have to be washed and de-loused before anything else can be done. Lice can spread typhus and this unpleasant job often falls to the nursing VAD's like May. If things become too hectic, we all wade in and give a hand and even Matron will sometimes roll up her sleeves and set to work. She is a wonderful woman, an example to us all and never stands on her dignity. We all admire and respect her tremendously. The mere sight of her upright, imposing figure, with her flowing, well-starched head-dress and cape that makes her stand out from the rest of us, is more than enough to make the men fall still and behave themselves. Because, I assure you, they can sometimes be worse than a handful of schoolboys, especially once they begin to get better.

Chapter 11

May 1st 1916

The whole camp fell quiet this morning because the sacks of mail had at last arrived from Base and everyone disappeared to read their news from friends and relatives. I scooped up my letters joyfully and ran off to our tent to read them as soon as I was free. It was marvellous to hear from home. Mother keeps complaining bitterly about the rising prices and scarcities of things back in Blighty and grumbling that all the maids have been sent off to do land work or are getting far too high above their station these days. Apparently there are hardly any able men left to do the garden and Father couldn't get his favourite whisky. How inconsequential all these trivialities seem here where men are dying daily of malaria, where we all suffer such discomforts and are lucky to have our daily rations supplemented by village produce sold at ridiculous prices by the avaricious natives.

Agnes adds a few words and says she is enjoying her teaching work and is too busy to write much and hopes I am well. Father's letter is as cheerful as always and he talks of his studies and his lectures and tells me he has taken up war work. What on earth can he be doing? ...he doesn't say. Surely he's not into espionage? I should jolly well hope not at his age.

The most marvellous letter was from dear Richard in France. He has to be careful of what he says but he and I have always had our own codes since we were children. We invented a sign language, which we employed during dinner as we were expected to sit in silence throughout the meal and also a written code that was a funny mixture of Latin-English, or words that meant something to us but nobody else. Generally, all letters are censored by one of the MO's, which I find horrid. I have no wish for all my inner thoughts or those of Richard to be scrutinised by any Tom Dick or Harry. But that's the way of it. God knows what they make of some of our more cryptic letters!

Richard seems well enough but I can tell that the dreadful conditions are wearing him down. He describes the disgusting conditions of trench warfare though he need not explain it as I see the results daily when our men are brought in on stretchers, suffering from dysentery, malaria, and God knows what else. Conditions on the Western Front are really different. There isn't the heat to contend with, nor the flies and mosquitoes but rain and mud instead. One way and the other it's all pretty miserable. He says he has taken to writing poetry. It's the fashionable thing amongst the men, apparently, a way of expressing some of the horror of it all. His descriptions make it all seem so vivid and I know he tells me all this but not Mother and Father for he would never want to alarm them. I look up from his letter and suddenly wonder what on earth we are all doing in these unfriendly far flung places? A cloud of black flies descends and I spend my precious time swatting furiously. In the end, I just get inside the mosquito net on the bed and share it with a couple of little green lizards that have found an abode there too. It's the only place to escape from the filthy, noisy insects. I think I'd rather have the German planes buzzing around.

Later this evening May and I took a walk down to the seaside. I felt a sense of peace in the softness of the early evening light when the air is far cooler and gentler. A breeze blew and we wandered along the shore, our minds on our letters and inevitable thoughts of home and happy days long gone by. May had heard from Bill and was full of his sayings and doings.

'He says his C.O. might let him come down the line to visit me soon,' she said joyfully, 'won't that be wonderful! I am so looking forward to it and I'm going to pray and pray so as to make it happen soon. Canon Jones will wonder what's come over me when he sees me in chapel so often.'

'All your other suitors will be jealous to see Bill,' I said with a smile.

'What other suitors?'

'Half the camp, I should think, from the corporal in the canteen onwards! Even Captain Willoughby has a soft spot for you.'

'Don't be so ridiculous,' said May blushing. 'I know I am a flirt but it's all just a bit of fun …you won't tell Bill, will you?'

'As if I would! I'm only teasing you, May.'

'Anyway, Captain Willoughby has a soft spot for *you*, as you well know.'

I looked at her in surprise. 'He doesn't like me a bit, May, don't say such silly things.'

'Oh, doesn't he? The trouble with you is you just don't take any notice of the men unless they're patients. Then you are as sweet as can be and they all think you wonderful. Poor things, they could die of love for all you care, you're so hard hearted.'

I looked at her witheringly. 'May you are just a sentimental thing and see romance everywhere. Don't try and change the subject. You are the world's worst flirt and you know it, May Spannock. Haven't I caught you sitting on the officer's beds and making them laugh till their stitches burst? You are a tonic for them all, you pickle.'

'Oh, I admit I fall in love a hundred times a day,' sighed May. 'We're so different aren't we?'

'How do you know that you truly love your Bill, then, May?' I asked, looking at her curiously.

May made no reply but sat herself upon an upturned boat on the beach and gazed out to sea. It was so beautiful, so calm, quiet and lovely. The sky was deepening to a vivid rose and purple and in the distance the sea had turned to that strange deep blue that was dark and mysterious. It was as if Night was arising from its depths like a magnificent Goddess; as if she was a living sentient being not just an absence of the sun. An old woman dressed all in black came wandering along the shore followed by a scruffy mongrel. She was still gathering flowers in her apron, wild flowers from the seashore. As she passed us she grinned, her teeth all black and broken and her skin wrinkled and ugly. She gave us both a flower from her apron and said some words of greeting in a harsh voice. Her act and look was kindly and I smiled at her and thanked her as I took the proffered flowers.

'What does she say?' said May flinging the flower down carelessly on the ground after the old woman had passed.

'She was saying something about *Proto Maia* ...May the First ...apparently, it's been a sort of Flower Festival today, a bit like our May Day, I suppose. Haven't you seen the wreaths of flowers hanging up on the doors of the village?'

May shook her head blankly. 'No, I didn't notice.'

'Eleni put one on the canteen tent flap for fun this morning. The wild flowers that bloom everywhere are gathered and made into wreaths and put upon the doors. Sadly, they soon wither and die, just like the youthful beauty of their women. But it's a lovely idea and for a brief moment does make everything look brighter and better.

'Well, I suppose it's a pretty idea,' May replied in a rather bored tone of voice.

'Aren't you interested in this country and its customs then, May?'

'Oh, I can't abide the people or this place, Dot! It's worse than I ever dreamt it could be ...I never thought such a hellish place could exist. They're smelly, dirty, covered in lice and flies. The villages smell a mile off and one is in terror of those frightful dogs of theirs. The city is busy and cheerful enough but expensive. And it's pretty smelly there too and the roads are so awful you're in fear of twisting an ankle any moment.'

'Well, don't wear those silly high heels then.'

'But I like to look nice. I long sometimes to have on a pretty dress and not this boring, old blue uniform. I want to be young and a girl having fun again and not always seeing sick men and washing wounds and changing dressings. I want to go home, Dot ...I want this horrid war to be over!'

I stared at her for I had never seen cheerful little May sound so downcast and unhappy, the tears trembling in the blue of her eyes. I put an arm about her and hugged her.

'Oh, May ...poor soul! I feel that too sometimes. But what can we do? You know you *can* always ask to go home, you aren't on contract like myself, you can go back any time you want.'

'*You* feel it too, Dot, *you* of all people? You are always so brave, so calm and sensible. You make me feel ashamed. No, of course, I won't go home till it's all over, one way and another. Bill has to stay, like it or not ...and so then shall I. I want him to be proud of me. I came with such good intentions and I'm already grumbling and groaning my head off. I'm so sorry!'

'Oh, don't be ...we all feel like that, it's only natural. None of the doctors grumble but they too must long to be back home with their wives and sweethearts. It's getting Bill's letter has upset you.'

'Yes, I think you're right. It is that ...I so long to see him. I do love him, Dot, even though I like to flirt with the handsome officers!'

'Even the Serbs and Greeks?' I laughed

'Well, they *are* gentlemen and very handsome some of them but give me an Englishman anytime. They all look alike to me these Serbs and Greeks ...all twirling their moustachios and eyeing one through and through, the saucy devils!'

I couldn't help laughing at her comic expression as she pretended to twirl imaginary whiskers and rolled her eyes fiercely.

'Life is horrible if you think about it too much,' she said suddenly and a slight shadow gave her normally animated features a momentary look of seriousness that somehow didn't become her at all. May was not made to think or feel anything but joyfulness, or to care for anything but having fun.

I felt in my heart that she was a shallow creature but still her charm and gaiety pleased me as it did all who knew her. Some are born to lighten those of us who have heavier and more serious dispositions just as butterflies are made to look delicate, beautiful and lure one after them as they dart gaily from flower to flower, never still, never at rest, elusive and lovely for a brief while. As she says, we are so unalike, but then opposites do attract one another. Perhaps I am too sober and feel things so much more keenly than May ever could. Her little depressions are soon over and like a cork, she bobs back up to the surface again. She doesn't want the depths of life but enjoys playing in the shallows like a child.

Sometimes, I wish I could be like her.

Chapter 12

May 4ᵗʰ 1916

Yesterday, on my afternoon off, I decided to take a ride into town with one of the ambulance men. I wasn't perturbed by all the rumours and horror stories about women venturing into the city though I know Matron prefers us to go out in pairs or more, preferably accompanied by one of the officers. The fact is I love to be alone whenever I can; everyone is so on top of each other in the camp and it makes me fidgety at times. When one is alone, one can take in the surroundings undisturbed by the inconsequential chatter of a companion. I assured myself I was afraid of very little in life and had great faith in my own good luck.

The driver dropped me off at the White Tower. I felt like a schoolgirl on holiday; it was such a freeing experience to be out of the camp and on my own. The bustle and noise was deafening at times with trolleys clanging along, wagons, trucks and those useful Army Fords we call the Tin Lizzie bustling about carrying stores and dropping of nurses, officers and anyone else who might have cadged a lift into town. Amongst this confusion, passed the horse-drawn gharries or *arabas* full of important looking officer who had just arrived and hadn't yet realised they were being charged the earth for their ride. Then there were the shouts of pastry sellers calling their wares, their sticky sweetmeats buzzing with flies. Turkish porters came by loaded with enormous weights from a piano to a huge wine barrel. Soldiers in their various uniforms strolled along the promenade, mingling with Greeks from the mountains in their long white pleated skirts they call the *fustanella*. In the dirty, dusty roads, oxen with loaded carts filled with anything from water melons to barrels of wine, Army mules and donkeys with a fat Turk on them weaved their way amongst the glorious confusion of races, sounds, religions and costumes. I loved it all and laughed with sheer delight.

I decided to walk through the city and up the hill towards the massive towering walls with their seven towers. A most forbidding citadel stands on the ramparts up there and is called the *Yedi Kule*. Here, so the story goes, people were imprisoned for years under the Turkish regime. By the time these poor souls were released by the Greeks, they staggered forth as old men whose families had all but forgotten them.

To reach this place, one first has to pass through the Jewish section of the city that lies behind the sea walls to the Via Egnatia. There seem to be synagogues everywhere. I passed through the busy area of the markets and business quarters and made my way through fascinating streets with dark little shops tucked away here and there and heard the hammering and banging of myriad coppersmiths as they fashioned their beautiful wares. Here big balconies hung out over the street and elderly Jewish ladies in their strange Sephardic costume sat up on high, sipping their coffees, and looking over curiously as I clambered up the hill. Little children also came out to look and pointed at me, jabbering and giggling, calling to me for *backsheesh, missie, backsheesh!* But I remembered my last experience and refrained from parting with money. How fair some of these little Jewish children are! It surprises me to see them as fair as any little English child might be.

The Sephardim Jews here speak a form of old Spanish-Greek, called Ladino. They had been driven out of Spain centuries ago and allowed to settle here by the Turks. It was a haven of peace for them here; they virtually made Salonika their very own city, a second Jerusalem, where they lived in peace and without persecution for centuries.

Past the Jewish area one climbs to the Upper Town where

the Turkish quarters lie. This part of the city is quaint and mysterious with its labyrinthine, cobbled streets. The houses are made of wood or stone with stout wooden doors set in high walls and closely latticed windows barred with wrought iron grilles. Here one might glimpse the flutter of a dark robe and know that the Turkish ladies sit in their harem behind these walls and look down on the streets at all the passers by, yet cannot be seen themselves.

Despite the heat, I enjoyed the climb up to the walls and once there stood staring down on the city, thinking many deep things, still caught up in my amazement at being there at all. In worldly terms it had all arisen from such an apparently insignificant happening as some Austrian Archduke being assassinated in a far off Balkan country!

In the distance lay majestic Mount Olympus. Its high summit, ever wreathed in misty vapours and drifts of cloud, was the home of the ancient, pagan Gods and I wondered if they were taking their revenge for centuries of Christianity when the Lamb of God had banished them all to the depths of Tartaros. Perhaps they were now rising from the deep and calling for blood sacrifices on a grand scale to feed their long held fury. Something greater than our tiny human selves seemed at work. Here was I, a puny mortal, close to the very home of these fierce, ancient Gods. England seemed so far away, another lifetime, another me.

The deep, booming moan of a ship in the harbour brought me back to the present and I felt it was time to descend the slopes to the main city if I wanted to fit in some tea and cakes at the King George Hotel before I returned. It was impossible to walk fast in this heat so one had to give oneself plenty of time. Slowly, I began to walk back down the twisting little streets, observing all the fascinating little details of the houses and the people I passed.

A man in baggy trousers and red fez was sweeping the roadside. He looked at me with curiosity but said nothing, just watched me silently, then returned to his work. The local people had stirred now from the somnolence of their midday siesta and were returning to work and play. Small back-street shops plied their business as they had no doubt done for centuries and I saw young boys carrying little trays on chains to various shop doorways. No doubt the proprietor was entertaining someone whose business he sought, haggling cheerfully over the prices with a cup or two of sweet, dark Turkish coffee and a plateful of delicious *lukum*. A *limonada* passed by calling his wares in his clear, sing-song voice and I was tempted to buy a drink from him but dear old Captain Dunning would have thrown up his nicotine stained hands in horror – so I desisted.

The colours of the houses were bright and cheerful but looked far better from a distance. Close to they were often peeling and cracked with little tumbledown areas. Little weeds and wild flowers grew out of the cracks or decorated the doorposts and small lizards sometimes darted out to settle on a stone and warm themselves in the rays of a bright sun that slanted round and over the tops of the houses, penetrating the deep shadows in the street. I stopped to look at these funny little creatures and smile to myself at the insignificant things of Nature, so utterly oblivious to our human raging and madness.

I now came to streets of larger houses, some two to three stories in height, surrounded with gardens fenced off by stout iron railings. They had large double doors with big iron knockers set in them. I wondered what lay beyond these doors. Sometimes one might be slightly open and one glimpsed some little courtyard shaded by flowering lemon trees. The strong, sweet scent of mimosa came to me as I passed one house. A small blonde boy ran out of from the half-open doors and coming right up to me, he stood there, thumb in mouth staring. From above a woman's voice called out to him in Ladino Spanish and looking up I saw a young and pretty Jewish girl, perhaps his nurse, who leant over the balcony. She smiled at me and I smiled back, patting the lad on his fair, curly head. He ran back into the courtyard and the doors glided mysteriously shut after him.

As I walked along one of the little streets, one of the big wooden doors opened. I paused briefly, ever curious to have a tiny glimpse inside for all these doors seemed to me to be like the caves of Ali Baba, full of unknown treasures, the strange compelling allure of forbidden, hidden things that has teased us since the days of Pandora and her Box. I was surprised to hear men's voices speaking in voluble Greek and not the usual Spanish. Out of the massive oak door strode a tall, slim and commanding looking man of about thirty who was dressed inconspicuously enough in dark baggy trousers with a black woollen kalpak on his head which most people wore now that the Turkish fez was no longer in fashion. For a Greek, as I deemed him to be, he was unusually tall and, despite the poor looking clothing, had a proud military bearing about him. He was followed by a smaller, older and bearded man with traditional, rich looking Jewish robes who must certainly have been the master of the house. He patted the taller fellow on the arm and then hugged him and seemed to be saying farewell.

'Goodbye, Takis,' I heard him say.'Take care and come again as soon as you can. Palomba misses you.'

'Doesn't Ishabel miss me too?' smiled the tall man.

'Well, of course, what a silly question. Take care, good friend.'

'Goodbye, Yussef.'

The two men embraced once more.

It was rude of me to pause and watch and I wasn't really aware I was doing so. I had disappeared somewhere inside myself and felt utterly unselfconscious. Sometimes it was like watching a film at the cinema; like a story, life went on before one and was so different, so interesting that I had to stand and watch it all.

The house owner now shut the door and the taller man turned round as if instinctively sensing my presence and gave me a sharp and penetrating look. His eye was so piercing, so direct, that I flushed with sudden embarrassment and yet I could not look away. We stared at each other in silence. His eyes were a deep, dark brown, almost black, with a hard, glittering cruelty about them that nonetheless attracted me. His face was sallow but unlined, his dark hair thick, waving in abundance over his head and he wore a small, clipped little moustache. His was a face that I felt I would never forget. It was not handsome, yet it had character, a sense of nobility about it, mingled with pride and haughtiness. His frame was slender but very strong and flexible.

Suddenly a sweet smile came over his features as he noticed my nurses' uniform. Those hard, dark eyes softened in the most incredible manner and became tender and feeling. I smiled back and he made a little bow, with just a slight click of his heels. I felt sure that he was a military man and wondered why he was not in uniform. However, it was no business of mine. I did know that the Greek army was demobilised and heard that it had been withdrawn from the city some time ago. He could be a Royalist spy; he could be anything. But, in that moment, I cared nothing for that.

He turned then and went swiftly on his way down the street and disappeared down one of the twisting corners.

'I will never forget your face,' I murmured to myself. 'How interesting you look! I wonder who and what you are and why you are here in this Jewish house. He called you Takis, so you must be a Greek...I wonder who you are?'

However, the incident soon went out of my mind and I walked on a little more speedily to the sea front and enjoyed my tea and cakes at the King George before making my way back to camp.

Chapter 13

May 5th 2.30am 1916

We were woken up early this morning by the noise of incendiary rockets going up into the sky and the bangs and booms of guns from the ships in the harbour. Careless of anything, we all came running out of our tents to have a look. Some sensible Sisters put a tin basin on their heads in case of any falling shrapnel. But we need not have worried for the action was all taking place high up over the bay. Searchlights were scouring the night skies and suddenly we saw them centre on what looked like a huge silver cigar.

'Good grief, it's a Zepp!' said May excitedly.

The guns blared from the battleships in the harbour and it was like fireworks going off as bits of tracer shells began to float to earth again. Suddenly the Zeppelin began to take a nose-dive downwards. We watched it fall swiftly away to the other side of the bay amongst the Vardar mud flats amidst deafening cheers that seemed to echo around Salonika from camps, hotels, streets and boats. It was really quite thrilling.

Hard to go to bed after all this so some of us congregated in the mess tent and made ourselves some cocoa and talked with great enthusiasim about the hit, wondering who had scored the bullseye.

May 7th

The news has come through that it was HMS *Agamemnon,* one of our British ships that scored the hit the other night with a 12 pounder in the forward bridge. It had only become the ship of a senior Naval Officer this April so what a stunning victory for the crew. Naturally the French, and Italians are trying to pretend it was their shot but no one takes any notice. Our engineers have gone over to collect the bits and pieces of the Zeppelin and mean to reconstruct it near the Tour Blanche so as to make out how it works ...it's really quite a coup. Evidently the German crew set fire to the airship and tried to escape through the swampy marshes but they were all captured, thank goodness.

The last remnants of the Serbian army are now straggling in to the city. It seems that some of them have never seen the sea before and are vastly suspicious of it. How strange it must be living in a landlocked area, never to see the sea in one's life! I am glad that I was born on an island where, in just a short journey by bus or train, one is ever close to the shores.

May 14th

'This is a very hot summer, we haven't had such a summer for twenty years,' Eleni told me today, wiping the sweat from her face. 'The grapes are ripening very fast on our vines.'

Not so good for us poor foreigners though, I thought, for the heat is absolutely unbearable of late. We have taken to wearing nothing but overalls to work in; they are a good protection from lice and mosquitoes. At night the nurses who go on duty look quite comical. They have to wear mosquito netting over their heads and long, protective gloves and some sort of puttees wrapped round their legs. A special tent had been rigged up for them at the back of the camp to sleep in peace when they come off duty –well, as much peace as can be had with dogs barking, hens clucking, people shouting, lorries and ambulances rattling around, plus the distant din from the city. In other words, a normal day in the camp.

All the same, night duty has its compensations for it is a mite cooler at least, especially if the wind blows over from the sea bringing a slight salty tang to the air. When one goes on duty at dusk, the fireflies light up the night like strange little lanterns shimmering in the air. As it grows darker, the stars in the sky are so clear that they seem ready to be plucked from the sky and set in our hurricane lamps. On moonlit nights the whole area is flooded in a strange, unearthly whiteness and the sea glistens in the far off distance. These wonderful sights cheer one's spirit when one walks into the wards ready to care for the poor restless, delirious, malaria-racked patients, taking pulses, four hourly temperatures, mopping down feverish limbs. Then after a long, busy night to come forth into the violet dawn and see the mist rising over the '*wine-dark seas.*' It has a mystery about it at such times which stirs me deep inside. It is as if for some strange inexplicable moment all the ancient heroes of Homer are still alive, they move yet about the landscape, and it is no longer the River Vardar but the ancient Axius. The Gods reign on Mount Olympus and we little human beings go about our business here below in fear and trembling of the thunderbolts of Zeus. It is a truly beautiful place. Yes, despite the heat, the flies, the mosquitoes, I am still so glad to be here.

May 17*th*

This outdoor life is doing us all a world of good. The nurses and doctors all look suntanned, fit and healthy despite all the hard work we endure. Captain Dunning still smokes like a chimney and his cough hacks away. He can be heard approaching a mile off so you are well aware of his presence long in advance of his arrival. Ethan Willoughby has shed something of his grey pallor and is beginning to look tanned and healthy and his eye has lost its sad, dullness. He's actually beginning to look quite attractive! I won't tell May that, of course, or she'll be off on her eternal matchmaking.

I suspect that he is really enjoying the work. There are certainly a variety of operations, and many of them complex and interesting. It's strange but if I am on duty and he is operating, Matron always asks me to go over and help him. The other day we had an emergency tracheotomy to perform on one of the children from the village. Willoughby actually came to me himself as I was walking around the officer's ward taking temperatures.

'Come along, Sister, I need your help with this child. I want you to hold her while I operate. The poor thing's scared out of her wits.'

'Yes, sir,' I said meekly and asked one of the other girls to carry on with the temperatures and followed him at once.

I did wonder why he never asked the other sisters. When I mentioned it to Matron she told me that he says he likes to have me there whenever I am on duty as he feels I am always so calm and unflappable. I wish that was true. I still find it hard to watch some of the operations. This one was pretty grisly and seemed to take ages to finish. Willoughby had to cut the child's throat and then slit the windpipe and put a tube in while I held the mite as tenderly as I could. I was thankful that we now had an anaesthetist as just a short time ago it would have had to be performed without an anaesthetic.

It still takes all my courage to watch these operations but I am getting hardened to them and my interest in the medical procedures manages to overcome my momentary squeamishness. It is at times like this, when I watch Willoughby performing his work, see his intense concentration, his utter dedication and love for the patients that I begin to feel true admiration for the man. He has the most beautiful hands. They are deeply expressive hands with a generosity and gentleness about them that belies his cold, defensive exterior. Behind this social façade, I can see that there is strength and courage and I truly respect that.

I sense that he in turn understands that I am very stoical by nature and capable of keeping my natural feelings in check, for to my way of thinking the necessity of the work is far more important than my selfish needs. Of course, all the nurses are being brave in just this way. Yet he does seem to have a special fondness for me these days and, both of us being of a serious and taciturn disposition, appear to work together very well. It is as if I know exactly what is required and how his mind works and therefore always ready with what he wants. He likes efficiency, and appreciates my swift appraisal of the situation. He never says so, never utters a word of thanks or praise, nor would I want him to, it would embarrass me. We understand one another in some strange unspoken way.

My tracheotomy patient needs very careful nursing for the tube becomes choked up with pus and blood and has to be constantly cleaned out through a hole using a swab in a pair of forceps. The dear, little mite is very good and makes no fuss or struggle. Only her large eyes express her feelings as she cannot make a sound. She looks very lovingly at me sometimes and I want to hold her and hug her but dare not as yet. Her mother and various other relations stand outside the window of her ward and make the most awful noise. The orderlies keep trying to chase them away but they will not go. The women weep and wail loudly as if already at the funeral they obviously expect to attend for as far as they are concerned a hospital visit means death; such is their experience of Greek hospitals! Thank God, the child recovered beautifully and was taken away by grateful parents who knelt and kissed the hem of my gown.

Captain Willoughby was passing by when all this was going on and came over to see what the fuss was about.

'This is the person you should thank,' I told the father, 'this is the doctor who cured your child, all I did was nurse her afterwards.'

The father turned towards Willoughby and bowed low. He thanked him profusely in a rattle of Greek like machine gun fire. Willoughby bowed back and smiled.

'No need for any thanks,' he said rather abruptly and went on his way.

For some reason, I felt I liked him even more because of this reticence.

Chapter 14

May 30ᵗʰ 1916

May has had her visit from her sweetheart, Sergeant Bill Myers. He came down with one of the field ambulances on Sunday which is our 'at home' day here in camp. He seems a very pleasant, well-spoken young man. He is brown haired with light brown eyes and an open, good-natured look on his face. Thankfully the Colonel of the Camp has been away on business this last couple of days and Matron who has a soft spot for May, waived Army regs about consorting with NCO's. She allowed May the afternoon off to meet her fiancé on the proviso that they didn't go into town together but stayed in the camp.

We held a tea party in our tent and invited some of the officers who are always keen to participate in such activities, especially if there was any cake to be had. As it happened, we had some very nice biscuits and cook produced an astonishing pink cake for us in which he had used goat dripping. It gave the cake a strange but interesting flavour. Bill Myers told us some riveting stories about the conditions our poor men have had to endure. He has a lively sense of humour and soon had us all laughing at the doings of his comrades and their various adventures. It was marvellous to hear of the high morale of the men despite illness, flies, long night marches and the peculiar extremes of weather that are to be encountered in that wild terrain.

'You haven't a clue how boring the whole thing is. Now and then we 'make play' at attacking 'the enemy' in the form of another battalion who takes the role. That sort of manoeuvre livens things up a bit at least.'

'You mean you pretend to fight yourselves!' asked May in astonishment.

'It's meant to be practice for the real thing. Little birds in the Birdcage we are,' joked Bill, 'but things have got a bit better than when we first arrived. We have some kind of order now, stores have arrived at last, and life is a bit more tolerable. But we've only just got a few mosquito nets and solar topees sent up, can you believe it? If the ruddy powers-that-be in Egypt had their way, we wouldn't have had a thing. They simply don't understand this terrain at all.'

'We all know about supplies!' said one of the men. 'We're all cheesed off about it! They really treat us as if we were living the life of Riley here, just because we're near a city. Have any of them ever come to see this bloomin' city? Do they think it's Southhampton or something? They should come over and take a look at this smelly, noisy dump.'

'Dead right you are,' agreed Bill, 'but what we can we poor wotsits do? I can put up with most of it but it's the boredom that's worst. We tend to gamble a lot, I'm afraid. One of our things is having races with the tortoises. There are hundreds of them up there on the hills, big fellas some of them, hundreds of years old, I expect. Occasionally we get together a Company concert …our own band has played in the Place de Liberte a couple of times and I can tell you that went down very well with the locals. Or a pretty good troupe comes round all the units. It's something we all look forward to no end. All our favourite tunes to sing-a-long to.'

'We have some concerts here too. Dot and I play on the piano for our patients once they start to get better,' said May.

'Yes, and it probably makes them ill again,' chipped in some wag.

'Nonsense!' said May crossly. 'Some of the other nurses make a little ensemble and one or two of them have really beautiful voices. It all sounds very pretty. The men say we sound like an angelic choir and they wonder if they have died and are in heaven! Isn't that silly? The officers like to dress up and do funny burlesques, that's what the men like best, of course. Our piano renderings aren't too marvellous though, are they Dot? ...but no-one complains! They really love *Home sweet Home* and all the old favourites.'

'Well, don't go and play *Tipperary* if the Serbs are anywhere about. I swear they think it's our National Anthem for they're always playing that ruddy tune for us wherever we go. I've even heard them singing it in harmonies, which is pretty queer to listen to ...not that it isn't an improvement on the original.'

'They can't help it,' I laughed, 'the Orthodox liturgy is in their souls. Yes, I've heard them singing like that too; I think they sound marvellous.'

'Not if they keep singing *Tipperary* in every village you enter!'

'But what *is* going on out there?' asked one of the men who had joined us in our tent for tea, 'are you fellows ever going to fight?'

'It's what we want, isn't it?' Bill said with a shrug and a sigh. 'We keep getting orders that we're going to fight but then along comes someone saying that the ADC says we can't advance after all for some reason or other. Usually it's all to do with supplies. An army can't march without supplies, especially in this God-forsaken place. Food and ammo ...we have to have food and ammo. Emergency supplies we do carry along with us but they're only meant to last a day. They are for absolute and *utter* emergencies. I've had mine since France.'

'Well, yes, I know. But what the hell are they doing about it back home?

'Search me, no idea. All I know is General Milne has taken over from Bryan Mahon who's pushed off to Egypt, but nothing seems to have changed much otherwise. We still make roads, put up barbed wire and bunker down with the mosquitoes for company. Those blighters get in everywhere and as for the lice! You just can't get rid of them.'

'I suppose you can't give us a clue where you are right now? Or if there's going to be any movements?'

'No, I can't, mainly because I haven't a clue. *We* aren't

expected to know what the big-shots are planning. We just get on with it and wait. All I know is that I half envy some of the chaps who managed to get sent home early on when the ships could get through to old Blighty because they were too sick with malaria to come back up the line. Otherwise, the way things are now, you just get better in some field hospital then back up the line till you fall ill again, then back again to hospital and so it goes on till one is too weak to do anymore.'

'Don't envy them,' I said quietly, 'they will be sick for most of their lives. The malaria is in their blood and in their soul, I suspect. God willing, you men will all come through this and soon be home ready to take up your lives again.'

Bill looked at me and smiled a little sadly, 'Well, Dot, you're right. I apologise, ladies, for such a show of weakness. It's just that one could go mad waiting and wondering. We are soldiers, we're honed up for battle and action. It's hell having to polish our bayonets and boots all the time and grow beans and tomatoes when we long to take a stab at the blighters. You've no idea how frustrating it can be.'

'Poor Bill!' said May sadly, taking his hand in hers and giving it a fond squeeze. 'We can't say that about life here. We're always on the go, aren't we Dot?'

'We are indeed!

'Sometimes,' said Bill with an air of extreme bitterness, 'I think the people back home have just forgotten about us. They've sent us here without proper kit or food or solar protection and here we are, stuck like idiots, dying of bloody dysentery and malaria instead. We're the forgotten army.'

June 1ˢᵗ

It was nice to see May with her man and her distress at parting with him was very touching. It made us all feel rather romantic and even Matron's eye seemed to have a gentler beam.

'To think we would have been married and living back home in a dear, little house, maybe had a child by now,' May sighed.

'It will happen, May. Like Bill, you just have to be patient.

Nothing stays stuck forever,' I said as philosophically as I could for at times even my optimism failed me and I wondered if this war was going to go on for ever and ever. Or would we all be wiped out by it, the world return to the Dark Ages once more and the 'poor inherit the earth'? On the whole, I *was* enjoying the adventure, the interesting work and the comradeship of the other men and women. One met so many different and fascinating people. Also I felt a love for this country that May and Bill and many others obviously did not. For me it was redolent with an ancient past that they neither knew nor cared about. It was dear old Blighty they wanted, with all that was familiar and safe.

Seeing Bill and then having to part from him seemed to make May very depressed. For some time her natural ebullience deserted her and she looked sad and downcast, scarcely eating. I took her in hand as much as I could and it was I who now became the gay and cheerful one while May turned silent.

She tried hard but something of her merry spirit seemed to leave her and she certainly never flirted with any of the men again much to their disappointment. She put Bill's photo by her bedside and stared at it every night, often for some time before turning down the lamp and falling asleep out of sheer exhaustion.

June 15th

We were roused very early this morning by our Austrian POW banging on a little tin at our tent door that serves us as our alarm. He had left the hot water outside in a can and I brought it in and started the morning ablutions in a rather grumpy mood.

'It's so early, what can be going on?' yawned May who was still lying in bed.

'I seem to recall Willoughby saying that some visitors were coming to see the hospital today so I suppose we all have to look ship-shape and hearty, so come on May, before this water goes cold.'

'Not much chance of that happening in this wretched heat,' she sighed as she dragged herself out of bed for, despite the early hour, it already felt humid and sticky. I sighed and agreed with her heartily as I wrestled with the little buttons of my white collar and cuffs and wished we had a more sensible uniform in this weather. I envied the Scottish Women's who were allowed to cut their hair short, wore really short skirts and much simpler uniforms and looked far more cool and comfortable and somehow liberated.

We went on duty and were amazed to see how everything looked so spick and span. The army of Greek ladies who came and cleaned had set to with a will already and all the patients were neatly tucked up by the night nurses and told to stay still and behave properly or else! The livestock which generally just roamed about the camp had been confined to various places, fenced off by wire netting from whence arose the pathetic bleats of our two little lambs used to their freedom and the furious clucking of six hens deprived of their favourite pecking places. The goats were always tied up but they often managed to escape and would cheerfully wander into one of our tents where they would sample anything left about from our newly starched and ironed collars and cuffs hanging on a little line to the odd handkerchief or stocking lying on a bed. And anyone foolish enough to leave a precious letter lying about might return to find nothing left but a soggy chewed up ball. Today, however, they were securely tied on short ropes and looked very dismal about it all.

'Who is coming, sir?' I asked Willoughby who was striding around the various wards and laboratories with his assistant making sure everything was up to his ideas of perfection.

'A Greek officer and a Greek doctor are coming to inspect some of our hospitals and take a few tips from our vastly superior way of running them,' he said. It was meant to be a joke, I suppose, but Willoughby had a manner of saying his jokes that always made them sound so flat and serious. Nobody ever laughed at them. However, I smiled to please him and went back to my work longing as always to giggle at his slight pomposity.

I had prepared a delicious egg flip in the tiny kitchen attached to the ward and was feeding it to a very sick patient when I heard a bit of a commotion at the door. Looking up, I saw Matron enter, followed by a Greek Colonel, his ADC, plus another gentleman in mufti whom I assumed must be the Greek doctor. Willoughby and another MO, Captain Sherwood, made up the rear and behind all this crowd came another man who turned out to be a reporter from some Greek newspaper. Despite the rather crowded nature of things, Sister Deirdre and I carried on quietly with our work. Having finished feeding my patient and wiped his mouth with care, I gathered up the utensils and began to take them away to wash.

'This is one of our very best nurses,' I heard Willoughby saying in his quiet tones and with a trace of a smile on his serious face as he came up to me. He was speaking to the party in general but the doctor in particular. I looked up rather shyly for praise always disconcerted me. I hated to be singled out in any way, especially with such an unlooked for comment from Captain Willoughby of all people! ...but smiled and laid down the bowl and shook hands with the Greek doctor. He seemed a very distinguished looking person with greying hair, handsome dark eyes and a strong handclasp. The Greek Colonel looked very splendid in his uniform and stood nodding affably. I'm afraid his name escaped me; it was one of those long, convoluted Greek names like Papadopoulandreou or something like that. Then I turned to his ADC who was introduced as Captain Costas Cassimatis.

I started in surprise and shock. It was the face I would never forget; the tall, slim, dark man who had stepped out of the Jewish house in the city, who had looked at me so deeply and intensely, and then disappeared out of my life ...or so I had supposed.

I gasped and went to say something but stopped myself almost at once. The Captain gave a half-smile and bowed to me but there was no recognition at all in his dark eyes. He looked through me rather coldly and his gaze went to the patient in the bed with more interest than he gave to me. I don't know why I should but I felt a pang of disappointment. Yet why on earth should he recognise me? All nurses must look pretty much the same to him just as we always jokingly said all Greek men looked the same to us. Though I knew now that that wasn't true for this man was quite distinctive ...to me, anyway.

I watched them go and admired once more his proud bearing, one hand behind his back holding his horse whip, a walk which was not stiff but almost animal like in its flexibility yet rather like an animal that is ready to move swiftly to flight or else, if cornered, to fight to the death. I felt he had lived a dangerous life; it seemed to breath from ever pore of his being. It was something our soldiers didn't quite have, this strange watchfulness, this sense of wildness and suppressed cruelty that peeped out from the nobility of such a face. I had seen something of it in other Greek and Serbian faces too. There was a curious candour but also a contradictory wiliness and slyness about them and also a feeling that these men had an endurance and harsh courage we might never match. They had seen so much fighting and hardship these latter years and the brigand blood was in their veins. These were men of the wild and inhospitable mountains not of the quiet, peaceful, uneventful British countryside.

The little party moved out of our hut and on to the next. I watched them go rather regretfully. I would never meet this man again, this Captain Cassimatis. I wondered why he attracted me so much. Who can say? I shrugged the incident off and carried on as usual.

Later on, Willoughby came over as I walked towards the Sister's Mess tent for a cup of tea.

'How come you knew that officer?' he asked almost sternly.

'Which officer?' I asked in surprise.

'The Greek chap ...you looked as if you recognised him.'

Good gracious, did nothing escape this man's eye!

I assured him that it had been a case of mistaken identity and that I had thought he looked familiar when he was not. Willoughby gave me a thoughtful look for a moment and then strode off. What a cheek! What business is it of his anyway? I am really fuming about it.

Chapter 15

July 6th 1916

There is news on the grapevine that some of the men are moving forward to the frontline at last and May thinks the Wiltshires will be amongst them which means poor Bill may see some action after all. Goodness, why are men so mad keen to fight all the time? I just pray that nothing will happen to him. But I suppose inaction is far worse for them when they are all keyed up and ready to take the enemy on. However, at the moment it is all just whispered rumour and we shall have to wait and see.

I decided to go into town again on my own yesterday. Perhaps I had some vague hope of bumping into Captain Cassimatis. I am really beginning to become as foolish as May. What on earth is the matter with me? However, my actual excuse is that I need to go to the Mondiano market and look for some material to cover over the boxes we use as provisional furniture and to make a couple of little bedspreads to cheer up our little sleeping area. May was still on duty as it happened and so I went with one of the officers and Corporal Smith who also wanted to visit the town, though from all accounts I had of the latter fellow, it was the Red Light district at Vardari that he was more interested in. I chuckled a little as I watched the Corporal salute and disappear down a side street with a muttered apology that he had to go and sort out some urgent business.

There seemed to be a lot of soldiers about the streets today; French, Sengalese, British, Italian and Serbs jostled, gesticulated and talked in loud and dramatic tones. Droves of donkeys and mules and little small mountain ponies laden with packs went by and odd bullock wagons covered with bulky tarpaulin. There is something in the air that makes me feel action of some sort is about to take place now that the Allied reinforcements have arrived at last. General Sarrail is up to something and I suppose we shall soon enough know what it is.

I went to the market first of all, the wonderful market in the Jewish quarter, which is also where the banks and the best shops and hotels are, the Jews being in charge of most of the commerce in this city. It was delightful to look at all the amazing assortments of colourful silks and materials and other objects on offer. There was some beautiful leatherwork and intricately wrought copper items made by the Turks too. But as Dunning had said, a great many utensils and electrical goods from Birmingham or Germany had found their way there; these being much coveted items to the native Salonikans, though pretty commonplace enough to us Europeans. Mirrors seemed to be almost priceless for some reason.

I bought my length of cloth and began to walk in the direction of the roundabout, which the Tommies called 'Piccadilly Circus' because so many roads branched off it. I then took a route down some of the side streets for they were always so much more interesting.

'*Simera ehei, avrio then ehei!* ('here today and gone tomorrow!') came the shrill call of an old Jew wearing a turban and flowing dark robe and with a long tape measure about his neck. He passed by me, walking beside a little mule that carried what looked like two little cupboards on either side.

They did seem to pile up these poor little creatures. Sometimes all one could see walking along the country roads were moving hay bundles with little hooves poking out beneath them. However, this animal was well looked after. The Jewish peddler knocked at a door and one of the servants came to open it. While the servant went to fetch his mistress, the old Jew, seeing my interest called to me,

'*Vene aqui, chicita! Orea tsitaki!*' ('Come here little girl, beautiful cottons!')

He beckoned me over and showed me his wares. The little cupboards were covered with doors of wire netting and through these one could see shelves on which were rolls of pretty, sprigged cotton. I nodded and smiled and looked appreciative of them and wished now that I had waited and bought some of his materials, which were far cheaper and prettier. He looked most disgruntled when I showed him I had already bought some stuff and shook his head at me angrily.

I walked on and my mind for some reason returned once more to the mysterious Captain Cassimatis. I wondered if I could find the place where I last saw him. The trouble was that very few of these twisting streets in this area of the city had names and they all began to look very alike after a while. I couldn't remember the route I had taken when I had first seen him and in trying to find it began to wander down some very narrow little streets with rather dilapidated houses. Great trellises of vines weaved overhead from house to house across the divide of the street making a green gloom below which, while shady and restful from the heat of the afternoon sun, was also rather mysterious and claustrophobic. Washing hung in some of the front porches and a few black robed women stared at me with the blatant curiosity of all these people, especially at the sight of a lone European woman.

I became rather lost in thought at this point and when I came to myself, I realised that I had now wandered far astray and had no idea where I was. It was the darkness that awoke me to my plight for the street I was now in seemed to have high, windowless walls on each side that gave an appearance of warehouses or storerooms of some kind and the smell of petroleum hung in the air. I could hear the faint sounds of the sea and the groaning boom of a ship and wondered if I was near the Jewish port. There was also the unmistakable sound of trains shunting so I knew I was somewhere close to the railway station. It was strangely deserted just here and I could hear the hollow ring of my heels on the rough cobbles. They were always rather hard on the feet, though still better than some of the dusty sidewalks or pitted roads of the city.

Suddenly, I took in with a start the squalor of this area and realised that I had completely lost myself. A slight, just a slight, quiver moved my heart. No, I was not afraid, I told myself severely. What was there to fear? I decided to retrace my steps and find my way back down to the harbour side.

I took the turning back but something went wrong and I was soon hopelessly lost in a maze of tangled little streets and alleyways which seemed to be leading back to the Turkish quarters. I saw a heavy door open in one of the ramshackle houses and out came a couple of navvies, talking earnestly to one another. They seemed raffish individuals, dark, dirty and evil looking. It was hard to tell what nationality they were, perhaps Greeks, perhaps Jews, but I had no desire to enter into conversation with them whatever their origins. They looked at me in surprise and then their eyes narrowed and they looked at one another. I didn't like their faces at all. I turned again and began to retrace my way and heard their heavy, rapid footsteps gaining on me. In that moment, I was utterly terrified and began to run, a really foolish thing to do. I could hear them pounding along after me, drawing closer so that I felt sure I could smell the drink on their breath. I would be raped and robbed, glad not to be murdered; everything dreadful seemed to flash before my eyes.

'Please God, help me!' I prayed aloud.

One of the men had caught up with me now and seized me by the arm. He was utterly horrible and his vile features will haunt me till I die. I screamed and tried to punch him in the face but he laughed and said something derisive in Greek to his accomplice. I felt disgusted as his fat, hammy hands began to wander over my body, looking for jewellery or my purse, his foul, garlic-laden breath in my face. I rallied myself and a fierce anger ran through me. I wasn't letting this brute have my purse or anything else and I tried to kick him and bite him and push him away by sticking my fingers in his eyes, which only made him angrier and nastier in turn. I really had very little sense; I suppose I should have kept still and quiet, but refused to go down without a fight.

I heard him shout angrily to his mate something to effect

that he would teach this wild one a lesson and he seized my breasts and twisted them so hard that I thought I would faint with the pain. I felt myself sliding down to the ground as my knees buckled beneath me.

It was then that a darkly dressed and equally dirty looking man stepped out of the shadows and a very nasty looking knife suddenly appeared in front of my assailant's neck. The ruffian's hands darted to his neck and it was his turn to look afraid as the steel bit a fraction into him and drops of blood began to drip down onto a dirty collar.

'Move an inch,' said a rough, rasping voice in very colloquial Greek, 'and you're dead meat, you foul bastard.'

I stood by and watched in horror as my apparent champion then proceeded to kick and punch and swear heartily at the fellow before letting him run off down the street after his companion who had taken to his heels long ago. It took me some time to recover my composure. My rescuer seemed about as rough and evil as the men he had rescued me from but he *was* on my side; at least I *hoped* that was the case.

'Thank you, thank you so much' I said in faltering Greek, 'you saved my life. Here, take some money.'

I offered him some drachma notes but he just stood and looked down on me for a few moments, seated in the dust, my hat fallen off heaven knows where, my hair beginning to tumble down. He was a tall man and I could scarcely see his face in the shadows and what I could see was weather-beaten and very dirty. He came closer slowly, as if not to alarm me, and taking my hand in his, pulled me to my feet. Then he wrapped my fingers about the notes and pushed them back at me. I stared at him standing in the shadows and tried to make out his face but his kalpak was drawn well down and its shadow fell across what looked like aquiline features.

He said roughly, 'You speak Greek? That's a big surprise. An Englishwoman who speaks Greek? But you know, you really must stop wandering about these streets all alone. This is a very rough area with robbers and thieves of all sorts. It's not a place for little English nurses like yourself.'

He then turned and looked as if he meant to go but I looked around me a little wildly and said, 'Don't go …please don't leave me! I don't know where I am. I don't know how to get out of here!'

The man hesitated and turned. I suddenly found that I had large hot tears streaming down my cheeks. It was ridiculous but I just couldn't help it.

'I'm sorry …just a delayed reaction,' I said in English, for my Greek deserted me at the moment. I wiped the tears away with the back of my hand and tried hard to look brave. I was so angry with myself for such feminine nonsense.

'Don't apologise,' the man replied in such good English that I looked up in astonishment, 'you're a brave, little girl, but very young and foolish too.'

His voice had changed and was no longer so rough but seemed far more cultured and quiet. Something inside my gut suddenly lurched in recognition. The man came a little closer.

'It seems as if someone keeps bringing us together, *petite souer*, and that I have had to appoint myself your protector. Are you always so foolhardy? So infernally curious?'

He took off his kalpak now and stood bareheaded before me and I at once recognised Captain Cassimatis, despite the fact that his face was so much browner and dirtier, his hair wild and unkempt. Seeing me start and about to exclaim something he put a finger to my lips and drew me back into an archway.

'Say nothing. Come with me.'

'My hat!' I said wildly, looking about for it. I had also lost my purchases.

'Forget your hat!' he said brusquely.

Taking my arm, he began to steer me away from that awful place and I followed him, half bemused, half-excited. It really was so strange that we should meet again, that he should be there just when I was in such need. It was truly as if he was my protector and God had answered my prayers. Not only at that dangerous and desperate moment but also my unspoken prayer that I might meet him again.

Chapter 16

Silently I followed Captain Cassimatis along the back streets, wondering where we were going but not really caring all that much, for I was caught up in the sheer sense of adventure. Also I felt a deep sense of trust; felt him capable of anything, a man with no fear, what the Greeks would call a *palikari leventis*. He seemed to know all the little back routes, the twists and turns of the alleys and arches and doorways, the ways to dodge people who might stare at a rough looking sailor hurrying along with a young British nurse in tow.

His disguise was so good that no one would have recognised the distinguished, upright Captain Cassimatis in this shambling, baggy-trousered ruffian with dirty face and hair. I had certainly not recognised him straight away but deep down with some female instinct, I knew who he was even as he kicked and swore at the rogue who had attacked me. I felt even then a strange kinship, a sense that he had something to do with me. I can't explain it. Something about him has always intrigued me from the start.

I wonder what exactly is his role. That he belongs to the Secret Service is obvious now and I assume he must be a Venizelist as he is in the Venizelist army. But who could say? Is he a Royalist at heart and spying for them or the Germans even? Our officers keep assuring us that there were dozens of pro-German spies about and how careful one has to be all the time. Somehow I feel that he is not one of these. Why would he have taken the trouble to rescue me if that was the case? Surely, he would have been delighted to let those nasty ruffians slit my English throat.

I pondered thus as we hastened through the alleyways until we reached a small door in a wall. Here Captain Cassimatis produced a large iron key from somewhere in the baggy trousers and opened the door. He pushed me unceremoniously inside and then with a swift movement shut the door and locked it again. We were in some sort of low-ceilinged, dusty passageway, lit only by a tiny grating high up. The Captain poked around on a high shelf and found a small oil lamp, which he proceeded to light up. Shadows sprang into being.

He now leant against a wall and produced a packet of cigarettes. He offered me one but I refused and he lit his up and drew on it with deep satisfaction. He then looked at me with a steady and appraising eye.

'You are very young, aren't you? You English women are such crazy creatures ...our girls would never behave the way you do, striding about, getting yourselves into such trouble. They have far more sense.'

I was stung by this comment.

'Well, in England we haven't quite so many evil ruffians as you seem to have here,' I retorted.

He shrugged and smiled a little.

'But,' I added humbly, 'I know I was foolish, knowing the dangers of *any* big city. The trouble is I just love to explore and find out about places and people. I wish I wasn't born a woman! Men have so much more freedom and don't have to be so careful.'

He gave a little laugh and patted my arm, 'You wouldn't really wish it; you're a charming *copellitsa,* a lovely young girl. See how I risk myself for you? As a man you have no freedom, you are at the beck and call of your country, your family, your work in life. You are just as capable of being murdered and robbed as a woman. What freedom is that? Am I free? I wish I was.'

His tone was sombre and a little sad. He ground the cigarette into the earthy floor and said, 'We're safe now, *copellitsa.* This passage leads to the home of my friend, Yussuf Yiakovides. That was the first time we met, remember? Outside his house.'

'I do remember. And you've been in my mind ever since,' I said candidly.

'I have? That's a dangerous thing to say. I have no wish to be in any one's mind at all. Maybe I should have left you to those cut-throats after all.'

'Why didn't you?'

'I cannot pass a woman in danger, it's not in my nature,' he replied with pride, 'on the other hand, due to my idiotic sense of chivalry, you are now a danger to *me* because you know me as Captain Cassimatis. You must forget that I am the same man. But can I trust you? Women are chatterboxes. Are English women any better than Greek ones?'

'Not at all,' I admitted,' we have our gossips and indiscreet women and men too. But, I *am* to be trusted. I will *never* give you away.'

I thrust out my hand to shake his but instead he took it between his own and held it for a moment or two, looking down at the floor as if weighing something up.

'For some reason, I *do* trust you,' he said at last.

'I want you to trust me,' I said eagerly.

'Remind me of your name again. I know we were introduced but it escaped me. Colonel Papandreou asked me to accompany him that day as I know good English …my father was very fond of the English nation and I had an English governess as a child. As soon as we walked into the ward, I spotted you. I was so shocked that of all the hospitals we might have visited that day, you should be there and moreover, that you immediately recognised me.'

So he hadn't forgotten me after all! I was so glad.

'My name is Dorothy Clark.'

'Dorothy …Dorothea, we would call you …a gift from the Gods. I have yet to judge quite what sort of gift you are. Are you going to be my Pandora?'

'I'm not opening any box, Captain. I owe you my life. Do you seriously believe I will betray you? You don't know me if you think such a thing. I may be young, but I am not a fool. I have some notion what you must be doing but I have been so sheltered all my life. I don't think I really *want* to know about it at all.'

'Well, that is certainly very wise. Yes, I trust you, Dorothea. God has thrust you in my path three times and something in me says this is for a purpose. I have no idea what it can be. But we Greeks are superstitious about such seemingly chance encounters. You are in my debt ...that is always useful.'

He smiled as he said this and then taking my arm again led me along the passageway. I loved the feel of his strong grip on my arm, his commanding presence. I felt so safe and secure with him and wanted nothing more than to be beside him forever. Was I falling in love with this man? Horrifying as it was for me to admit it, I knew I was.

The passageway led through a concealed trap door into the back of a house. We came out into a kind of kitchen or washing area.

'Most of these passageways were made by the Christians when the Turks first occupied us,' said Cassimatis, 'they sometimes had to escape underground.'

'To follow their religion?'

'In the old days the Turks were fairly easy going about religious freedom. They liked to tax us infidels and weren't at all enthusiastic that we should convert to the Muslim faith. Lots of people did so at first to dodge the taxation and then practised their religions secretly. Many Jews did this and are considered as Muslim but still secretly practice a kind of Judaism. No, for us it was the fact that the Greek knowledge, language and customs were being forgotten and lost. So schools were set up in secret to keep alive the Greek spirit. We no longer need these hiding places for this purpose and many people have forgotten about their existence. They are useful passages to those who know about them,' he added with a chuckle.

'Wait here a moment,' he said and opening the little door went through into a room beyond. I could hear the faint murmur of voices for a few moments and then he re-appeared.

'I'll leave you now. One of the servants will take you upstairs and give you some refreshments and anything else you want.

I've arranged for you to be taken safely back to your hospital camp. I have your word that you will not betray me?'

'You have my word, sir.'

He gave a strange little smile and said quietly, 'If I had not trusted you, you know I would have killed you?'

I went pale and silent for a moment.

'I don't think you would have.' I said in a firm voice, looking up at him. 'You're a gentleman.'

'Am I? That is real praise from an Englishwoman, a girl of good breeding, like yourself. But don't be so sure. I am everywhere, a child of the night, seen and then unseen. I am not my own person anymore but belong to my nation. I am a Greek patriot first and foremost. If I have to I *will* kill you. Not for any personal reason …no, not for that …little *copella*, little Dorothea …' and suddenly he took my chin in his hand, lifted my head up and gave me a swift kiss on the lips.

'*Adieu, ma petite,*' and then he disappeared back into the passageway from whence we had come.

I wanted to weep. I might never ever see him again.

Now I know how May felt when her man had to return to his unit.

The brief meeting, the uncertainty of meeting again.

The agony of loving!

I now went into the room beyond and a manservant was waiting there for me. He bowed low and ushered me to an upstairs room. The furnishings were modern and European rather than the oriental scene I had envisaged. There were sofas with pink velvet covers, gilt mirrors and framed pictures on the walls of various Spanish scenes. An old serving woman came to me now and brushed my clothes down with care, removing as much dust as was possible, even passing a cloth over my dirty shoes. She brought me a bowl of water and I washed my face and hands and dried them on a towel so soft and fluffy that I was envious, used as I was to the rough things we used in the camp.

My breasts still throbbed with pain and I unbuttoned my dress a little to see what damage that wretch had done and saw massive bruises beginning to form already. The woman gesticulated to me to show her and I did so and she looked horrified and said something to me in Ladino, that queer mixture of Greek, Hebrew and Spanish. I shrugged and grimaced a little and she nodded in sympathy. As she was dressing my hair which had tumbled all over my shoulders and looked quite wild, a small, middle aged lady came in, dressed in the rich and quaint old Sephardic costume, followed by a younger woman in a white muslin European dress. This was obviously the mistress of the house and she smiled at me and clapped her hands and another servant appeared with food and drink on marvellous plates of silver. A little brazier had been lit and coffee was brewing in a long handled copper vessel.

'Please do eat whatever you would like,' she said in French, 'is this adequate? Would you like anything else?'

'I thank you with all my heart,' I replied, 'but I'm not hungry. I would love some of the coffee, that's all.'

The lady served me herself and passing a tiny cup of sweet Turkish coffee and a little sesame cake to me, she told me that her name was Palomba and that she was the wife of Yussuf.

'This is our daughter, Ishabel,' she said, and the young lady bowed and smiled at me. She was a truly beautiful girl, her eyes large and dark and lustrous, her red lips warm and sensual. I remembered Costas Cassimatis saying 'and does Ishabel miss me too?' and felt a pang of jealousy. Was he courting this lovely young Jewess?

'Costas tells me you have had an unpleasant experience near the docks,' said Palomba, 'no-one should ever be alone round that area …Jew, Turk or Greek, the men there are rough types and often vagabonds. The Ashkenazi are the worst, they're pimps and take lovely white girls away to the Turkish harems. You are lucky to have escaped.'

'I certainly am,' I said with a shudder as I remembered the feel of those hateful hands.

The servant had finished my hair by now and spoke to her mistress quietly, pointing to me. Palomba looked angry and shook her head in dismay then sent the girl off with a command.

'I've asked Buena to fetch you some special ointment. She says you are covered in bruises.'

When Buena returned, she offered me a small, silver pot.

'You poor child,' Palomba said, 'here, take this with you. You may be a nurse but my mother's old remedies are not to be beaten! It's a salve made from various herbs. Try this tonight and the bruises will be almost gone by the morning.'

I thanked her and took the tiny, intricately wrought pot of ointment.

'Keep the pot, don't worry,' said my hostess seeing the doubt in my eye as I held the lovely object in my hand.

'Has Captain Cassimatis been a friend of the family for long?' I asked as I sipped the coffee.

'His father knew Yussuf's father many years ago. They were in the wool trade together. Yes, we are old family friends.'

I dared not show any further curiosity about Costas in case they thought I had some ulterior motive. I would never know the facts. I would have to spin my own romantic ideas about him.

It was time to go. I had already been out far longer than normal and May would be worried if she came off duty and I was not there to greet her. I knew that I could say nothing about my adventures, not even to dear little May. She was not very discreet, I'm afraid. No, I could tell no one about all this.

A smart, old-fashioned landau came round to the front door. I was ushered in and driven back to camp in style. I asked the driver to stop and let me down just outside the camp so that I might walk the last mile by foot. It was hard work getting rid of him as he said he had been told to take me right into the camp. I assured him that I wanted to stretch my legs a little. He looked puzzled at such English madness but obeyed and turned the horses and went off back down the dusty track to the city. It would be bad luck to bump into Matron or someone and they would certainly wonder why I had come home in a carriage instead of with one of the ambulance men.

Just my luck, of course. Captain Dunning came driving by in his old Buick and seeing me walking along, offered me a lift.

I could hardly refuse and managed to fend off his questions as best as I could. He seemed convinced I had had a tiff with some young beau and been obliged to walk all the way and he teased me without mercy all the way back to camp.

July 8th

Palomba's ointment worked well and the bruises did disappear virtually overnight. There is not a great deal of privacy in a tent and I hadn't wanted May to see the state of my poor bosom. We had rigged up a curtained area as a wash place so this did afford some screen. Thankfully, she saw and suspected nothing for she was at present still caught up in her own gloom.

I, however, was made of sterner stuff than May. The whole adventure had been terrifying and yet so exciting. I did not regret it in my heart, despite the foolhardiness of my actions. All the same, my sense of duty was strong and I knew that I had taken some very foolish risks and thought of all the trouble I might have caused had I come to harm, all the worry to everyone, the shock to my poor parents. It came home to me how very thoughtless I had been. In future I would confine my walks to the seashore and the hills around here. And even then, one had to be a bit wary of the crazy, dirty looking shepherds on the mountains who could be highly rude and unpleasant and were inclined to be vagabonds and thieves from all accounts.

I knew I could never return to the area where Yussuf and Palomba lived. My heart longed to, but I had promised the Captain. I knew that I must forget him; forget his very existence.

I cannot, of course. I can *never* forget him. I know now that I will never marry for it would be impossible to find such a man again. I will remain single all my life and devote myself to nursing.

July 10th

Such a strange thing happened today. As I was busy writing up my daily report for the doctor, one of the orderlies came in and said that a little ragamuffin was waiting outside with a parcel for me.

'The little bleeder insists it has to be given to you personally,' he said with a laugh. 'Reckon you've got an admirer, nurse?'

'Of course not,' I snapped, but my curiosity aroused I followed him out and a little ragged lad of about ten came up to me and handed me a soft, well-wrapped paper parcel. The orderly hung about as if waiting for me to open it but I glared at him and took it back into the ward with me. I would open it later away from curious and prying eyes.

When I had finished my reports, I went back straight to our tent and opened the parcel. To my joy there was my hat nicely brushed though a trifle flattened. Also a little handkerchief I had dropped, all washed and ironed. Nestling in the middle of the hat was a pretty little bottle of perfume that smelt utterly delicious and very Oriental …like patchouli or some such rich and sensual scent. A small card also appeared with 'A gift from the Gods' written on it and nothing else. I smiled to myself and held the card against my lips.

Chapter 17

July 20th 1916

May has heard from Bill whose unit has now gone to the frontline and is helping to relieve the French troops near Kalinova. He tells us that the trenches there have to be blasted out of solid rock. At least they are spared the frightful mud of the Western Front but he says that the dust is not much better. It's a fine insidious, invasive layer that creeps everywhere and seems to cover everything they eat and drink, parches the throat and dries the skin. There seems no way of finding comfort if one is a soldier but perhaps that makes it easier to die, if only to get out of such a nightmare existence. Surely Hell itself couldn't be worse than this?

All this means more casualties and hard work all round. And still the wretched mosquitoes spread their foul diseases and create havoc amongst soldiers and nursing staff alike. At night there is such an interminable whine of the wretched creatures about my net that it keeps me awake. I don't mind the frogs or the dogs …but I hate the sound of the mosquitoes!

The air is so hot, sticky and humid; a pall of disease seems to hang everywhere. We are all taking five to six grains of quinine daily and it is the most foul tasting stuff. A wretched mosquito bit my eye the other day and it became so swollen that it made me blind as a mole for a day or two. I tried some of Palomba's ointment on it and amazingly, the swelling went down almost at once. I wonder what on earth is in that ointment and mean to take it to the lab to be analysed. For some reason, I haven't caught malaria as yet. Some people do seem to be immune to it; I hope I am one of them.

The ambulances bring in stretcher after stretcher of roughly bandaged creatures who look scarcely human, their faces are covered in fine white dust like chalk and flies drone round them constantly, even crawling into their mouths if they are too sick to move. The poor men just lie about looking wretched and gasp for a drink with parched and croaking throats. We have plentiful supplies of limejuice and sparklets for them, which they gulp down as if it was the best wine or beer.

A Red Cross Kitchen has at last been opened up at this hospital saving the nurses a good deal of work preparing special diets. It was a problem trying to cook messes on a primus stove that kept blowing out in the least wind. The new cook has arrived from old Blighty, fresh for action. It turns out she is an Hon somebody or other in civilian life and now she takes orders meekly from us nurses, many of us being from far lower stations in society. This war has put everything and everyone on their head, that's for sure. Despite 'talking so posh' as May puts it, the new cook does concoct some delicate things for the poor invalids, mainly jelly, junkets, custard and Bengers but she turns out a good egg flip when eggs are available. The invalids' throats are far too dry to manage anything more solid. The men are wonderfully brave; they try so hard not to complain and are so immensely grateful for all we do.

'I haven't seen an Englishwoman's face for so long,' said one lad wearily, looking up at us as if he had just arrived in heaven, 'it makes me want to cry but that would be real silly.'

'Why should it be silly?' I asked as I began to wash him down and gently helped to remove his filthy clothes from him. He had had the misfortune to meet up with a Bulgar shell and the poor soul's leg and one side of his body was in a terrible mess. There was shrapnel embedded in his head and his shoulder. He was lucky not to have been blown to bits but as it was, he would never walk again. He was only seventeen.

He seemed more worried about his dirty clothes than his wounds. He looked ashamed about it all, 'Sorry, sister, some blokes are better at washing their kit than me,' he apologised. 'My Ma would have a fit if she saw me now. Proper dirty and that; she wouldn't half yell at me.'

'You all arrive the same, officers and men,' I said soothingly, 'don't worry about anything, just lie still and rest while you can.'

'It's good to be here, sister,' said the lad with a deep sigh as I changed his blood-soaked dressings and got him to his bed in the bright, clean ward where he sank back into sheets for the first time in ages and immediately fell fast asleep.

Later, he told me that he came from Bethnal Green and his mother was a parlour maid in a big house. His Dad was fighting in France and he had three sisters who were all working in munitions factories.

'They tell me their faces and hands get all yellow with the stuff they use and people call them the 'Canaries' he said, 'well, Rosie, she is always singing about the place so it seems a good name for her, don't it?'

We operated on him and he seemed to settle but then one night he took a turn for the worse, became very delirious and kept talking about going home, describing his street, the house he lived in, how he wanted to see his Ma. I hated to tell him that few of the hospital ships were going home just now because the U-boats were proving too dangerous. With luck he might get to Malta where he could convalesce.

Sadly his severe wounds became complicated and he died a few days later. It was not that often that we lost patients. I always felt so sad when we did so, despite all our care and efforts.

Most of the men are treated at the Aid Post by the medical officers of their battalions who pull out teeth, administer quinine and look after some of the malarial and dysentery cases. But those who are too ill to journey on with their units are sent down the line in the field ambulances to the nearest casualty clearing station or else to one of the hospitals around the city. If some poor soul has the misfortune to fall ill while on the march, he knows he just has to keep going no matter what for there is seldom any transport available, only a few stretchers that could carry him and they may be needed for other more urgent cases.

July 22nd

The sweat runs in streams down my back as I make my rounds and I look forward so much to when I can go off duty and take a lift down to the seashore for a bathe. We all bathe a good deal, it is cooling and refreshing, though even the sea can get very warm in the daytime. The best times to swim are early morning or late evening.

I have also heard from my darling Richard who is somewhere in the area of the Somme; he tells me that the Germans have been driven back at last and the French have regained Fleury and Thiaumont. The Roumanians have at last decided to join the Allies while the Italians, who have been fighting the Austrians, have now declared war on Germany too. So all this is cheering news. Here in Greece, that wretched coward King Tino still tries to sit on the fence and be 'neutral' …he seems to vacillate constantly and must have the worst advisors in the world. Why can't the man declare himself one way or another?

Meanwhile in Salonika, the Venizelists are in a high state of ferment. There are Venizelist Nationalists and Venizelist Marxists and heaven knows what else and an atmosphere of treachery, discontent and suspicion. It makes me all the more aware of how I need to keep my secret about Captain Costas. I wonder which of these factions he belongs to? Well, I shall never know. If only we could meet again somehow, there is so much I would like to ask him to explain, if only to tell Papa who writes and says as far as he can see the Royalist Greeks will have to join the war, like it or not and probably will be coerced into action in the end. He asks me if I have any idea about the state of affairs out here? Does anyone?

It's a queer thing that the Germans have infiltrated every European country through their princes. Here Sophia is the sister of the Kaiser, the Russian Tsarina is German and so is our own Royal Family. One wonders if this was all some ancient plot to try and draw these countries to help Germany build her longed for Empire ...but perhaps that is too far-fetched a thought! It's just the way things have come about. The Jews may well be the 'Chosen People' ...and a lot of good that seems to have done them ...but the German tribes seem to have been appointed as a force for destruction and for bringing down the declining order of things, yes, since the ancient days of the Huns and Vandals. Their God is assuredly Ares.

July 28th

Yesterday, the men in the canteen were discussing the Serbian situation when some of us joined them there for afternoon tea. A Serbian officer was there whom the other officers were entertaining and we all listened to him with deep interest as he told us about their retreat that terrible winter of 1915.

'The Serbs are truly an amazing people,' said Captain Dunning through his usual cloud of smoke, 'they can march for days with little or no food and seem to have some sort of fierce spirit that drives them onwards defiantly.'

'Yes, we have spirit,'said the Serbian officer with some passion, accepting a cigarette proffered to him by one of the other officers, 'but even the best of men sometimes feel hopeless. It is *teshko* – hard – it's hard to think how it will be back home or what will be left for us to return to. The men have this demoralising uncertainty hanging over them all the time. Will anyone or anything be left to come home to? We do not know. We do know if the Bulgars will have revenged themselves on our innocent families, devastated and emptied our villages that have been there for hundreds of years. Many of our people have fled. And many of them lie dead in the snow. They say that the Skumbi River was littered with the bodies of men, women, children, animals; people who fainted and died of hunger and had no strength left in them to cross over to safety and who fattened instead the wolves and birds of prey. Serbia is a graveyard! But we will not give up – we will fight on till none of us are left! When all has been lost then there is no longer any fear left in a man. There's nothing to fear or protect any more, nothing left but the burning desire to regain the soil of our fathers. That's why we refused to surrender to the Bulgars and Austrians or accept their ludicrous peace terms. It is fight and be damned! Revenge, that's what we live for now.'

'You *are* very brave men,' said Canon Jones, 'and if we needed proof it lies in the fact that your army has now regrouped, been brought back to health and fighting strength again. I gather it's taken some time to re-organise and the French have done wonders in providing artillery and rifles. I believe the British and French between them have helped to provide food and clothing?'

'Yes, that's the case,' said the Serb, 'we have all been helped by the Allies who set up little food stations along the last part of that nightmare journey through Albania. They gave us just enough food to keep us going for we had been starving for days and to eat too much would have killed us ...some men did die from eating too much too soon ...died just before reaching the end. Such madness! '

'But they can hardly be blamed,' said Sister Lorraine compassionately.

'No, no ...no blame, just desperation. We would have lost even more men if it was not for this help. It was like reaching Heaven to have a place that we could rest and return to health and strength again. God's blessings on all the good men!' added the Major fervently crossing himself as he spoke.

They are such wonderful people, the Serbs, so simple, direct and truthful and proud in spirit and bearing. Our men, who had never met a Serb in their lives before, took to them immediately for we British love straightforward, honest and uncluttered men.

'I invite all you gentlemen to our *slava* tomorrow!' said the Serbian officer enthusiastically and the men laughed and looked at one another.

A *Slava* is a sort of regimental feast, usually on a saint's day or a name day, I think. Or else they commemorate some battle in the past for these proud people never forget their defeat by the Turks. Apparently, the feasting would begin at 9.am and go through a variety of rituals and ceremonies and toast after toast is made, dish after dish brought to be eaten; then all the men dance the *Kola*, a queer sort of sideways shuffling dance. Apparently it requires no effort to stand upright as your partners hold you up which is just as well as, according to Captain Dunning, everyone French or British is pretty far gone by then. The upshot is that not an officer comes back to camp in a fit state for work the next day. But no one dares refuse to attend.

Chapter 18

A few of us went down to the beach today to take a dip in the cooling waters. May came too and enjoyed herself greatly. She has cheered up a great deal since her latest letter from Bill saying that he is well and that the troops were now pushing forward on the offensive along with Sarrail's troops, all heading towards Lake Doiran.

'Thank God he is all right. I worry so much that bad news will come, it's just too awful. He's had an attack of dysentery, poor darling, but says that all in all the brief rest in the field hospital did him good. It was bliss to be in nice, cool sheets again, he says! They all say that, don't they? The long marches are just a nightmare of heat and dust with hardly any water to drink. They feel so thirsty all the time, it must be awful. Apparently, they have been shooting hares in the mountains and it makes a nice stew for them. The diet must be so monotonous, mustn't it?'

'Ours isn't that much better. If I see another treacle suet pudding I shall scream! I wish they'd send one of those hares down the line to us,' I said with a laugh.

'Yes, but they have bully beef *all* the time, think how boring that must be. Sometimes, Bill says, they buy fruit and tomatoes from the local villages. But it must be boring as can be. Just look at this, Dot, isn't he sweet?'

She carries his latest letter about with her all the time and the whole hospital gets to see the news. We often exchange and read each others letters. In some ways we are like one big family and love to share one another's stories of our homes, parents, sweethearts and children.

I smiled and took the sheet of paper with its pencilled scrawl and read

'I hope you are well too, my darling girl, and as busy and cheerful for the patients as you always are for me. I don't mind sharing you with them just now. But, oh, how I look forward to the time we shall be back in dear old Blighty again! We shall have a lovely little house just like the one you admired so much on Beniton Street. You will make it just perfect for us both until a little one …or two! …comes to join us there. Won't it be bliss? Just keep that dream in mind as I do when things get that bit too much to bear.

Goodbye, darling girl, your ever-loving Bill.'

'That *is* sweet, May,' I said giving her back her letter.

Somehow, I felt sure that Captain Costas would never write a love letter like that. It was so typical of our Englishmen, home loving, gentle and rather sentimental. These poor lads have known nothing of such horrors before. Britain has not been invaded in years, our battles fought by our armies and navies overseas, scarcely touching the population in the way that the people here have been touched by constant unrest, warfare, brigandage and the occupation of hundreds of years. It makes different people of them like a fire that hardens them into steel, tougher, hardier, crueller than us, though oddly childlike and superstitious too, for they are often ill-educated and unsophisticated. We British think ourselves practical and realistic as a nation but my feeling is that we are actually very idealistic and sentimental about many things, especially about this dreadful war. However, something in me whispers that this is nothing more than the age-old struggle for land and power rather than anything idealistic or liberating.

It was wonderful to have these few snatched moments of peace and calm by the seashore. We went back to camp with the others and then May and I took a little walk in the hills before lunch. The sweet scent of wild thyme arose in the late afternoon heat and drifted in wafts of fragrance towards us. Hearing the faint tinkle of goat's bells, I looked up and on a distant slope I could see a shepherd with his flock of scraggy sheep and a few goats. He was sitting on a boulder, his savage looking dogs at his feet, and seemed to be looking in our direction as he drank from his skin bottle and munched heartily on his goat's cheese. I have heard some tales about these shepherds who are said to be rough fellows prone to stealing if they get half a chance. They look filthy, with unwashed hair, wearing heavy coats no matter how hot it is, wads of cloth wrapped about their legs and thick boots because of the snakes. Some wear the *fustanella,* which may once have been white but is anything but that now, a dirty grey more like. I had not seen any shepherds around here before and hoped he would go away. I don't think he would have dared cause any trouble for we were too close to the camp. All the same, his brooding presence spoilt the peace of the scene.

September 3rd

It's been so busy I haven't had a minute to write up anything. Things are getting so difficult in Salonika with these Venizelist activities and stirrings. Our usually reliable Eleni did not turn up for work the other day and on Monday, I was asked to come to Matron's office in the hopes I might help translate. I found poor Eleni there in tears accompanied by some rather unpleasant looking 'officials'. Eleni explained that she had quarrelled with her fiancé and broken off her engagement, an almost unheard of thing in these parts for an engagement is as good as a marriage. He had revenged himself by informing the authorities that she was 'not for Venizelos'. She had thus been frogmarched off to prison but had managed to persuade the authorities to bring her here so that we might explain how good and loyal she really was.

We felt sorry for the poor wretch who looked terrified which was scarcely surprising given the horrible atrocities we hear do happen. I assured the officer in my best Greek that the girl had always praised Mr. Venizelos to the skies and that it was her nasty ex-fiancé who was the real problem. (None of this was strictly true but then she had never actually ever said anything *against* Venizelos either!)

The men listened politely and seemed rather astonished at my very ungrammatical command of Greek but I don't think our testimony went for much as we never saw Eleni again. She is probably still languishing in jail, a victim of spite. I just pray nothing worse has happened to her. Matron said that there was really nothing we could do. Such a thing could never happen in England and it is distressing to think it can happen anywhere, especially in a country that had once been famed for its democracy and fairness with an inborn love of freedom despite years of tyrannous occupation.

Well, I think the love of freedom still burns in them but personal freedoms are daily swallowed up in the present climate of acquisitive greed on the part of the statesmen for more and more gains in Asia Minor. I keep my mouth shut, but my feeling about Venizelos is that he is a very wily and cunning man.

I am still troubled about poor Eleni and wonder if I could risk asking Costas to help in the matter. But how? Perhaps I could send a note via Yussuf Yacovides, surely someone must know where he lives. No, no …I *must* forget Costas exists. I might get Eleni into more trouble than before. I feel so helpless.

September 20th

What a mixture of news. The Serbs are still striving to gain their land, slowly, slowly moving forwards towards Monastir but the poor Roumanians who declared war on Germany in August are now doing very badly which is terrible to hear. Captain Dunning says their army is just not up to modern warfare and they still go galloping around on their cavalry charges with swords drawn and simply get mown down by the machine guns.

'Just like us at the start,' he said sadly, 'but we soon learnt our lesson. To think we used to have our swords sharpened by the regimental blacksmith and we used to make petrol bombs in old tin cans! We're moving away fast from all that. And yet the warfare now is sheer madness. It has become so technically sophisticated that it reduces fighting to a stalemate. Both sides are so well armed and on the defensive that there is no hope of any movement at all. At least one stood a chance when it was armed combat, man to man and may the best man win!'

'Indeed,' said another officer who had been in the Boer War, 'there was nothing like the sight of a cavalry charge sweeping down the hill at the enemy, sabres flashing in the sunlight, by God! Pride, courage, and man to man. We soldiers respected the Boers ...they were great fighters. One had some respect for one's adversary and skill. Now look at 'em. The poor fellows don't stand a chance when they go over the top. They're mown down like hay. What sort of fighting is that? What kind of manoeuvres can one make in these circumstances? The generals work it all out on their maps and move men about as if it was the old days of sending in the cavalry or the cannons and let 'em have it. But the idiots forget that there is totally unknown terrain to consider, totally new weapons in use.'

'And we have the end result ...men blown to bloody bits ... my apologies, young ladies, but that's how it is,' said Dunning shaking his head in despair

The Allies have given the Greeks an ultimatum and asked for the total de-mobilization of the Greek Army and the dismissal of the Greek Parliament. Naturally the King ignores them. It is impossible this situation ...something has to happen.

Things have become riotous and most unpleasant in the city and we are all keeping out of it just now. The Venizelist supporters have begun a reign of terror and are smashing and looting and people are disappearing daily. It is truly awful. I do hope Costas is not involved in this sort of evil but something tells me that is not his role, nor his nature.

Well, Venizelos has left Athens now and gone off to Hania in his native Crete with his henchman Admiral Koundouriotis. The cat is truly amongst the pigeons and we all wonder what the next step will be. Whenever the copies of the 'Balkan News' are brought into camp we all rush to see it and it circulates round as rapidly as gunfire!

October 1st

An odd thing happened today. As I was walking through the village I saw the lad who had brought me the parcel with my hat in it. I went up to him and caught him gently by the arm. He looked most alarmed, poor lad, and seemed to act like a simpleton when I asked who had given it to him.

'I didn't do anything wrong!'

'No, no, child, it's fine, you did very well. I just want to ask a few questions. It's all right, you aren't in any trouble! Just tell me who gave you the parcel.'

'A man,' he said.

'Was he a Greek?'

'Dunno.'

'Was he from the village?'

'No.' He shook his head vehemently

'How was he dressed?'

He shrugged, 'Dunno ...trousers, hat, like everyone.'

'Was he a very tall man?' I raised my hand to indicate height but the boy just looked at me and shrugged.

I wondered if it had been Costas. I decided to take a chance. I took some money from my purse and held it up before the lad's suddenly awakened eyes.

'If you ever see this man again, ask him if he knows anyone who can help Eleni Stavropoulos who is in prison. You know poor Eleni, don't you?'

'She's my cousin.'

'There you are! Maybe the man can help. Ask him if you ever see him.'

The boy looked reflective.

'Don't think I'll ever see him again.'

'Well, keep your eyes open,' I said and gave him the money.

'All right, he replied and off he scampered.

Venizelos has sailed back to Salonika in some triumph via the Greek islands, which support him strongly, and established what he calls a 'provisional government'. Lots of supporters from all over the country are joining him here including army officers and political figures. That will please the Allies but they are afraid to recognise his government officially just yet as Constantine still holds his government in Athens and the Russians tend to be on his side as his mother was a Romanov. Things have calmed down in the city, which is a relief as it is the only place where we can go for any real shopping or entertainment.

Much to my joy and amazement, Eleni came into camp the other day and came over to me and knelt down and kissed my hand fervently.

'You are my saviour,' she declared.

'Oh, thank God you're free!' I said, raising her up and putting an arm about her. She was woefully thin, her lovely plump face almost hollow. Only her fine lustrous eyes were the same but now had an expression of deep suffering in them that alarmed me. I hoped she had not been harmed or violated in any way but didn't like to ask her. I prayed that the sadness would go with time.

'I would still be there but for you, dearest lady,' she said, 'Yiangos told me you had asked for my release. They obeyed you.'

'I don't think the authorities took any notice of *me*! But who is Yiangos?'

'My young cousin. He passed your message to someone he said he knew and a day later, the men came and let me out.'

So the child did know the mysterious man who had given him the parcel. He had kept very brave and quiet about it and earned himself some cash into the bargain. My opinion of Yiangos went up. I felt he might be a useful contact. That the message had somehow got through to Costas who had immediately acted on my word thrilled my heart. I felt a certain delight in this strange cloak-and-dagger life I now had. No one else in the camp knew about it. It was my own precious secret.

Chapter 19

November 19th 1916

I nearly bumped into Captain Dunning as he came hastening out of the Officer's Mess Tent today and he seemed so excited that I stopped and stared and asked him if he was all right?

'My dear girl, such news!' he puffed as he slowed down for a moment, his face so red from the exertion that I feared he might collapse at any moment.

'What news, what news?' I cried, caught up in his emotion though not knowing why.

'The Serbs have re-taken Monastir. They're back home!'

And the sound of cheering soon echoed about the camp as the news travelled around like wildfire. It was the most wonderful piece of news in ages. We all had the biggest grins on our faces that day as we remembered and toasted in a bottle of Captain Dunning's best whisky our brave and wonderful Serbian friends.

November 25th

Now I am beginning to understand what they mean about the frightful winters in this place. The heat was certainly bad enough but now that the infamous Vardar winds are really storming up, life is becoming difficult in a quite different manner. These winds can last from two to three days at a time and create immense havoc. They seem to blow through everything, freezing one to the very bone. Several tents were blown down in one violent night and the rain lashed down, churning what had been a choking summer dustbowl into thick, yellow mud. We wear long rubber boots to get from place to place and skirts and trousers become filthy in no time. Nothing feels dry, our clothes, our blankets, all permeated with the soggy damp of the relentless rains. Often there is a shortage of paraffin rations and we have a nightmare trying to light those wretched Perfection stoves that blow out in the least wind let alone a hellish blast like this one. There is something highly depressing about it all. It is such an inhospitable land. At times like these, how the heart longs for the cosy fireplace at Downlands, one's feet on the fender, staring dreamily into the flames with a cheerful maid bringing in a pot of tea and scones with jam.

Oh, forget such images! For all I know, I may never ever see them again.

Captain Willoughby has kindly offered to take me into town with him for I want to see if I can purchase some really nice *loukum* to send back home for Christmas. There's precious little else to buy here and Pa has a very sweet tooth. I don't know what to get for Mama for she is extremely strict about sweet things as she is about any sort of food. She'd live on bread and water if she could; she has no interest at all in eating. Agnes, I know, will love some of Floca's famous chocolates but they would be wasted on Mama. Eleni, our village friend, has promised to embroider me some pretty tablecloths for her. The Greek ladies do embroider beautifully and make the loveliest tatting to edge their cloths. To my mind, the women here are very creative but their exquisite work is little valued.

I asked May if she wanted to come into town with us but she had some letters to write and kept making innuendos about leaving me alone with Ethan. Really she is so silly at times! I am deeply fond of him as I am of most of the officers here. He is a brilliant surgeon, he has my deepest respect and we have shared some very difficult moments together working in the operating theatre. He has sworn fluently at me in trying moments, he has hugged me in successful ones. I feel we are comrades but he is not special, not a man I would care to spend my life with. There is only one man that appeals to me and he is out of my reach. I try not to care about it too much. There's no point.

Willoughby took me to Coukis where he said one could get the best *Rahat Loukum* in lemon, caramel, pineapple, raspberry and more flavours; the very best with burnt almonds in them too. I bought some for Papa and my mouth watered so much looking at all the delicious flavours that Willoughby smiled and bought a little box of best rose flavoured *loukum* as a little gift for me. That was truly gentlemanly of him.

'It's not Christmas yet, Captain,' I said gaily, accepting the gift with great delight.

'Ladies should receive presents all the time,' he said with a smile, 'especially pretty ones.'

I looked up at him when he said this. It wasn't his habit to make me compliments. Quite often it was friendly insults. Now that we were not at work but relaxing, a softness and an air of quiet protectiveness had descended upon him as we made our way down the noisy, muddy streets, past the clanking trams and the din of the iron rimmed wheels of bullock carts that veered slowly in and out of the chaotic traffic. Occasionally a smart car or an army truck would go racing by and we would all get out of the way or else be splashed all over. Old *arabekyas* with sad, mangy horses in the shafts, driven by sallow Turks wearing the red fez, rolled along in this glorious confusion. Everywhere the wheels churned up the mud and our footwear was filthy. But little, skinny *loustros*, or shoe-shine boys, popped up in the doorway of every important establishment and offered to wipe clean one's shoes.

'Shine, Johnny, shine!' they called, their cheeky faces grinning from ear to ear. So, as we entered Flocas, we availed ourselves of this service and nicely smartened up went to try and find an empty table amongst the throng that crowded the place. Flocas was considered by common consent to be the more chic café in the area with the military and the sailors alike and the officers liked to bring their wives or girlfriends here.

'These Israelites and Greeks are greedy and rapacious and not that friendly either,' said Willoughby, 'they charge us the earth in here. If only we could have our own club as the French do and not have to eat out at these ridiculous prices. The men billeted here find it is getting out of all proportions with the hotels charging best London prices and the stores taking on all the airs of some famous department store in London, Paris or Vienna. This place is just the limit at times.'

'I suppose people would always be out to make a profit if they could,' I replied, 'isn't that human nature?'

'It wouldn't be allowed at home,' was the short reply and I suppose he is right.

'Don't you sometimes wish you could be out of this madhouse?' said Willoughby with a strange little sigh.

'Yes,' I admitted, 'sometimes I just long for home. Yet it is such an amazing adventure. It's frightening and all the rest; it is sickening to see the men so ill and dying. That is awful. But I admit, I am finding it fascinating and if we all live, it will be our heroic experience in life.'

'Hardly heroic, is it?' snorted Willoughby. 'I do understand the men when they say they feel cheated to see their comrades die of malaria or invalided home because of some wretched bug. They feel that to die in battle is part of the game, the scheme of things. Maybe it's something of our ancient Danish and Saxon blood that feels Valhalla may be waiting for the heroes who fall in battle. But to come all this way and die of influenza or malaria is sheer bad luck. There's no heroism in that.'

'Well, of course there is! It's a time of true grit and heroism. We are *all* of us heroes. We have all offered ourselves up for sacrifice. May's lad, Bill, says the men keep going even when they are about to drop even though they might long for a brief rest in a field hospital or whatever. They insist they are fine even when they are dropping by the wayside and try to struggle on. They *are* heroes. Think of those men who go off on bombing expeditions knowing they will never return, the fighter pilots in their matchstick planes. They know they'll get killed eventually. But they stay cheerful, they toy with death; my brother says they laugh at it. They're like Gods those men. He wishes he had joined the Flying Corps now. How glad I am he didn't! He wouldn't have stood a chance, any more than the rest.'

'No, he wouldn't,' Willoughby admitted, 'yes, I think we all perceive *those* young men as heroes. But we doctors and nurses only do what we would always do. We're not heroes.'

'I think our patients would say otherwise,' I smiled, 'though I agree with what you say. But when *you* are battling to save someone, sir, then I see you as a real hero.'

I looked at him earnestly and spoke with a frank honesty for I meant what I said but regretted saying it almost at once. A slight flush spread over Willoughby's pale face and he looked at me in such a way that I felt a sense of immense panic. He took my hand in his and kissed it briefly. I was so amazed that I let my hand fall back to the table like a fool. I know I blushed scarlet but it wasn't from maidenly something or other. More from shock.

'Don't look so horrified,' said Willoughby with an embarrassed little laugh for I must have been a comic sight. 'You must know I care deeply about you, Dorothy?' he said *sotto voce*, now looking at the tablecloth almost bashfully, which horrified me even more. Love makes such idiots of people.

I was saved from a reply by the arrival of the tea and cakes. It gave me a moment to think. This dalliance had to be squashed straight away. No more outings on my own with the good Captain.

'You do know that, don't you, Dorothy?' he persisted again when the waiter had moved on to another table.

'Please don't, Captain,' I replied.

'You feel nothing towards me?'

'Of course I do! I admire you wholeheartedly and feel you are a wonderful comrade. But that is all.'

He smiled a little, 'Well at least you don't hate me.'

'How could I? Please, sir, don't confuse love with all this. We've got so much work to do and I couldn't bear to think that you felt this way. Just let's be comrades as before.'

'I'm too old for you, is that it?'

'It has nothing to do with it. I simply want us to be friends, to be comrades as we are now.'

'For such a young woman you are incredibly sensible,' he murmured, 'maybe a mite too sensible, but I wouldn't have it otherwise. You are right, very right, Sister Clarke. We must remain as good comrades while this war is on. It would never do to let one's personal feelings interfere with our uncanny ability to work so well together. And who knows, after all this …perhaps your feelings might change in a different setting, a different time and place. Everything here is heightened and changed and our normal attitudes disappear. I shall certainly ask you to join my team in London if, God willing, we ever are allowed to return there.'

'That's so good of you, thank you sir.'

'It's purely selfish, I assure you,' he smiled, 'I know a good nurse when I see one.'

We fell silent for a moment and my eye wandered briefly away from him and around the tables. Then to my intense dismay, I saw Captain Cassimatis seated at another table with a couple of pretty young women. From this distance I couldn't be sure, but one of them whose head was turned away from me, looked like Ishabel. Perhaps the other was a friend or sister. My heart leapt so suddenly that I gasped. Willoughby looked at me in surprise and turned his head to see what I was looking at.

'Did you see someone you know?'

'I …I don't think so. People often seem to look familiar. No, it's just a trick of the light.'

Willoughby turned in his chair and scrutinised the area. 'I do believe you're right,' he said slowly. 'It's the chap who came along with the Greek Doctor. You thought you recognised him before.'

'It's just that he reminds me of someone I know or knew,' I said lamely and wished that Willoughby was not so frightfully possessive of me. Can you imagine my marrying the fellow? He would drive me mad in a week. I so hate to be watched over.

Captain Cassimatis seemed to sense he was under scrutiny and his eye turned slowly and lazily towards us. I felt sure he had seen us already and felt troubled and annoyed to think he might have witnessed Willoughby's declarations. He probably thought I was very fast being out with a man on my own. Or worse still, he might think we were courting. However, he showed no sign of recognition, his glance brushing over us. He returned his gaze to the young lady next to him and resumed his animated conversation. I felt the most intense jealousy I have ever known before. It was truly stupid. But I envied her right to sit beside him and talk with him easily and happily. Laughter drifted to us from their table. I felt no more desire for the cakes and pushed them away.

'What is it, my dear?'

Willoughby had become formal again for which I was very grateful I had no wish to be on intimate terms with him.

'It's nothing,' I said with a forced little smile, 'I feel a little tired. Maybe we should go now, if that's all right with you, sir.'

He gave me a stern look that made me want to squirm.

'I'll finish my tea first,' he said.

Sometimes he made me feel like a small child with a very strict father. I have no idea why I reacted this way …it was just something about him. In some strange way, he reminded me of my dreaded mother in a male form.

While Captain Willoughby finished his tea, and a very slow job he made of it as if to prolong my agony for some fiendish purpose of his own, Captain Cassimatis banged noisily on a plate to attract the waiter. He paid his bill, bowed to the ladies and then left. As he brushed past our table, Willoughby caught his sleeve and spoke to him, 'I believe we have met, sir? How are you?'

I swear he did this on purpose to study my reaction. Somehow, though for what reason I couldn't begin to imagine, he seemed to have some gut instinct about us both. Bother him. Perhaps it was the idea that he was in love with me that made him so ultra-sensitive.

Cassimatis stopped and looked at him, then bowed and smiled at us both.

'I believe I do recall, sir …yes, at the British hospital? I'm afraid I forget the names …'

'Yes, at the Hospital, that's correct. Captain Ethan Willoughby at your service and this is my nurse, Miss Dorothy Clarke. Won't you join us?'

'I think it's time for us to go back, sir,' I broke in trying hard to look calm and collected.

'There's no hurry, my dear,' said Willoughby infuriatingly. The man was impossible and happy to torment me. I just knew it. I felt furious at that moment.

Captain Cassimatis caught the wrathful flash of my eye and couldn't prevent a tiny smile from twitching the corners of his mouth. My angry gaze shifted to him now. I was fast becoming really tired of men and we had work to do back at the camp but Willoughby was giving me a lift back so I had to wait for him or else be very rude and leave on my own. That would have looked odd. I stayed put most unwillingly.

The two men chatted briefly and then as Willoughby turned and clapped his hands for the waiter, Cassimatis said, 'I must leave now, make my *adieux* to you both.'

He took my hand and appeared to kiss it in a perfunctory manner but I felt him slip a tiny piece of paper into it with a deft movement. I closed my hand and swiftly put it in my lap. Even the watchful Willoughby didn't notice a thing being embroiled with the waiter and the bill at that moment. Taking his leave, Captain Cassimatis walked proudly on his way with that wonderful lithe movement of his. My heart was thumping so wildly, I felt sure that it moved my coat or could be heard like some huge hammer striking. I kept my face as impassive as I could and thankfully we left at last and headed back for the old Buick, which Willoughby had borrowed from Captain Dunning for the outing. We remained quite silent on the way back, I pleading a headache, that ally of the importuned woman.

As soon as I got back to my tent, I fished the paper from my pocket and opened it in haste. I had never felt so excited in my life. The writing on it was in English and said, 'Tonight at the village cemetery? Look for the shepherd and be alone'

Chapter 20

When I came off duty that evening, I slipped under the barbed wire at a convenient spot known to many a saucy nurse who wanted to stay out late at night and not be caught by Matron. Taking the long and muddy track that led up the hill I skirted past the village. Dusk was gathering very fast and the wind already blowing fiercely and I shivered and wrapped my thin serge coat all the tighter about me, cursing the stupidity of some rigid Dame or other back home who refused to depart from standard uniform and allow us British Warm instead. How I wished someone would bring the old dears out here and let them see what real cold felt like! I took my little hurricane lamp with me but didn't dare light it yet in case the fierce wind blew it out. By lucky chance, May was doing a bout of night duty and sleeping in the accommodation set aside for the night nurses. I have to confess that I was grateful for this just now. I was not in the mood for answering questions and could slip unobserved into my tent later.

Despite the gloaming and the lonely, treeless expanses around me, I felt quite unafraid. I knew the path well and since the business with Eleni, the village people were now my good friends. They would all be indoors by now and as I approached the village boundaries, I saw the little lights that flickered from oil lamps and paraffin stoves here and there behind a half-open shutter and smelt the rancid and garlicky odours of lunchtime leftovers being re-heated for supper. My only terror was that I might have an unpleasant encounter with one of those nasty, fierce village dogs that they left unchained at night but though some of them set up a din on hearing my hurrying footsteps, they soon subsided. I swear animals can recognise different footsteps or sense what is about and most of these brutes knew my sight and smell as I was a fairly frequent visitor to the village.

There was a long and rather scrambling and undignified descent down to the cemetery on the other side of the village. As I regained my feet, I stood up and looked about me, my heart pounding with a mixture of anticipation and fear. Suppose no one came? The place was deserted. *Look for the shepherd*, the note had said. Why on earth should I look for that filthy, scruffy fellow? Perhaps he was to give me a message from Costas and was one of his spies.

I stood irresolutely, trying to shelter behind one of the large family sepulchres and looked out over the hillside. It was darkening swiftly and the sun was setting in glorious vivid colours over the Hortiach mountains. In the far distance to my right, I could see the glitter and gleam of waves as they tossed on the wild and angry sea. The wind blew so hard that I had to take off my precious nurse's headscarf in case it bowled away. Hearing a soft sound, I spun around and stifled a cry at the sight of a dark figure emerging from the shadows, gliding like a ghost at night. It was the shepherd all right; I could smell him from here. He put a finger to his lips and came towards me swiftly. I was alarmed for a moment and wondered if I had walked into some awful trap. But suddenly I knew with the deepest sense of relief, that it was my own Costas that approached me. I held out my arms and gave a little sob of joy and longing. He took me in his arms and kissed me with such passion that I felt my head swimming.

'Dorothea *mou!*' he murmured and we clung to one another.

'I love you, Costas, I love you!' I said, half laughing with a delirious kind of joy.

'Shh! You crazy girl! You're not a bit like an Englishwoman. I thought they were cold and frigid beings,' Costas laughed too as he kissed my face, neck and any other bits of flesh visible outside my winter coat.

'What do you know of Englishwomen!' I retorted. 'I believed all Greek men to be brigands and cut throats.'

'E!…so we are!'

We both laughed and he sat me down beside him on his thick woollen shepherd's cloak beside the sepulchre, which protected us from the night winds. It was becoming dark now and a Full Moon was rising and casting a marvellous, cold, bright light upon the bay. The French and Italian ships, despite the repeated warnings to turn off their lights, shone as brightly as could be, waiting targets for an enemy foray. It was a tranquil and beautiful evening in spite of the bitter wind.

Costas took my hand, pressed it to his face and kissed it repeatedly as if he couldn't abide to let it go.

'My sweet child, my beloved,' he kept murmuring and with my free hand I touched his face and marvelled at this glorious moment of intimacy. I had dreamt of it but never felt it could happen. It all seemed unreal, a delirious dream.

'I apologise for my appearance and the foul smell,' Costas said after a while, 'but I have to keep in character, you know.'

'You *are* a bit like an old cheese,' I laughed, 'but I don't care at all. I look a bit of a mess myself. The wind creates havoc with one's *coiffure!*" …for my soft, fine hair was beginning to tumble over my shoulders again, which it tended to do with the least provocation.

Costas took the straying locks of hair and tugged them gently so that they fell undone around my shoulders, scattering hairpins on the ground.

'You are so beautiful, so delicate,' he said, 'the wind is not the only culprit. Blame your beauty …it wants to take your hair in its hand as I do!'

I was unused to such extravagant compliments and put my hand on his lips to stop his nonsense but he just kissed and nibbled at my fingers. I loved the warmth that exuded from him like a wonderful fire; his was a hot and passionate nature like my own. Yet it was a contained passion, which was infinitely more exciting.

'Thank you, Costas, thank you so much for helping Eleni. I hope you weren't angry with me for trying to contact you but I felt so sorry for the girl. You were my only hope. They wouldn't listen to us but just dragged her off, poor lamb. What sort of justice is that?'

'I was glad to help you and your methods were very neat and discreet. I might engage you yet as a spy for Venizelos. The boy is the son of a friend of mine in the village and often runs me errands. He doesn't know who I am, of course, for I am always different …as you know.'

Well now, that was two employment offers I had had in one day and I couldn't resist a little smile.

'Mind you, it might have been better if they *had* shot her,' Costas mused.

I looked horrified.

'Who? You mean Eleni? Why say such a thing?'

'She's fit for nothing now, no-one will marry her now …the prison guards …well, let us say they *played* with her.'

'Oh, don't! That's so wicked …and her wretched fiancé put her there. I hate him! He must have known what would happen.'

'She has brothers …they will avenge her but she'll be lucky if they don't kill her too. The family honour has been stained now.'

'Honour! …an excuse for male bloodthirstiness!' I fell silent I was so inflamed. Then a thought crossed my mind and I added half joking, half serious, 'Well, Costas, you didn't kill me, as *you* threatened …unless you plan to do so tonight?'

He looked at me for a few moments before replying softly, 'Ah, true, I did say such an evil thing to you. Did I frighten you? Were you afraid of me? Or angry?'

I considered. 'No,' I said at last, 'I understood your position. I'm sure one of our own officers would have said the same in your place. Duty comes first with me too.'

'You are not afraid of anything, Dorothea,' he said with admiration.

'Costas, I'm afraid of so much. I'm afraid this wonderful moment with you will soon pass and I may never see you again. I was afraid you loved Ishabel.'

'Ishabel?' he looked puzzled and then laughed his deep, throaty laugh. 'Jealousy, ah, jealousy! Ishabel is the loveliest girl but I would never marry a Jewess. We have known one another from childhood …we are like brother and sister.'

I sighed with relief. He gathered me in his arms again and said, 'I'm glad you are capable of jealousy. It shows you love me deeply. And I am jealous of the long faced doctor who was kissing your hand today. An Englishman never kisses a woman's hand unless he is intimate with her. Is he your fiancé? Is he your *lover*!' he snapped out these words at me and looked so ferocious that any other woman might have been alarmed but I just laughed at him as he had laughed at my own anxiety over Ishabel.

'Lord, no! He is our Chief Medical Officer. A marvellous surgeon, a wonderful doctor and I care for him a lot – we work so well together. I may well work for him in London when all this is over. But that's all, that's all, Costas. '

'I think he loves you madly, his eyes were riveted on you … but then the world should love you. I adore you Dorothea. Do you know that? I have never loved a woman as I love you. I've known and made love to many women, I confess it. But never really loved till now.'

'Well, I *would* have been surprised if you were a virgin,' I replied equably. I was beginning to feel very comfortable with him and ready to tease a little. He was so intense about everything.

'No woman wants a virginal man,' he shrugged, 'but I am jealous of *your* virginity. Has some Englishman made love to you? Are you affianced in England or married?'

'No, to all those questions. I am as pure and unsullied as the Virgin Mary.'

'But, *she* bore a child, didn't she?' said Costas, stroking my face gently with his hand.

'Oh, Costas, what *are* you saying?' I said, half shocked by his cynical attitude.

'Would you ever yield to me, Dorothea? Would you ever let me be the man who took your flower, made you his wife …his true wife? We say that the man who deflowers a woman is her first and only real husband. No-one else ever counts in her heart. I want to be that man for you.'

'I want you to be my husband if God wills it,' I said with passion.

'We *will* marry when this war ends. We will marry, I promise it.'

He paused for a few moments, looked into my eyes and then said, 'I have to tell you that I *have* been married.'

I looked back at him and my heart sank. Was he telling me his wife still lived? I remained silent and downcast.

'No, she is dead,' he said, as if reading my mind, 'she was killed in Athens by a Venizelist sympathiser about six months ago. We had been separated for three years and she hated me with all her heart. I think she wanted a child and I couldn't seem to provide her with one. So it made her turn sour and bitter. The truth is she was probably barren – she wasn't very young. I have a feeling she was much older than she told me and that was five years older than myself. Yiota was an ardent Royalist and intended to denounce me to the pro-German lobby at court and that would have been the end of me. She never got that far.'

I drew back a little and stared at him. 'Did *you* kill her?'

'I might have done but I was spared that sin, at least.'

'Did you love her?'

'No, I married her for her money.'

I couldn't help laughing a little at his sheer honesty. I preferred that to the sort of pretence most people put up to avoid accepting blame for anything they did. Costas was so like myself. We both called a spade a spade and were not sentimental but neither were we callous. My belief is that those who are truly hard of heart will weep for hours over the death of a pet dog but have no pity whatsoever for the sufferings of their own kind. But the unsentimental and apparently cool types are those who have real compassion for others; they are the ones who will do anything practical they can to alleviate distress, the Good Samaritans of this world. I detest sentimental people; they are deeply cold inside and will cheerfully pass by on the other side.

'Costas, I love you so much.'

'I love it when you say that, but say it in Greek ...*s'agapo, se latrevo Costaki mou*!' he said pleadingly. 'Say you love me again.'

I obliged and he pulled me towards him and we began to kiss with urgency, half frantic for one another's lips but when his hands began to unbutton and wander within my coat, I pulled myself back and made to stand up.

'No, no, Costas, no!'

'My shame, Dorothea …forgive me for losing control,' he murmured and he helped me to my feet. We embraced again. It was hard to part from one another. I felt like a wild animal longing for its mate and so did he.

'I want you and only you to take me, Costas,' I said with candour, 'but this isn't the time or place. It's freezing! '

'Yes, nurse,' he smiled, 'yes, my wise little nurse. Mind, if I fell ill, I could come to you to nurse me well again and take you into my bed with me then.'

'Oh, for goodness sakes. Be sensible.'

'*Dieu*! I've been sensible all my life, sweet one, *glikia mou*, my little love. For once I feel wild, youthful and ridiculous. Allow me to enjoy it for a few, brief moments. How good you are for me.'

'I loved you the moment I saw you,' I said wonderingly. 'I always thought love was to do with the heart. My heart has ached, all right, longing to see you again, but the feeling right from the start seemed to come from here,' I pointed to my gut region, 'and be connected as if by a magical string to you there,' pointing to his own. 'It's the strangest feeling. That's how I always seem to see through your best disguises. I just feel that string between us tugging fiercely away.'

'Yes, it's the same feeling for me. The same, just the same. Dorothea, this is meant to be. Sheer madness. *Quel coup de foudre!*'

We embraced again and then he took me by the arm and we walked back up the track together. In the distance we saw the eerie sight of the headlights of a stream of lorries taking supplies up and down the hills to various camps. For some reason I couldn't fathom, the village dogs remained silent except for an occasional little whimper or howl. Perhaps the goaty smell of a shepherd was a familiar one as these men generally went out with their flocks at night, especially in the summer, in order to escape the daytime heat.

Once within sight of the camp, shining white and peaceful in the moonlight, Costas paused and hugged me to him.

'I will contact you when I am able,' he said, 'but, dear one, don't get in touch with me again in any way. I will do what I can to meet you and you must have trust. Believe me, I will be on fire till then. We *must* be together even for a mere hour. I will do what I can. When do you have time off?'

'It varies and I can never be sure. I am due some holiday leave and could take that. It may have to be after Christmas though. I've been here since March and we're supposed to be allowed three weeks. We can't go home on leave but I certainly should be allowed to go to the Nurses Rest Home on the Kalamaria Rd.'

'Would you be allowed to go and stay with a friend in the city?'

'Meaning you, I suppose?'

'Meaning my mother's old house in Salonika. She would love to have you stay with her. I could visit you there now and then without any problem. We have a boat and I can take you on trips around the bay, you could have a wonderful time.'

I looked dubious, 'Well, I suppose it would be all right. I would have to ask Matron, she is quite a duenna and responsible for us girls. But what of you? Would it be safe for *you* if I went to your mother?'

'It is safe. I have a sister and a brother in law who can come and visit too so all will seem fine. You will have to think of some story of how you met my mother. I will arrange for you to go and visit her some time soon.'

It sounded very exciting. It would be marvellous to go to a Greek home in the city. I hoped Matron would make no objections but couldn't see why she should. Other people went to see friends in the city, admittedly British friends – but all the same. 'It does sound wonderful, Costas.'

'We shall do what we can, we must meet again and have some private time ...out of the wind and rain!'

He left me with regret and swiftly melted away into the night shadows. I think we both felt torn apart inside at the separation but it had to be. It was the deepest, wildest yearning I had ever experienced in my entire life. I wanted to join with this man's flesh, be with him forever and ever.

I scrambled under the barbed wire and walked back into the camp, stuffing my hair under my cap as I went. I lit my little hurricane lamp, which was vital in order not to trip over the guy ropes or fall into one of the trenches around the tents. The night nurses were all on duty in the wards and the sentries no doubt nodding in the Mess tent. No one challenged me and I slipped silently into my tent, brushed my teeth and went to bed. It was impossible to sleep. The experiences of this whole, strange, dreamlike day played over and over in my mind like an old gramophone record. From the gentle, almost timid declaration of Ethan Willoughby to the wild passion of Costakis and his urgent embrace. How different those two men were. At last, exhausted with emotion, I fell asleep and had to be shaken awake by the orderly in the morning.

Chapter 21

December 19ᵗʰ

The geese and ducks are being nicely fattened up for Christmas and all sorts of cheerful concerts and merry things are being prepared. We are busy making paper chains to hang around the wards and there will be little packs to give every wounded and sick soldier with crackers, puddings, a Red Cross gift bag and a card in the language of the recipient. It is such fun to get these things together and to imagine the pleasure they will bring. The men will be so surprised and delighted.

It has been a very busy month. Trying to work in the winter weather is such a struggle. The water in the basins and jugs freezes up and the whole place is difficult to walk around for if it rains, it all turns into a quagmire and one is slipping and sliding in the mud. Somehow or other we manage to perform all our duties with remarkable efficiency. Many of the staff catch colds or go down with influenza. Though I might look small and fragile – or so I have been told – I seem to be a tough one and thank God that I have not had a day's illness so far. Sometimes I think my mother's hated Spartan regime has stood me in good stead. She never pampered us and was always very strict about rising early, washing in cold water and eating simple, plain food. She would never light a fire anywhere except the sitting room and father's study and perhaps in the library. Our bedrooms were always cold. So the difficult conditions don't make me turn a hair whereas many of the girls complain bitterly and have asked to be sent home. Those not on contract are allowed to do so. The rest of us have to put up with it.

Things have taken quite a different turn in the madness of Greek politics. The Royalist Greeks in Athens apparently fired on the Anglo-French Allies as they approached the port and this has proved their undoing. The Allies see it as a very good excuse to blockade Athens. People think Venizelos has encouraged the Allies in this with hopes of ending the rule of King Constantine

December 26ᵗʰ

Christmas has been such fun. Church in the morning with Padre Tudor Jones, who gave a fine, uplifting sermon and prayed earnestly for the war to end soon. After we had dealt with our various morning chores, dinner was served. The menus were all very elegant and properly printed out and tables with lovely tablecloths and beautiful plates and glasses were laid in rows in the canteen. Goodness knows where they had managed to requisition all that stuff. Some artistic soul had even found lots of ivy and pine branches and decorated the tables with these. It all looked truly festive and cheering. We had a regal meal. There was Consommé Royal, Roast Turkey, Goose and Beef. Puree of Apples; to follow this there was English Plum Pudding, Mince Pies and Mandarin Surprise, then Canapes, and Coffee. What a glorious feast!

Then there was a marvellous theatrical show put on for us by GHQ and it was really professional. The men took parts, both male and female and looked very good. It made me think of Shakespeare's days to see the young lads act the part of pretty maidens! The older men dressed as pantomime dames took on more exaggerated and comic appearances and there were many cat calls and comments from the men though I have a suspicion they would have been a good deal more lewd and ribald if we nurses had not been there too. There were a couple of comedians who kept everyone in stitches and some really marvellous singing from the Serbs and Russians who rival our Welshmen in harmony. Naturally they did 'Tipperary'. May and I winked naughtily at one another and laughed so much. After the performance we all cheered loudly and banged the tables in appreciation.

I have had my menu autographed by as many people as I could. I mean to keep it forever as a cherished memory of the most amazing, friendly, cheerful, happy Christmas of my life.

Ethan asked me to autograph his own menu and bent towards me and kissed me tenderly on the cheek. 'Happy Christmas, Dorothy.'

He had been perfectly well behaved and made no reference at all to his declarations in Flocas Cafe. It was as if it had never happened. Now as he gave me this little kiss and Christmas greeting, there was such a wealth of deep feeling in his voice that I laughed a little and tried to lighten his intensity.

'And to you, sir,' I said cheerfully, 'it's been such a marvellous day and the men look far better for it.'

'They do indeed!'

'Let's pray for this war to end,' I said, 'but all the same, it has meant finding such wonderful new comrades and friends. It seems even evil things can produce some good.'

'Yes. I have found you Dorothy,' said Ethan, 'and I *don't* mean to lose you.'

I smiled a little and looked down but made no reply. What could I say? I couldn't upset him as yet. I had to work with the man. He little knew that I had it in mind to stay here in Salonika forever once the war was ended; that my private ambition was to be the wife of Captain Cassimatis..

He seemed downcast by my silence and stood by me for a moment longer staring into space and then he patted my shoulder a little awkwardly and walked away. I hated to hurt him. He was a wonderful man. But I simply did not love him.

Chapter 22

The Black Diary

January 3rd 1917

The wounded and sick come down on the hospital trains, field
ambulances or even occasionally brought in on a travois, two
long poles on which a stretcher is slung and pulled by mules.
The mules are quite capable of tipping the whole thing up as
they rather resent this particular duty. The men are in a filthy
state, crawling with bugs and fleas and almost dead with cold.
They have to be thoroughly shaved of all hair, yes all! ...a job for
the orderlies, I assure you ...and then washed first in kerosene to
kill the lice, rewashed to get rid of the awful smell, temperatures
taken, clean dressings put on, clean pyjamas and into bed. Then
cups of hot Bovril or Oxo and lots of hot water bottles are doled
out. If there is frost-bite we have to check immediately and if the
skin and tissues have remained whole they can be treated with
oil of turpentine, covered with cotton wool and gentle heat
applied to restore the circulation. Sloughing wounds have to be
treated with eusol and paraffin dressings twice daily. But
gangrenous limbs have to be watched very carefully in case the
inflammation becomes more severe in which case it might be
necessary to amputate the limb. Sometimes the men sob bitterly
to think they will lose a limb while others simply accept their
fate with sad resignation and British phlegm.

I am busy some days from 4am to 6pm and feel very tired.
I am grateful for Franz, our friendly Austrian POW, who acts

as our orderly. He seems to dote on us, especially May whose fair hair and blue eyes probably remind him of some pretty, little Gretchen back home. He always makes sure that we have a hot water bottle in our bed when we get to our tent. Sometimes he puts in two or even three when it is really cold. I can only wonder whose he has taken for our sake and pity some poor soul shivering as they get in bed minus their bottle! He has also dug a little ditch around the bell tents which helps to drain off the water and keeps us reasonably dry in there at least.

Despite all this, when the snow begins to fall it drifts into our tents through every tiny crevice it can find. It is so dispiriting to come off duty tired and weary and then have to crawl into damp beds, but there's nothing else for it. One of the nurses woke the other morning with her hair frozen to the pillow but May and I had the sense to wrap our heads in shawls to keep them warm and managed to escape that fate at least. We always find that our hot water bottles and our sponges have frozen overnight and it takes a while to thaw them out in the precious jug of hot water, which rapidly turns cold in its turn. So some days we just don't wash. It's too cold to take off one's clothes and we put on coats and shawls and anything else we can find and look like great shapeless lumps rather than women. Some of the officers are such angels and let the night nurses borrow their greatcoats as ours are just useless. One enterprising nurse bought herself a fur coat in the market and looks like the Yeti.

The trouble with the snow is it covers everything over so thickly that the night nurses are always in danger of tripping up on the guy ropes and falling in the ditches and apparently one poor soul did just that at some other camp high up on the hills and was only just rescued in time before she died of cold. The agony of the circulation returning to her frozen limbs was so awful that she begged to be allowed to die. Thank God neither May, nor I, are on night duty this month.

Apparently this is the first snowy winter they have had in a long time. Just our luck! Does everything conspire to make our life here a torment? The shops have been shut in the town and people die in the streets and are simply left there till the snow thaws.

January 14th. 1917

On New Year's Day the local people were celebrating quietly with a lot of praying and icon kissing going on everywhere. Down in the city there was a salute of 21 guns, which we could hear up in the camp.

Let us see what this New Year will bring us …will it be the end of the war yet? From all accounts it seems unlikely that any breakthrough will occur in the stalemate for a long, long time. Sometimes I wonder if it ever will. Life in England seems to be a distant dream and we all feel we are here forever.

I had a lovely letter from Papa. Agnes sent me a note and some photos of little Reggie who does look a bonny baby. Mama wrote her usual long letter admonishing me to do this and that for my health, wear this and that and take care not to eat anything she considers to be dangerous. As if we have any choice! She doesn't know the half of it, bless her. I never elaborate on conditions here as I don't want to alarm them back home and neither does Richard. However, her attitude is that it is 'poor Richard' who suffers and is doing all the hard work fighting the Hun while they at home have endless trouble getting butter and other commodities. *Poor* things. I sound a trifle sour but really the attitude of those back home seems to be that they are having all the problems and we are all having fun and games out here in Salonika just because we aren't fighting major battles and being blown to bits every day. I suppose they would like that better than the endless waiting, the sickness, the cold, hunger and misery the poor men have to suffer.

Papa loved his box of *Rahat loukum* and Mama says she was delighted with her embroideries. I wonder if she *was* delighted that much, I think she is just being polite. She isn't a frilly sort of person but what else to send her? I have sent Richard my cigarette ration and he tells me he has shared it out with some of his men. May gave hers to Bill and most of the nurses gave theirs to soldiers they knew. I also sent Richard some *loukum*, a lovely meerschaum pipe on which was written 'made in Germany'… and various other little things that I knew would be useful or amusing.

His reply came the other day and it troubled me. It lacks his usual cheerful sound. The winter in the trenches has been a real nightmare over there too. It doesn't bear thinking on, but I *do* understand what it is like and it is good to share each others sufferings. A trouble shared is a trouble halved as they always say.

'I don't want to grumble, Dot, heaven knows my men endure it all with me and we are in it together. I can tell you all this because, darling Sis, you know what things are like out here on the battlefields and in the trenches. You know how the men suffer and how many die and the diseases and the despair at times. You know about the mud and the heat and the conditions we have to bear. I see brave, young men with trench foot and they know it means they'll lose their leg. We are constantly knee deep in mud and water, standing for hours in it in the freezing cold. And that's the least of it. I dare not tell them at home…just don't want to worry them. It's worse, isn't it, when one is waiting at home and can't do anything to help? We're in the thick of it, you and I, and we are at least doing something, sharing what we feel with our colleagues and fellow soldiers. So don't breathe a word of it all to the dear ones, Dot, there's a chum.'

He has also told me that there has been no repetition of the amazing fraternising of last Christmas when soldiers from both sides crossed into No Man's Land and greeted one another with a true comradely Christmas spirit. That sort of behaviour didn't appeal at all to the wretches who send the men in as cannon fodder for the greedy, power-mad purposes of their leaders. Ordinary people want peace and contentment; love is in every man's heart deep down.

I haven't heard from Costas yet and try hard not to think about him too much. I confess that late at night as I try to keep warm in bed, he comes to my mind and I relive all the moments we have had together, over and over, till even these bright images grow so stale that I know I have wrung every nuance from them. I yearn to feed my hungry heart with new ones. If only he would send me a message, anything. I am always so terrified that something untoward might have happened to him in these dangerous times.

Papa sent me a new diary for Christmas as the red one is full. This one has a black leather cover with gold letters on the front. I wonder where he managed to get it in these hard times and do appreciate his thoughtfulness. For some reason the dull black cover fills me with a sense of foreboding. I much prefer my red one but we can't be choosy about these matters. I know I am being quite silly. However, I am starting the New Year with my new diary.

Jan 20ᵗʰ

My presentiment over the Black Diary was not so foolish it seems. Our sweet little Eleni has died of pneumonia today and I asked Matron if I could go to her funeral.

The custom here is to dress the body all in white like a bride and place it in an uncovered coffin. This is then carried shield fashion on ropes supported by her male relations. Off we all went in a procession to the cemetery led by a man in a trilby hat and frockcoat, presumably the undertaker, and behind him came the village priest and his boys carrying candles. Behind this crowd came the train of keening relatives. Before they took Eleni away, I stood by the open coffin and looked at her for a long time and kissed her pale face. She looked so peaceful at last. I would always be haunted by the look in her eyes when she first came out of prison and by the knowledge of what happened to her. I know it's an unchristian thought but I hope the brothers *have* avenged her.

Her mother came to me and kissed my hand and thanked me repeatedly for bringing Eleni home to her village for her last brief moments in this world. After what Costas had told me, perhaps death is a blessing for her. I am glad that at least she died at home surrounded by her grieving friends and relations and not lost in some unknown, filthy prison, abused, tormented by hateful, evil men. I am grateful to Costas for his help too, but of course could not say so to the mother. She probably knew anyway.

Was this what my foreboding was about? If so, why is this sense of unease still there? Perhaps my nerves are wearing thin; I do feel quite tired of late.

Feb 5th

The wild geese are flying over again and flowers are beginning to appear on the hills which are now covered in crocus and anemone, while a soft green covering is beginning to spread over the sombre winter landscape. It looks so beautiful as if stretching and waking after a long, long sleep.

Matron has said that I can have off a week in March and go to stay in the newly established Nurses Rest Home. I gather it is all very cosy and smart in some beautiful old Turkish house with a garden all around it. It sounds delightful but it would be very difficult to meet with Costas there. I wasn't sure what to say about staying at his mother's house as I still haven't met her and have no idea quite where she lives. It's all a bit difficult.

However, next time I passed through the village, I captured my young go-between again. I then told him to tell the man we both knew that Nurse Clarke was going to be on leave in Salonika in March and he could contact her at the Nurses Rest Home just off the main Kalamaria Rd. I felt my confidence ebb even as I sent the boy off with a whole drachma note clutched in his hand. Maybe after all, it had been a dream and Costas no longer cared. A flash in the pan …a man thwarted of his lustful desire? Was that him? Was he so shallow a person? Or had something terrible happened to him?

Feb 10th

I was laying some wild anemones on Eleni's grave today when the little lad, Yiangos, came up to me and put an envelope in my hand. To my surprise, he refused the money I offered and told me he had already been paid enough. How proud some of these village people are! Even at so young an age they show generosity of spirit, unlike the greedy townspeople.

I walked through the little cemetery and sat myself down in a sheltered spot on a wall. The note was on elegant paper, the address at the top written in English and was from a Mrs Nina Cassimatis. She asked me to do her the pleasure of coming to tea with her whenever I might be allowed an afternoon off. The way the note was worded it made it seem as if she was an old aquaintance. I was sure Costas had written it. It looked like his large, sprawling hand. I wondered with a little disquiet in my heart if there really was a mother still alive. Surely he wouldn't say so if there wasn't. How could I doubt him even for a moment? The address looked legitimate enough. I looked it up on the city map later and found out where it was. It was in the smarter, residential quarter on the eastern side of the city.

I took the note to Matron and asked if I might visit on my day off. She looked surprised.

'How do you come to know this lady, Sister Dorothy?'

'We became acquainted in Salonika while I was sightseeing,; I said glibly.

I hated to lie, I so hated it. But there was no choice.

Oh, Costas, why am I letting you drag me into your web of secrets and espionage and lies?

I wondered if Matron would recall the name Cassimatis but she seemed not to do so. She said I could have off Thursday afternoon unless anything untoward happened as long as I was back by seven pip emma.

I wrote a polite note of acceptance and took it along to the canteen to be posted and delivered to Mrs Nina Cassimatis.

Word soon gets round the camp and several people have asked me where I am going and to tell me all about it when I get back. May is especially curious and it is all I can do to fend off her persistent questions.

'She just …took a fancy to me, that's all. It's probably because I can speak some Greek. That seems to make friends wherever one goes.'

I feel sure May thought I was up to something but I showed her the elegant, polite invitation and that seemed to satisfy her that I was not going on some mysterious assignation. As for myself, I had no idea what was in store for me, but then I always enjoy that state of affairs.

To my vast annoyance, Willoughby spoke to me later in the day and said, 'So you have managed to meet the Captain's wife? I assume it is the same Cassimatis.'

'It's his mother, not his wife.'

'I see.'

'Really, is nothing private in this place?' I said with a little flash of anger. 'It's worse than a country village! Of what interest is it to everyone who I choose to visit on my day off?'

'It *is* like a village here in some ways,' smiled Willoughby, 'and no, nothing is sacred, is it? Of course people are interested; we are like a big family. And it is always wise to tell people where one is in case of any problems.'

I still felt rather cross and made no reply.

'Aren't you getting a bit involved with this Greek lot?' said Willoughby in that rather stern manner that always grated on me.

'This Greek lot …what a way to talk about people.'

'Dorothy, you don't know who they are, what they might be up to …now, do you?'

I was rather troubled by his uncanny manner of putting two and two together. I hesitated and wondered if it might be wiser to confide a little in him and ask for his discretion.

He was watching my expression carefully. All of a sudden, he took me by the arm and steered me to one side away from the eyes and ears of anyone else. I stared at him in surprise and some alarm. He looked at me for a few moments with that serious, intense expression that he always wore.

'I worry about you, Dorothy, you are so young and suggestible. This is a foreign country, the people, however interesting and even in some ways childlike and loveable, well, they are alien to us and our way of life. We can never be sure if they are friends or enemies ready to stab us in the back. They aren't to be relied upon or trusted and would sell their children or their grandmother for hard cash. Isn't it wiser not to become mixed up with them in any way?'

There was an urgency in his words but I still felt them to be patronising. I couldn't help wondering what he suspected or what he knew? Had he discovered something about Costas and myself? In a way, that wasn't the problem. What troubled me most was that I might compromise Costas in some way and bring him into danger from his own people in these uncertain times when the Greeks seemed more bent on cutting each other's throats than worrying about the enemy outside. I bent my head and wasn't sure what to say. Willoughby watched me like an eagle, sensing my turmoil in some way. He waited patiently for me to speak. In the end I took the plunge.

'Captain Willoughby, sir, I don't know what you suspect or what you know. But please, promise me you won't mention any connection …won't connect my visit to see Mrs Cassimatis with the Captain. Or mention it to Matron or anyone else. I don't say this for my sake at all. There are reasons for my not being completely open. I can't explain just now.'

'He is a secret agent, I expect,' said Willoughby shrewdly, 'most of these Venizelist officers are up to something or other.'

I gave a quick, little nod.

'Please don't mention it, sir. Will you promise?'

He considered for a few moments and I saw him struggle. He must have felt that he should report all this to our own Intelligence men. From the start of the campaign, the spy problem had been a continual harassment that our military police dealt with very efficiently. I didn't blame him at all. Even I was not quite sure what Costas was up to or whose side he was really on. I gazed up at Willoughby anxiously, willing him to trust me. After a few moments he looked at me again.

'All right. I give you my word, as you ask it. But I will break it if I sense you are in any trouble. I'm worried that you might be getting embroiled in something beyond your understanding, my dear. These men are dangerous and not to be trusted. There is no knowing who is spying for whom and what they are up to half the time …I wonder if they know themselves. These Greeks don't like us here …especially the Royalist bunch. I don't think even the Venizelists like us that much but put up with us because we guarantee that Salonika won't fall into Bulgar or Turkish hands again. I think they hate the Bulgarians almost more than the Turks. My dear girl, how on earth have *you* become involved?'

'No, no …it's nothing at all sinister. I promise that I am not involved in anything underhand. Just a coincidental meeting and an invitation from a nice old lady who loves my funny Greek,' I said with what I hoped was a disarming smile.

He looked at me for a long time with his candid, searching eyes. I felt a slow flush creeping over my face. How I hate the man; he s always poking his nose in my business as if he had some right to. I turned and marched off to my tent rather rudely I'm afraid. It really is not up to him to tell me what to do. Matron is satisfied and that's all I care. But I had many unpleasant dreams that night and felt troubled in myself. Then I thought of my desperate yearning love for Costas and quelled the sense of shame. He has to tell lies all the time and yet he is still a man of honour.

All the same, I know that my own lies are purely selfish and are just because I want to see him so desperately. So very desperately that it hurts.

Chapter 23

Feb 22ⁿᵈ 1917

I felt quite nervous about my visit to see Mrs Cassimatis. I really wasn't at all sure what to expect or what was going to happen. I half wondered if Ethan Willoughby was right and I should never have become involved in all this. I came here to nurse and be useful, to sacrifice myself on the altar of good works and here I now was, my mind on nothing but the rather exhilarating thought of seeing Costas again. He was a stranger in a strange land; a man who might be a murderer or a villain for all I really knew. And I had felt myself to be so invulnerable. How right May was, we fools are the types that fall the hardest. I used to smile with vast superiority to myself about May and her flirtatiousness, thinking her shallow. Now I felt real shame for thinking so of her. She was proving the loyal one, the willing one. I felt myself to be very base at this point and troubled in my soul.

The day dawned and during that morning I slipped into the tent that was our little chapel and went down on my knees before the altar. Someone had picked a bunch of the first little wild flowers and arranged them in an empty ideal milk tin. This simple offering brought tears to my eyes; other people were so good and noble and just now I felt so dishonourable. Putting my hands together in submission, I prayed to God for guidance. Was I being selfish and stupid? Was I, Lord?

Of a sudden, a very clear image of Costas came to my mind. I hadn't seen him for some time and so his features had blurred in my memory. Just at this moment it was as if he stood before me in my mind and my heart leapt with strange joy. I knew then that I loved him with all my heart and soul and that God was not angry with me at all. We had met for a purpose and that was all that mattered. I would follow this road come what may.

Canon Tudor Jones came into chapel as I rose from my knees and looked at me in surprise. I smiled at him and said good day but didn't stop for paternalistic advice or pastoral help. My feelings were now quite clear to me.

The afternoon came and I made sure that my blue walking dress was ironed and smart, my collar nicely starched with what little arrowroot I could beg from the cook so that for once it was nice and stiff and tidy and not floppy and bedraggled. It made such a difference. I had been told that Kyria Nina would send her servant to take me into town so all I could do was wait. As I finished pinning up my hair, May came in and said excitedly, 'Goodness, Dot, your friends must be very well off! They have sent such a smart carriage for you.'

The arrival of an elegant Victoria with its two fine bay horses certainly caused a stir in the camp and several people stopped and looked at it with interest. Both the equipage and the horses looked smart and well kept in contrast to the rattling old *araba* and the pathetic looking mules of the city drivers. I sighed a little. Could things be *more* ostentatious? Perhaps Costas was being clever, who knows? Certainly Matron could not suppose that I was going anywhere that was not respectable or that I was not being cared for.

I really hated being the centre of attention and yearned to crawl away somewhere. But go I must, so I strode out with assumed confidence and the smart Turkish servant in his red fez opened the little door and ushered me onto the wonderful black leather upholstery to the cries of envy and encouragement of various orderlies and officers who were there. I felt myself blushing but tried to be calm. Out of the corner of my eye I spotted Ethan Willoughby who had come out of one of the laboratories to see what the fuss was about. Well, he certainly couldn't say it was all a cloak and dagger operation. His face was impassive but I caught his eye and he smiled and waved at me encouragingly. I can't say why this pleased me so much but it did. Somewhere deep inside I always want his approval.

We set off for the city over the terrible bumpy, pitted roads. The driver negotiated the potholes with ease and it was the smoothest ride I had ever had on this ungainly track. The weather had been wet of late but now the sun began to shine forth in a pallid and watery manner, while the irritating wind dropped at last and a soft stillness seemed to take over the countryside. The fields full of wild flowers glimmered in the sunshine, a glorious yellow, purple and white carpet. The mountains rose in their rugged glory, mists still wreathing and drifting around their summits, and for once all was soft, fresh and newly cleansed. It looked so very beautiful. I have to confess I love adventure. It stirs my heart and soul and I was beginning to enjoy myself already.

We drove into the city and away from the seafront and the Jewish areas bustling with commerce and activity. We came at last to a beautiful wide paved street on the other side of town with well-kept terraced houses on each side, some tall, some smaller, all brightly painted and shuttered tightly against the afternoon sunshine. Little vines or jasmine grew around some of the balconies and doors and sweet scented pots full of marjoram and basil rested in the porches. No unsightly washing draped here! There was a sense of space and quiet elegance such as I had not yet seen in Salonika. It was so different to the rambling, twisting mazes and the dilapidated wooden houses of the Turkish area that I had previously explored. Different again to the beautiful big villas with their well kept lawns and gardens and tennis courts that lined the road to Karaburun and belonged to the wealthier Jews. Here was a sense of upper middle class gentility, neatness and lack of ostentation.

The carriage stopped before one of the tall, narrow, three-storey houses and the coachman came and opened the door for me and helped me down. As if by some pre-arranged signal, a manservant came out of the house and ushered me indoors into a wide, cool, dark hallway with gleaming black and white veined marble flooring.

A small, slender lady came forward to greet me. She was dressed in European manner in a very elegant and well cut black dress. Her hair was pure white and wound into a low bun on the nape of her neck, her eyes deep brown and though she appeared to be in her late sixties, her face was almost unlined. In her ears were little pearl earrings like tiny droplets. Round her neck was a long rope of tiny, evenly matched pearls. Everything about her was discreet, calm and dignified. I felt at ease with her immediately for there was something warm and receptive in her manner despite the formality of her greeting.

'Welcome to my home. So nice to meet you, Miss Clarke,' she said in almost perfect English as she extended her hand to me and took mine in a warm clasp, 'come ...come and sit with me and tell me all about yourself.'

I followed her up the stairs her into a well-furnished salon that might have been in Paris or London except for the abundance of embroidered or crocheted articles, which the Greek ladies seem to favour so much. Lovely modern pictures in gilt frames adorned the walls and the room was comfortable and tasteful. Large windows draped with heavy red satin curtains opened out onto a wooden balcony that spanned across the entire house looking down onto the courtyard below. One could presumably walk around to another room from this balcony or take another staircase that led down to a pretty yard full of flower-pots and lemon trees.

Mrs Cassimatis sent for coffee and cakes and meanwhile a servant brought a large ornate tray with two tall glasses. One contained the long spoons which one used to eat a strange, bittersweet jam in a dish. The other glass, which was filled with water, was for the spoon to be put in after use. A glass of very clear cold water was also served with this to wash down the sweetness. This offering of sweet jam is the customary reception that one has in any Greek home and one simply has to take it or offend one's hostess forever. I swallowed the jam and washed it down with the glass of water and actually quite liked it for a change. It tasted of quince but with a certain aroma about it.

Mrs Cassimatis smiled a little

'This is one of our best jams . . *glico kidoni* …do you like it? I know it isn't your English custom but when in Rome as they say. Greeks hate to turn anyone away without something in their stomachs. We never ask if they like it or not!'

I assured her that it was utterly delightful.

'And the water tastes so good and so cold,' I said in wonder. It was a delight to taste water that was neither chlorinated, nor the foul, brackish stuff that the villagers offered.

'Of course. It comes from our own well out there in the yard. We do have water in pipes nowadays but personally I prefer to drink the clear lovely water of our well. My neighbours come and ask …'can we have some of your *oreio neraki,* Kyria Nina, some of your lovely water? It's the best we have ever tasted.' I don't trust that the tap water is clean, it always has to be boiled. But the water from our well goes very deep and is pure as crystal.'

Coffee arrived and some wonderful creamy French pastries rather than the usual sickly sweet Turkish type cakes, all nuts and honey. I did appreciate these pastries very much. They were delicious.

I am an adaptable person by nature and felt relaxed and comfortable. Nina Cassimatis and I began to chat away as if we had always known each other. Feeling at ease as I did, I soon began to express my feelings about Salonika, my home life, the war and many other topics and found my hostess a very good listener. Yet, deep down I kept wondering if I was being looked over and reviewed by this charming elderly lady. She surely must know what her son Costas felt about me, or did he want her opinion and approval first? There was no sign of him at all and she made no mention of him. I did not dare to mention his name either. It all seemed so strange and uncertain.

'How beautiful your home and gardens sound,' she said as I described my beloved Downlands to her, 'I am sure you must be longing to be back there, longing as we all do for this war to end?'

'I long to see home, of course,' I said and hesitated, wondering if she was sounding out just how enthusiastic I was for a Greek life, 'but I confess, I do love it here. I feel a sense of being at home here where the other English girls don't. They see the mud, the flies, the malaria but I see colour, romance, liveliness. It appeals to my romantic nature. I long to see the rest of Greece and tread the path of the ancients some time, see all the marvellous places that Homer brought to life for us.'

'Sometimes I wonder if Greece belongs to us or to the rest of the world,' mused the old lady, 'during the Turkish occupation, we became rich and powerful, many of us. My family, certainly. We were rich aristocrats in the old days . . .not now; now we have left all behind and fled the City, fled our beloved Constantinople. My family would meddle in politics, you see,'she said with a sigh, 'they would meddle! But it's in our blood ...we Greeks are political animals.'

'We were safer,' she continued, 'practising our Orthodox religion under the Turks than we would have been had the Papists got hold of Byzantine. I swear we hate the Catholics ten times more than the Muslims or Jews. To the Turks we were all 'people of the book' and they treated us with some respect.'

She paused to pour me another tiny cup of sweet Turkish coffee and press another cake upon me.

'But you know, the Greeks forgot their ancient heritage, the people forgot everything, just living from day to day, mostly quite happily, Turks, Armenians, Jews, Serbs, Bulgarians, Greeks and more ...all mixed up together in a big soup of people. That's why they call a mixed dish of fruits a '*macedoine*'! What a mixture! Yet all friends in those olden days not enemies as now. Ask anyone in those days before the Revolution what nationality they were and they would look at you in surprise and say ...'But I am a Christian' ...or a Jew or whatever ...because this how the Turks ruled. They saw their conquered lands in religious terms not national ones. The Muslims are very religious people. They insisted that one practised one's faith whatever it was and practised it well.'

'And so we would have forgotten all about our ancient heritage apart from a few stories and old piles of stone to remind us of a dim time in the past when Greece was the glory of the

Mediterranean. Isn't it strange that our heritage was kept alive outside the Ottoman Empire…that backward, sleeping, lazy mass of nations and peoples! Like an old dog it was, asleep in the sun. It was those of us Greeks from the City, it was those Greeks who travelled abroad, who found their heritage once more in the universities, amongst the learned men of Europe. Ancient Greek was better known outside Greece than in it. They brought that heritage back and woke us all up and reminded us of our glorious past again. So Greece is free now of the Turkish yoke. Thank God that our beloved Greece is free! But now we have war, war, war…hate, killing, death and disease. E! …what can you say?'

Mrs Cassimatis smiled at me and shrugged and spread out her hands in a little gesture of dismissal.

'Yes,' I replied, 'each nation does seem to have a character of its own, though it is made up of such diverse individuals. But when they face an attack from outside they suddenly seem to act as one body, one nature. Look at the Germans …I always used to like the few Germans I knew. Now as a race they have become arrogant and warlike. As a nation I feel we British are idealistic and honourable. Individuals may not be but I think as a nation we *are* fair-minded.'

'I agree, I agree,' said Mrs Cassimatis, 'and we Hellenic Greeks are philosophers at heart. Philosophers, just as in the days of Plato. The Hellenes are thinkers and always will be.'

'So you are from Constantinople?'

'I am indeed. But my husband, Petros, was a Thessalonian, born and bred here. Well, they say the Thessalonians are bold men! He heard of me – we are distantly related – and came over to the City to have me as his bride, just on the strength of my portrait. I was very young and a beauty then.'

And you still are a beauty in your way, I thought, looking at her with admiration.

'Here's a photo of us when we married, 'said Mrs Cassimatis, going over to a drawer and taking out a large, old photograph. I smiled at the stiff, unnatural poses of the bride and groom, she seated on a chair, her ankles neatly crossed, her dark eyes so beautiful, her hair then a thick wavy mass beneath the bridal veil. Petros Cassimatis had been a tall, elegant man with a thick moustache, wavy dark hair and solemn eyes. I could see how much Costas resembled him and it made me feel such a longing to see him again.

I could sense Mrs Cassimatis studying me with equal interest as I looked at the photo and wondered what she was thinking. I smiled and handed it back to her again.

'You made a lovely couple.'

'Ah, my Petros!' she said fondly, looking at the photograph for a few moments before replacing it in the drawer. 'He was such an amazing man.'

She went on, 'You speak of the character of a nation. Our men are still the soul of honour and great courage. Our women the same. We need to go forward not live in the past, be part of Europe and the world again. For this reason above all our family approves of that old Cretan rascal Venizelos. He is determined to bring us into the 20th century and out of the medieval past and this is why we support him.'

Mrs Cassimatis rose and I wondered if this was the end of my 'interview' and half rose too.

'No, you stay here for a little. I have bored you long enough with Greek politics. I am going downstairs to speak to my cook and consider what we shall have for our evening meal. I wish you could stay?…no, I guessed you would have to go back; you have your work and duty. However, as you well know, there is another person who wants a few words with you,' she added with a sweet little smile.

My heart leapt and a faint flush rose to my cheeks, which did not go un-noticed. Mrs Cassimatis gave a little laugh and taking my hand in hers said, 'I have loved meeting you Dorothea – you will allow me to call you that? But take care, my child, take care.'

Her voice suddenly dropped a note and became quite serious and she looked at me for a little while without speaking. I returned her gaze steadily. Then she turned and left the room and I saw that despite her age, she had the same lithe, supple walk as her son, Costas

I sat and waited. Then, feeling quite nervous, I arose and began to walk about the room, twisting my hands and breathing rather fast. Of a sudden the door was flung open and in walked Costas. I couldn't help it; I clutched my hands to my heart and went quite pale. He was in civilian clothes today, looking so slim and handsome. One never had any idea how he would be dressed, what role he might play each time. But I had loved him even when he was dressed in baggy trousers and cloth cap. He stood at the door and looked at me and then held out his arms. I ran into them like a child.

Chapter 24

We hugged one another speechlessly. Costas held me away a little and looked long and intensely into my eyes.

'It has been so long, *agapi mou,* so long.'

'It has been weeks,' I said with a little pout, 'I've missed you so much!'

'And I you, little treasure.'

He tucked my hand in his arm and we strolled about the salon together. It felt so right and wonderful to be arm in arm together.

'There is such news coming through about Russia,' said Costas, 'matters go from bad to worse, strikes, famines, unrest. No wonder the people there are rising and they say the Revolution has definitely begun. It won't be long the way things are going before they throw out the Tsar. As for this country, time to get that idiot Constantine out of his palace. Time for our own revolution!'

'Goodness, it is frightening,' I said,' where will all this lead to? It seems impossible to imagine that we British might revolt against our own King and Queen. No, no –it couldn't possibly be. Yet that seems to be the trend nowadays. How the world is changing, changing so swiftly.'

'I long to go into action with the Allies,' said Costas, looking quite fierce, 'we Venizelists all want to be involved. Men, officers flock from Athens to join the Nationalist Army but we can't move yet due to all this political wrangling and constitutional nonsense. Soldiers are men of action but statesmen make and end wars and move armies about like pawns on a chessboard. Left to the soldiers, wars would soon be fought and won and everything decided and settled in no time. Those politicians are idiots – they keep us inactive, drive us to desperation.'

'Costas,' I said, clinging to his arm in sudden fright and gazing up at him, 'I don't want you to go to war – I don't want to lose you, to risk your life! I know that's stupid and wrong of me. I was so proud when my brother Richard set off for France, I'm still so proud of him and all he endures so cheerfully but we had no idea it would all go on so long or be so dreadful and so frustrating. Everyone seems to feel they are frustrated, bogged down, desperate to make a move but unable to do so. It's the oddest war. At home Pa says they call this Salonika Campaign 'a mere sideshow'. They have no idea what the men here suffer. It's so unfair. And here in Salonika the men call it 'The Doctor's War'. We fight Mother Nature herself in all her terrible vindictiveness. Oh, God what a fool I am, I don't want *you* to go into battle too.'

'My life is always in danger, Dorothea *mou*, always,' said Costas looking down at me and pausing to stroke my cheek and hair and lift my face up for a kiss, 'I am not afraid. I hope I am a man of *philotimo* a man of honour, never afraid of anything. But now that I know you, now that I have met you, I care more to stay alive. Is that a good thing? It has unmanned me.'

He spoke half-jokingly but I sensed that he did feel to some extent that he had lost his sense of a bachelor's freedom from care. A mere woman I might be but felt the same and said so.

'I cared only about my nursing work, about being of service and I too feel that now I only want to be here with you. I don't know if that is a good thing either.'

'Well, we seem to suffer from a crisis of conscience then, both of us. We are all soldiers, now, all helping to liberate the world from tyranny. And, of course, we will never fail to do our duty, we both know that. Meanwhile, Love is the glory of man and woman and is that which rescues us from despair, loneliness and hate. It brings the world together like Romeo and Juliet. We are from different nations, you and I, but we love with passion and longing, the feeling transcends the differences in our age and culture. We love, Dorothea! – we love! And that is the most important thing, more important than war, glory, honour and death.'

However, I wasn't so sure. 'You speak of Love but it should mean what the Red Cross stands for – *caritas, agape* –.loving one's fellow men, seeing all men, even the enemy as brothers. You speak of our personal, selfish love, Costas, you speak of just two people in love.'

'And what then? Doesn't love begin between two people? It begins with individuals, everything begins with individuals. What is in this heart is in the heart of the world – good, bad, love, hate. God, you speak so coldly!'

'I'm not cold, Costas, I am just being thoughtful and detached about it all.'

'Oh, you English women …and I thought you were a woman of passion.'

'I *am* passionate. You *know* that.'

He loosened me from his arm and held me away for a moment. His eyes seemed to burn me and his long fingers dug into my arms painfully but I said nothing, just looked back at him with a fearless calm. If anything my stoic composure seemed to increase his excitement. Rather than alarm me, his fierceness made my blood race and my heart beat. But I wasn't going to show him that. Let him rage and fume!

His eyes narrowed and he tucked my arm back into his and we resumed our walk in silence. I responded by squeezing his arm close to me.

After a while, he said in a sad voice, 'If only I could keep you here forever, release you from this dreadful work you do. So unwomanly, so unwomanly for you to deal with men in such a state. What made you want to be there amongst the blood and filth and horrors, a well brought up girl like yourself? Why don't you leave and come and live here with my mother? She loves you already, tells me you are a beautiful and good girl. Come, Dorothea, be her companion and live here.'

'Costas, for God's sake, you sound like my mother! She had a fit when I chose to come out here. Would I have met you if I hadn't come? You know you don't mean all this; surely you love me because I am what I am, as I do you. Do I say a word against your spying activities, the underhand things you must have to get up to? I understand you have been given a mission and have to execute it like any good soldier. Well, I'm proud of what I do, proud to be, as you say, a soldier in my own way. I am not a pacifist. I am not a malingerer. No, Costas, I signed a contract and I will fulfil it. I came here to help my fellow men. I can't turn my back on all that and live in comfort and laziness here. It's not in my nature.'

'Ach – now I see your passion, but it is not for me. It is for your duty.'

Nonetheless he smiled and kissed me tenderly. 'No, I know it is not in your nature. I am just dreaming. After the war, will you come and live here with us then?'

'As your wife?'

'Of course as my wife. But will you marry into the Orthodox Church, accept our faith? Here only a church marriage is legal.'

I paused a little and considered the matter.

'Yes, after all, we all worship the same God. What can it matter what church we worship Him in? Yes, I will marry you in the Orthodox Church.'

'How beautiful you will look!' he exclaimed enthusiastically.' We shall exchange wreaths and be king and queen for the day. My dear love, it will be the happiest day of my life.'

'Oh, and mine too,' I said fervently.

'And we shall have many sons, many sons, Dorothea, handsome and wonderful and two beautiful daughters to keep you company ...'

'Oh, Costas, you are running miles ahead already. Dear heart, let us at least wait till this war is over; none of us knows what will happen.' I said tapping him playfully on the nose.

'But that's it. We *don't* know. I may be killed, who can say? Dorothea let us marry now. I cannot wait, can you?'

I hesitated at this. 'Costas, don't rush me ahead like this. No, we'll wait till the war is over.'

He sat me down beside him on the sofa and stared ahead for a long time. I wondered if I had offended him but remained still and quiet, my arm still entwined in his, my hand held tight against his heart as if he would never let it go. His passion seemed to throb through him and although he said nothing I felt caught up in it, taken outside myself. It was hard to keep a hold of who and what I was. Being with Costas, was to become a part of his own burning fiery nature, caught, consumed in his own being.

'We can consider ourselves affianced, can't we?' he said at last.

'I'm not sure which of us proposed,' I said with a little laugh, 'but I am more than happy to be so, to be your fiancée.'

'In Greece we are as good as married. There can be no other now for either of us. We shall exchange engagement rings properly when you come here.'

'*When* am I coming here?'

'You said you had a week holiday?'

'Yes, indeed.'

'Won't you spend it here with us?' he asked, with such a pleading and delightful expression that my heart melted away. How could I ever refuse him anything?

'Your people won't mind? They can say nothing, surely?' he added.

'Well, no, not really …'

'Then it's settled, *n'est ce pas*?'

'All right.' I had to laugh a little. He was obviously used to be being obeyed and having his own way, yet was so utterly charming about it.

'Costas, we don't really know one another. Is this madness on our part?' I said with sudden misgiving.

'Oh, the English! –always so cautious,' he said almost angrily. 'If you only have a part of the love and desire I have for you, you wouldn't say such a thing, Dorothea.'

He stood and pulled me up to face him.

'Do you or do you not love me?'

I stood there and looked at him. He shut his eyes for a moment and gave a quick, impatient sigh. It was almost as if flames came from him, as if he was surrounded by vivid, bright light. He was a man of such extraordinary power and passion. I had never known such a man in my life and yet I knew that this same power and passion resided in my own heart and was reflected back at me from him. He was a mirror into my own soul. He *was* my soul. I had recognised this face from the first moment he had turned and looked at me outside the house of Yussuf the Jew.

'Costas, I *adore* you,' I said.

The breath rushed out of him again and he pulled me to him and held me tightly.

'My darling, my beloved, the love of my life,' he murmured and kissed me with a strange fierce ardour that had at the same time a sense of desperation about it.

After some time, I said regretfully, 'I must go back soon, Costas.'

'This is the hardest thing …to let you go from my sight,' he said, 'but you *will* come next week. I shall send Nouri to get you the carriage and drive you back to the hospital. You will see what a wonderful holiday you will have with us. I have managed to arrange a few days leave too and will be with you whenever I can. We shall have a wonderful time! The best time we may ever have, who knows. And we shall exchange our rings; then you are as good as mine. At least in Greek eyes.'

'And in English eyes. I don't go back on my word, Costas.'

'I know that. You are a girl to honour and trust, an angel.'

'No, *not* an angel,' I said firmly, 'not an angel, just a very foolish but truly loving girl.'

Chapter 25

March 8th 1917

I am at the Cassimatis house and sitting writing up my diary in a beautiful little bedroom. The room is in Turkish style with wonderful kilim rugs on the floor and walls, huge, intricately wrought copper and brass jars and ornaments everywhere. A long, gilt framed mirror decorates one of the walls and a mirrored dresser stands against another with washing implements and other toiletries. There is a lit brazier in a corner emitting a soft warmth as it is still chilly in the early morning and late evening.

A long, low divan sofa and unusual little triangular corner seats piled with embroidered cushions take up another wall making a cosy and intimate alcove with a low carved round table in the centre. The brass double bedstead takes up a large space; it seems a vast bed after my little pallet in the bell tent. But oh, to be sleeping in a real feather bed again! No one can imagine the bliss of it. Now I see why the soldiers always sigh with delight when we put the poor souls to bed, no matter how much pain they might be in. It is letting the bones sink down into a comfortable yet supportive softness for a little while. We spend so much time holding ourselves up, being alert, moving about and busy all the time.

I open the shutters of my window in the morning and step out onto the wooden balcony that overlooks a large courtyard full of pots of flowers. There is a small, carved fountain in the centre from which the water runs in pleasant streams into a basin below. An enormous ancient wisteria with a stem as thick as a tree clambers around the yard and up the walls of the house and winds around my balcony. The first of its green, delicate, frond-like leaves are appearing and bunches of long purple flowers are beginning to bloom already. I can see that there will be roses and jasmine too.

At the back of the yard under a huge old fig tree is the famous well with a bucket that lets down into it to draw up the waters. Often this bucket is filled with bottles of wine and lowered into the well to chill for our meal later. No expense seems to be spared. I am being treated as an honoured guest and utterly spoilt. Will I ever want to go back to the hospital and its mournful sights again after this? Maybe this is Costas's hope and intention …to lull me into this delightful *houri* like stupor of indolence and luxury and make me forget my duties. I realise that I have kept myself going for such a long time with no rest, no pause. And now a pause such as this will make it very hard to take up the reins again.

Yet mine is not a slothful nature and all this relaxation, wonderful as it is, is sure to pall in the end. However, I mean to enjoy every moment of my blissful holiday. Kyria Nina is so delightful; if only I had a mother like her, so caring, thoughtful and considerate. She is all warmth and praise and love in contrast to my own cold, critical and straight-jacketed parent. Costas has a young sister also with a husband and a little boy and I met them briefly the day I arrived. For the moment they have returned to their home in Kavalla. Now the house is just for Kyria Nina and Costas and myself and it is a delightful place to be in.

The kitchen staff seem bent on making me any English or French meals I like but I am keen to try out their own cuisine. They tend to cook in the Constantinople manner with lots of pilaff, cous-cous and sweetmeats – all very delicious indeed. Kyria Nina informs me that the Turkish cuisine is one of the best in Europe and I am inclined to agree.

The kitchen is on the ground floor next to the servant's quarters. With its copper pots and bowls, its huge jars and big chests full of spices, it is a most interesting place. I think though that my favourite room is the quaint bathhouse tiled in green Thessalonian marble, which is on the ground floor behind the kitchens. I love the unutterable luxury of having a douche with really hot water and in utter privacy. A huge copper brazier is heated up in this room and from this one ladles steamy hot water all over oneself as one sits on a stool set on a wooden slatted dais. The room becomes lovely and steamy like a Turkish *Hamam*. The maidservant was keen to come and help scrub me but I assured her I could manage very well by myself. So she hands me in a soft, fluffy white towel and I sit and pour water over myself and feel in a seventh heaven.

Kyria Nina has given me some lovely clothes to wear about the house while she has my things nicely laundered. The clothes all look new to me for they certainly don't belong to her daughter who is small and plump while I am small and thin. But Nina assures me that they belonged to Christoula before she had the baby. Apparently she has a fondness for chicken pilaff and honeyed *baclava* and has put on weight since her marriage as her husband spoils her a great deal. I must take warning from this as I hear that oriental men like their women plump. I most certainly won't allow Costas to fatten *me* up in this way! It is so nice to wear a pretty white muslin dress again though I know I cannot go out in it. I shall have to wear my uniform when we go out in public. Still, at least indoors I can pretend the war is over and look pretty again.

There is electricity and fans are installed which help turn a breeze around the rooms as the noontime heat begins to build up. Everything is very modern; there is even a telephone.

March 10th

Costas has arrived and has a few days leave so he is now able to relax a little. I cannot believe I am here at times, in this house, with this man of whom I had not even dreamt some months ago. And this man is to be my husband?

This morning I am sitting with him in a small back room,

furnished with divans along the length of the wall and with little coffee tables before them. There is a large, heavy walnut desk in a corner and I have seated myself here to write my diary. This room overlooks the gardens below and I can hear the trickling sound of the fountain in the courtyard and the soft sigh of the breeze in the trees. There is a sense of great space, peace and quietness in the tranquillity and privacy of these old Turkish houses. The sense of seclusion without being isolated soothes one's soul. I pause with my pen in hand and stare out of the windows and then turn my eye upon Costas and watch him, lounging upon the divan amongst the embroidered cushions with his dressing gown still on, one foot tucked beneath him oriental style, reading the newspaper. At his side a little brazier has on it the inevitable long-handled coffee pot bubbling away and he smokes a thin French cigarette.

People in these countries seem to stay in their state of *deshabille* till noon at least. I suppose it is cooler and more comfortable. I am so used to dressing immediately that I find it a trifle odd. I prefer to be ready and on the go, while these languid and delightfully indolent Orientals are disinclined to be alive till the evening when coolness descends with the night and the social side of the city suddenly comes to life and cafes, restaurants, theatres and the one cinema are all filled to capacity.

Costas is usually a very active man but it is as if a switch has taken place and he now assumes this lazy, relaxed Oriental mode as casually as if he had never been the tense, intriguing man I met outside Yussuf's house, as if he was not the violent and rough navvie who had sworn and punched the ruffians who had attacked me, nor the smelly old shepherd on the hills. I would always love that smelly old shepherd! Nor at this moment is he the alert, dignified, upright, military man who came around the hospital with his commanding officer.

Who is he …who is the real man? I look at him now and watch the dark eyes concentrating on the page he is reading, the slight hollow under the high cheek-bones, the wave of his thick, dark hair. His face is balanced in its proportions and though not handsome in the classical sense, yet has a fineness and delicacy that I have not noticed in him before. His mouth is surprisingly soft and sensual. It is his eyes that can be so hard and cruel but the mouth betrays a different person, a lover, an easy liver, a man who likes his food and drink and sensual comforts. Where has *that* man come from? I had not seen *him* there before!

Suddenly those dark eyes flickered away from the page and he caught my glance. There was laughter in his eyes now and I saw he had a roguish look as well. Gone was the steely, hard coldness. He smiled at me and flinging his newspaper aside, he caught up my hand and kissed it.

'I could be afraid of you, little one,' he said with a laugh, 'you are taking me to pieces, writing away about me in that little black book of yours, and I am afraid that you may not like what you see, may be wondering why you are here with this mad fellow?'

'I am just taking you in,' I replied, laughing also, 'for you know, Costas, you are never the same man, ever. Today I mean to have you pinned down – wriggle as you may – for you are just like Proteus, the Old Man of the Sea, who changes shapes constantly. Today I mean to hold on fast and see your real shape.'

'Hold me fast as you like, hold me forever!' he said with feeling.

'I will, I will, Costas.'

'And so you shall. The priest comes today and we shall exchange our rings and this will then be our formal engagement. Ishabel, Yussuf and Palomba will be here later and my sister and her family will come over too. No one else – only those who know and love us. We shall celebrate in style; the champagne is in a bucket now, cooling in the well. It is a marvellous day to be alive. I am so lucky to have met you. God brought us together …it was all meant to be. With the Arabs, I say *Inshallah!* It is all fate and meant to be.'

'I feel that too. It makes me feel better for sometimes I do consider I should be thinking of my real purpose of coming over here rather than thinking so much of you,' I said, half teasingly.

'Well, *don't* think of that purpose now. Duty, duty! You Northern peoples are so guilt ridden – the English, the Germans and Austrians, the Scandinavians – the whole lot of you!' Costas gesticulated with both his hands in that wonderful way Greeks have of emphasising their point. 'You are so afraid to enjoy life, to grasp it by the throat as it were, force it to deliver joy and happiness even for a short time. Forget that dreary Protestant conscience you all seem to have. I will make a Greek of you yet, Dorothea, a real Greek woman. When this war is over I shall teach you to sing and dance and be happy.'

'I was not unhappy before,' I said with a smile for his earnestness, 'but you are right, we do have a strong sense of conscience in our country. That's not such a bad thing to my mind. Please don't include us with those hateful Germans and Austrians! It has always been the secret of *our* success. We are prepared to work at things, we are very dutiful, *we* don't run away from things and mutiny like the French and Russian soldiers have done by all accounts. I don't think our men would dream of doing that.'

'Don't fool yourself. They are afraid of being shot that's all,' said Costas cynically.

'I suppose so but that fear didn't stop the French did it? I think we have something they don't have, that even you Greeks don't have ...obedience. Above all, *obedience*. We tend to do what we are asked without constant rebellion and questioning. I think too that we have strong, stubborn determination to do the job well and see it through to the bitter end. I know I feel like this. I am always happy doing my work. It gives the deepest satisfaction.'

'More than being with me?' he asked, jealous as ever.

'No, no, not more than being with you, Costas. This is the happiest day of *my* life too.'

He seemed dissatisfied with this reply as if he wanted me to burst in flames and immolate myself with the madness of love as he himself seemed ready to do. It was almost as if he wanted to devour me at times, there was such a wild frenzy in his eyes.

'*Agapi mou, manoula mou*, I wish I could put you in a little box and carry you around with me everywhere. No one, nothing else could have you then!'

'That's very selfish of you, Costas. I most certainly don't want to be put in a little box; I like my freedom.'

'Hmmm . . . was his reply and he looked at me sideways, narrowing his eyes speculatively. I felt a slight frisson of fear. Would he be a possessive man? Would he try to incarcerate me, make me dress for the rest of my life in black because some Greek second cousin had died? Would he refuse to let me work at what I loved best –nursing? What was he really like?

I had no idea but I did know this. That I loved him as I had never dreamt I might love a man. I knew that in my turn I was equally possessive of him. Somehow, I felt sure he would not be old-fashioned or coercive. His mother's educated, cosmopolitan attitudes *must* have influenced him. She was by no means a repressed, enslaved Greek peasant woman but conducted her life in her own manner.

He seemed to catch that moment of uncertainty that flickered in my heart and his face went dark and stormy. Yet it was when he looked just like this, dark and almost evil, that I loved him most. How strange we women are. He was so unlike anyone I had ever known in my life and I found his sudden moods and infinite shades of feeling fascinating. Englishmen seemed to be dull and pallid in comparison.

However, he said nothing more but called the servant to tell him to get his clothes ready instead.

Later that day the guests assembled in the salon and small cakes and liqueurs were handed out to them. Then a small table was placed in the middle of the room and on this table was placed an ikon. On the ikon Costas placed two gold rings. He looked at me as he did so and smiled. The priest duly arrived and everyone, except the Jews, kissed his hand. I felt obliged to do the same though it felt a strange thing to me. I could see that my acquiescence met with approval.

The priest was a solemn looking character who seemed to

view me with a vague sense of mistrust for which I did not blame him in the least. Not only was I not Orthodox but I was a foreigner too! He was handed some refreshments which he enjoyed in a perfunctory manner, put on his stole, neatened his bun and combed his long beard with his fingers. His nails were long and in my opinion none too clean. Then he settled his hat on his head and put on his official expression. I did not have my father present so Manolis, Costas' brother-in-law took the part of my father and he stood with me on one side of the table, while Costas and his mother stood opposite. The rest of the guests formed a circle with us. The priest muttered prayers and crossed the rings three times above the ikon. Costas took my hand in his, looking at me steadfastly while the priest passed the ring alternately over our fingers and then finally put one of the rings on my finger and the other on that of Costas. We all kissed the ikon, the priest's hand and one another and the guests greeted Kyria Nina with the words 'na sas zeisei!' …'may they live for you!' Ishabel who was as yet unmarried was also wished well …'here's to your wedding next!' …and that was it. Nonetheless it all felt very special.

Costas looked at me with such immense tenderness and whispered to me that I looked so beautiful that I felt my sense of self failing me within, my heart plummeting into my stomach. Then I understood what he meant about keeping me in the little box. Yes, I too wanted him with me all the time, all to myself. Should I abandon everything and everyone, all I believed in, to come here and be with him? It was so tempting. I knew as we performed this little ceremony that *this* was our wedding. Anything after this, church or no church, would simply be a legalising ceremony but *this* day we made our vows, our exchange, our coming together as man and wife and I know Costas thought this too and that all those present considered us as good as married now. My Protestant conscience was totally gone with the warm glance of those dark eyes and would never return again.

It was good to meet up with Yussuf and Palomba and the lovely Ishabel once more. I felt as if they were my old friends also and they treated me as such. Costas recounted again the tale of the ruffians who had attacked me amidst exclamations and gesticulations on all sides but we could laugh at this now and almost be grateful for the incident which had brought us together once more and introduced me to these good and dignified Jewish people.

'How lucky I am that you were about just then,' I said in wonder.

Costas whispered to me later that he had early on spotted me 'crashing around in that unwholesome area,' as he put it. Fearing for my safety, he had followed me for a little way, lost me briefly, then hearing my screams, had arrived to prevent any further mishap.

I was delighted by this.

'Why, you're my guardian angel, Costas!'

No longer jealous of Ishabel, I was able to talk freely with her and discovered that she was very well educated in many European languages, literature and modern ideas and was altogether a delightful person. Costas's young sister Christoula also came with her little baby. His sister was a sweet little creature, small, plump like her mother and very vivacious. Her dark eyes shone with merriment and mischief. She seemed so different to Costas! She was what the Greeks here call *tschakpina*– charming and lively. She was not unintelligent but her outlook on life was narrower than that of the more cosmopolitan Ishabel. Her world and conversation centred mainly on her husband and child and she struck me as a woman inclined towards her own pleasures and comforts. I liked her but felt she was a little uncertain of me and even a little jealous in some way. Perhaps she had always been used to her brother's undivided love for her and now this had to be – well, not even shared – for Costas ignored her and played with the baby while his eyes were constantly fastened on me, watching my reactions and smiling with delight to see me so at ease in his environment and with his friends. I felt she was a little spoilt and used to everyone's attention and didn't like my being the special one for now I *was* part of the family. My only regret was that my father had not been here to give me away for the engagement. How perfect this happy moment would have been then,

Costas was outnumbered by women but he didn't seem to mind. He laughed and joked in a way I had never seen before and the baby on his knee looked up at his uncle with rapt, goggling brown eyes, its mouth dropped open as if astonished also. Gone was that serious, hard face; now Costas was wreathed with smiles of joy. He kept looking over at me and smiling and now and then when close to me he would run his hand over my posterior seductively, apparently un-noticed. But I'm sure everyone knew. I couldn't help wondering if Ethan Willoughby would behave like this. It would be considered very bad form and of course he wouldn't. He would have been so immensely polite, gentlemanly and boring. I far preferred the thrill of that secret, intimate caress that throbbed with longing and desire.

The food served was so delicious. The Jews had brought some of their own specialities with them, *huevas enhaminados* , long narrow boiled eggs which were traditional food for them on Sabbat and at feasts, fruit candies, sesame cakes and *keftikes,* a kind of meatball. There were various kinds of pilaff with chicken, lamb, nuts, sprinked with cinnamon that gave a delicious aroma, *imam bayildi* made with aubergines and *yalantzi dolmas* which are little bundles of rice wrapped in vine leaves. We drank champagne and sang and laughed and Costas and Yussuf danced in turn slow, marvellous dances, so male, so concentrated, so into themselves. Then Costas took a handkerchief and put a corner between my fingers and taught me some steps of a Greek wedding dance all played to the accompaniment of a servant with an instrument that looked like a dulcimer. It was heady music, heady food and wine and I felt my 'Englishness' slipping away from me like a hateful garment that I had worn all these years. My blood pounded, the music in its long drawn oriental rhythms, its repetitions and wailing notes seemed to pluck at my heart and stirred a wild, intense emotion in me. Desire palpitated between Costas and myself and the onlookers watched us dance together with silent fascination. Our eyes were cemented together, the blood tingled its way through the separate veins and flowed like electricity through our hands as we touched fingertips. We were in a world of our own just then, the room melted away around us and we twirled in silent concentration, the deep, intense concentration of desire.

Bravo, bravo! E –*vre* Dorothea – you have *kefi* – what a girl you are!' they said when we had stopped and they applauded us loudly and happily.

It was a wonderful evening. The hours flew by, till Yussuf rose up with regret and said, 'Well, we'd better get going home or they will be bringing in the *siktirpilaf*, e, Kyria Nina?'

Everyone laughed and Kyria Nina explained that this was an old Turkish joke. The *siktirpilaf* was a rice dish with stewed prunes that would be brought in at the very last as an indication that guests had outstayed their welcome!

After the guests had left with much kissing and embracing and requests to come and see them, we sat and chatted with Kyria Nina and then, feeling rather tired I went to my bedroom, taking a book with me from the little library. They had a surprisingly mixed library with French, Russian and Italian literature and works by people I had only dimly heard of. There was also Shakespeare, Milton of all things, and Byron, of course. Byron, the Philhellene, who had sacrificed his life to help the Greeks in their struggle for Independence and whose memorial was at Missalonghi where he had died.

I undressed and put on a delicately embroidered, gauzy muslin shift that had been laid out for me on the bed. Then I sat down on one of the little sofas brushing my hair and idly picked up Byron and began to read a little of *The Corsair.*

> *Sunburnt his cheek, his forehead high and pale*
> *The sable curls in wild profusion veil*
> *And oft, perforce, his rising lip reveals,*
> *The haughtier thought it curbs, but scarce conceals ...*

I smiled to myself. I suppose Costas is a corsair type too. We women do seem to like these sorts of vagabonds. As I read I heard a faint tapping on the door. I laid the book down and whispered a quiet, 'come in.' For I knew full well that it was my husband come to take his bride.

Chapter 26

My honeymoon week is over and it has been the most wonderful, few, brief moments of my life. I think nothing will ever give me the joy of this time ever again even though we will marry in the glorious Agios Dimitrios one day – or so Costas tells me. We both feel that this week *was* our wedding week and felt the solemnity of it in our souls, enjoyed our love together.

We were left alone to enjoy this brief respite. Kyria Nina was in the house, of course, but joined us only occasionally when we indicated that we had surfaced from our blissful state long enough to enjoy other company. The servants looked after us to perfection, with fond smiles for their beloved master and his little, foreign fiancée then left us discreetly alone. These days none knew what the end of it all might be and if lovers would ever meet again, if promises could ever be fulfilled, wonderful as they might sound. I let Costas paint his wishful pictures of our future life together but in my heart I felt a strange, sad sense that somehow it might never be. Perhaps it was all too good to be true and my natural British sense of disbelief in too much happiness prevailed upon me.

Costas took me sailing round the bay in his boat, the *Helidoni*. We had some delightful lazy days on deck, floating over the glorious blue of the Aegean. I am not ashamed to say that we made love all the time; we couldn't stop touching, kissing, gazing upon one another as if gazing on some newly discovered planet that had suddenly appeared in our mutual universe. I had no idea that lovemaking could be such joy. Mother had never spoken much about these matters and when she did so made it all sound so terrible and dreary and dutiful. She had never mentioned the delights! As a nurse, I had seen the end products when doing some midwifery and have to confess it never inspired me very much. I don't think I am a natural with small children. The operating theatre has far less horrors for me than teething babies. Costas takes great care for I really don't want to end up expecting a baby at this point. It doesn't bear thinking about.

Coming back to camp is the hardest thing I have ever had to do. To tear oneself away from Heaven, to come back to the innumerable discomforts – and they really feel like discomforts after so much delightful luxury – to leave my beloved, never quite sure when we might meet again, is so painful. I have taken off my ring and wear it about my neck on the fine gold chain that Costas gave me. We both agreed that it was wiser to keep our engagement secret for a while. I have written to Richard about Costas for *we* have no secrets from one another. Today, I must write to tell Father and Mother about it. I wonder how they will take it? I know Mother will be furious with me. She will detest having a foreign son-in-law. Father will love it, especially a Greek with whom he can talk politics and art and music for hours on end. For Costas has the most erudite conversation and seems to know so much about so many things. He has travelled all over Europe and I feel as if I have scarcely lived when I hear his stories, his adventures and his truly hair-raising escapades. He is better than a hundred books.

I also do believe I am beginning to understand something of Greek politics at last. In as far as anyone can understand the Macedonian mind. The trouble is that Serbia, Bulgaria, Turkey, Greece have all had great dynasties at various times in history in this area and can all lay some claim to Salonika or various other towns that are so hotly fought over. Costas is just as violent and adamant that this and that belongs to Greece and that no-one else should have a look in. Why don't they all forget their

176

ancient past, bury it along with their ancestors and carry on with modern life?

The news has come through that the Russians have indeed begun their revolution and Tsar Nicholas has abdicated. Could such a thing happen in dear old Blighty? It's a horrible thought but somehow I don't think it likely. Our temperament is so different and despite everything we have never suffered as the Russian people have suffered under the Tsar.

March 21st

Returning to camp, I am flung into the midst of a vast influx of malarial cases and we toil from dawn to dusk caring for our poor men. Costas told me that though this illness is in the spleen and livers of the native people, as one can tell from their sallow faces and occasional distorted limbs, yet it had not been such a fast spreading problem before the war despite the amazing lack of even rudimentary hygiene amongst the villagers.

Now all this was changing, the lazy Turks no longer masters, the villages and populations now stirred and moving like a slow, bubbling, fast growing tide around a land scarred by wars and inner turmoils. Add to this the movements of the Allied soldiers, themselves unused to the land and its deprivation, who thus succumb swiftly to the diseases and malaria is being spread to the villages and overtaking the hungry, unkempt inhabitants, slaughtering them with as much thoroughness as the Turks or Bulgars have done. Sometimes one marvels that there is anyone left. This, plus the fact that our men can no longer be taken home to England, keeps the foul disease circulating. The men get better, return to base camp, become ill again and the infected blood is spread by the nasty little mosquito to other soldiers, and so it goes on. It means that our hospitals are crowded out with both soldiers and civilians.

Sometimes it seemed to me as if some vast cataclysm is taking place amongst the peoples of the earth. It is like the stirring of an underground volcano, spewing forth its heat and fury. All the nations are being mixed up and moved about. A giant game of chess is taking place perhaps. I watch the poor men come in by the dozens, brought to us to wash, cleanse, feed, and nurse back to health only to send the poor souls back up the line again to join their units. The men do not expect anything else; they are as caught up in this as we are. It is so vast, so huge, so beyond the ordinary ken of us men and women that we are swept along with this impersonal dark tide; all normal reactions and feelings disappeared.

It is not that we are acting in a mechanical fashion for all the feelings are there working away as we mop feverish brows and cover dead faces...alas for the dead faces and the grieving mothers and wives! Compassion drives us on, a sense of something greater and more important than ourselves and our usual petty concerns. Would those one time concerns ever really seem important ever again? I cannot believe that they would or that any of us fighting in the thick of this war could ever settle back to what we once called normality.

Chapter 27

March 30ᵗʰ 1917

Ethan and I were working together today on a difficult operation and I had to wipe sweat from his face constantly for the weather is already turning so hot. He swears a good deal but no-one takes notice of that ...surgeons are allowed to let forth as many expletives as they want. Poor Ethan, he looks so very tired. I don't believe he has taken any leave, certainly not more than a day or so. And his health is not that robust at the best of times.

He has not asked me a thing about my visit to see Costas. Nor does he know that beneath my dress and neatly starched apron, my engagement ring burns its indelible mark of love and passionate longing into my flesh. Sometimes when I feel very weary and sick of it all, I think of the ring and it seems to come to life on my breast. Just my fancy, I don't deny that, but it makes me long so much for Costas that I have to turn my mind away forcibly for he is always there in the shadows of my mind and heart, waiting to move forward into my consciousness.

When I am working I dare not let his image rise up before me. However, the moment I finish my duties and step out of the wards, his face comes to life before my mind's eye and I feel such an upsurge of longing. He is out there somewhere in the city and so near yet so far away from me. It is at times as if a huge gulf divides us. He might just as well be in another country. I dare not write or phone or act as if he was even alive. I can say nothing to anyone yet this secret joy burns in me and consumes me and makes me fearful for him, fearful for myself. It is a joy and a terror combined.

I lie awake for hours at night, thinking of him, reliving our moments of love and happiness. Yet, as soon as I button on my collar and cuffs, pin my nurses cap on my head and walk into the ward to resume my duties, I put him firmly out of my mind. I am absolutely sure that he too dreams of me with great longing but rises from his own bed and resumes his own duties whatever they might be, shutting his memories firmly away. Sometimes I feel as if he is there beside me, so close is his presence at night; his breath seems to stir my hair, his voice whispers in my ear, desire floods my whole body and it even feels as if he enters into me once more with all the passion of his ardent nature. I know then for sure that he thinks of me and that we are together in some subtle manner although our bodies are separate. I understand for the first time what is meant by the marriage sacrament, what it is to be of one mind, one soul, one flesh.

I awoke to find May standing, towelling her face and staring at me through the mosquito net this morning.

'What's the matter?' I asked, sleepy and yawning.

'When are you going to tell me what is the matter with you, Dot?' she said.

'Nothing is the matter …what do you mean, May?' I said. I looked down and my hand rose involuntarily to my breast to conceal the ring.

'I've already seen that…it's no use hiding it,' she said testily. 'It's none of my business, Dot, but you have been acting so oddly lately and I see you wearing this ring round your neck but saying nothing. You spend the nights tossing and turning and moaning and groaning so's a girl can't get any sleep. I'd rather you snored or something. So …well, aren't you going to tell even me? You are engaged to someone. Why the secret?'

I was abashed by this discovery. How useless I would have been as a spy when I couldn't hide a thing or control my sleep at night! May seemed to read my mind and said with a little smile, 'Can't hide things like this from another girl, Dot …we know the signs, don't we?'

I parted the mosquito nets and rose up, flinging on my dressing gown for it was still chilly in the early hours of the morning. Thankfully the flies had not really got into formation as yet and a mere few of the wretched things that were more enthusiastic about getting up in the morning than myself, batted against my face as I poked my head out of the tent flaps. The faint flush of a pearly pink dawn showed that camp activity was already well under way. The cocks began to crow, a sound that had always had an eerie ring for me since my childhood. It always made me shiver and it did so now.

I went back into the tent and sluiced myself with the now lukewarm water that Franz had left for us earlier. I must have slept through his clanging on the tin outside the tent. I shook my head to clear it a little and felt an immense sense of weariness and sadness fall upon me.

May was watching me as she pretended to be absorbed in pinning her hair up in a bun.

'Well?' she demanded.

'May, it's not that easy to say anything ...'

She turned to face me, her blue eyes brimming now with tears. 'I thought we were friends, Dot, real friends. Living like this makes people more aware of one another. It's as if we are sisters. I feel more close to you than I do to my sister Mary. It's sharing this whole situation –the life and death situation we are in. Not just the situation of the men we look after but our own. You and I might be dead tomorrow –well, we might! We don't know the future. Fritz may get it in his head to bomb the lot of us one night. I don't want to die, Dot! I'm really afraid sometimes. I so long to be back home with my Bill; back home and safe. What I'm trying to say is, we can't really hide things from each other. You and I, we know each other now, we've been living so close for a year and more. It's not good to hide things, to have secrets, Dot. It's not your nature. It's making you look tired and drawn.'

'We all look tired and drawn,' I said rather crossly. I didn't really feel like being interrogated or making confessions at this time of the morning and wasn't too sure how much I could trust May. It was unkind of me, I know, but I had to consider Costas above all. I would have died if something happened to him because of my foolishness.

'I *am* engaged, May,' I said slowly as I buttoned up my cuffs and began to fix my belt about my waist.

'It's Captain Willoughby!' she said her eyes shining. 'I knew he loved you. Knew it from the very first. He keeps *on* playing 'A Bachelor Gay' on the gramophone. You know ...'

And May began to trill the words ...

when he fancies he is past love,
It is then he meets his last love
And he loves her as he ne-ever loved before!

I laughed, she was so comic, but rolled my eyes and sighed a little. May was such a sentimental and romantic girl. I just knew I couldn't tell her everything much as I yearned at times for a confidante. She was right, of course, secrets are such a burden to carry and it is always a release to talk with another.

'No, May darling, not Ethan.'

'Oh,' she said, her face falling in disappointment, 'and I'd set my heart on it. He does love you, I can see it whenever his eyes fall on you. You never give him a drop of encouragement, so I did wonder how he had managed to persuade you.'

'He did tell me once that he cared about me,' I said with reluctance for I am a very private person by nature and rather hated to have my inner self laid before May's curious eyes.

'And you never told me!'

'Well ...I think you were doing a turn of night duty at the time so I didn't get a chance ...and then I forgot.'

'You forgot! Really, Dot, you are so strange at times. I would have so wanted to tell you if that had happened to me. When Bill proposed, half the town knew of it.'

'Exactly,' I said with some severity. May flushed a little and fell silent.

'Dot, you think I am a tittle-tattle, I know that, but I haven't said a word to a soul about my suspicions of you and Willoughby or mentioned I've seen that ring or anything. You *can* trust me.'

'Just as well you didn't mention it to a soul as it is totally unfounded.'

'Well, yes,' she admitted, then added frowning, 'no, it wasn't totally unfounded if he proposed.'

'He didn't get that far, May. I don't want that kind of thing here in camp. Partly because it interferes with our work, partly because, as you so rightly say, it's the strangeness of the situation. He wouldn't love me back home, we're so utterly different. But we do work well together and admire and respect each other immensely. He has offered me a job working with him when we get back home. That's far more the sort of proposal I prefer from him. Since I made it clear that this was how I felt, he has behaved like the gentleman he is and said no more.'

'I think you would get on so well. You're more alike than you think, Dot.'

'May – we're nothing like each other!'

'People never see themselves as other's see them,' said May sagely, 'anyway, this is all your cunning distraction away from the main event which is that someone here *has* proposed to you, or else you have met an officer in town who has led you astray.'

May was joking, I knew, but her stab in the dark made me draw breath as if she had smacked me in the face. May's eyes narrowed and she gave a knowing little laugh,

'Aha, so that's it! No wonder you've been so keen to go into town on your own!'

Her expression changed and she added, 'Has that Greek woman you went to got something to do with it? God, you're not involved with some Greek fellow, are you? You've been so disturbed since you got back from leave.'

I took May's hand in mine and looked deep into her blue eyes. She looked back and fell silent.

'May, darling, this is not a laughing matter, it's so serious that I feel frightened of it all at times. I *have* met someone and fallen deeply in love –I admit this. I never looked for it, never expected it, it simply happened. And you are right, he is not anyone here in the hospital. Please don't try and put two and two together and make five. It troubles me. I am not allowed to divulge anything about him. You can guess why. Walls have ears, May, even tent walls. One day, when all this is over, I shall tell you everything and you can be godmother to our first baby,' I added with a little smile.

May stared at me for a moment. 'I said you were the type of person who falls hardest, didn't I?' I nodded with a smile and she turned away and asked no more. She has made no more allusions to the matter since then and I have preferred to let her imagine that it is an English officer in the Secret Service or some such thing. Sadly, a barrier of some sort has arisen between us because of it. Secrets are terrible things and so divide people. What can I do? I prefer to be safe than sorry. Besides my mind is on Costas and May's not talking to me so much is quite a relief; her inconsequential chatter and gossip do tend to get on my nerves at times. Just now, I want to be alone but that is an impossibility in a place like this where we are all on top of one another day and night.

April 2nd

I have had such a wonderful letter with congratulations on my engagement from Richard and he assures me that he looks forward to meeting my fiancé very much. I beam at the mere thought of introducing Costas to my relations, especially my beloved brother. Richard has something of the passion and fire that Costas has in such abundance; he has the same fierce energy, patriotism and that immense ability to enjoy life despite all hardships and problems. He often sends me jokes and little amusing anecdotes of his life in the trenches and his letters are nearly always cheerful and positive.

I know, more than any at home could ever know, how very different things really are. Yet, Richard finds time to notice the soft feeling of the wind on his face, the beauty of the moon rising over the strange battle scarred plains where he tells me that the twisted, blasted stumps of trees rise out of the mud like tormented souls. Richard so loves nature and beauty and I know he feels a terrible sadness at the sight of this pointless devastation where fields of corn once nodded in the sunshine. Yet, he can still see beauty even amongst this ugliness and thank God for his gift of somehow rising above it all. As Costas would put it, he is capable of grasping life by the throat. No feeble blood in my brother! He is immensely British and proud of it but he is not a man of prejudice. He is what Costas would call a *palikari*… a word of indefinable meaning that implies a man of bravery, honour and even more than that.

Papa has also written to congratulate me and is equally delighted to have a Greek son-in-law with whom, as he says, he can discuss Greek history, politics and classical works. I could just imagine him with Costas, locked for hours in the library at Downlands. It made me smile so much and such longing arose in me at that moment to be back home. In my mind's eye I saw the beautiful, ivy covered house, Papa walking along the long drive and looking up at the trees with Babbidge our gardener, discussing what might need to be done to the shrubbery or to the lawns. (Babbidge was deemed too old to go to war but I hear they are now taking men of fifty!) I saw the rolling fields and the Cotswold hills in the distance just as I could see them from my bedroom window. For a moment I was there so strongly that I felt as if my heart might stop. I wanted to feel the cool English air on my face, walk down English lanes and see the vivid green of the fields and gentle hills rather than this rough, boulder strewn mountainous terrain with its dark brown rivers and its humid, disease laden air. For a moment I really hated it here. How then would I live here all the rest of my life with Costas?

The memory of my beloved flooded back and obliterated all those nostalgic pictures of home but not entirely. My heart felt pulled asunder in that moment. I would have to persuade Costas to spend some time in England as well as in Greece. I felt sure that once he saw my lovely home, saw my father and brother he would have no difficulty in our setting up a home nearby and we could visit Salonika whenever he wanted to. He was used to living abroad, surely he would not mind England?

Foolish daydreams! I amazed myself for harbouring them and for my disloyalty to Costas and to Salonika already. What sort of a person was I? I sometimes wondered if I really knew myself at all. May was right, we never know ourselves as other's know us. Our ideas about ourselves seem often to be totally false and white as snow when the reality is a good deal more muddied and confused.

Chapter 28

April 25th 1917

I think we all knew something was brewing up for it has been muttered that General Sarrail was about to begin his Spring offensive for some weeks. Now the men have actually made a move at last. The Battle over Doiran began at dusk yesterday and since then casualties have been coming down the line in droves. We have no idea yet as to numbers or how many men and officers have been lost but it must be a great many judging by the way they keep arriving in lorries and ambulances which disgorge their occupants wherever they can find room. We have taken over a hundred already and I know that Matron says we won't be able to take many more and will have to send them on elsewhere.

April 28th

Today we performed 90 operations and everyone had to be on hand to help out with the theatre work and the after care. The surgeons are exhausted but they carry on regardless. Ethan works on and on like a Trojan. He simply refuses to rest, hardly goes to bed. His face is drawn and thin and emaciated but he will not stop. I have to confess my heart goes out to him. He is such a wonderful man. I wish I had his stamina but feel I can manage no more for today and simply want to crawl into bed. May, bless her, also works so hard. She too looks rather pinched and drawn and I know full well she is terrified. We all know the

Wiltshires are in the front line near that terrible Jumeaux Ravine from which the enemy hurl down their fire upon our soldiers struggling up the rocky, treacherous terrain. She is terrified that at any moment her beloved Bill will be brought in with the wounded and she might be faced with an amputee or worse but she says nothing, just keeps going like the rest of us. If there is anything at all to gain from this mad bloodshed, it is the sight of such strength of character amongst those one is glad to call one's friends.

May 1st

It seems that the Devons have suffered the most casualties trying to take that wretched hill they call Petit Couronne. But the Wiltshires and Hampshires have had their fair share too. Oh, they all have, they all have – our brave boys! The men brought in are shell shocked beyond belief as well as badly wounded. Thankfully Bill is not amongst them. We all breathe a sigh of relief.

May 3rd

This is a black day here in camp. May has been given the news that Sergeant Bill Myers has been killed, flung against the rocky face of the hill by an exploding shell, and she is stricken with grief. She carries on her work as always but her eyes are red with weeping. No one knows what to say nor is there time to say much. I know that May will take a long, long while to recover from this terrible blow. Despite the merry charm of her nature that makes her seem light and flippant, there is a gritty side to her, a depth of real loyalty and I know she loved her childhood sweetheart with a slow burning, undemonstrative, yet deeply dependent kind of love. They had been together since they were in their early teens.

I saw her quietly weeping over his letters one night and my heart swelled for her. But we all had to get on and there was no knowing when the same thing might happen to any one of us.

Many nurses there had already heard of losses of brothers, fathers, and other relations on the Western Front. My heart was always fearful about my own beloved Richard. May God protect him! Please, please God, make him come home safe and sound.

May 10th

A brief couple of hours respite today. I went walking over the hillside to look at the wild flowers rather than going to the canteen for a cup of tea as the other nurses were doing. I simply have to get away from the hospital and everyone else once in a while in order to retain my sanity. May was busy washing out some of her clothes this morning and didn't want to come with me when I asked her.

'I am such rotten company just now, Dot,' she said. 'You go for a walk, it'll do you good and I know you like to be alone sometimes.'

'Oh, May, don't say that. It makes me feel bad. The walk might do you good too.'

'No, no – you go, Dot.' She tried to smile but it was a sad smile. I realised that she too needed time alone to do her grieving. I put an arm about her and squeezed her shoulders tenderly. Neither of us said anything, there was no need.

It was still quite early in the morning as I walked along the track past the village. The weather had already turned hot but not as yet the terrible unrelenting heat of the summer. In fact at this hour of the day it seemed almost perfect for a fresh wind blew along the hills, cooling my face.

I looked out towards the distant sea and felt my heart expand with the blue vastness of the ocean, the timelessness of its existence compared to the fleeting briefness of our human life. The restless madness of men! Rather the rolling waves, the breeze on the face, the sense of being alive and a conscious partaking of all this beauty. I felt utterly present in this moment and with a sense of involvement with something impersonal and yet tremendously alive and beautiful.

I drew a deep breath and thanked God. Men blame Him

and wonder why He does not put an end to all this misery. It is such nonsense. God has given us foolish creatures free will. If He was to step in every time we did foolish things then we would never learn. It's just like a good parent who has to stand back occasionally and allow his child to experience life, even danger. It is painful to do so, but how else can a child ever learn to take care of himself except by learning to use his own instincts in a situation, or by using his mistakes as lessons?

The warmth here in Salonika is such that scents waft up and seem to be tangible, part of the air and the heat and the richness of the atmosphere. Now the sweet odour of the wild thyme and chamomile blossoming on the slopes assail me and it is a scent I shall always associate with Greece. I stopped to smell this delightful scent that mingled with the salty tang of the sea and the freshness of a breeze that quite suddenly sprang up and patted my cheeks like an old friend. It made me think of Psyche floating down to meet Eros from the mountain-top where she had been abandoned by her parents. Zephyr, the soft West wind, had taken her in his arms and brought her down to meet her lover and her immortal fate.

I always tended to look up at the hills rising above me when I was here just in case that old shepherd was back again. I had not seen him there ever again, a disguise no longer needed. Now I spotted an old man wandering along the deserted track and my heart skipped a beat for a moment. I watched him avidly as he walked along, picking up the strangest odds and ends along the way, a fallen handkerchief, little round stones, some sheep's wool caught on a briar, which he then placed in a little bag. As he drew nearer he looked up at me with red-rimmed eyes and a face lined and wrinkled beyond recognition of what might be termed human skin. A wispy white beard completed his image of the 'Old Man of the Mountain'

Seeing my eager face watching him, he stopped for a few moments and peered back at me then muttered some imprecation at me, crossed himself against what he evidently regarded as an Evil Eye then bent his back again to his task of filling up the little bag. Goodness only knows what he found to put in it or what he meant to do with it. That he regarded me with deep suspicion and hostility was evident. I smiled to myself and thought how foolish I was to see Costas in every strange face and form, expecting him just to turn up from nowhere, but I sighed also. When *would* I see him again? God alone knew. I so yearned to see and touch him, the longing was so intense in that moment that I turned and flinging open my arms shouted aloud to the listening hills, 'Costaki *mou* …where are you, where are you? I so want you near me. Speak to me, dear love, send me some token. Oh, *please*, my darling, please!'

The old man might have heard me or not, he just hurried on, no doubt convinced that some mad foreigner had been let loose upon him and he had better go home quickly.

Chapter 29

I turned back now and began to wend my way up the steep path towards the village. I still had another hour before going back on duty and decided I had better return to camp, perhaps write a letter or two for it was some time since I'd had a respite or enough energy to think of putting pencil to paper. I felt again that sense of unutterable tiredness and dispiritedness sweep over me as I clambered over the rough stones. These days it was hard to be cheerful. Bad enough were the daily sights of men who had lost limbs, parts of their head or face, or who were still sick with malaria and assailed by the depression that came with that nasty disease. Bad enough being cheerful before the men and never daring to let them see the horror in your face as you uncovered their terrible injuries. They watched you like hawks, waiting for your reactions because, thankfully, they couldn't as yet see themselves. Seasoned nurse as I now was, I still felt my stomach turn at the sight of some of these injuries. Yet one had to smile and bustle about and be as matter of fact and normal as could be.

On top of this, May was so sad all the time though, poor lamb, she never grumbled or groaned about anything. Yet the heaviness of her silent sorrow was like a reproach to the living. I would far have preferred her to wail and keen like the Greeks did over their dead; it was more natural to let forth one's pain and anguish in this manner and surely wiser than keeping it all within oneself, gnawing away at one's very substance like an evil monster. We English are so foolish. Why do we find it hard to let go and show our feelings as these people here do? It seems so much more normal and spontaneous.

As I came towards the tiny, whitewashed village church, I turned aside to sit and rest for a moment on a low, stone wall under the shade of an olive tree. The morning heat was already rising, almost tangible now. Waves of that soft Mediterranean warmth enveloped and permeated me, full of scents, carrying sounds, stupefying and lulling the senses to a state of sleepy lassitude. My head began to nod a little as I sat like a cat, sunning itself. Then I heard a voice call my name and my mind slowly re-focused into the present. The little boy Yiangos came running towards me calling, '*Despinis* Dorothea! *Despinis* Dorothea!'

Suddenly I was alert. 'What is it, Yiangos?'

'Come with me, come quick! We need you.'

Alarmed by the urgency of his voice, I followed him, wondering what awful disaster had befallen the village.

'*Ellate, ellate, Despinis!*' urged the boy, running on ahead of me.

He brought me to a house I had never visited before. I knew it wasn't his home, a mere tiny little hovel on the outskirts of the village. This freshly whitewashed two-storied house with its wooden gallery was large and comfortable by Greek standards. These were wealthy people with olives in the large garden that surrounded the house, a beautiful thick leaved mulberry tree and other fruit trees at the front. There were some vivid blue painted pots by the door full of red geraniums and a huge bush flowered on the other side of the door, its deep red flowers like large open mouths. A beautiful chestnut horse was tethered in the back yard and it lifted its head from the manger to look at me as I approached. It whinnied softly and returned to its food. I stared at the horse for a moment and then followed the boy inside the house via the back door that led into a neat kitchen with bright copper pans on the walls. There was no one around and a strange silence pervaded the house that made me feel uneasy.

Something odd began to gather within my stomach, a sense of what …fear? …anticipation?

'In there –.go and wait,' said the boy opening a door for me and pointing inside.

I entered the rather bare looking room. The shutters had already been closed outside though the windows were open and a breeze ruffled the lace curtain. Slanting bars of sunlight crept through the shutters. I stood for a moment wondering where everyone was and what was going on, adjusting my eyes to the semi-darkness. There was a large double bed in the centre of the room and a big deep chest against the wall, perhaps a trousseau chest still full of the linen collected by a bride. Before I could wonder to myself what I was doing in this room, a figure disengaged itself from the shadows and seized me from behind. A hand closed tightly over my mouth before I could utter a sound.

I felt a jolt of fear rise up in me. What trap had I been led into? I struggled for a moment but of a sudden caught the familiar scent of the hand held over my mouth and began to shake with silent laughter, my whole body and being relaxed and I fell back against the form behind me in a submissive surrender. The hand came away from my mouth and moved over my body instead, caressing my breasts, while a voice murmured in my ear, '*Agapi mou*, my love . . .'

I turned round to face Costas and beat on his chest with my fists. 'You utter wretch. You frightened the life out of me!'

'Not so easily done,' he grinned. 'You are such a brave and foolhardy girl. I knew you would come but I didn't want you to scream and bring all the neighbours running. Forgive me.'

'I'm not so sure I will,' I said pushing him away, 'you're just wicked, Costas. You delight in teasing me.'

'Aren't you glad to see me?'

'Well …' but his kiss silenced my efforts at teasing in turn. Something fierce and lupine flared up in us both. Clothes flew around the room and we became like two wolves, starving for food. We fell upon the bed together panting and tearing at one another, consuming one another, raging with hunger and need.

Exhausted we both lay drenched in sweat on the now crumpled white sheets of the bed. The wind outside made the light through the shutter slats waver and play upon the ceiling. In the corner of the room high on the wall was a little shelf and on it was an ikon with a small brass oil lamp burning before it. I hadn't noticed it before but its gentle little light had a soothing effect. It lit up the halo of beaten silver nailed about the head of the Virgin and her Child, making a strange, dappled pattern through the little holes in the lamp. Apart from this, the bed, the chest and a couple of small wooden chairs, the room was whitewashed, bare and simple. A bright rug of woven wool covered part of the stone floor.

'Whose house is this, Costas?'

'Some very good friends of mine.'

'Is this their bed?'

'It is.'

'I presume they know we are using it?'

'Yes,' said Costas with a little smile, 'I have permission, Dorothea. Is it a problem?'

His hand stroked my thighs and stomach as he spoke and he looked down at me, smiling, handsome, so utterly beautiful. I raised my arms and pulled him towards me again. The wolves had been fed and now it was the turn of the turtle-doves.

As we emerged from the room blinking, I looked in dismay at the now rather crumpled dress I had put back on.

'I can't go back like this.'

'Xanthi will iron your dress. Go and take it off and put on the dressing gown behind the door.'

I obeyed him and a middle aged serving woman appeared when called from the kitchen and took my dress away with a nod and a slight frown on her face. I didn't get the feeling that she approved of our activities at all. But I was too satiated with love to care about her opinion.

'I must be back soon,' I said with regret, as an old, wooden clock in the hallway chimed the hour. 'Tell me, though, how did you know I was here, Takis?'

'By pure chance. I had to visit the person who owns this house, on business. I kept hoping to see you whenever I got the chance to come here but I know how busy you have all been with the latest battle in the valley there. I have heard the news, seen some of the poor men. Some we brought over ourselves – my mother offered her horses and mules.'

'That is so good of her.'

'E –.well, she's that kind of selfless woman. Anyway, I came today as if impelled for some reason, hoping against hope that the Fates would draw us together.'

'And I prayed for you to come when I was on the hill, Takis – I prayed so hard.'

'You see – we are soul children! That's how it is for some lovers, they don't even need to have a telephone. Then that old fool, Giorgo, came rushing down the street so fast he was falling over himself and said he had met a mad foreign woman who was talking to the air. He kept crossing himself, saying she had put a spell on him and Heaven knows what, the silly old fool. I felt so sure he must mean you as I know you often walk down round there, alone or with your friend.'

'Well, I did pray aloud to the hills – to Zeus himself, I suppose. So he wasn't that mad.'

'Bah –.the village people are all superstitious fools,' said Costas with the contempt of the educated agnostic, 'but hoping against hope, I sent our little Yiangos to see if he could find you and bring you here.'

'I thought I'd never see you again. Sometimes I feel so afraid, Costas, so afraid I'll never see you again.'

He gathered me in his arms.

'Sometimes I do too,' he admitted. 'We must trust to our luck, we have been very lucky so far, haven't we? When things work out this way, then one can only say, Aphrodite herself is on our side.'

I smiled. 'Yes, she seems to be. But she is a strange Goddess, at times, Costas. I put no faith in these fickle Gods any more.'

'No, nor I – but don't think of all this. That we have been able to meet at all is marvellous. Ah, *chrysi mou*, your beauty, your perfume, your sweetness –how I love you!'

The dress arrived now, beautifully pressed. I put it on, tidied my hair and Costas took me and set me up before him on his horse, still patiently waiting in the yard.

'I had a strange feeling it was your horse,' I said, 'but thought I was being foolish. Because, sometimes, I keep thinking I see you but it is always someone else.'

'And every time I see a blue nurse's uniform, I look again in case it is you turning a corner, seated in a café, being where you ought not to be. But no, it is someone else and I feel something die inside me. Love is a painful business.'

He took me close to the hospital camp and set me down to walk the last few hundred yards alone. I watched his horse canter off across the rough track with a huge pang of sorrow. Too soon the ecstasy ended and the agony returned to fill the long mournful gaps between our brief meetings.

May 15th

I feel so troubled about May. She seems to be fading away before my eyes. I try to make sure she is eating and sleeping properly but I feel sure she touches little food. Once I would never have believed that one could fade away with the grief of love like the Fair Maid of Astalot. It always seemed to be a poetic fancy. Yet now I saw it happening before me and understood it too. I would feel like this if Costas was taken from me but also knew that we had to keep our strength if we were to nurse these wounded men back to health. That was the important thing. But I can't upbraid May in any way. She works as hard as ever.

Others have noticed the change in her too. Ethan Willoughby is so very gentle and kind to her. He is such a good man.

'I don't like the look of her these days,' he said, staring after her disconsolate figure as she dragged herself over to the laboratory to fetch some samples for him. Her step was usually so brisk and upright. 'She looks quite ill and will succumb to something if she goes on like this.'

'I don't know what I can do,' I said helplessly, 'who would have supposed she would react quite so badly?'

'She's not emotionally strong like you Dorothy,' he said, giving me one of his keen looks. 'There was always something very dependent about May. It's as if the main prop in her life has been pulled away.'

'Yes, I suppose so, but I don't know how strong I really am. I haven't been tried yet,' I said and felt a spasm of anxiety in my heart.

Ethan looked at me as if he meant to ask something but refrained. I have a feeling he was going to ask about Costas. I'm glad he didn't.

May 20th

All of a sudden the other day while May was crossing the ward, she collapsed at Sister Moira's feet. The orderlies were called and she was taken off at once. She has fallen ill with malaria and confined to bed. Matron, who refuses to discriminate against the VAD's, has sent her to Sick Sisters. There she is made as comfortable as is possible.

I go to see May whenever I can take time off. Her pale white face stares out at me, sometimes almost uncomprehendingly, from the sheets. She is often shivering under the pile of blankets despite the heat outside and becomes delirious and talks about her home and parents and Bill in an incoherent and incomprehensible jumble of ideas and memories. She seems to believe Bill is still alive and I listen to her ramblings about the house they mean to have, the sofa her Aunt Edie promised to buy her, the silver spoons her mother has put aside. How in the face of death can the mind produce such stupid desires and recollections? At first it horrified me that we are nothing but bundles of foolish memories, which seem to mean more than all our greatest and best ideals. I listened to May almost impatiently. Was this what we all came to in the end? But little by little, I realized that it is these small, everyday, inconsequential things that make up our humanity. They make us the feeling individuals we are.

'Is Bill coming to see me?' May asked in a fairly lucid moment, her blue eyes looking huge in the shrunken cheeks and pallid face.

'Not yet, darling, not yet,' I murmured, mopping the beads of sweat from her face. Then a sudden recollection would come to her as she became less delirious and she would cry out in utter pain and anguish,

'Oh, but Bill's gone. Bill's gone, Dot!'

No longer held back by English phlegm, she would sob weakly, tears streaming down her cheeks onto the pillow and making little damp pools around her head.

I felt utterly helpless in the face of this enormous grief. It constricted my own throat too. She would turn delirious again as if to blot out the memory of this awful reality and I would have to give her another injection of quinine, which thankfully knocked her out.

May was young and strong and she rallied round despite her desire to slip away from this world and not face the empty void without her Bill. She was still very weak and, added to the awful depression that comes with malaria, was her own unhappiness. She was a shadow of her former self and was packed off to one of the convalescent homes by the sea front to have some time to recover and readjust. She was told she could go home if she liked but it was still too dangerous to attempt to leave the shores just yet. However, May refused.

'I would rather come back here and work,' she told me, 'it takes my mind off things. I don't know how I shall bear being home again. It would be wonderful to see Mother and Father but ...' her voice trailed off. She had no need to say more.

It seems lonely at times without May around. I miss her far more than I supposed. At times she annoyed me and I yearned for some time alone without her chatter and her incessant cheerfulness. Now it was so quiet, no smiling face to greet me and perk me up in the morning when I felt like nothing on earth. May had always risen cheerful and ready for work, ready for the day.

Everyone missed her and spoke of her with fondness and asked after her. She was one of those lovely people that brings light to others without their even knowing it till it is taken away.

I wished now that I had confided in her more but knew it would have been a big mistake. She might have spoken in her delirium and been overheard by some Greek clerk or a cleaner or washerwoman.

Besides May I miss Costas and, without the distraction of her merry conversation, think of him more than ever when alone in my tent at night. Now I have no idea where Costas has got to. He may even have gone off with Venizelos for all I know. What is he doing, what mad adventures is he having? He is as much at risk as any man on the front and more so, perhaps. Any night a dagger might pierce his back or a gun blow his brains out, his body dragged away and none of us the wiser. He would just disappear into the horror of some nameless grave, flung down a well, or in some dank old cellar. It made me shudder to think of it. I have to trust that he is a wily fox and knows his way around the city and its underground passages, can see in the dark, smell danger a mile away.

He has friends amongst the Jews and Armenians, the Turks and the Serbs. He is one of those strange people who can become almost anything he wishes, can look like any character he chooses. He is truly an actor and an escape artist and this is his real talent. I wonder if direct combat does appeal to his nature. Perhaps he prefers the stealth, the ferreting out of information, acting many parts and the sheer duplicity of his espionage work. I feel sure that our own side would dearly love his services for he not only knows many of the local dialects and ways, not only is a master of disguise, but knows and understood the Eastern mind which our men do not. He is a Greek but a Greek of Macedonia whose mother came *apo tin Poli* –.from Constantinople itself, that gem of desire and longing in Greek hearts. He has all the cunning and duplicity of the Levantine mind coupled with the elegance, education and manners of the Western world.

At times I feel regret that there is something underhand about the things Costas is obliged to do. I want him to be a real soldier like my Richard, want him to go out and grapple with the enemy face to face. Reflection tells me that this was not possible in this day and age of trench warfare and modern weapons. One had to be more subtle, cleverer than the enemy. Bravery is not to be found in one to one combat, may the best or luckiest fighter win. Bravery now lies in comradeship, solidarity and obedience, flinging oneself forward in the face of sudden and certain annihilation, knowing one will be lucky to survive. There is no skill in it. It is sheer guts that drives the men on, a strange, blind obedience to something greater, yes, far greater than the Generals who command the armies. The Generals are puppets too. Yet on their shoulders falls the terrible burden of decision, of knowing that they have to send men off to certain death. The only way to break through the stalemates and impasses created by both sides is by assault, sheer weight of numbers. And the weight of numbers, of mowed down bodies, is a sacrifice on the altar of a dark and terrible God.

Chapter 30

May 30th 1917

'Seems that Thessaly has changed allegiance and gone over to Venizelos,' said Captain Dunning the other day.

'Just as well,' remarked one of the doctors, swilling back a hasty cup of tea before rushing off to his ward, 'the Royalists were hoping to reap the Thessalian corn and fill their granaries with it. That would have made them self-sufficient for six or seven months and then who knows what trouble they might have caused?'

'Sarrail seems to have swung the matter nicely. Amazing how these Greeks change their politics every five minutes.'

'Well, poor bastards, I can't say I blame them. They're interested in self-survival.'

Everyone here in Salonica is now buzzing with the latest news that the Allies are in Thessaly and that they have taken over in Athens now that Constantine has been obliged to abdicate due to his unconstitutional activities.

The case against him is severe. He should have made his mind up long ago to go with the Germans and be done with it if that is where his real loyalties and interests lay. At least then everyone would have known where they stood. It is almost impossible to play the neutrality card in a war of this scale …only the Swiss seem to manage it and that because they truly are neutral by nature and also because they have one of the best trained armies in the world. Even the Germans wouldn't dare tackle them. As for the Greeks, they are by nature passionate, political, changeful and about as neutral as a tiger facing an elephant.

June 13th

As always news travels fast and we have heard today that
Constantine has finally given up and fled to Switzerland with
his Queen and the Crown Prince, leaving the country in charge
of his second son Alexander. He hasn't formally abdicated and
one wonders what repercussions this might have. I suppose he
hopes to return to the throne in due course. All the same, there
is a general sense of relief amongst the Allies and as for the
Venizelists, their joy holds no bounds. I am afraid reprisals will
now take place against the Royalists as they did against the
Venizelists last December. It's really awful that people here can't
be allowed to hold a different political point of view without
having to be robbed, butchered and tortured because of it.

June 15th

Yiangos brought me a note today. My hand trembled as I took it.
Costas asked me to try and come to the village and meet him
there the next day if I could. My two hours time off was in the
mid-afternoon and so I sent a note back saying I would come
then. Most people in the village would be having their siesta at
this time and all would be quiet.

June 16th

All day long, at the back of my mind was the delirious thought
of meeting Costas again. It was such a long time since we had
last met and I yearned for the touch and scent of him. Yiangos
came to greet me as I approached the village. The wretched
village dogs had spotted me too and set up a furious racket that
threatened to bring out all the inhabitants but no one stirred,
not a shutter opened to see what was going on. It was like a
morgue. The dusty track that formed the main street was
deserted, the hot sun beat down and my rapid movements
roused clouds of flies from every available pile of dirt and dung.
However, that part of the village where Costas's friend lived was

a smarter, better kept area and there was no filthy sewage outside the house; all was nicely swept and had been watered down that morning. A large mulberry tree cast a pleasant shade over it and it was a relief to step inside the clean, cool, close-shuttered house and away from the heat and those wretched flies.

Costas was waiting for me as before in the bedroom. I have no idea whether his thoughtful friends were in some other part of the house or had gone elsewhere, nor did I much care. I was simply grateful for their kindness in lending us their home like this for a brief hour or two. As before, we fell upon one another with a peculiar frenzy of lust and longing.

'I feel as if I have been starved of you. I can't have enough of you,' whispered Costas.

We were reluctant to finish our love-making, reluctant to take flesh away from flesh.

'I wish we could stay joined like this forever,' he murmured.

'Oh, Takis, if only we didn't have to part.'

'If we were always together I would be like Ouranos coming to take glorious Gaia every moment,' he said with a little laugh, 'and then you would have me castrated as she did in order to have some peace.'

'Takis, what a thought. You're quite mad. I would welcome you all the time ...but I suppose that story means that lovers have to be separated for anything to be born. There is no space for anything to be born if one is always joined in a coupling, an eternal embrace. It is Chronos who separates them, isn't it? Time brings everything to an end and castrates eternity.'

'He is the Grim Reaper, he brings all things to an end,' said Costas unhappily. He looked down on me, leaning on his elbow. His eyes were sad and I felt close to tears.

'You ...you're going away somewhere ...'

'Let's not think of it, *agapi mou*, just now we are in eternity.'

He entered me again and again ...we simply couldn't let each other go. At last with a tremendous burst of energy, he filled me with his seed, which he had never done before. I fell back on the sheets, panting and with the strangest feeling that this sublime experience was the most special and perhaps at the same time, the most frightening moment of my life.

Later, when we had washed and dressed, Xanthi brought us some coffee to drink and some small cakes to eat.

Costas sipped his coffee, lit a cigarette and said, 'You know the King has fled?'

'I had heard.'

'Thank God! Thank God the wretched man has gone at last. Ach, now things *will* change, Dorothea *mou*. I have been promoted to a Major, with a company to command, a proper soldier now. No more skulking round Salonika for me. I am glad. I made it clear I want to fight and help the Allies to be rid of the Bulgarian scourge. You have no idea how our people want to fight along with the British ...we so love and admire your people. You are the best and bravest. Do you know that Mr. Venizelos says Britain is the only really civilized country in Europe?'

'Does he really? It's generous of him to say so,' I replied, 'and your words about our men cheer me so much. Our men are not demonstrative but they are dignified and resourceful. Because we don't blow our own trumpets, people think we are a quiet and feeble lot. They are just beginning to see what dogged determination can be about. What saddens me is that the folks at home still have no idea what we have to put up with here. They still think we are lazing about and having a good time. My brother tells me that when some units from here were sent to France after that last attack on Doiran, the men were asked if they 'had been over the top yet?' ...their officers were furious considering that so many of their men had been slaughtered in that latest futile offensive. Richard, of course, was able to confirm what they said and opinions changed a good deal.'

'It is time we set about correcting these false impressions between different countries,' said Costas. 'Before this war, the people of this area knew little about the British but that is changing fast. Now they are much admired and old Yussuf openly admits that he wishes the English might take over Salonika rather than the Greeks. He feels they are more impartial towards the Jews and, of course, he is right. Most Greeks dislike the Jews – mainly because we are ourselves as greedy and crafty as the Israelites so look on one another as competitors,' he added with a laugh and a slap of his hand on his knee.

Then his face became serious again and he went on, 'I and my men are to go to Athens in a few days and reform our units. Venizelos will declare war officially on the Central Powers and the whole Greek army will at last be behind the Allies. The country will no longer be divided and on the brink of a Civil War as it was with that pig-headed Constantine.'

His calm words brought home to me a more personal fear and I looked at him aghast, ' I am glad of your promotion but Takis – Athens is so far away. At least here I could see you now and then but Athens – when would I see you again? Oh God!' I began to weep at the mere thought of such a parting.

Costas put out his cigarette and kneeling before me, wiped away the tears with his hand and taking my chin, lifted it up and kissed me.

'My dearest, my dearest soul – no need to cry. No need. Soon with our brave Greek soldiers on your side, the Allies will push back these wretched Bulgars and Austrians back where they belong …preferably into hell!

I struggled hard and held back the tears though I felt like wailing and keening as loudly as any Greek might do.

'If only it was soon, Takis. If only the war was over.'

Chapter 31

June 30th 1917

Most of our wounded men are now convalescing or have been sent back up the line. Now that the summer heat is at its worst, a wave of men suffering from malaria and sand fly fever are coming in thick and fast. However, it has to be said, that due to various wise precautions matters *have* improved; dysentery is less of a problem at least. I gather that a great deal of care is taken by the men to keep things covered and clean, latrines dug deep, waste stuff burnt at once and general hygiene much better But not a lot can be done about that wretched little lady, the female Anopheles mosquito. She has the cheek to take a tasty meal of blood from us in order to feed her young and in return gives us a horrible illness. What sort of gratitude is that?

May has come back to work again and despite odd lapses when she sometimes has to leave the dinner table in the middle of a meal and retire to her tent for a couple of days, feeling awful and totally indifferent to life, she is in fairly good form. The work does help her and she keeps as busy and uncomplaining as ever. It is so good to see her and everywhere patients and orderlies call out greeting to her. Even the Greek women who help about the place smile and wave. She seems so surprised at the warmth of people's love for her. It does her good and restores her feeling for life and humanity.

Sergeant Thompson, who rules the Mess with a rod of iron, is especially gentle and saves her his chocolate ration though May insists on giving him matches and cigarette rations in exchange. She no longer has Bill to send it to and is happy to pass it on to the bluff, kindly Sergeant. He was always was a bit sweet on her and I have hopes his attentions may help a little in showing her that there are other men in the world and she need not resign herself to being an old maid in memory of Bill. It sounds heartless, I know, but it is reality. We have to go on and cannot allow the past to drag us down and hold us from living.

So seeing the dimple back in May's cheek when the Sergeant says warm and flirty things is a pleasure to me. I want to hug the good man.

Richard's letters are not as cheerful as they used to be these days. They are far more grave and subdued though on the surface he says nothing very interesting or important. He just describes the life of the trenches, the mud and mess and monotony of it all. Our private code is more than useful in these circumstances and Richard uses it when he wants to tell me things that would otherwise be censored. It had made me laugh when I first understood what he was up to. I had almost forgotten that special language. I suppose it is our own form of mutual espionage.

Thus I learn between the lines that morale is not always that high, patriotism at an all-time low. The men just want to get through it all and go back home. They almost don't care who wins the wretched war. Sometimes they wonder if the war will ever end or will they be forever stuck in this nightmare vista of blasted landscapes, mud and barren plains? God seems so far away to those men out there – at least the well-mannered God of the English Church with His sleepy Sunday requirements, the droning vicars' sermons, the lugubrious hymns. The men still have church services but for many of them they appear out of place now. The old words that may once have stirred souls to nobility now seem almost meaningless in the face of the hourly certainty of death and the terrible discomforts of body and mind. The soul no longer has a meaning for most of these men. They couldn't care less about it. A cup of hot tea is a good deal more important.

The Germans use the most atrocious and appalling of weapons. They have taken to using a mixture of shells, which include mustard gas and sneezing gas. The latter makes the gunners sneeze and weep so much that they have to take off their gas masks and then they are hit by the nasty effects of the mustard gas and its choking contents. It is absolutely foul stuff that blisters the skin, can destroy the eyes and if inhaled causes pulmonary oedema. God, what evils men conjure up with which to destroy themselves!

It seems that they are soon to launch a major offensive to capture some village and its ridge. As always, the idea of movement and action is welcomed by everyone. Better than sitting and being shelled with mustard gas anyway.

July 15th

Venizelos and his government are in Athens and I know that Costas is there with them, the Greek army reunited and preparing itself for whatever lies ahead. Costas assures me that he will be back again soon but we have no idea when that may be. I resign myself to the long separation with a heavy heart. Athens feels so far away, my only wish that I could be with him there. He assures me that one day he will take me all over Greece to see all the ancient sites, and glorious views. There is one consolation and that is that we can be open about our relationship now. He writes as often as he can and lets me know how he is and what is going on in the capital.

As I feared, the Venizelists have routed out the *epistrates*, those armed civilians who supported the King, and summarily executed them. Trials, if they take place at all, are usually a mockery and the outcome determined in advance. The ferociousness of revenge and reprisal flows over Athens and other loyalist areas like a bloody tide. Costas does not like it any more than any other civilised man but is powerless to stop more than the worst excesses. He tells me that it has even been forbidden for people to sing *'Son of the Eagle'* a song written for Constantine when he liberated Salonika. Some old man stood on his balcony and sang this song over and over in his cracked, feeble voice but a couple of soldiers became so incensed that they shot the poor old fellow where he stood. For singing a song! What an intolerant race they are. How easily they forget what has been good. They live totally in the present moment and in this moment the King they had hailed as a hero yesterday is now an outcast and a traitor.

Well, that is the fate of Kings everywhere, I suppose. I don't think we are much better if one reviews British history with any kind of honest detachment.

July 20th

We have just returned from a visit up country. Everyone was invited to attend the Divisional Horse Show held on the edge of the Struma plain. Captain Dunning took four of the nurses, myself included, in his rattling old Buick. It was a magnificent day in every way and a treat to see the beautiful well-trained horses put through their paces by the flower of our manhood. Impossible to praise enough the manner in which our men conduct themselves and are the admiration of all. Our Allies are astonished at these well-organised shows that DHQ put on from time to time. Maybe we British aren't as useless as they first imagined.

Beautiful too to see the Struma Valley in its entirety. It is an impressive sight, especially when we passed the Lagenza Lake and saw the mountains reflected in the still waters. Though it is mainly treeless, harsh and barren, not even any scrub to cover the brown earth, yet it has a stark and majestic loveliness as it lies tranquil in the heat of the day with a sky of the most astounding blue.

July 22nd

I have had a letter from Richard who tells me that preparations are underway for a massive advance that will break through the entrenched German lines. Morale has improved considerably and the men are almost eager to go over the top. Richard has lately taken some leave and says everyone back home is much the same. Mother still complains about the war-time shortages and rising prices, Father is buried in his books and lives in some distant age when other wars troubled men's existence and Agnes is quite happy and dear little Reggie doing well. Her stupid husband, the Honourable Henry, is involved in some sort of work in the Civil Service doing as little as possible and changing his life style as little as he can. No particular surprise there.

Richard said he half wished he hadn't gone home for it made going back to the trenches all the harder. He is grateful he has no sweetheart to leave behind as some of the men do for it would have made it all the more difficult. He understands fully how painful my separation from Costas must be.

'But there you go, little sis, we all have to make our sacrifices and carry on. I know how brave you are and what a stickler you are for your duty. You're my brave girl and I miss you so. I felt it in full force when I walked down the lane to Cottersley and saw the old farm, warm and peaceful in the sun's setting rays, the cows being brought home in the loaming, everything in many ways as it was except that the local girls are running the farm now and have become milkmaids, shepherdesses, plough the fields, do everything that the men do with just as much skill and tirelessness and don't grumble a half as much as some of the fellows did. If anything they seem to thrive on it all and thoroughly enjoy being so useful.

Then to come back to all this. It was hard, sis, it was so hard! How I look forward to the time when we can wander up that lane together again as we used to in the old days, go and ask for eggs at the farm and take them home for tea. And how I look forward to meeting your brave Greek Officer. He sounds very dashing and I can tell how much you are smitten.'

Oh, my darling Richard, how I miss you too! I also long for a walk up the shady lane and the sound of the cattle lowing and the rustle of the leaves in the breeze, the sight of snowdrops, the bluebells in the woods and the verdant garden in summer.

I haven't been feeling too well lately which is unusual for me. I felt so sick this morning that I wondered if I had at last succumbed to malaria. But another thought suddenly presented itself and I am absolutely terrified by it. Could I be expecting a child?

God, that would be absolutely awful. I just pray I'm not.

July 30th

I am certain now that I am expecting Costas' child. I have missed twice and my nipples have changed colour and look quite different. The morning sickness is decidedly unpleasant. I have to grit my teeth and not let anyone know how I feel. Lassitude has hit me and I feel so tired every day, my body invaded by some strange thing I never really wanted. Only the thought that it is Costas' child makes me feel less horrified. It was born from love, from that amazing moment when he poured his love into me. That is how children should be born – from real love and lust, not from some jaded act of duty or momentary pleasure. This thought alone consoles me. I have said nothing as yet to Costas, for who knows, I might miscarry. I rather hope in my heart I will and do the maddest things, clamber hills, carry heavy items, but these little creatures are stubborn and determined as I well know and hold fast in there.

I feel sure May senses something. She looks at me with a strange eye some mornings when she finds me retching over the pail. Wisely, she says nothing, not wanting another of my rebuffs. Perhaps, I can confide in her now Costas has returned to proper soldiering, is in Athens and in a safer position.

The other morning she came over to me after one of my bouts of sickness and gently washed my face with a damp flannel. This little act made me burst into tears.

May led me inside the tent again, shut the flaps and said, 'You're expecting, aren't you, Dot?' in such a matter of fact way that I was astonished.

I nodded, wishing the earth would swallow me up.

'Is it that obvious?' I asked miserably.

I felt desperate about it at that moment. I would have to give up nursing. It would be such a disgrace to the Red Cross to send a Sister home for this reason. Though I felt myself to be 'married' to Costas, in the cold light of English and even Greek law, I was not. I had little claim on him. He might not want me pregnant. I didn't know what his reaction might be. I felt sure he would be glad but at the same time, when would we meet again, when would we ever be able to marry? I didn't want my child to be illegitimate. Doubts assailed me. Did I really *want* to marry him and live in this wretched place forever? At this moment, I wanted more than anything in the world to be back home in Downlands, curled up with my favourite book on a settee in the library or roaming the woods and the fields with my darling Richard as we had done in our innocent youth. I wanted to be a child again but I was to be a mother, with all the responsibilities that would entail, all the curbing of freedom and independence.

I sobbed and sobbed. It is awful to realise that you are not the good person you imagine yourself to be. I had come out full of noble thoughts, ready to sacrifice myself for my country and fellow men. I remembered how scathing I had once felt about girls who 'got themselves into trouble', how judgemental about their lack of will power, their stupidity. Yet I had blithely fallen into the arms of a man who was, when all said and done, a complete stranger. At this moment I felt nothing but hate for Costas and men in general. What had made me love him? He was just a mad Greek! ...but even as I thought this way, the memory of his gaunt but fascinating face rose before me again and I knew it couldn't have been otherwise. It was destiny. I had had no choice and would have acted the same way whatever the consequences.

Drying my tears, I smiled a little at dear May who had lovingly taken my hand in hers. She was the best of friends. She made no comment, uttered no criticism just looked at me with deep compassion. I so wished I could be like her. I knew I was a very judgemental person and felt, if nothing else, I had learnt a lesson in kindness.

'We'll be late,' I said, struggling to my feet.

'It doesn't matter. You don't feel well. I'll tell Ward Sister you want to lie down a bit and then you come later.'

'All right, just for a few minutes. I'll be along soon.'

I lay on the bed and feebly waved the flies away and felt nothing but wretchedness engulf me. What was to become of me now? I suddenly wanted to go home so very much, to get away from all this. Yet how would my parents take it all? I was terrified of what Mother would say. Father I knew would be accepting and as for the rest of the world, well they could go hang. Anyway, it would be a grandchild and that would be lovely for them. Once they saw the child they would be glad and so would I. Costas would marry me after the war. It was my fault for not agreeing to marry him when he had spoken of it. Perhaps even now he might obtain leave and come back to Salonika and marry me. Yes, that was it! I would write and tell him at once and suggest the idea.

Chapter 32

August 1st 1917

I have written to Costas and told him the news and await his reply with trepidation. Meanwhile I carry on as best as I can from day to day. I am sad that I cannot feel the joy I should over this child that grows within me. It ought to be a happy time, restful, eating the best food, helping the little one to have as good a start in life as possible. Instead I have to work like a skivvy, fall into bed exhausted each night, my heart full of sorrow and a deep sense of shame pervading my every waking moment.

I sometimes sit alone on the hillside thinking through it all wondering where I went wrong? The answer is I didn't go wrong but followed my heart instead of my head. I feel I could not have done otherwise, given my reckless and wilful nature. Can we change our natures and act against the deepest impulses of our heart? Is it wrong to love with such passion? If so then I have wronged and the Lord must judge me accordingly when I present myself before Him.

That is my argument in my favour but then another quiet voice comes and whispers in the other ear. Love, it says, is the Christian virtue. This love of mine is a purely personal one and through abandoning myself to it without a thought, I have endangered the life of my unborn child, my own life too, and will bring shame on my unit, friends, family and country. My mind tosses and turns over these thoughts in despair.

What sort of an ignoble person am I?

This afternoon I sat on the hillside in my favoured spot, watching the wriggling and varied wildlife that unheedingly lived out its existence around me, while tearing myself to pieces within. Hearing a step, I turned to see Ethan Willoughby coming along the track, smoking his cigarette and looking remarkably peaceful. His air of purpose made me realise that he had spotted me and was coming to join me. I looked wildly around. I wanted to run away but there was nowhere to go.

He came up and sat beside me and carried on smoking in silence. I was relieved. He didn't seem to want to speak, just be companionable. I was grateful for that and giving him a half-smile, continued to gaze out over the sea. His strong, silent presence gave me such comfort. I took a deep sigh and told myself that he was a good man, a real friend, a true Englishman.

After a while, I felt his penetrating gaze upon me and he seemed to be studying me. I pretended not to notice and kept staring out to sea but felt tears rise to my eyes that fell in slow drops down my cheeks.

'Can't you tell me what troubles you, Dot?'

I sighed again. It was all I seemed capable of doing.

'Is it all getting to you, my dear?'

'Oh, Ethan!' I burst out and turned to him.

He put his arms about me and held me tight. For a while I just sobbed like an idiot on his shoulder, while he patted me awkwardly on my back.

Eventually, I pulled myself together and smiled at him a little.

'My darling,' he began but stopped, his own face contorted with feeling. 'I hate to see my brave lass so dismal,' he went on with a supreme effort to stop himself from turning sentimental that somehow wrung my heart more than a hundred declarations of love. Was it possible to love two men? I did feel a great deal of love for Ethan in this moment, Costas so far away, everything so confused and troubling. Ethan was someone I understood, an Englishman, a gentleman. Did I really understand Costas and the Greek mentality? He fascinated me, everything about this glorious, cruel, pitiless yet beautiful country did, but in my heart of hearts I was English and would never fit in here. Never!

The tears began to fall again. I was committed now. There was no escape.

However, I could tell Ethan none of this. I didn't want his face to avert, his features to stiffen with disapproval. He would think me a slut. He would not be my friend anymore.

He took my hand and rubbed it gently but remained silent.

'I'm so sorry,' I said at last. 'I'm just tired out, Ethan. I don't know how you manage to keep going the way you do, you never seem to rest.'

'It has to be done,' he replied, 'the work has to be done. I *can't* stop to think of myself can I? And to be honest,' he added with a deep sigh of his own, 'this is all there is for me to live for.'

'Don't say that!'

He looked at me for a long time. Tentatively he put out a hand and brushed the fallen wisps of hair back from my face. 'You know how much I care, Dot. Would you ever consider marrying me when all this is over?'

'It's impossible,' I replied. I hadn't meant to sound so abrupt and seeing the look of hurt in his eye, hated myself even more. 'There are reasons, Ethan. You know I *do* care about you – a great deal. But I cannot marry you.'

'I think I understand,' he said stiffly and rising, helped me to my feet.

Oh, if only you did, Ethan. If you only knew the truth, you wouldn't want me then!

August 10ᵗʰ

Despite my cruel rebuff, dear, kind Ethan arranged with Matron for me to have a couple of days at the Nurse's Rest Home next week. It's true, I hadn't had a break for a while and I was so grateful for the thought. Meanwhile this morning, a letter arrived from Costas. I was relieved to find that he was delighted with my news, looked forward to our first son and would come as soon as he could. He said he couldn't promise that it would be very soon as so much had to be done to reform and re-train the new divisions that were to join our own troops next year. According to Costas, once the great Greek army came on our side, the battle was as good as won. I smiled and prayed that this optimism was well founded.

'But chrysi mou, don't stay in that filthy work you do! Why not leave now and go to live with my mother in the city? She will take such care of you and be so delighted about her expected grandson (for I feel sure we have made a fine, brave Greek boy here). Do go! I shall feel so much happier knowing you are safe and happy with our Mama. Can they hold you still? Can't you just leave? Surely even you must feel you have done your duty by now? Ach, my little Dorothea hanum, my little wife, I so long to see you!'

As it happens my original contract was for six months only and has not been officially renewed. May and I have been given a chevron to sew on our shoulder to show that we have completed a year's service and we simply carried on. The paperwork hasn't been done and no one has had time to be bothered. I suppose Matron assumes we will stay unless we become too ill to carry on. The way is open and I can leave at any time now. I toyed with the idea; it seemed the only sensible course to take. Soon enough I would be heavy with child and incapable of working these long hours and I would not wish to be seen in that condition. I would be sent away in disgrace. Why not take matters into my own hands and leave honourably? I feel regretful in a way. I so wanted to have my second chevron! But that's just my nonsense and to be truthful, a part of me is weary of it all, my conscience dulled by exhaustion and sickness.

I decided to go and see Kyria Nina while I was staying in the city for the couple of days leave and discuss the matter with her.

August 16th

The Nurses's Rest Home is in a beautiful house, once the residence of the former Turkish Governor of Salonika. It has a delightful garden surrounding it and broad steps of white marble leading to the front door. Inside it is luxurious, comfortable and cool with armchairs one can sink into and good books to read – I haven't read a decent book in ages. It is a blissful change to the harsh routine of camp life.

I feel myself to be very lucky but can't help thinking of the poor soldiers up the line who have not had a day's leave since they had arrived, except for sickness. Only the officers are able to manage the occasional three day visit to the city during which time they have a hundred commissions to execute for the men in their unit. They always carry these out as conscientiously as they can and return laden with vital and important things like beer (only that thin, flat Salonika brew but better by far than chlorinated water) whisky, razors, clothes pegs, gardening tools and all the other weird necessities of camp life. Oddest of all are purchases of silk underwear and white stockings! These latter items for the use of those clever men who have formed an amazing troupe of entertainers and are planning a new pantomime for us all at Christmas. They take their parts as females most seriously and it has to be said are far more attractive than the local soubrettes and act a good deal more convincingly than a great many actresses on the London stage. We all look forward to these brilliant and professionally produced shows, which cheer up bored and frustrated men in the trenches and enliven the spirits of the hospital staff alike.

I rang Kyria Nina today and asked if I could visit her. She was full of warmth and kindness and said she had heard the good news about the baby and would send Nouri with the carriage to fetch me over to stay the night. I could have easily walked there as the house was quite close but Nina wouldn't hear of it. Something in me relaxed at this response and I felt as if all was well after all and would be taken care of by others.

I had to ask permission of the Matron in Charge as we are supposed to be in by 6.30 pm. She is a frosty number and pursed her lips at this request, looking at me with disapproval over her glasses. I could tell she was not at all convinced of my motives but suspected that I meant to go to some low class cabaret at the White Tower and disport myself with the officers!

However, I finally convinced her and a call to our own Matron secured the required permission. It was at moments like this that the rebel in me arose and wanted freedom so much. It was annoying to be treated like a child when I was supposed to be on leave.

Nouri arrived later that evening and took me to Kyria Nina's house. I was delighted to be back there and immediately felt a sense of comfort and well-being. Nina was motherly and fussed in just the right amount, making me feel special and important not the guilt-ridden creature I had become of late. The servants were all pleased to see me and welcomed me, telling me they had prepared specially the delicious foods they remembered I liked. I was so touched by their attention and outpouring of sincere love. The beautiful memories of those happy days when Costas and I became engaged flooded back as I sank upon the bed in my room and thought of our first lovemaking. It was impossible to feel regret or guilt. No need to torment myself with that unloving, harsh 'Protestant conscience' as Costas would have put it. I loved him, he was my soul mate and we were to have our first child. It would be wonderful.

August 17th

The next day, after a deep and untroubled sleep, I rose early and made my way to the bathhouse. The maid, Christina, supplied me with towels and told me the water was now nice and hot. I revelled in the steamy *hamam* and felt clean, refreshed and for once at peace with myself. I put my engagement ring on for there was no longer any reason to hide it anymore.

Kyria Nina joined me for breakfast and we sat together in a room overlooking the garden now full of scents from the roses and jasmine, twittering with the sound of canaries in little cages. Contentment seeped through my whole being.

'You look beautiful, my daughter in law,' she said with her sweet smile as she regarded me, 'motherhood suits you. You look rosy and lovely. Here have some more *bourekakia*,' offering me some buttery shortbread cakes that were utterly delicious.

'No, no, I shall be fat as a prize pig if I stuff any more of your good food down myself,' I laughed. 'You all spoil me so much.'

'Well, we love to spoil you, *coritsaki mou*, my pretty daughter,' she replied taking my hand in hers affectionately and patting it, her face beaming with pleasure, 'our Takis has given us a child at last and that is the best news I have had for a long while. And he has made this child with the woman he loves. That is also important. People will gossip as they do but *we* care nothing for that. My family has always gone its own way and thumbed our noses at the narrow-minded creatures of this world. I am happy for both of you. I wish only my Petros was here to see this happy day. What a wedding, what a christening we shall have! All these happy events to look forward to.'

These days, everything anyone said made me want to weep. I struggled not to give in though her words really moved my heart. She could not be more different to my mother who would eye me askance in this state of *deshabille*. Yes, I had even taken to sitting about in my dressing gown, Oriental style! And be *most* disapproving of the fact that I was pregnant. As if this natural and delightful state of affairs was some sort of disgusting ailment. She would have made it feel so. I realised in this moment that all my present unhappiness stemmed from that cold, British upbringing that pretends to ignore sexuality and its inevitable products as if they did not exist.

It was not Mother's fault. In her turn she had been brought up in such ignorance of these matters that it's hardly surprising that she is shocked and disgusted by the reality. How grateful I am that I was born in more liberated and educated times and above all that I had taken to nursing, learning to love and understand the human body and its manifold needs and dispelling that cloud of ignorance that surrounded most women of my class.

We sat and chatted away all morning and Kyria Nina told me many amusing and romantic tales of her relations in Constantinople, the life she had led there in her childhood. My delight in all things Greek was aroused once more and I saw how very warm and spontaneous the Greek character is compared to our own. I also knew that I could never be quite like this. The natural constraints of my own English blood would always prevent my becoming as exuberant and overflowing as the Greeks. Yet the two types of nature went together nicely and complimented one another. I felt that Costas and I would do very well after all. Our child would combine these two splendid races within himself and would be bilingual and at ease with both.

Chapter 33

I did not feel at all sleepy that afternoon and asked Kyria Nina if she wanted to come to the market with me for some shopping. She said that she felt tired and would lie down a little as it was so hot but would send Giorgos with me to help carry the parcels.

'You are not to carry as much as a pomegranate home,' she admonished me, 'be very careful. Are you sure you want to go out in this fearful heat? Why not lie down? You are meant to be resting.'

I had to assure her that I already felt rested with just the one peaceful night's sleep though it was also because my mind and heart felt at rest again. My energies had returned and I wanted to enjoy as much of the city as I could while I was here.

I was driven into the city centre and a servant accompanied me, walking behind me some paces. I felt quite the Grand Duchess! However, I wanted to go and have tea at the Nurse's Tea and Reading Rooms. There was a particular book I wanted to look up. So I made my purchases and sent Giorgos back with the parcels, telling him that I would take an *araba* and find my way back later. I bought a copy of the *Balkan News* from one of the lads in the street and tucked the thin pages in my belt, meaning to look at it later on and feeling cheerful for the first time in ages. As I walked along Venizelos Street who should come tooting and honking by in a cloud of dust but dear old Captain 'Drains' Dunning?

He shouted to me and told me to climb in.

'Where are you off to?' he asked.

'Debating where to go for a cup of decent tea.'

'Well, let's go to old Floca's, get some sea air. Their tea isn't too good but the ice cream is superb. By Jove, you look better already, dear girl. You looked all washed up the other day. I could tell you needed a break.'

All the pavement tables were occupied so we squeezed our way inside Floca's and managed to find a couple of seats at the back. I preferred to be indoors despite the heat as the wind had decided to blow up a gale. It did little to dispel the heat and just added to one's discomfort by blowing choking dust into one's face instead.

'Phew, thank God for that! It's a hell of a scorcher as usual,' said Dunning as he whistled and shouted and banged on the table till a waiter at last arrived and took our order.

As we ate our ices and chatted about this and that, someone came in and announced that a fire had started over in the Turkish quarters and was burning a treat.

'Poof, a few Turkish houses! That will clear the place a bit more and good riddance,' said a Greek with a shrug of indifference.

'They're always starting fires that careless lot! It gets rid of the rats, human and otherwise,' was another callous comment. Nobody seemed at all concerned.

Captain Dunning lit up his inevitable cigarette and a couple of other officers he knew joined us at our table. An interesting conversation began about nothing in particular but it had us all laughing merrily. I felt a sudden pang to think I was going to leave all this. I would miss these men; miss my nursing friends and the life we all shared as comrades together. Uncomfortable and hard as it was, the work felt rewarding and useful. I still yearned to be of service to Mankind. My old guilt feelings came pouring back again. A decision will have to be made soon and I must stick to it, the only logical decision being to go to the Cassimatis family and begin the new life I and the Fates had chosen.

When we left Floca's some time later, we were startled to see a large plume of smoke arising from the north-western corner of Upper Town where the Turks lived in those ramshackle hovels of theirs. So it was true about the fire.

I looked at the rising smoke and said worriedly, 'It does look rather a blaze and the wind seems to be fanning it in this direction. I hope they can keep it under control.'

'Good Heavens, it's just a little fire,' said Dunning, 'not that the local fire engines are likely to do a lot of good, they couldn't put out a cigar. It'll stop at Via Egnatia anyway. It's a broad street and it won't have anything to feed on once it's reached that.'

'I hope you're right,' I said.

There was a terrible clamour going on and people had begun to stir from their afternoon siesta and were coming out to have a look. Many clambered up to their roofs and watched the entertaining spectacle from up there. The opinion seemed to be that the fire would burn up all the native quarters, which was no great loss. Get rid of a few more of those damned Turks and Jews! Music sounded from the bars and parks, people ate, drank, danced and carried on as always. These self-absorbed Macedonians reminded me of Nero fiddling while Rome burned. I did not feel quite so phlegmatic about it.

'Captain, let's go to Via Egnatia and see what we can do,' I said.

'My dear girl, are you mad? What on earth can *we* do?'

'I don't know,' I said unhappily, 'but there seem to be a lot of carts and wagons dashing about, people must need rescuing … maybe we can take some of them in the car.'

'Those smelly creatures in my car!' said Dunning in horror but his natural sense of justice prevailed and he agreed to drive down the Via Egnatia and see if anyone needed picking up. When we got near there we began to see the first stream of refugees pouring along the street, their faces registering despair and grief, clutching their foolish belongings as if they were gold dust. One woman held a mirror and a brass bowl against her chest and appeared oblivious to the wailing infant yelling and clinging in terror to her skirts. An old woman was wandering about, calling for her family, looking lost and bewildered. Others pushed and jostled along, dropping their useless and heavy goods at last, in order to lift their children who screamed to be picked up and carried. To my disgust I saw men load up their womenfolk with the precious sewing machine and other items, then leaving them to struggle along in the crowd, took themselves off speedily to save their own lives.

The noise was unbelievable. Men were shouting to each other, women and children screaming and behind all this one could hear the crackling roar of the flames, the crash of timbers and glass shattering and smell the acrid smoke which billowed up into the air and was driven by the fierce wind down the streets which formed tunnels for it. It was like some strange dragon breathing out through its' nostrils.

'Good God!' said Dunning in amazement. 'This thing's beginning to look pretty bad.'

People knocked on the car windows and tried to get inside. We took on board some children and a couple of old ladies, repulsing those who wanted merely to save themselves and their goods.

'*Aide! Imshi*...scram!' yelled Dunning as a fat old Turk tried to push aside some of the children and get himself into our car. He was shoved aside in turn and we slammed the doors and set off as fast as we could, and that was a snail's pace for the roads were crowded with lorries, cars, bullock wagons and any other means of transport available. We decided to head for the Monastir road and out of town rather than the seashore, a wise decision as it afterwards proved when the wind changed course and took the fire right down to the very edge of the sea walls.

'We'll take them to the Mess of 244 MT Company ...that's down the Monastir Rd. somewhere. They can look after this lot and give 'em some tea,' said Dunning.

On the way, I spotted a little girl sitting by the roadside looking strangely quiet and still as if in contemplation. More likely the poor mite was just too stunned to move. No one took notice of her but streamed around her. She looked up at us as we paused and her huge, pleading brown eyes filled me with such tenderness that I called to Captain Dunning to stop.

'I must pick her up. We can't leave her there!'

'We haven't got room for anyone else.'

'I'll sit her on my lap.'

The child seemed to be afraid to move but I picked her up and took her with us to the MT Mess. Here we unceremoniously dumped our human cargo and the men took the children in very tenderly and plied them with biscuits and juice while we went back to fetch others. This activity went on for hours and the fire kept gaining ground pushing the hapless refugees from one street to the next.

The fire had no boundaries, unlike us human beings. It had no preferences at all and moved steadily across the thirty foot broad Via Egnatia, fanned by the fierce wind that created a draught pushing it along. It flickered, leapt, crashed and consumed its way through the business quarters. It was an insatiable, crackling, roaring monster and the noise was deafening. I thought …so this is how the Fire of London or Ancient Rome must have looked. Magnificent, terrifying, unstoppable! Out of that red blaze the long, white minarets stood out for a while till they too fell into the flames and sparks lit the air like a shower of fireworks falling to earth.

Night had now begun to fall though it hardly seemed the case with the lurid glow that lit the sky. Oddly enough, due to the freak wind, the rest of the Turkish quarters were no longer in danger and the fire was instead gaining ground in the Jewish Ghetto. I was terrified for Yussuf and his family. But it was hopeless trying to find a way through to his house, even if I could recall where it was. I prayed that they had all escaped and were safe somewhere and kept looking out in case I might see them. Robbers were already looting shops and amongst them were drunken French and Italian soldiers. The half-crazed Jewish proprietors s were flinging their goods out into the street in some mad hope of saving them that way. Beautiful rugs, copper vessels and all sorts of other articles came out on the pavement and were snatched up by the looters.

By now the British troops had joined in rescuing the refugees and our Tommies were piling women and children onto their lorries and trucks and carting them well away from the fire Thankfully, our men refused to be involved in the looting and put all their energies into fire-fighting and rescue operations.

We plied to and fro, taking as many as we could pack in the car, consoling bewildered and troubled people. Dunning had forgotten his distaste and good-naturedly shoved foul-smelling infants and old ladies into his car and raced off as best as he was able through the crush to safety. It was almost impossible to move and we could not use the Rue Venizelos as our firemen had laid their hoses along there in an attempt to rescue the old Jewish bazaar. Just as we were leaving we heard the crash of timbers as its long roof caved into the inferno below.

To our astonishment, some of the residents refused to leave their houses and sat pathetically clutching their bundles of goods in their hands as if the Gorgon, herself, had petrified them into stone. Their lethargy astounded us, but we realised it was the result of centuries of apathy under the Turkish rule. They didn't seem to understand what was happening to them. One Turkish fellow locked his door and was about to abandon his house with all his harem still locked inside but Dunning grabbed his keys from him and ran back to let the women out. He had a hard time persuading them to come forth. They preferred to burn alive than break their purdah. What mad people!

In the end, exhausted, my face blackened with smoke, my mouth dry as a bone, and full of cinders, I let Dunning carry on with the rescue operation and stayed behind with some others to feed the children. We found food that had been dumped by fleeing merchants and brought it with us and gave people cakes and fruit as the Mess had almost run out of their supplies by now. Meanwhile the BEF canteen brought out drinks and tins of biscuits for those who had gathered on the promenade. As the fire began to move towards the sea front, lighters from the ships in the bay came out and took to safety those terrified creatures that were now trapped on the quayside with a solid wall of flame behind them and not a moment too soon either.

In the end, the soldiers had to use dynamite to make a fire break and would have done so sooner but the Greek authorities were very resistant at first, convinced as they were that the solid buildings of the business centre would withstand the flames.

But the fire, as I said before, had no pity or discrimination and roared on through the houses as if they were made of matchwood. When the fire reached the sea wall early in the morning, Floca's, were we had been having ices yesterday afternoon, was gone with the BRCS HQ, the Nurse's Reading Rooms, Orosdi Back's Emporium, the beautiful, smart shops and hotels and all the Serbian Relief Fund stores. Salonika was a stricken city.

Chapter 34

I awoke to find Captain Dunning bending over me anxiously. I was lying by the roadside surrounded by children and other refugees, my head in the lap of one of the little girls.

'Thank the Lord! ...I thought something frightful had happened to you,' said the Captain as he helped me to my feet.

'Oh, goodness, I'm so sorry,' I said. 'What time is it?'

'It's 4 ack emma, my dear and I feel we've done enough. Let the army get on with it now.'

'Is the fire out?'

'God, no! It's still billowing away, it'll be days before they have it completely under control. We can do no more. But I can't see how I'm going to get you back to the Nurse's Home. It's right the other side of town and the centre is blocked by the fire, plus hoses, engines, lorries, you name it.'

My mind went to Kyria Nina who, to be honest, I had forgotten in this last few frantic hours. I had not been overly worried for her safety as her home was well on the other side of the city. Now it occurred to me that she, however, would be worried about me, wondering if I had been caught up in the fire and even injured. There was no way that I could communicate with her.

'What on earth shall I do?

'Well, there's nothing for it – you'll have to come back to camp with me. We'll have to take the long route across the hills but we should be there in a few hours.'

He helped me in the car and we drove up hill in a roundabout manner till we at last reached our hospital camp. People crowded round us asking questions about the fire but I was too exhausted to respond and beginning to feel queasy and light-headed.

One of the Night Sisters took me away, gave me a cup of sweet tea, then led me to the Night Nurses rest hut and told me to go to bed and talk later. I was most grateful and hastily undressing, washed my face and hands with some cold water left in a basin, tumbled into a free bed and was asleep in moments.

When I awoke, it was broad daylight outside. My watch told me that it was well past midday. I could easily have turned over and fallen asleep again but I was desperate to get word to Kyria Nina and made myself get up and dress. Some of the Night Nurses were also rising now and looked at me with curiosity but said nothing. I went off to Sister's Mess to have some tea and scrounge a piece of toast for I was famished. There Sister Moira sat me down and in exchange for my thrilling first hand account of the fire, gave me a bowl of porridge and made me some bread and dripping which was delicious.

'How amazing that you were there to see it all, Dot,' she said as she poured out my tea, 'we could only watch from up here and wonder what on earth was going on. Goodness, that'll be something to tell your grandchildren.'

'I suppose it will,' I said.

'Frankly, I think it's not so bad a thing. I always said that filthy city needed scrubbing out or burning down. Who'd have thought it would actually happen though?' she added, 'not that I don't feel for the poor creatures who have lost their homes, of course. But you said all the hotels and markets have gone. Well, they deserve it. The extortionate prices those greedy people have charged our officers just to billet in some seedy, dirty hotel! Everything has trebled in price and they have become rich with Allies gold. I feel it's a judgement on them.'

'I can't help but agree with that but it was still terrible to see the fear on their faces. I won't forget it till I die,' I sighed, 'and these poor souls have suffered a good deal of late caught in all these wretched political wrangles and wars. As if it isn't enough to have the war to deal with without having to house and feed all these homeless souls now. I doubt the Greek Government will do much for them, it's a task that's bound to fall to the Allies.'

Today I felt surprisingly free of the morning sickness that usually assailed me; in fact I was beginning to feel quite bright and perky. This baby is a mighty tenacious little one. All that frenzied dashing about would have made any other woman miscarry. I put it down to the tough outdoor life of these latter months, which has made me far stronger and healthier than I have ever been in my life.

I wondered how to get a message back to the Nurse's Home and also to Kyria Nina. I wasn't even sure if the phone or telegraph lines were still operating but decided to go and ask Matron if I might try her phone.

She was most concerned and glad to find me well.

'You and Captain Dunning have done some amazing work and we are very proud of you both,' she said, 'you may have another day's leave to recover. I feel you deserve that much at least. The city is out of bounds now. The army is having its work cut out dealing with all the homeless inhabitants.'

She told me that she would let the other Matron know that I was now back in camp but allowed me to ring Kyria Nina which thankfully I was able to do as that side of the town remained untouched by the fire..

'*Doxos sto Theou*! Thanks to God you are well, dear one,' was her greeting when she heard my voice. 'I was frantic with fear wondering where you were. I sent Nouri and Giorgo to see if they could find you but they said it was impossible to get into the city centre because of the fire and all the streams of fleeing people. You rest, my love, but come as soon as you can. Oh … we have your things here! I will send Giorgo over with them when he can ride through the city.'

I left Matron and went off, free for the day. What bliss! I would write some letters and go for a long walk in the hills and with this end in view began to make my way towards our quarters. May now came running over to me from one of the wards and hugged me speechlessly.

'Thank God, you're safe,' she said echoing Nina's words.

Then out came Willoughby from another ward and taking my hand in his, kissed it and told me I was a heroine. A few other people passing by crowded round and plied me with questions again.

This attention was all too embarrassing.

'We didn't do much,' I protested, 'you'd have all done the same. It was just pure luck the Captain and I were there and he had some transport. I wish we'd had a Ford van and could have packed in more people. As it was they were all sitting on each other's laps.'

At last, I managed to extricate myself from these kind and well-meaning people for it really did seem to me to be an unnecessary fuss.

I sat for an hour or so and wrote to Richard about my news, read the couple of pages of the now stale *Balkan News*, which I had discovered amazingly still tucked in my belt. I wondered if their offices had been affected by the fire and if we would have ever have any more *Balkan News*. An orderly brought me over a cup of tea and that was very welcome. Then I decided to go for a long walk and really think things through.

From my perch on the hillside, I looked down over the scene of devastation in the city. Smoke was still rising in billowing clouds but the towering walls of flame appeared under control now. How terrible a business this was!

I then sat and wrestled with myself like Jacob with his angel. The upshot of this inner battle was that I would wait another month until just before I was beginning to show and then tell Matron about my condition and ask for my release. I knew this was what I had to do but I quailed at the thought. Just as I had everyone's good opinion of me, I was to lose it.

Did it really matter?

Yes, unfortunately I was vain enough to care about their opinions. These were people I loved and admired.

Chapter 35

August 20ᵗʰ 1917

The corner where stood the Bank of Athens and the offices of the *Balkan News* was actually untouched by some miracle and within a couple of days the paper boys were out in what was left of the streets shouting their old cry of 'Johnny, Johnny!... .Bawkanooze!' It was a special edition at five pence a copy to help the Refugee Fund. I asked one of the ambulance men to bring me one as a souvenir.

Alas, the 5ᵗʰ century Church of the patron saint of Salonika, the famed and beautiful Agios Dimitrios, had been burned to the ground. No wedding there for me now! Fortunately the beautiful 6ᵗʰ century church of Agia Sophia was untouched, though the fire came close enough to it, saved only by the wide courtyard all around.

The thousands of refugees, mainly Jewish, were immediately helped by the Allies who organised camps for them. Our men gave up half their rations to help feed them and supplied 1,300 tents and taught these people some of the rudiments of elementary hygiene while they had them under their wing.

The *Balkan News* told us that our efforts were received with admiration by the Salonikans who wrote glowing praises in their own papers about the affectionate and loving care with which our men helped old and young to safety and the immense efficiency... '*the marvellous and amazing quality of this great race*'... with which tents were erected in neat lines and people housed and fed in the twinkling of an eye. We British have many faults but at our best we *are* a compassionate people and I feel our men deserved this praise.

The nurses are forbidden to go to the city at present but Captain Dunning and Captain Sherwood went in the other day and brought back the sad news that their beloved Officers Club had been razed to the ground.

'It was the only place you could get a decent comfortable chair and a reasonably priced meal apart from the French Club,'groaned Dunning. 'We shall miss it, I can tell you. This place is God-forsaken enough without losing that little haven.'

'It's such a sight now,' said Sherwood, gloomily, 'there wasn't much to enjoy before but now there's nothing at all. It was the only place men on leave could have a bit of life and a change from the endless view of the barren hills and the shelling and all the rest of it. Scarcely any of those poor Tommies have had leave since they came –. and they think they're worse off in France! At least they can get home or go to Paris. I mean *Paris* – how does this stinking hell hole compare with Paris!'

'It doesn't compare with anything decent,' said Dunning, 'and you should see it now. It's like a city of the dead, everywhere is deserted, silent; it's really peculiar. No more happy times in Floca's being charged the earth for an ice cream and cake. No more third rate cabaret in the White Tower.'

'That hasn't burnt down too, has it?' I asked in dismay.

'No, more's the pity. But it has shut for the moment. Half the performers have gone back to whatever ghastly holes they came from. Nobody ever used to listen to them anyway. It's sad though to see some of the finer buildings now blackened shells and twisted girders, the cafes and restaurants all reduced to rubble. God, I shall miss Orosdi's …it was the only place to get little but important things like decent shaving soap or a flannel and a pair of braces.'

I asked him if he would inquire what had happened toYussuf Yiakovides and his family next time he went in. The good Captain managed to track him down in one of the refugee camps. He spoke to Yussuf who said that he meant to re-open his business as soon as he was able and had meanwhile managed to send his family off to Athens to a relation who lived there. That was a relief and I was able to write and give this news to Costas who I knew would find them and help them.

'Things are already perking up in the city. They don't hang about, you know. The coppersmiths are back amongst the ruins and plying their trade and so are the other shopkeepers who have anything left to sell, 'said Captain Dunning with a grin. 'They may spread out their hands and shrug and say 'All finish Johnny!' but believe me, nothing stops these Jews and Greeks earning a bob or two!'

September 1st

This latter month I have been working hard and putting my all into whatever I do. Perhaps it is some sort of guilt offering for the fact that I must shortly leave. All too soon the awful moment arrived when I knew I *must* speak to Matron and confess all.

I stopped her one day as she was making her tour of the wards.

'May I speak with you later, Matron.'

'Is it important?'

'Yes, it is important.'

'Very well, come and see me after lunch.'

I could scarcely eat my meal, being so full of trepidation. Everything was sawdust in my mouth. I made my way to her quarters and knocked on the door, feeling that I would rather face the Bulgarian army than Matron.

When I entered, I found her sitting at her desk, her little spaniel, Tinker, curled up near her feet. I stooped and patted the dog, feeling it might be an ally. Its soft brown eyes turned up to me and reminded me of the little Greek child we had picked up that awful day of the fire. I wondered irrelevantly how the poor child was and if she had ever found her family again.

'Well, my dear, what is it?'

I stood there and struggled to find the right words.

Matron looked up from her papers and frowned a little.

'Take a seat,' she said, realising that I had something personal to tell her. It was unlike me to seem so lost for words.

236

I sat down and said slowly, 'Matron, I am expecting a child.'

Now I had her full attention! …but I wasn't grateful for that. She looked at me shocked and uncomprehending at first and then her face actually flushed a bright red. She rose and began to pace about the room.

'You are absolutely sure of it?'

'I am three months gone now.'

'And who is the father?'

'A Greek Officer.'

'Even worse!' exploded Matron who was angrier than I had ever seen her. I was going to have this at home too, I thought ruefully, though my mother was seldom angry and would show her disapproval in a cold and silent manner. Matron was a warm person and her anger blazed over me alarmingly. I felt quite afraid of her but managed to keep composed and still and not disgrace myself by bursting into tears.

'Even worse!' she repeated. 'If it was one of *our* men we would get Canon Jones to marry you on the spot. But how are we to deal with this man if he is in the Greek Army? Have you told him?'

'I have told him.'

'And his reply?'

'He was delighted and means to come and marry me as soon as he can get away from Athens. We *are* officially engaged Matron. And he told me it is as good as being married here in Greece.'

'Did he indeed? And you swallowed that? I can't believe that you of all people have let me down, Dorothy!'

I was amazed to hear her use my first name.

'I always trusted you, felt if anyone was sensible it was you. If you were to dally with anyone, I thought it might be …' here she paused and I felt sure she meant to say Captain Willoughby but she thought better of it..

'Well, at least you are engaged. Where is this fellow now?'

I objected to my future husband being called a 'fellow' in this contemptuous manner but replied quietly, 'He is busy in Athens and can't come for the moment as they are re-forming the Greek Army.'

'What nonsense. Enjoying the flesh-pots of Athens more like! I am sure his C.O. would give him compassionate leave if he asked for it and he could get himself here in a few days and marry you, having got you in this condition. The man ought to be court-martialled.'

'Please, don't say that, Matron. I don't want a fuss made if it can be helped. Please don't bring him into it. The blame is not all his. If anything the blame is mine and I accept full responsibility. I wanted to ...to ...I went into it all with my eyes open.'

'And without thinking of the shame you bring your country, your profession, your family! You may well look woebegone. I can't believe this of you of all people. And I trusted you to go to that Greek woman. They are so strict about these things I felt sure it would be safe. I suppose you met this man there?'

'Yes, he's her son,' I replied, feeling that I couldn't possibly relate the earlier events leading up to that particular meeting. Looking back with the cold light of reason, an angry Matron and the present situation, I felt it had all been madness itself. What had possessed me, taken me over? Had I really had my eyes open or been carried away with a sense of romantic adventure?

I sighed deeply.

'You sigh. But you have ruined your life, my girl.'

'He *will* marry me I know. And he would like me to go to live with his mother and have the baby there. May I not be discharged Matron and go there? Then I will be off everyone's hands.' I couldn't help adding with a little petulance, '*They*, at least, seem ready to accept me and my child with joy and gladness.'

'Is that so? Then I cannot begin to think what sort of people these must be that you mix with so freely. People who are not at all dismayed by such behaviour? You can't trust these people, Nurse. You don't understand them or know them. They are a wily lot, changeful. Look how treacherously they have behaved to the Allies. Now they are on our side! But when we first arrived they did all they could to thwart our efforts, betray us, milk us of our money. No, you cannot go there. You are still under Army command and a British citizen. Unless, of course, this man marries you, in which case you belong to *them* ...and Heaven help you is all I can say.'

She sat down now and looked at me for a while in silence.

Her face softened a little, her first anger over.

'You are a brave girl, Dorothy, and a very fine nurse. I intended to promote you to Ward Sister eventually. Your conduct, apart from this, has been an asset to us. I don't pretend I am not baffled and disappointed. I felt I had better judge of character than I have displayed, but that's war, that's life, I suppose. I intend to send you home. It's the very best place for you in this condition, you will have far better medical care than here where the conditions are so very bad. How are you and baby to survive another of these dreadful winters here? Your Greek friends may be very kind, I don't know ...but do you seriously feel you would settle to a life here?'

'I love Salonika, I love Greece!'

'Salonika! What is there left of Salonika just now? You saw it go up in flames and the ruin it's in. All those unhappy people to feed and care for. This is *not* the place to be, with the uncertainty of whether we will win the battle of not. We will, of course, but just supposing the Bulgarians and Austrians *do* get here? How would you fare then? No, you must return to England at once. I shall not discharge you dishonourably but simply inform HQ that you are no longer fit for duty for health reasons. That much I will do for you as you have shown yourself such a good nurse in other ways and have stayed out here far longer than many others. I think you deserve that.'

Her words were beginning to have their effect on me. I had to think of the child for once, not myself or even Costas. Suddenly, I knew it was the right thing to do. My heart leapt within me at the mere thought of home. I could face my parents and sister's disapproval but they would stand by me, I was sure of that. It was my family, my own people, whatever they might be like.

'Thank you, Matron.'

'I mean to send back May Spannock as well. She is not at all recovered from her illness and needs to go home. You came together and you will return together. A strange fate.'

Oct 8th

May and I are preparing to leave the camp and set off home. To my surprise May also seems relieved and is glad we are going together.

'I've had enough,' she said. 'This fire seems to be a symbol of it all being over for us. I long for Old Blighty, Dot. I long for my familiar surroundings again. We can meet up sometimes,' she added, 'I'm so glad we became friends.'

'You will come and stay with us at Downlands,' I said hugging her warmly, 'and be godmother to the baby.'

For, of course, May knew the real reason for my return. The others did not and were puzzled. They assumed we were being transferred to another hospital so we let them form that opinion and shrugged off any enquiries. There were many exhibitions of regret from the various good friends we had made and people came wishing us luck and a safe journey.

May's sergeant brought her a huge box of chocolates that he had bought at Floca's before the fire.

'Meant to give it you at Christmas, Nurse May,' he said looking a trifle sheepish about it.

May looked at the box as if she wanted to cry.

'How good of you,' she whispered and the Sergeant looked even more embarrassed than ever. But somehow I felt her emotion was not over him or his gift at all.

Ethan Willoughby was not so easily satisfied. I did my best to avoid him, fearing his direct look and questions but he cornered me yesterday and asked me if I would go for a brief walk with him.

'I'm – busy. Busy getting ready to go.'

'I ask for a few moments of your time, that's all.'

'All right,' I said somewhat ungraciously.

We walked out of the camp and followed the path some way before he spoke.

'I know full well that you aren't being transferred as others suppose. Why are you going home, Dorothy?'

'There are reasons, Ethan, and I can't explain. Please don't ask me.'

'Very well, I accept that ...but I have my suspicions.'

'Well then, you may keep your suspicions to yourself.'

'Don't be angry, Dorothy. I apologise. It is none of my business. But I *want* your welfare to be my business. I am glad you are going home and out of all this ...but I will miss you so much. You are my best nurse. You know I think that.'

'It's purely due to your personal regard,' I said with a little smile.

'Well, partly. But not entirely – for you *are* very good. You keep your head so well in theatre.'

'But not in the theatre of life!' I said bitterly.

'That is a quite different drama,' he said with a shrug.

'You are young,' he went on, 'and like all young women, you are romantic and have probably read too many Marie Corelli novels.'

My mind went to Costas and our wonderful moments of passion. Was this all my imagination, the product of reading foolish novels? Even Matron had almost convinced me that it was all just so much romantic nonsense. That would be the opinion of all the old fogeys who were past falling in love or so straight-laced that they had never even known love. I pulled myself together with a sudden air of determination. I was *not* that sort of girl at all. I loved Costas and would never, ever love like that again.

I had not been allowed to visit Kyria Nina though I so wanted to see her again before leaving. I think Matron feared I might desert if I saw her. However she allowed me to phone her and tell her the news. After all, she *was* going to be the child's grandparent. Nina was deeply upset but saw the sense in my going to my own home and parents and out of the terrible situation that Salonika was now in.

'I shall pack up house and go to Athens myself,' she said. 'I want to be with my son and other relations I have there. This place is cursed, I swear! But when this war is over, come back, marry Takis and we shall see our baby then,' she said. 'These are strange times but the war cannot go on forever. God bless you my child!'

Would I ever see Costas again? I had sent him the news that I was leaving for England and had no reply as yet, not a word, a telegram or anything else. It almost seemed as if Matron was right and now that he was away from me, his feelings had cooled down or altered. I refused to believe he was so dishonourable but if it was so, it was so. It didn't alter my own feelings at all.

Ethan annoyed me at this moment. I felt he had no right to act as if he had some sway over me, or interest in what I did. But this had ever been his way. He was such a possessive man.

'You really don't understand, do you, Ethan?' I replied at last.

'I don't know that I do,' he said, 'but I do know that I love you, Dorothy, and always will. I hope you can accept me as your friend, at least?'

'I do, of course I do.'

'When all this is over, and if I live through it, may I call on you at your home – as a friend?'

'We would be delighted to see you, Ethan. You *will* live through it! Don't even think such a thing. But who knows,' I added in mischief, '*I* may well return here once the war is over. '

'You may feel obliged to,' he said, taking my hand and looking at the ring on it and I knew that he had guessed the state of affairs in that uncanny manner of his but didn't seem to be at all judgemental about it. I was surprised yet it was also a deep relief that he took it so. His opinion did matter to me, despite my annoyance over his paternalistic attitudes.

'No, not obliged,' I said, 'I will *want* to return.'

'How can you like it here, Dorothy?' he asked, bewildered. 'It is so uncivilised. So barren and ugly; the people unreliable, if not downright shifty. I *don't* understand, you are right.'

I looked about me at the curve of the hills rising up to the broken top of Mount Hortiach then over to the sweep of the bay down below. It was barren it is true but it held a solemn beauty of its own. The sense of vast, treeless space and mountain wilderness appealed to something in my soul. It was impossible to explain. I felt a sense of freedom when I looked upon it.

'It's ugly? When the violet coloured mists float over Mount Olympus like veils drawn by the Gods? When the light streams like gold around it at sunset? Or glitters on that Homeric deep, dark sea below us? Ethan – you spend your life in this tiny, dutiful place inside yourself where you don't see these things as I do. You don't look up at the bigger things, the larger picture. Your mind is on your work, your ability to deal with all the minutiae of surgery and that is how it is and should be. You need to be like that or you wouldn't be so brilliant a surgeon. But I see the vast, lonely expanses about me and revel in them. That's why we are so different and fail to understand one another.'

He fell silent at this and his gaze followed the outflung sweep of my hand that embraced the view I was describing.

'You are right, Dorothy,' he said sadly, 'my life has always been spent with my eyes down on the ground. This is why I love you …you raise your eyes up unto the Lord like the David who wrote the psalm and in turn open up my eyes to the bigger picture.'

There was no more to say and we turned back together and walked silently back to the camp.

May and I took our leave of them all the next day and left for England.

Chapter 36

October 10ᵗʰ 1917

Our passage home was on a most unpleasant, crowded train without glass in its windows and uncomfortable seats. After a tiring day's journey we arrived at the rest camp that had recently been set up at Bralo and stayed here for a night before proceeding to Itea, a small port where stores and troops came via Italy, now the only safe route left open to us. I did not dare ask if we could visit Delphi despite its being so very close though my heart yearned for the experience. There wasn't time as we had to catch the boat leaving on Friday for Taranto.

The CO at Bralo was bluff and kind to us but oozed deep disapproval of women being involved in the war effort. It reminded me of Ethan. When we had first met, he too had had this attitude and then changed his mind when he saw how useful we could be. He had admitted it many times and laughed at his own short-sightedness. Not the good Colonel though. It's just as well he didn't know half the story or he would have felt more than justified in his opinion.

There was a gramophone in the camp and they played many records all evening, ending with good old Tipperary. Dear old Bert Farrington warbled away about Piccadilly and Leicester Square and how his heart was still in Tipperary. It made me feel so incredibly sad. It was the other way round for me. *My* heart lay in Greece. As I lay in bed that night, the words from that foolish but touching song stuck in my head and went round and round for long time ...

for love has fairly drove me silly
Hoping you're the same ...

The journey to Itea was by motor lorry along a narrow and winding pass in the Parnassus mountains. Up and up we climbed to the very summit and there before us lay the blue, glittering waters of the Gulf of Corinth and the little port of Itea. The road climbed back down through olive groves and pretty little villages quite unlike Mistres, the rather squalid village near our General Hospital. The people here were wealthier and better fed. Yet, that dirty, tumbledown little village I had grown to know so well would always hold for me the sweetest memories of love. Our child was conceived in that place. The child's soul would always be in Greece because of this.

My heart was full of regret at leaving. Not only this wonderful, wild, savage and incredibly beautiful country, but more, oh, far more – the love of my life, my beloved Takis! He never sent a word to me and despite my efforts at not minding, it hurt me deeply. I said nothing of this to May but she sensed my anguish and smiled at me and kept squeezing my hand comfortingly.

October 18th

The journey was of little interest to me once we boarded ship. I recall little except sleeping on my bunk most of the time. Taranto was a pleasant city, crowded with soldiers and bustling with activity but neither May nor I were inclined to look around. We were both anxious to be on our way.

From Taranto there was a train journey to Rome and we did some sightseeing there for who can pass through the Eternal City and not take a look at the Colosseum and St. Peter's? But our hearts weren't in it. Something within both May and myself had been extinguished by all the suffering we had seen. We had become accustomed to the terrible conditions and they had taken their toll on us emotionally and physically.

Then on to Boulogne. Being on Free French soil made me realise how close I was at last to dear Richard. Where was he at this moment? If only he too was coming home with me and all this turmoil and anxiety was over! I could well imagine how terrible the daily conditions were for him and wondered if he was fighting somewhere at that very moment, shells bursting about him, rallying his men and taking them forward along some German artillery line. It didn't bear thinking on, life was so precarious and at times my heart was full of dread for his safety.

We were all aware that our men were attempting to reach some village called Passchendaele in Belgium. They were after some ridge round there but progress had been held up by terrible rainstorms and other problems that were turning the fields into quagmires. He had all my sympathy. I too knew the feeling of sinking into the mud of Salonika when the fine summer dust turned to a thick clogging mass. But where he has had a wilderness of ruined fields and the mangled stumps of trees to gaze on, we had the view of the magnificent Mount Olympus clothed in all weathers and shining like a beacon of hope.

Now that we were nearly there I wanted to be home with my family, in my own little room at Downlands, away from everyone's gaze. A dark depression was seizing me in its grip very fast and I had to battle hard not to give in to it. If only Costas had written to me or got a cable to me, anything, anything but this terrible silence on his part.

October 21ˢᵗ

At last we were standing on the platform of Waterloo station. It felt the strangest thing in the world to be there; such a sense of safety and familiarity. May and I looked around the crush of people, searching for familiar faces. May spied her parents and gave a yell and jumped up and down like a little girl, waving frantically. They elbowed their way through the throng towards us.

'Oh Ma, how marvellous to see you …Pa, give me a kiss!'

The three of them were cemented firmly in a big hug. I was so glad to see her look so happy.

'Ma, Pa – this is my dear friend Dorothy, I told you about.'

She introduced us. Her parents were two very pleasant looking people with gentle and friendly faces. They shook hands with me and exchanged pleasantries but as I smiled and spoke I kept glancing about looking for my own Papa.

I spotted him as he fought his way towards me. It is indescribable that feeling of seeing a face so familiar, so comfortable, so dear to one! I felt a little child again. Papa would take care of me. I kept my wits about me as best I could for I wanted to shout for joy. We hugged one another for a long time.

'My little girl!'

Papa looked at me quizzically and patting my cheek, added, 'My dear, you are so thin! What happened to my plump, pretty little girl? '

May's parents declared that they too were shocked to see how thin we had both become.

'Well, you've lost weight too, Pa,' May declared, playfully prodding her father's stomach.

'That's what comes of living on less food,' he said ruefully, 'very good for the figure.'

We said our goodbyes and fervently promised to meet up again as soon as we could. Papa and I then set off in the familiar old brougham.

Homeward bound.

Downlands.

I held Papa's hand, looking at him speechless with relief and joy. Tears of emotion welled up in his eyes too. He kept shaking his head as if in disbelief that I was actually there with him, at last.

'My little Dot,' he murmured every now and then.

I gave a deep sigh and relaxed back onto the seat. It was good to look out at green fields instead of bare slopes. Good to see the trees again, trees still clinging to their autumn colours. A fine rain formed strands of mist over the landscape and turned it to a gentle haze. This was a peaceful, gentle countryside, mournful perhaps but soothing after the flies, ants, mosquitoes, heat, fierce winds, fires, floods …all the drama that was Macedonia.

'You'll have plenty to tell us but first you need a long peaceful rest after all that travelling,' Papa said.

'I'm *so* glad to be home, Papa,' I said.

October 22nd

It took some time for me to realise that I was in my own little room at Downlands this morning. It all felt so strange. The house seemed somehow smaller. I was so unused to being indoors in an English house. I snuggled gratefully into the comfort of my bed listening to the homely sounds of people up and about downstairs. Sara was still with us and also Rose the cook so we hadn't been entirely deserted. I would go down to a real English breakfast though there would be no butter or sugar but who minded little things like that after all the deprivations I had been through?

How far away Macedonia now seemed! It was hard to relax in all this ease while my comrades were still over there, coping with the flies and the winds and all the other discomforts of camp life. I missed them sorely.

For today I decided to unwind and just enjoy being home. I spent the day walking about the house and grounds, enjoying the familiar sights, the nooks and crannies that held those special memories of childhood and early youth. Then I took a walk down to the village and Cottersley farm. It all looked so still and quiet. Life appears to be much as before except for the sight of strapping, rosy-cheeked young women working about the farmyard. They don't look familiar but I suppose they are local lasses.

That evening after dinner we all sat in the parlour, Mother, Father and myself. Agnes and Henry had come along with their little boy Reggie. It wanted but Richard and then one could pretend that nothing had happened and there was no war or unpleasantness anywhere. A huge fire had been lit especially for me. The logs roaring and crackling were a beautiful sight though they reminded me of the fire I had witnessed. It made me shiver suddenly.

'What is it, my dear?' asked Papa. 'You still feel the cold? You *have* come from a far hotter country.'

'It's not the cold so much – believe me, it will be far, far colder than any English winter in another month. It just makes me think of that awful night of fire at Salonika. I and an officer were literally in the middle of it all.'

I went on to tell them about it and they listened with deep interest.

'It sounds terrible, my dear, so risky! I still cannot imagine what possessed you to go there at all. So far away from home. You young people today are a mystery to me,' said Mother shaking her head in disbelief.

'I must say, rather you than me,' Agnes agreed, 'but you were lucky, I suppose, going to an easy posting rather than the kind of thing the fellows have had to put up with in France. You *asked* to go there, of course.'

I was stung by these remarks, implying as they did that I had specifically chosen an '*easy*' posting. Easy indeed!

'Agnes, you are talking utter rot as usual,' I said angrily. 'You have no idea at all over here what things are like in Macedonia. What's going on, don't you people ever read the papers?'

'They say very little about the Salonika Campaign,' said Papa. 'The general impression is that nothing is happening and it's all just a sideshow, the men are just enjoying themselves.'

'I can't believe that's what they're saying!' I was so indignant that I turned a vivid red and felt my heart jump. Everyone looked at me in silence.

'You have no idea then,' I repeated, 'no idea, no knowledge of the fact that men are dying of malaria, dysentery, fever and that these men will return home broken and unwell for the rest of their lives? They may not be so many casualties from shrapnel and mortar wounds though, believe me, many men *have* been wounded, especially in the attack on Doiran in the Spring. They are sitting targets, the Bulgarians hold the hills on high and look down on our men and laugh at them. Sitting targets! They have to be entrenched for months, nothing can be done in the height of summer for it is too hot and too malarial. The men up the line have had no leave. They cannot come home or go to have fun in Paris as the men do from France. They have what little is on offer in Salonika, and even that has been burnt down now. They are out in that hot or icy howling wilderness where the wind blows so hard it goes through the bones. One's feet are frozen …people die of cold in the winter.'

I paused for breath and almost wept with rage.

'Do you know how hard we all work some days? How a man like Captain Willoughby has had to work from dawn to dusk dealing with not just our own men but also the Greeks civilians, the Serbs and many others? Ethan is unwell himself and oughtn't even to be in active service but they are taking all our doctors away to the Western front right up to the age of 56. So we are left with the older chaps or else unfit men like Ethan. But that doesn't stop him or any of them giving their all. I won't have it said that that is an *easy* posting – I *won't* have it said!'

They all stared at the floor after my outburst and looked embarrassed. It was not our habit in this family to be so impassioned but I could hardly help it. It wounded me deeply to think that this was the general attitude. It is all very well dying for your country but not for a country that refuses to recognise your valour.

'My dearest Dot,' said Papa after a while, 'it is just as well you are here and can tell people these things. You scarcely mentioned any of all this in your letters so cannot blame us for supposing things were a lot easier. Mama was glad of the fact. But now it seems you have been worked far harder than we imagined.'

'I don't complain, papa. Not for myself. I loved the work and I loved the people and I still wish I was there. I wanted to give my all, my life even, if it came to it. Other nurses have died there of malaria and pneumonia. I have been so lucky health-wise – thanks to Mama's strict regime,' I added with a little laugh. They all laughed with me and the tension lifted.

'My feeling is,' said Papa wisely, 'that little is said about this campaign because we want to keep the Bosch guessing a bit. Perhaps some major offensive is being planned now the Greeks have at last joined the Allies. Our men are keeping the Austrians and Bulgarians busy and that means less available troops for the Central Powers. Don't worry, Dot, the Salonika Expedition will get its recognition in time, when it is all over and the full story is told. At present we are all as much in the dark about what is happening as are the enemy. At least I hope that they are.'

'That makes sense,' I said mollified.

'Now,' said Mother, after a brief pause during which Sara brought us in some coffee, 'we would like to know a little more about this young man you say you are engaged to.'

'Can't we leave it for tonight, Mother?' said Pa. 'Let the poor child rest a little.

'It's all right, I had better get it all over and done with, I suppose,' I said, putting my cup down with a sigh.

Where to begin? I knew I couldn't tell them the full story of how Costas and I had met. Mother would be horrified and Father alarmed at my foolhardiness. No, that would have to remain my secret forever. It was my own splendid story, an exciting and romantic tale that belonged to Costas and myself alone. No one would ever know about it. So I stuck to the fact that we had met at the hospital and then later in town and how I then met his mother and got to know Costas better. While sticking to the truth, I nevertheless drew veils around the reality.

'But you hardly know this man, Dorothy. He is a foreigner.'

'I do know him, Ma; he's the man I love.'

Mother sniffed loudly to indicate what she thought of that. 'Does he come from a decent family?

'A *very* good family. And wealthy too,' I smiled.

I showed them my only photo of Costas and told them some of Kyria Nina's tales about Constantinople. Despite herself and her utter disapproval, Mother looked interested. Agnes, of course, looked unimpressed. Henry was one of the local gentry so she felt herself vastly superior. There has never been much love lost between my elder sister and myself. She rose after a while and said she was going to put Reggie to bed and then retire herself.

'Come on Henry,' she said in her no nonsense manner. Henry, who never liked our company much and always did as he was told, followed her out of the room.

I was glad of this and when I had my parents to myself, said quietly, 'I have something else to tell you, my darlings. I know you won't be happy about it.'

'Well, what is it?' asked Mother sharply.

I hesitated. It was such a difficult thing to say and I looked at them both knowing that things would never be the same once these words were uttered.

'I am expecting Costas child …in another five months. That is the reason I had to come home.'

My parents looked at me stunned and silent.

I looked back at them defiantly. I no longer felt shame. It had happened and everyone was going to have to put up with it.

October 27th

It has been hard to bear my mother's cold attitude.

'You have always been a disappointment to me, Dorothy,' she said after my announcement and rising, walked out of the room. She almost refuses to speak to me. Thankfully, Papa is his old self and treats me with love and understanding. I am more than glad he is not the typical *paterfamilias*.

I assured him that I meant to return to Salonika after the war and that I would live with Kyria Nina till Costas and I married. Yet in my heart, I wondered whether this was just a hopeless dream of mine without basis in reality. I didn't dare tell father this but he sensed I was not happy.

However, this morning all my terrible desolation and doubt has been dispelled. I have received a letter from Costas!

Ma Cheri, where are you now? I send this to your English home – I think I have the right address – hoping it will reach you. I was devastated by your news, the news that you were abandoning me and running away from me

I was running away from him! Was he mad?

When I read your letter I went straight to my CO and asked if I could have some leave to return to Salonika on urgent business. He wasn't too pleased but eventually said I could have three days. So I took the train and arrived at Salonika, rode straight to your camp and when I got there I met your long faced Doctor friend ...'

Ethan! How did Ethan always seem to be around when Costas was there! These two seemed to have some peculiar connection that drew them constantly together. Their feelings for me? ... perhaps, my feelings for them? I cared for Ethan greatly. The three of us seemed twined in a strange and inexplicable love knot.

...and he told me you had left two days earlier for Itea from which port you were to sail to Italy. He said it was a new route because of all the U-boats. If only you had come via Athens, we could at least have met before you sailed. It was too late for me to travel to Itea. I had to be back in Athens. It was too late. I missed you and now I feel fearful that once in England you will never want to come back to me again.'

Takis, how could you believe such a thing!

His letter made me so happy that I sat down and wept and wept. It was a release of so much pain and distress in the soul. He loved me after all. He had not abandoned me. Thank God for that! I picked up a pen and immediately wrote a reply to him in Athens.

In the innermost depths of my heart though, I wondered why he hadn't come to me when I first told him I was expecting a child. If we had married, I could have returned to Athens with him and all would have been well. Or would it?

November 1st

Perhaps the blackest day of my life. By some strange coincidence this is the last page of my Black Journal. Fittingly it began with Eleni's death and it ends with Richard's.

Is life worth living now he is gone? My bright and beautiful brother. My brave, brave brother. Lost in the mud of Passchendaele.

Nothing else to say.

PART TWO
ANDREW'S ODYSSEY

Chapter 1

September 1936

He had bided his time. And in that time he had made careful preparations. His mother might well want him to go up to Oxford next year but he had other ideas. Andrew had made up his mind that having finished at Somerfield College, he was going to cast forth into the world and set off on his own personal Odyssey. He was going to Greece to find his roots.

Since he had read his mother's diary Andrew had been a changed being. No one understood why because it was his own dark secret. Now he too had a hidden knowledge to equal that of his mother. He had entered her heart and soul and she didn't even realise it. Every time he looked at her smiling and talking he relished it. When her eyes took on that faraway look, he knew very well on what inner landscape they were gazing. She had no more secrets from him now! Whenever she came to Downlands, slipped off to the sweet privacy of her room and shut her door, he in his mind was reading her diaries with her, living her love affair with his father. It was a delightful and yet terrifying thing, like a sacred and mysterious violation. It didn't give him happiness but ate at his peace of mind. He became thinner and thinner; his face was gaunt for one so young.

His grandmother and mother worried about him and he was fiercely glad of it. Now they cared! This was the result of their good work. And somewhere in their deepest soul they knew it too. They knew what was eating him up.

Andrew had studied Greek history avidly. He tried to

understand the complex politics and the characters involved in all the recent coups and counter coups. He had purchased a map of Greece and a Greek dictionary and had learnt hundreds of words. This, coupled with the Ancient Greek he had taken up at school, gave him at least a rudimentary knowledge of the language and the country he had never seen but which sang fiercely in his blood and called to him from across the sea. He also spoke French, Italian and German fluently. Persevering at languages had been his major obsession and his tutors felt he could make a career in the Foreign Office if he wanted.

Ethan, not surprisingly, advised him to go in for medicine. His mother wanted him to study law. Well, they could forget all of that. A career was not what he cared about. His whole being was consumed with but one desire. That desire was to return to his homeland, to Greece, to search for his remaining relations and to see the place where he had come to being. He yearned above all to find that very spot, that very bed in which his parents had conceived him all those years ago.

Leaving Somerfield had been the happiest moment of his life. Now he was a young adult, free to do pretty much as he wished. He had achieved good results for he loved to study and work hard and being a loner, had devoted his time to this end. The comments and remarks of his peers at school who called him 'swot', 'paleface', 'bookworm' fell on deaf ears. In the end, his total absorption and an air of a person who is not quite in this world of men, silenced them. They couldn't make him out at all. His intensity was un-natural and even his masters told him that he should get out more often on the rugby field, take some fresh air. But those game-playing days were over. He had a view in end. He worked towards it like a person possessed.

After the last handshake, the last goodbye, Andrew left school life and his boyhood far behind him. The fact was that he had left it behind at the age of fourteen and had simply suffered being with these children, as he saw them, until he could escape. His initiation into manhood had been the rape of his mother's soul.

Returning to Downlands where he could be guaranteed some peace and quiet, Andrew began to sort out the details of his Great Plan. He had been saving his small allowance and had a few hundred pounds in his bank account. He needed to get a passport. For this he would have to obtain his birth certificate, which was still in his mother's possession. He could write to Somerset House for a copy but felt that he preferred to ask his mother for it. It was time to let her know his plans before she started telling him what *she* wanted him to do.

Dorothy had asked her son to come to their London home to visit them so they could discuss what was to be his future. He felt a grim sense of pleasure in knowing that he would confound them all with his plans. It would create a regular bombshell and he felt sure he would get little support but braced himself for the encounter.

Ethan had driven up to collect him from Paddington Station and the two chatted amiably on the way back. They got on well together. In fact, Andrew's liking for Ethan had increased after reading about him in his mother's diary. He was a good fellow, one to respect and admire and his advice was generally sound. Naturally Ethan wanted him to be a doctor. Medicine was the man's vocation in life. However, being a doctor had never been Andrew's calling. He wasn't sure what his calling was or what he would do when he got to Greece but he was determined to stay and work there in some way or simply travel about doing odd jobs wherever he found them. His desire to enter the army had ebbed away long ago. Soldiers were just cannon-fodder; it was not all bravery and glamour at all. Anyway, what was the point of being a soldier in peacetime?

All the same, the world was large and exciting. His own life might be short for all he knew and he wanted the exciting adventures his parents had had. Things were unstable abroad, everyone knew that but Andrew was young and this didn't bother him. The world was always unstable as far as he could see. There was Communism rife in many areas; everyone was terrified that the Chinese would fall for this rampant ideology and that, coupled with the Soviet States, they would become an overwhelming force against the West. Some felt that Fascism might be the answer for keeping the Communists at bay in Europe but no one was quite sure what Hitler and his party were really up to. Was Hitler a good thing or a bad thing?

Andrew knew that Dorothy was against Hitler with all her heart, troubled by his anti-Semitic attitudes.

'How can people have such fanatical attitudes towards other members of the human race?' she would say in despair, as she read various accounts of the persecution of Jews that were taking place in Germany.

'It's a strange thing,' Ethan said, 'that it was the Jews who began the cult of the 'scapegoat', putting all their sins and darkness upon a sacrificial goat and then driving the beast out into the desert to die. They hoped that by doing this they would cleanse themselves of all their sins. Now this concept is turned against them and they have become perpetual scapegoats, driven out of this place, that place. They have become the Wandering Jew.'

The Wandering Jew! These words sent shivers up Andrew's spine. They had the sound of wily, restless, rootless Odysseus about them and resonated in his deepest being. Jewish journeying to what end? ...to find their Promised Land. And what would happen when they did find it? What happened to Odysseus when he came to Ithaca...surely such a searching, uneasy, questing human being could never be satisfied with the final goal? Was it the journey that mattered or the end result? Andrew sympathised with the Jewish race and knew why his mother did so, though for different reasons to his own.

That January, George the Fifth had died, and his son Edward was now King. King Edward seemed a caring man, his face constantly troubled and furrowed with lines, as if the mantle of Kingship was a very heavy burden for his shoulders. One had the feeling he was always trying to shake it off. His rounds of Europe still had the playboy feel of his younger days as Prince of Wales. Yet, when he visited the miners in Wales or went to other deprived areas he looked as if he really understood and cared about the grinding poverty and lack of work. England had become so unutterably dreary and depressing. Poverty and despair seemed to be everywhere.

'Was this what we fought for?' Ethan would say at times, 'this madness! Now we've got civil war in Spain, nasty clashes in London with that bunch of thugs, the Mosleyites. Then that dreadful chap Hitler spouting off his bombastic stuff in Germany. There'll be another war, you mark my words!'

'Please, Ethan, don't say that!' Dorothy replied with a shiver whenever he said this, 'darling, don't be so despondent all the time. There can't be another war. Surely reason will prevail.'

'War is not about reason, my dear, when did reason ever prevail in human affairs? It's about emotions, about greed, power, humiliation. The Germans felt humiliated and what I'm saying is they are out for revenge. They want European blood on their altars as well as Jewish scapegoats. Their God is a dark one. He wants blood. He hasn't had enough of it in the Great War it seems but is thirsty for more.'

'For goodness sakes, Ethan – how you talk! You'll alarm the children.'

Ethan shrugged angrily. Like all men of his age, he was disgusted by the prospect of another war.

Andrew listened to all this talk with avidity. What if there *was* another war? The idea both fascinated and horrified him. It probably wouldn't affect him in Greece though and Greece was where he was heading for.

He decided to take the plunge at once and speak to his mother that very night.

'Mother,' he said going up to her after dinner. She was seated on her own in the parlour, the youngsters now in bed, 'I would like to have my birth certificate.'

Dorothy put down the newspaper, took off her glasses and looked at her son with a puzzled air.

He was so like his father. The thought came to her unbidden and, for some reason, she felt a sudden wave of anxiety. Something in her elder son's face made her feel afraid. He was like a grown man at eighteen. His eyes were not that of a young fellow at all. It had been impossible to reach into him this last few years. On the surface he had been as attentive and courteous as before. Yet she sensed that something had changed in his attitude towards her and had no idea why. Standing before her, looking at her with those hard, penetrating, piercing eyes, so like those of Costas, her son felt distant, a million miles away from her, as if a great barrier had come between them.

'It's in the iron box upstairs,' she said, 'I'll find it some time if you want it.'

'I want it now, mother.'

Should she tell him a little about his father, she pondered? It was time, of course, but she was so afraid of his reactions. Why stir the boy up now? Let him get his degree, settle his life, find a nice girl and marry and then all would be well. She put the idea out of her head as she had done a thousand times before.

'What do you it need for?'

'A passport.'

Dorothy fell silent, her eyes studied a patch on the carpet and her face slowly drained of colour as if she would faint. Andrew looked at her without love or pity. He knew that what he had to say would undermine her totally but that didn't trouble him any more.

'I intend to go to Greece.'

'I knew it!' burst out Dorothy, her hand to her heart in anguish. 'And what good will it do you? You're an Englishman now.'

'No, mother, I am not an Englishman. I don't even know if I am a Greek. But I need to discover what being a Greek means to me. Can't you understand that?'

'When do you plan to go?'

'Next month if possible.'

'Next month! But what of your education? Your exams for Oxford?'

'Mother, I am not going to go to Oxford. I don't want it; I don't care about it. A career is not what I am searching for.'

'I understand you might want to go there – to see Greece. But why now, why not gain all your education first of all and then go? Doesn't that make sense? You are young now and headstrong – just like I was, I'm afraid to say. Oh, Andrew!' she burst out, 'don't do this. God, I think I understand my mother's feelings better now than I ever did then.'

'Yes, you *were* headstrong and wilful, Grandma said so. And I *am* your son. I will go and nothing you say will stop me. Look what adventures you had! I need to go there and find what I can out about my father, find my grandmother and my aunt.'

Had she ever mentioned Nina and Christoula to him? He often came out with odd little comments as if he knew her better than she knew herself. Dorothy was unsure. His certainty and air of knowledge un-nerved her. It is as if he could reach into her very entrails and was going to pull them violently forth, gutting her whole existence.

'And how will you find them? No-one knows where they live anymore,' she said despairingly.

'I'll start with the addresses I've got.'

'What addresses have you got?'

'The ones I found,' was his calm reply.

'Where did you find them?'

'In your precious box, Mother. In your wooden box.'

Dorothy rose to her feet, dropping her glasses on the floor. She clutched the chairback as if to steady herself and stared at her son in stupefaction.

'Are you saying …are you telling me that you have opened up the box in my room at Downlands?

'Yes, Mother.'

Andrew's stoicism flinched in the scream of distress and rage that came forth from his mother's throat. It was like the cry of some animal in extreme pain.

'You wicked boy …you wicked boy! How dare you!'

She flew at him and smacked him hard across the face.

'You wicked boy!' she repeated and burst into tears.

Ethan came running into the room, alarmed at these un-natural sounds.

There stood Andrew with a red weal across his face looking defiant and stony, Dorothy sobbing as if her heart would break.

She sobbed in such anguish that Ethan was afraid she might have a heart attack.

'What the devil's going on?' He took his wife by the shoulders and she tried at first to push him away. Ethan held her tightly and let her cry on his breast until at last she had spent herself and clung to him like a drowning person.

'What is it, Andrew …what's happened?'

'I've told mother that I am going to Greece and won't go up to Oxford,' said the young man rubbing his cheek but still with that air of sullen defiance that Ethan had never seen in him before.

'For God's sake, Dorothy! Is that all? Why are you taking on so?'

'It's not just that,' she burst out afresh, 'he has been prying and spying on his own mother, reading my private things … things I had locked up that were for my eyes only. What right had he to do that, the sneaking, disgusting boy? What sort of boy have I brought into this world?'

'Is this true, Andrew?'

'Yes sir, it is true. I found her diaries and I read them ages ago. I don't deny it and I don't apologise either. I was driven to it. I had to understand about my father and what he was and how he died and where. Mother has never told me a single thing. I knew nothing. I *look* foreign, don't I? And people, yes even you, have always treated me as a misfit. I am not one of you. I belong nowhere. I want …I *must* find where I belong!'

Ethan led Dorothy to her chair and made her sit down.

'Sit down, Andrew, let's discuss this whole business.'

'I'm not discussing anything!' said Dorothy enraged.

'Dot, be quiet. You must listen to the boy. You owe him that, at least. Why on earth have you never spoken to him about his father?'

Dorothy put her hand to her mouth and tears again welled up in her eyes. She had never been a weeping type but it was as if a lid had been taken from a bottomless well deep down inside her that was now spewing forth water in a boiling, bubbling torrent that could not be stopped or prevented. It was the secret hidden well of all those years of feeling, sadness, grief and loss, impossible to contain any longer. Her son had released something but that something was too painful, too awful to contemplate. It seemed to make her whole life meaningless now. It was ridiculous and she knew it and knew too how much she had wronged her son. Yet, like him too she felt no pity or compassion, ensnared as she was in her own pain and sorrow.

'I want him to leave the house. I don't want him here at all.'

'Dot, Dot – come on, this is your son, your boy. He's acted badly but you *must* see things from his viewpoint.'

Andrew was astonished that Ethan was taking his part and felt a sense of some comfort from this. He might look as if he had hardened like steel but his mother's tears touched a raw nerve in his heart. He had so adored her when he was a child. He stifled the feelings at once. He had to hate her or he would not be able to function. It was too late now anyway. She would never forgive him for his sin. He knew that. But then neither did he forgive her.

Dorothy arose and left the room without a backward glance.

'Take him back to the station, I don't want him here!' she repeated as she went out.

Ethan looked at Andrew who had turned a deathly white now. His compassionate heart melted at the sight of the boy. Poor, unhappy lad! How right he was, he belonged nowhere and now his own mother wanted to turn him out of her life. Ethan knew she was in the wrong but what could he do?

'Andrew, you have behaved pretty dishonourably. You should have challenged your mother, made her tell you what you needed to know, not read her private papers.'

'I tried!' the young man burst out. 'I tried so hard to ask her and speak to her but she has never let me speak. She never truly listened to me, or what I needed. It is as if I have existed only as a part of herself and her own past and have never had a mind or heart or feelings of my own. I have existed for *her* to live not her for me to live.

Ethan felt his own heart constrict and remained silent for a moment.

'It might have been better then if you had spoken to me. Perhaps I could have helped you, told you a few things.'

'You are her husband,' Andrew said almost accusingly, 'I couldn't ask you. I didn't know how.'

'You didn't know how? I have tried to be a father to you, Andrew.'

'Yes, sir – and don't think I'm not grateful. I am. You have been kind, very kind but . . .'

'But I'm not your father.'

'No, sir.'

'Yet, I did know your father.'

'Sir, tell me about him now,' pleaded Andrew, 'was he a good man?'

'He was a very honourable man and by all accounts a brave soldier.'

'What do you know of his death?

'Sit down, Andrew, sit down by the fire and I'll give you some idea of it all,' said Ethan.

Chapter 2

Ethan took out his pipe and lit it up. For a few moments he puffed at it and his eyes had a speculative, far away look about them. Andrew sat in the armchair his mother had just vacated and stared into the fire. Ethan began his tale:

'The Greeks had joined the Allies by 1918 and were forming their own divisions. Your father, who had previously been involved with Military Intelligence, wanted to fight in battle and was promoted to the rank of a Major in the Serres Division. The Italians and Russians and, of course, the Serbs, had joined the French and British by then, so things were looking a bit better.'

'The situation was like this. There were Germans, Austrians, Turks and Bulgarians all ranged against us on the frontiers of Serbia, Greece and Bulgaria. The Bulgarian army still held the mountain ranges over Doiran and the important Rupel Pass. We all knew that we needed Bulgaria to fall for then Austria and Turkey would also capitulate ...it was all rather like a line of dominoes ...one falls over and knocks out the other. The Germans always had the manpower to kick us out of the Balkans if they had wanted to but at this point in autumn 1918 they'd had losses in the West and didn't have enough manpower available to help out Bulgaria. As for the Bulgars they were fed up with years of Balkan wars and content to sit on their backsides along the mountain ridges, looking down on us and laughing their heads off at what seemed to them to be our feeble manoeuvres to dislodge them. 'Come on, Johnny,' they used to yell at us, 'Come on, you goddam bastards!'

'They were fine, dry, comfy and well fed up there in their

trenches. We were ill-fed, depleted and made weak by disease and the long, boring wait for action which always gets on a soldier's nerves. It was necessary to wait for the right moment to strike at them and that moment came in September 1918.'

'We only had four divisions by this time; some of the others had gone off to Palestine and other places. The Greeks, when they joined us, took over the Struma Valley and we pushed on up the Vardar river. Here our men held their own despite the awful difficulties of the situation. The odd thing is the Germans never took our forces in Salonika very seriously. I think they really thought they were keeping us nicely out of the way in our 'Birdcage' and that we were of no importance in the theatre of war at all. And that was their big mistake. At any time they could easily have sent us into the sea as they always mockingly threatened they would. They had the ease of supplies overland and the guns and manpower. We had to bring everything, and I mean everything, by a slow, dangerous and difficult sea route.'

'People think now that the Bulgarians simply didn't *want* to push on into Salonika ...they knew the Germans would never give it to them but to Turkey if they got it and they would lose their men by the thousands for nothing. The Allies were hardly going to let it go without a damned, good fight. They knew that too darned well and didn't want to risk it. Plus the Germans kept hoping that Constantine would get us from the back and we would be caught in the middle of two hostile forces ...and believe me for a long time it was just like that. We could never be sure of the Greek intent at all. Not till Venizelos won the day and swung the whole thing round.'

'Your father worked for Venizelos as I expect you know, and he also helped our own Military Police to catch spies. The place was crawling with them at first till General Sarrail put his foot down about it and put the city under martial law. As the country was supposedly neutral we still had the Bulgarian and German Embassies in Salonika having a field day passing on the info to their friends in Athens. But thanks to those early German aerial bombardments over Salonika – which showed that the country wasn't the least bit neutral! – Sarrail was able to load all the

Embassy staff on a ship along with their families and chase the beggars out. Yet still spies stood openly in the cafes of the Place de la Liberte and conducted their business!

'Well, it was easy for Costas to mingle with them. He was a master at disguise and knew all the Macedonian dialects and languages. He helped us greatly at the time, we discovered later. We caught a lot of the beggars thanks to his tip off and advice. I don't think your mother knew about all this. She really knew very little about him.'

'But to go back to the war. The Germans were mad not to try and take the Balkans. It would have really strengthened their hand. People over here took a long time to appreciate that the Salonika Campaign was the keystone to the war. Knock out the Bulgarians and all the German Allies would fall and only that way would Germany itself surrender. The whole edifice would crumble. And that's what happened.'

'There was an idea here at the time that the Balkan Army just wasn't fighting at all. If they had fought all the time, as they did in France, well, there simply wouldn't have been an army left. No one here understood the difficulty of the terrain in Macedonia. The trenches were just as awful as those in France, the weather as inhospitable. Our men sat under the scowling slopes of Pip Ridge and the Grand Couronne, entrenched in solid rock or on the tops of hot, dry barren hills, battered by shells, mortars, snipers, barrages and all the rest of it. Life was hardly cosy.'

'You have to go and see this place, the Doiran front, to understand that the hills our armies hoped to scale and capture were well nigh impassable, worse than any others, even those in the Dardanelles. They were sheer, bare, rocky and rolled along in a series of undulations for miles. Not a tree in sight. Nothing. Up on the Grand Couronne was an iron and concrete look out post, which we used to call the Evil Eye. There sat the Bulgars with their superior guns, overlooking our armies and able to blast out of existence anything that tried to climb up to them. Below was the Jumeaux Ravine – an awful, evil place – the very name makes me shudder, so many of our men died there. It must have been like hell itself when the huge shells exploded in that place. God, it must have been like hell!'

Ethan paused for a moment and his eyes clouded over as he recalled the men he had tried to save all those years ago, men long dead, long gone. Such heroic deeds and wonderful men! Andrew felt his own heart constrict as he watched him grieving.

'You never forget it,' Ethan said, 'you never forget it all, Andrew. Thank God we didn't really understand just how strong the Bulgar positions were until we had defeated them or we'd never have had the nerve to attack them. But attack them we did.'

'We had by now the nine Greek divisions coming into line. Your father's men came with the Serres divisions and they joined our boys in front of Doiran. By apparently concentrating here, we deceived the enemy who never suspected that our real target was to be on the Moglenitza range in Serbia. By now all the Allies were yearning to move in on the kill and we had those Bulgarians worried, I can tell you! They weren't at all sure what we were up to, where the attack would come from.'

'It was a beautiful day on the 18th of September but by noon it was a 100 degrees and no shade. That was nothing. The place they say looked lovelier than usual for there was this strange, barren beauty about these hills with their vivid blue skies and glorious sunsets. On that fine morning the guns were already blazing by 5 am and into that inferno of smoke, dust and flame went our men accompanied by the Greeks, all knowing damned well that they were going to die. Our men were the lambs to the slaughter. Their role was to hold the enemy here while the French and Serbs did their bit further up the line where they were least expected.'

'The Greeks went down to the lake; we were to push up over the hills and by God we really hammered those Bulgarian positions! The problem was the enemy could see everything that we were doing; even at night it was clear and visible. We set up smoke barrages, which helped. Our men were driven back along with the Greeks but still the Welsh Fusiliers went charging on, their Celtic blood was up, by God! –on to attack the slopes of a

270

hill they called 'The Feather'. Some Greeks joined them on their way up and stayed with them. As far as I know, your father was said to be among them. The smoke and dust cloud had so far hidden them from the enemy but quite suddenly it lifted and our men were in full view. They were only 250 yards from the summit. Despite the machine gun fire mowing them down left and right, these brave and exhausted men who had just clambered up those steep hills, rushed the enemy trenches where the enemy had been sitting doing nothing but keep a look out. These brave, brave men …Greeks and Welshmen …reached the summit only to fall there and be slaughtered. From these men only eighteen unwounded men and one officer managed to return. They were as brave if not braver than the men at Balaclava but who will ever recognise the deeds of those brave Welsh and Greek men that day? No Tennyson to sing their song.'

'I will recognise them!' said Andrew, fired by all these tales. 'I will recognise those men and my father too! I will find out more and write about them. If only I had known all this before.'

'Your mother wouldn't have known all this. You should have come to me, Andrew – or I suppose I should have come to you. You were far too young at first and then after all, it didn't seem my business to talk about it to you. The main stumbling block is the fact is we didn't *want* to talk about the war afterwards. It was all too dreadful. We wanted to forget and come back to normal existence. But there's no such thing. Everything has changed, everything is different. Men who have seen such sights can never be the same again. Looking on Hell changes you. Changed the women too. Your mother saw the results of the previous battles and knows what it was like out there. What a brave and wonderful woman she was, your mother! She too has changed from that strong, young nurse I first met out there. You must forgive her, Andrew …she has changed too.'

Andrew knew nothing about forgiveness. His heart was fired up with the tales of war.

'The sacrifice wasn't in vain, though?'

'Of course not. The next day the Scots took the place of the Welsh and they did manage to capture Sugar Loaf and the

Tongue. The Greeks got the Orb and the Hilt and consolidated their positions despite the counter attacks from the Bulgarians. Eventually though the Scots had to leave their positions and though about fifty per cent of the men managed to get out of it, the Highlanders were stuck and pretty well decimated … seventy-five percent of their men mown down. But believe me, those Bulgarians had some heavy losses too. They fought like savages themselves.'

'They say that the dead men made a track up the hill and the ridge was strewn with bodies. Our armies had cut off the Bulgarians to some extent so their men had been four days without food, which they didn't like a lot. Yet, it seemed that we had gained so little, lost so many men and the chaps were exhausted and wondered if they had failed after such a long wait for action. You can imagine their feelings when they counted the loss of all those comrades in arms. The Serbs meanwhile pushed on into their own country with a fury borne of hatred and cut off the communication lines of the Bulgarians. Our planes kept up a hammering too and eventually the impossible happened. The enemy was at last in retreat, abandoning those stony heights they had held for so long. Our men failed? Never! It was their ultimate sacrifice that had helped the Serbs to move on almost unhindered. But what a sacrifice …' His voice trailed off.

'And my father lies amongst them. I will never see or know him,' said Andrew sadly. 'Was his body ever found?'

'I don't think so, I don't really know. Men were blown to bits and many were not found. He never returned so he was reported as missing in action.'

'Yes, I know. I suppose I just hoped there would be a grave I could visit.'

'You really mean to go to Greece?'

'I do. I need my birth certificate but I know Mother won't give it to me now.'

'She will. I shall ask her to do so. You will stay tonight, whether she likes it or not. Perhaps by the morning she will have calmed down and be more approachable.'

But Dorothy was not more approachable. She handed over the

documents Andrew needed but said not a word to him. He *did* feel her anger; it would be a lie to say he did not. He felt it keenly but there was nothing to be done. Nothing could be changed.

When Ethan dropped him off at the railway station, he handed Andrew a large roll of notes.

'Take this cash, it might be handy.'

'Sir, I can't take this!'

'Of course you can, and will. Don't be a proud Greek. I am the only father you have now. Let me help you a little. Keep in touch with me at my club if your mother refuses to write. She's always been headstrong but time will heal it all, I feel sure. She isn't a person to hold a grudge.'

Andrew shook Ethan's hand and accepted the cash. What a good man he was. Andrew felt a deep gratitude that Ethan took him seriously and was treating him like a man and not a child.

As if reading his thoughts, Ethan said, 'I'm on your side, Andrew. A man has to find his way in life. He can't hang on to women. They would keep us forever like sons, like little boys. My mother was just the same, she hated my wanting to be an Army Surgeon. They don't want us to grow up, fight, make love, get into the thick of life's battles. They want us to be soft, tame and domesticated. Men are still wild animals at heart, Andrew, remember that, but in equal proportion to their wildness they are also noble and brave when the occasion calls for it. Have courage and find what it is you seek.'

After a few days, Dorothy began to regain her composure a little. She considered herself to be a reasonable person who seldom allowed her anger to run away with her. It came quickly; it went quickly. Plus her nature was forgiving and gentle. She couldn't bear to think that the love her son had once had for her had in some way been destroyed and that her own actions had been the cause of it. It was true that her son had invaded her deepest heart. He had forced to rise to the surface matters that she had kept locked away even from herself. Her immediate feeling was to rush to Downlands and take the wooden box with all its contents and burn it in the garden.

She knew she had to ask herself, why was she impelled to keep re-reading these diaries, looking at pictures of times dead and gone; mere memories. Her life with Ethan was loving and caring and fulfilled. She had her other two bonny children and a comfortable life full of social activities and good works and contentment. Yet something in her heart was never satisfied. It wanted something else. That something was indefinable. It was like a wound that never healed but oozed blood slowly drop by drop, ebbing her life away with it.

Ethan did not attempt to discuss the matter with her. He had not known of the existence of the diaries and he wondered now about them, wondered what they contained that was so explosive. He guessed that Dorothy had written of her affair with Costas and he respected the fact that this whole part of her life was impenetrable and secret, her experience alone. That was *his* wound. He was painfully aware that she had never quite surrendered herself to him. She loved him and cared for him as no other woman might do. He was glad and grateful for this, more than glad that she was his wife. No one else would ever have done. He had never loved any other woman but her except for his own dear mother. All the same, he had sensed that at times Dorothy's soul was elsewhere.

Neither of them ever spoke of the past or their days together in Salonika. Now Andrew had opened the Pandora's Box and a subtle barrier had formed between them. Dorothy could no longer hide behind that enigmatic mask of hers. Ethan and Andrew knew her long held secret and that meant that she could never again return to that magical place that had sustained her for so long. Where now could she go? Where escape? She felt desperate and trapped.

All the same, she couldn't hate her own child, her firstborn; the son that had sprung from so deep a love. She must speak to him before he went. Who knows whether he would ever return to England again? He was far more Greek than English, perhaps he would never come back to her but find his relations and be absorbed into their culture. It had once fascinated her, that culture, but now it made her shudder. People were right, the Macedonians were savages.

She rang her mother at Downlands.

'But he isn't here? I thought he was with you?' her mother said in surprise.

'No, he went a few days ago, Ethan dropped him off at the station and we assumed he was returning to Downlands. Where on earth can he have gone? He can't have left England already.'

'What do you mean, left England?'

'You mean he hasn't told you? Hasn't dropped his bombshell? He plans to go to Greece immediately.'

'Not go up to Oxford?'

'Not go up to anything. He is leaving, he is utterly determined.'

'What on earth has brought this madness on the boy?'

Dorothy's voice rose a little higher as she tried to control her emotion,

'He wants to find his roots he says, he won't wait, he won't listen to reason!'

'Surely, he'll come and say goodbye to me?' said the old lady, troubled.

'He cares for *you* so I expect he will,' said Dorothy bitterly, 'he didn't bring much with him when he came here so he's sure to come and get his clothes and things from Downlands. He can't mean to travel that light. When he does arrive, tell him I rang and ask him to contact me. We had a …a frightful row and I want to speak to him before he goes.'

'You really think he will go; he's not just being difficult and acting like a stupid boy?'

Dorothy recalled Andrew's face, the set jaw, the hard and glittering black eyes. 'He means it all right. He's not my son for nothing. I *don't* want him to go – yet I know he has to do it. He has to lay all this to rest. We've denied him the truth for too long.'

Lay it all to rest for me too, thought Dorothy with a sigh.

The old lady was silent for a moment. She had her own guilty secret and it struggled in her breast. Denied the truth for too long!

'He must come back and see me before he goes away, he must!'

Chapter 3

After Ethan had driven off, Andrew stood in the forecourt of Paddington station and considered. There was no point in returning to Downlands as there was still a good deal he had to settle in London. Grandma wasn't expecting him yet and an early return would mean awkward explanations, which he preferred not to make. Maybe he would find a room at the YMCA or somewhere and stay for a few days sorting out documents and other matters, buying himself some walking shoes and various travelling necessities. How decent it was of Ethan to help him with some cash! That was just what he needed. He had better make sure nobody could steal it. Just now the bulging roll of banknotes was feeling very vulnerable in his pocket.

He found a shop and purchased a small black cloth bag with drawstrings, which, when the opportunity arose, he would use to put his money in and tie around his waist, beneath his trousers. Then he took the Underground into town and got off at Knightsbridge. Some vague idea floated about in his head of trying to find his godmother, May Spannock. He had asked Ethan about her and Ethan had told him that she had long ago moved to London in order to train as a full time nurse. She now worked at one of the London hospitals, St. Bart's, he thought. He had an idea she lived in Knightsbridge but wasn't too sure as it was some time since they had seen May.

'Montpelier Road, it used to be but I can't recall which number. An upstairs flat in one of the large houses there.'

'Did she ever marry?' asked Andrew.

'No, she never married. It seems she wanted to devote herself to her nursing career. Your mother saw a fair bit of her for some years but they haven't been in touch for a long while. May was never too well; the malaria still gets her now and then, as it does me. It might be a nice idea to see her before you go. I don't think she's seen you since you were quite small.'

I'll see her in case she dies perhaps, thought Andrew sadly. Yes, he would love to meet his godmother and ask her about his father.

'She never met your father,' Ethan said, 'I am the only person who met him, ironically enough.'

Ethan also gave Andrew the last address he had written to in Athens when Costas had been alive.

'I think it was your grandmother's place. It may not be much use after all these years, but you never know, someone or other may still be living there who is related to you or who might know where they have gone.'

'It would be wonderful to see my Greek grandmother.'

'It would, indeed!' Ethan said heartily.

Andrew sat down in a Lyons teashop sipping thoughtfully at a cup of tea. He had found Montpelier Road and was considering his next move. Would he knock at all the doors of houses made into flats and ask for May Spannock? Would she welcome him or even want to see him? It would be a shock for her if he just turned up on the doorstep like this but he had better get used to shocking people as this was the sort of thing he would have to do when in Greece. There he would have a language barrier to contend with also.

As he munched on a slice of rather dry jam sponge, he suddenly heard a familiar voice call over to him,

'Good grief, Drew, old chap! –whatever are *you* doing here?'

It was Andrew's turn for a shock and he looked around to see his cousin Reggie hastening over to him, hand outstretched in greeting. Various eyes turned towards them curiously for a brief moment.

Andrew rose and took his cousin's proffered hand and the two men stared at one another in some surprise.

'May I join you?'

Andrew nodded and indicated the empty seat beside him. Reggie sat down and his face beamed with pleasure.

'So good to see you! What are you up to in this neck of the woods?'

'I might ask the same of you.'

'Well, I live here, don't I? Got a flat over by the station. Been there about six months.'

'I didn't know.'

'How would you? Haven't seen each other in an age. I stopped coming to Grandma's at Christmas, just couldn't bear it any longer – so frightfully dull, you know. So naturally, we haven't been in touch. What are you up to nowadays? Left Somerfield, I suppose and going on to Oxford. You always were an old swot.'

'No, I'm not going to go to Oxford. I mean to travel instead.'

Reggie regarded Andrew as if he had just fallen out of the moon.

'Have you informed the old uns of this deep decision?'

'I've told my mother and stepfather.'

'Good Grief, I'll bet they hit the roof!'

'Yes, rather,' said Andrew painfully for he still ached with his mother's anger, 'they chucked me out.'

'You've got guts, I'll give you that,' said Reggie admiringly.

'How about you? I gather you didn't get to Sandhurst?'

'No, I didn't,' said Reggie, 'and my own Ma wasn't too pleased I can tell you. I think Pa was delighted not to have to keep me any longer when I told them I just wanted to get a job and get on with life.'

'As far as they are concerned then, we're both failures,' said Andrew with a bitter smile. He wouldn't have thought Reggie had it in him to rebel like that.

'Oh, I don't think they think that anymore,' Reggie declared with a certain smugness, 'I decided to go into journalism and I've made a bit of a name for myself. It's a fair salary and even get to travel a bit.'

'You always had the gift of the gab,' said Andrew.

Reggie laughed, 'That's what they all say. So you see Dad's spot of Irish in me is handy after all. Kissed the blarney stone.'

A smiling and pretty little 'Nippie' came up to take his order.

Reggie grinned at her, 'Are you busy tonight?'

She just dimpled and smiled but made no reply. The waitresses here were used to being flirted with. He watched her with a gleam in his eye as she went on to the next table.

'Very nice indeed, what do you say, old thing?' he said. Andrew shrugged and finished his cup of tea.

'I see *you* haven't changed much,' he said witheringly.

'God, no! Always like a pretty face. What an old monk you're becoming! So, you're travelling? If that's the case, why are you skulking about round here? Where do you plan to go? Where are you staying?'

'I was planning to try and find someone who lives around here before I leave,' Andrew said, 'but I'm not sure exactly where she lives.'

'Oho – a girlfriend, eh?'

'No! A friend of my mother's, you fool!'

'Oh, blow that for a lark! Why not come and stay at my place for a bit? I've a good sofa. Do you for a few days, if that's what you are after. You can go and hunt the old dear up later.'

Andrew gave the matter thought. Reggie's sofa would do as well as anything else and it would save some cash too.

When Andrew had sorted out all his affairs, he debated whether or not to try and find May Spannock. Should he waste time looking for her – what after all was she to him? He had some vague recollection of her when he had been small but she had never come near him after that. She had deserted him like all the rest of them.

However, rather like Poirot reconstructing a scene and bringing together all the participants, he felt a need to gather together all these people and experience them for himself. Accordingly, he returned a day or two later to Montpelier Road and began to investigate all the houses that were obviously converted into flats, reading the nameplates, knocking and asking for information. At last, he came to number eighty-three and glancing along the little nameplates above the bells he saw the name Miss M. Spannock. He had found her.

It was early evening but he hoped she might be in. For all he knew she was still at work. He rang the bell and a tinny-sounding voice spoke on the intercom.

'Who is it?'

'It's your godson, Miss Spannock …Andrew Clarke.'

'My what?'

'Your godson, Dorothy Clarke's son.'

'Good Gracious!'

The bell buzzed and he pushed open the front door and went on up the stairs to the top flat.

Standing at the top waiting for him stood a woman of about forty-three. Her hair was still fair but greying so that the colour looked faded and washed out and there was an oddly unkempt look about her. She stood and stared at Andrew for a long while and he waited patiently as she scrutinised him there at the stop of the stairs.

'Well, come on in then.'

She led him into a large sitting room that was comfortable and clean but piled with odds and ends in inappropriate places. Magazines lay in heaps on the floor and knick-knacks seem to fill every available table or shelf. A nurse's apron lay over a chair. There were photos everywhere of her family, of a young man in uniform whom he supposed must be her dead fiancé Bill, and some of Dorothy and May when they were younger women.

May saw him stop to look at the pictures and nodded,

'All my memories,' she said.

She waved him to a chair and he lifted a heap of sewing and books out of it before seating himself.

'Sorry for the mess,' she said, 'I didn't expect any visitors. So you're Andrew? A grown man. It's a long time ago since I saw you, that's for sure.'

'You haven't seen my mother for a while then?'

May sighed, 'No, for some reason we haven't been in touch for a few years apart from the odd letter. I don't know why – people just drift apart. How is she – your mother?'

Andrew would like to have said his mother was well but was she? He had left her so angry and upset.

'She's in good health,' he ventured.

'In good health. Well Dot was always in good health. She was one of the lucky ones,' said May.

She rose, 'I'll make a cup of tea.'

As she bustled about in her little kitchen, waiting for the kettle to boil, Andrew took another look at the photographs. How different May looked now to that pretty, sweet-faced girl. She had aged swiftly and badly and her face looked wrinkled and tired and there was a yellow tinge about her skin that he supposed was due to the recurring malaria. He had seen this sallow look in Ethan as well when the spleen re-injected its poisons into him every now and then. Some people recovered fully but others were never really rid of it. Both May and Ethan had been in a weakened condition when the disease hit them. Perhaps that was the reason why they had never really shaken off the fierce, loving bite of that lady mosquito.

May came back with a tray of tea. She swept another lot of papers off a small table and put it down.

'I haven't been much of a godmother, have I?' she said as she poured out the tea, 'visiting you, bringing you presents and all that stuff. I'm sorry about that. I suppose I just couldn't bear it when you were small, then Dot had the other two as well. Silly of me; we old spinsters just get morbid.'

Taking the cup, Andrew looked at her keenly and saw the tired eyes had a wistfulness about them.

'What made you want to come and see me all of a sudden?' she asked. Her approach was as direct as ever and Andrew smiled a little.

'Because I want to piece together my mother's past,' he said, 'I want to discover myself through her eyes, through the people she knew and loved.'

May frowned a little. 'I don't follow you. I was never of any real importance in your mother's life.'

'But you *were* great friends.'

'We lived for over a year in close proximity. We slept together in a small tent. We were young, we were enjoying a mad adventure that had been thrust upon us. But we had little in common, really. In the end, I think we both realised that there was nothing much to say anymore.'

'So you drifted apart?'

'Yes …people do. They feel close in certain circumstances and then their life changes. Your mother married Ethan. I think it was then we found we had little in common any more. I was only interested in my work and your mother was enjoying a quite different lifestyle; she came from a very different social background to mine. We never quarrelled or anything like that, just became …indifferent to each other.'

'I'm sorry about that.'

'Well, it's life.'

Andrew felt strangely sad. He didn't know why he should. Silence fell between them for a moment.

'Anyway, what about you? You must be what –18 now? You've finished school?'

'Yes, I've left Somerfield College.'

'And what are your plans?'

'I intend to take a boat to Marseilles and go from there to Piraeus, thence to Athens. Then I am going to see if I can find my grandmother there. Or any other relations I can find.'

May looked at him thoughtfully.

'You *are* half Greek, of course. Is this your mother's mad idea?'

'God no! She's having a fit; she threw me out of the house when I told her.'

'That's odd. I'm surprised she isn't coming with you. It was all she ever wanted, to live in that God forsaken country! She nearly killed herself when she heard of your father's death. She would have gone back then I'm sure, but her mother wouldn't hear of it. I think she'd have left you, left us all because of that man.'

'My father?'

May nodded. 'Yes, her beloved Takis. I always knew your mother was the sort to fall like a ton of bricks if she fell in love.

She was never one for half-measures. She never loved poor Ethan. She married him in the end but it was never for love.'

'Why did she marry him then?' asked Andrew, puzzled.

'Oh! – some day you'll understand. I understand. I don't blame her at all. But I would never do that myself.'

Her glance fell on the picture of Bill Myers. Andrew followed her gaze.

'Bill got killed, didn't he?'

'Hmph – you've learnt your history all right! That was my Bill – an upright, honourable and wonderful man. There will never be another man like him; men today are disgusting creatures. I simply have never met another like him. Nor do I want to. My Bill ...' her voice trailed away.

Another of those yesterday people! They all clung to the past. What was the matter with them all?

Andrew drained his cup and stood up. There was only a dried up and embittered woman here. She had nothing to tell him nor did she seem interested in him at all. He wasn't sure what he had hoped to find, but it wasn't this shadow of a cheerful, happy young woman who had once been his mother's dear friend.

May rose too and as she showed him to the door, she suddenly clutched his arm and said, 'You're going to Greece? Will you be visiting Salonika?'

'Of course I will.'

'Will you go to the Lembet cemetery and look for Sergeant William Myers of the 7th Wiltshires? Will you put some flowers on his grave for me?'

'Yes, yes, I will.'

A look of relief passed over her face and for a moment lit it up so that she looked young again.

'I'll go myself some day. I keep promising myself. But it's a long way off and such a dreadful place; you've no idea. I hated it there and so did Bill. If only he was buried here and not so very far away. It's so far away. Why do you want to go there, it's a filthy place! England is so safe, so normal, so clean.'

'I have to find out for myself.'

Andrew turned and went down the stairs, his promise already forgotten and she watched him go, her eyes full of tears. If only the wretched boy hadn't come to remind her of all that was past. She shut the door behind her just as he slammed shut the front one.

Chapter 4

To his surprise, Andrew rather enjoyed Reggie's company. He still found his cousin a man of shallow, sensual charm but he was cheerful and full of the city gossip. He seemed to have an endless succession of girlfriends ringing him, apparently unable to exist without his company, and he revelled in it all. He showed Andrew some of his gossip columns for the Daily Express and they were witty and pleasant.

After all, Andrew thought, life isn't all about being deadly serious. Just at the moment, light, frothy chatter, glittering Hollywood films full of song and dance were what everyone wanted as if to distract themselves from the dark and gloomy undercurrents that rumbled beneath the surface of Europe like some chained monster waiting to be unleashed.

'I did enjoy covering the exhibition at Olympia,' Reggie said, 'pity you didn't get there, you know. Just your sort of thing.'

'Yes, I'd have liked to go. I always used to like messing around with wireless sets when I was a kid,' said Andrew regretfully.

'I remembered you made a set at one time and we tried to contact some people in Lapland but all we got was a lot of crackle and distorted speech. You did chat for a while to some fella in Norway. You are a clever chappie! I would have no idea how to go about doing such a thing. Even the girls keep telling me I'm a man of words and not action. However, radio's had its day, I say. They have television now; saw it for the first time. *That's* going to be the medium for the future, the new opium of the masses if you ask me – what potential! It can reach millions like radio but it's like having your own little cinema in the front room. Why go out at all? I'll bet it hits the film industry too. It's absolutely, bloody amazing! '

'Damn, I should have come to London sooner, I forgot all about it.'

'You forgot!' snorted Reggie, reaching for a new bottle of malt whisky and beginning to open it swiftly and skilfully, 'how the hell did you manage that, you idiot? Where's your mind been lately? If I didn't know you, I'd swear you were in love. Here, have a tipple.'

Andrew had never drunk whisky before and took the well-filled glass in a gingerly fashion. He had to confess that he found Reggie far more the man about town now and was for the first time at a disadvantage with his cousin. That soft, lazy boy he had so despised and occasionally beaten up just for the pleasure of it and whom he had looked down upon when they were both callow youths, was now a man at ease and comfortable in this adult world on whose threshold Andrew stood. He would have to start getting into the new role and learning a few tips.

He sipped at the drink and coughed as the fiery substance burnt its way down his throat. Reggie watched him and gave a huge laugh, tipping his own glass back and swallowing great gulps of it.

'Time to enter the world, Drew old boy! Here's to your travels. Cheerio!'

'Cheerio!'

'That's better! Get a couple of snorts down you! That'll make a man of you in no time. That's the thing with journalism, you have to be able to drink other folks under the table and then wrestle their stories out of them when they're in a stupor. Then you get the scoop and they get nothing. Cunning, eh? I can out-drink most of those hard-bitten old Fleet Street journalists. Dad got me going early so I had a good head start. He always let me come down to join them for dinner from an early age and let me drink wine and brandy with them. I don't think Ma liked it a bit but Dad took no notice. Don't want the boy to be molly-coddled, he used to say, want to make a man of him! And being a drinker is Dad's idea of being a man. Mind you I don't want to end up like some of those Fleet Street chaps – they look as if their liver's made of blotting paper. They look ghastly some of them.'

Andrew tried a larger gulp, which made him cough all the more. The feeling of the warm amber fluid carving its way down into his stomach felt good. It was just the kind of fire he needed at this point when he had to marshal all his courage and all his resources.

Reggie turned his whisky glass round in his hand speculatively and then refilled it.

'Come on, get it down you, do you good! You look all washed up, old chap. Good job Uncle Reggie came along in time to rescue you. You swots are all made of milk and water, live in your heads too much. You need some of this stuff in your belly.'

He refilled Andrew's glass and they clinked their glasses together again.

The whisky had a curious effect on Reggie. He didn't become noisy, hilarious or foolish but seemed to dive down deeper and deeper inside himself as he drank.

'Funny business life,' he said after a while. 'I enjoy it. I enjoy things the way they are for me. Life's comfortable and I always seem to have the luck of the Devil ...I get work, get women. What more can a fellow want?'

'Surely there's more to life than that,' Andrew replied. His head was beginning to expand with the warmth of the whisky and it suffused all his limbs so that he felt as if he could hardly move. It felt good, very good.

'Like what? Well, yes, there are, I suppose, high ideals and all that stuff. Didn't get them far in the War, did it? Look at Uncle Richard. Mum said he couldn't wait to get off to France and be blown up. They were all like that at first. Poor fools!'

'You're judging things from a material standpoint. I think it's worth dying for honour.'

'You're talking out of your hat, if you don't mind my saying so, Drew old chap. Would you really want another war? All that mud, shells exploding around you and lice in your hair? Really want the glory of a coffin? I find the idea terrifying. I don't like the way things are shaping up in Germany. I don't like it at all. Couldn't bear the thought of another war. Come to that, I don't like the way they're shaping up here either.'

'What do you mean?'

'Have you been living on Mars lately? Haven't you heard of the Blackshirts? Don't you see the poverty and the misery everywhere? I was up North recently, visiting the Fortescues at Bletchley Hall for a bit of shooting. Well, you know me, I was out looking for some stories but it wasn't what I wanted or expected at all. Things look bleak, really bleak for those poor bastards. The shipbuilding industry has gone to pot up there and the men are all laid off. Nothing but the means test for them now. They look beaten down. It made me feel bad seeing these men standing about street corners with that awful, haunted look in their eye – while I went off to the Fortescues for a splendid six course dinner, footman laying out my evening suit, the lot.'

Andrew stared at his cousin in surprise. This was the writer of frothy gossip columns? Uncle Henry had never given a damn for the poor and Agnes professed to but simpered over tea with her lady friends instead. Had Reggie developed a social conscience?

'Oh, well,' said Reggie with a self-conscious little shrug, 'it's always been the way – rich and poor. Glad I'm on the right side of the fence! Anyway, let's change the subject, it's far too depressing. What are you planning to do when you get to Greece? Tell me all about your plans. By the way, I have the phone number of some Greek journalist I met when I was in Paris. Lamb, Limb – somebody. Can never get my tongue round those names. He's with the Athens News and may be able to give you a hand. Remind me before you go.'

Chapter 5

Andrew returned to Downlands later in the week having been thoroughly initiated in the joys of whisky drinking by his cousin, hangover and all.

'Drink plenty of milk after a binge and you'll be right as rain,' his cousin promised but it didn't work a hundred per cent. However, it seemed to get better and easier to down the stuff as they went along and Andrew felt very worldly for the experience.

Reggie was all for completing his education by taking him to a brothel as well but Andrew drew the line at that. He was always terrified of venereal diseases and the idea of such women made him feel ill. The idea of paying for something that should be given with love and returned with love! It was all so cold and calculating. Reggie's easy fascination with women always amazed him. Andrew liked to look but not touch, preferred to admire from afar.

At his request, the taxi dropped him off at the large wrought iron gates of Downlands and he walked along the wide driveway once built for horses and carriages to ride along, feeling the cool evening air upon his face. As usual the house was in semi-darkness, Grandma sitting in the twilight waiting for night to fall. In the distance, he heard a welcoming bark and Joe came tearing down the path to greet his master, jumping up ecstatically.

'Oh, Joe – I'm so going to miss you!! I wish I could take you with me.'

He had already decided that he would take Joe to the farmer at Cottersley where he could live outdoors and help guard the hen houses. Joe was a good ratter and would chase a fox a mile away. He had already spoken of the idea to the farmer who had agreed. It would feel awful taking his dog there and having to leave him perhaps forever and he didn't look forward to his betrayal of dear, trusting Joe. But there was nothing else to be done about it and the dog would be happier working on a farm.

Sara had already opened the door and stood smiling, waiting to greet him. The sight of her gaunt figure, familiar grey head and welcoming smile made him feel sad. For the first time he began to have qualms about his rash decision. However, he hardened his heart again. He wasn't a child anymore. He didn't need comfort and women to mother him like that fool Reggie who couldn't live without them. Here at Downlands, he felt assured again, his old self and not the young man in the city, unsure what to do or how to behave. He now felt sickened by the fast, loose life his cousin led. Writing his rubbish and deadening his conscience with women and whisky! Was that what he called life? How could he have admired him even for a moment?

He gave Sara a little kiss and she giggled for he wasn't a little boy any more but a handsome young man. She took his coat off him.

'Mrs Clarke's in the sitting room, sir. I'll tell her you've arrived.'

There was no need. His grandmother had heard him and now came out of the room to greet him.

'Can't see a thing,' she said tetchily, 'put on the lights, boy.'

Andrew switched on the dim hall light and she peered up at him. She had just been having a little nap and looked a little awry and taken unawares. He smiled and took her in his arms and gave her a kiss.

'Oh, get off, boy,' she said but she pecked him on the cheek nonetheless and led him into her sitting room.

'Sit down, sit down,' she said, 'Sara bring in some tea. And that marble cake that Andrew likes.'

They both fell silent as they often did and Andrew's thoughts went far away as he watched the coals in the fire collapse in the grate, forming red-hot palaces and caverns. He felt a sadness that he was leaving his grandmother, his childhood and the only place he felt he could call home. What adventures awaited him, what would he find?

'Your mother rang,' said Grandma Clarke after a while.

Andrew looked up and his face darkened, 'What did she want?'

'She said you'd had a row. Told me you were planning to leave us all and go off to Greece.'

Andrew looked away again.

'Yes, I am, Grandma.'

'No, I won't even try to talk you out of it,' the old lady sighed. 'You're as pig-headed as your mother. She admitted as much. The Clarkes are all the same.'

'I am not a Clarke anymore, I am Andreas Giorgos Cassimatis' he replied with pride.

'I see. You reject your English side, now.'

'Yes, I do reject it. I am going to Greece and it will be very soon. I have the tickets and will sail on Monday.'

The old lady looked at him and her eyes filled with tears. She was losing him too. They all went in the end; they all went away.

Andrew did not notice her tears and probably would have remained unmoved; his heart had become flinty hard again.

'Your mother wants to speak to you before you go.'

'There's nothing to say,' he replied and lapsed into silence.

His grandmother looked at him and frowned but said no more.

The remaining few days seemed to fly by so quickly. Andrew was packed; he had taken Joe down to the farm. Leaving his dog was the only thing that had brought tears to his eyes. The taxi would soon arrive to take him to the station. Now he went in to his grandmother to make his farewells and found her sitting before the fire. She looked very small and lost and suddenly quite old.

'You'll be going off to your other grandmother now, I suppose,' she said without looking up.

'I mean to find her as soon as I can. Grandma, don't be upset. I will write to you, I promise. I want to thank you for all you have done for me all these years. You've always been so good to me.'

'Have I Andrew? I have loved you my boy. You haven't been the easiest of boys, mind. In you I recognise myself at times. You have an iron will and so have I. You love this house, don't you?'

Andrew sighed and looked about him at all the old familiar objects.

'I do, it's been home to me.'

'It *has* been home to you, it has been. And always will be while I'm still alive. You know you can come back here. I think you'll soon tire of Greece and Greek ways. This is where you belong but you're too young and stubborn to realise it yet.'

'Maybe. I'll have to find out, won't I?'

'Yes, you need to find out though I wish you had the sense to complete your education here first. But never mind, that's impatient youth for you.'

She wanted to tell him something else but she couldn't bring herself to do so. Unsaid words hung in the air but she turned her head away and said no more.

Andrew entered the taxi and Rose and Sara stood beside her waving and sniffing back their tears at the thought of Master Andrew leaving them for good. Andrew smiled a little and waved as the taxi moved away. He sighed deeply and settled back on the seat and felt his heart thumping. He was setting off on the longest journey of his life and fear mingled with excitement. He was taking the very journey his mother had begun all those years ago before he was born. It was a strange, strange feeling.

His grandmother watched the taxi disappear round the gates and wondered why she had not told Andrew about the three letters she had received from Greece six months after his father's death. They had been from Athens, probably from his grandmother or some other relation. She had never tried to read them, simply thrown them in the fire. She hadn't wanted to stir up her daughter all over again and have her leave and take the baby with her and go back to that wretched pace. It wouldn't have done Dorothy any good to re-open all those wounds again. Just as she had hoped, Dorothy had married Ethan Willoughby and put all that madness behind her.

Now she wondered why she had done such a dreadful thing and she wondered why she hadn't been able to tell Andrew about it. Oh, well, he would find what he wanted, if there was anything to find. If only it could all be left to rest! She sighed and went indoors into the darkening house.

Chapter 6

Andrew stepped off the boat at the port of Piraeus and walked down the gangway to the quayside where the customs agents were patiently awaiting the stream of passengers. After dealing with the necessary formalities, he took a firm hold of his small bag of belongings and made his way along the energetic, noisy quayside full of jostling navvies and stevedores unloading the large cargo ships and ferrying sacks, boxes, barrels and other produce hither and thither. The air was full of animated discussions and shouts and epithets.

The other boat passengers who were being met by friends or relations now parted company and went their varied ways. A Frenchman whom he had befriended in Marseilles came alongside him and bid him adieu.

'I am staying in Neo Faliron myself,' he said affably, 'I have some friends there. You are welcome to come if you have nowhere to go. I am sure they could find you a bed for the night.'

'That is very kind of you but I prefer to make my way to Athens before nightfall and find a room there.'

'Well, in that case, go as soon as you can. Don't hang about the wharves. I certainly don't advise you to stop in any of the cafes along here.'

'Why's that?'

'Pouf!' said the Frenchman with a look of distaste, 'the place is crawling with Greek refugees from Asia Minor and believe me, monsieur, they are scum, utter scum. The cafes here are hashish dens, full of vice and evil. Keep away if you value your life.'

He pointed out the way to the Metro and Andrew, alarmed by these tales sped on, almost expecting an attack in broad daylight. The long, dusty harbour side was edged with cheap shops, cafes and market stalls. He saw several men sitting outside the waterfront cafes looking rough and down at heel in their baggy clothes and cloth caps, but they simply regarded him with a mild curiosity as he went by in such a tremendous hurry.

He felt foreign and alien, even more than he had been in England. Nothing was familiar, the language sounded coarse and grating to his ears used to classroom Greek (a classical Greek that, let's face it, was probably never spoken as English teachers and schoolboys attempted to pronounce it!). The men he encountered everywhere seemed equally coarse and rough and yet there was a vibrancy about them, manliness in their look and strength in their bearing. They seemed to exude raw, animal spirits.

Facially he knew he fitted in at last and didn't stand out as foreign. People spoke to him in Greek and expected him to reply in the same language. They looked surprised when they heard his accent, unable to place where he was from.

'Ah, you must have come from the States!' they said knowingly, 'come back to see the Old Country, eh?'

He would smile and nod as if this was the case rather than answer all their innumerable questions. They were such curious people. Always wanting to know where you were from and where you were going and what you were doing. He had never before experienced the warmth of direct, childlike curiosity and it was tiresome but at the same time friendly and pleasant. He felt a sense of expansion in his heart because of it, as if sensing a kindly welcome.

Andrew took the Metro up to Omonia and stepped out into the centre of a large square with tall buildings around it. The area around the Metro entrance was a large paved circle with illuminated columns rising at intervals from its circumference and a few straggling flower-beds. Several streets seemed to lead away from this central place. However the name Harmony Square was something of a misnomer for the place was incredibly noisy and active. Cars hooted constantly and people seemed blissfully unaware of the need to move but stood in the middle of the road or pavements chattering, gesticulating and completely absorbed in their affairs. The shops and cafes scattered around bustled with movement. Trams clanged, cars hooted and vendors shouted their wares. But it felt cheerful and invigorating and for the first time in a long while Andrew felt at ease as he looked about him and absorbed all the lively commotion.

The hills rose around the city, enclosing it as if in a loving embrace. That must be Mount Lykavittos rising up like a little island in a sea with the tiny white church of St. George perched atop of it. He wanted to explore but the evening was now drawing in and feeling thirsty he entered a small café in Omonia Square which looked inexpensive and clean enough. Some old men were sitting in chairs on the pavement sipping their small glasses of ouzo and gossiping about all the passers by. They regarded the young man with curiosity and one of them raised his glass, 'Welcome stranger!' he said in a croaking old voice. 'How are things going, my lad?'

'Very well,' said Andrew with a nod and a smile. He ordered a coffee.

The proprietor bought the coffee and inevitable glass of water over after a while and then affably perched on a nearby table ready for a chat.

'You're a stranger here?'

'Yes.'

'So where are you from? You look like a Greek –.or an Italian maybe. But too wild in the eye for an Italian. You have Greek eyes, all right.'

Andrew laughed, 'Good, I like to hear that! My father was a Greek from Macedonia.'

'Ah, no wonder. They're a fierce bunch that lot! You don't sound like a Macedonian yourself though.'

'I've never been there.'

'No offence to your father, but don't bother. Stay here in Athens and be civilised.'

'You think so?'

'E, but of course! I tell you they're wild men from the mountains up North. We Athenians have a spot of common sense and some education. I think you must be from America, the way you speak Greek as if you'd got a frog in your mouth. Your father emigrated maybe?'

Andrew didn't want to go into his whole life history with a mere stranger so as always he nodded and changed the conversation.

'Do you know a place where I might stay tonight? I don't mean to be there long, just for a night.'

'Sure, I have a cousin, Petros, who has a hotel round the corner, nice and cheap ...I'm coming, I'm coming, man!'

Here he had to break off as another customer was banging the table violently to attract his attention, ' ...round the corner there,' he said, pointing down one of the streets, 'just look for the Aphrodite Hotel and say Manolis sent you.'

Having found the Aphrodite down a small and dingy looking side street, Andrew secured himself a little room for the night. It was not the most salubrious of areas but it was certainly cheap enough. He unpacked a clean shirt and hung it up and then made certain that his precious money-bag was well hidden. He couldn't be sure if it felt safer to leave it in the hotel or carry it about himself. He certainly didn't trust Petros the proprietor who looked a seedy, villainous individual. So he took some cash with him and hid the rest beneath the wardrobe, slipping it underneath the slightly raised legs. No one could see the black bag there, even from the door and no one would be likely to look underneath such a narrow space.

He wandered about the city, cheerful in the glow of the lights from the cafes and theatres and delighted in the fact that all the Greek population was now out and about, families enjoying themselves in the cool of a late autumnal evening, strolling the streets with an attitude of careless and unhurried delight. It was so different to cold, harsh England with its depression and poverty and misery. Here all seemed light and bright and happy.

In Syndagma Square virile young men sat in cafes, attending the smart, pretty, middle-class young ladies accompanied by their duennas. Shy exchanges, hands clasped briefly under the table, glances passed between lovers when the chaperone's eyes were elsewhere. Children laughed and ran around on the pavements, clutching balloons that escaped into the night air and chattering like little birds. Their parents sipped wine and nibbled olives, sheltering indoors from the chilly air and proudly watching their offspring while holding animated conversations with their friends. Andrew felt quite warm dressed in a tweed jacket; they were all wrapped up in their coats and hats. To the Greeks it was winter while for him it felt delightful and mild.

Fascinated, he watched the Athenian intelligentsia and the wealthy pouring out of the theatres and smart night-clubs. Ladies in beautifully cut and expensive clothes and furs, jewels about their necks and arms, were greeting old acquaintances with enthusiasm and delight. The gentlemen wore smart dinner jackets and bow ties and as soon as they came out in the road, cigars and cigarettes were lit up and smoke exhaled with pleasure. It looked for all the world like a scene outside the Opera House at Covent Garden.

He did not feel he belonged to this upper-class social scene, never had done so, even back in England. There was something just a little artificial about the glittering society of the wealthy but they were always a species worth watching. He far preferred the ordinary Athenian families. There was a sense of solidity about them, of pleasant, comfortable existence without too much fuss and ostentation, normal human beings, living normal, cheerful lives.

After enjoying a simple meal of an omelette, black olives and some bread and wine at Manolis Café back in Omonia Square, he asked the owner if he could use the phone. Then he made a call to Dimitris Limbourides, the journalist contact that Reggie had given him. A woman with a clear, pleasant voice replied and said that Mr Limbourides had been out at the theatre and was unlikely to be home for a while but she would leave him a message to call at Andrew's hotel tomorrow morning. Contented with that and tired with his travel, Andrew took himself off to bed at the Aphrodite with hopes that the not too clean sheets were not the depositories of any unwanted life forms left by the previous occupants.

In the early hours of the morning a banging on his door startled Andrew awake. He called 'Come in' in English, forgetting for a moment where he was. A man entered the room, switched the lights on and coming to Andrew, cheerily pumped his arm up and down and introduced himself as Dimitris Limbourides.

'I got your message,' he said, 'good to meet you! Welcome to Athens.'

'Er, thanks,' said Andrew, peering at his watch. It was four in the morning. Did these people never sleep?

'Ah, I woke you too early,' said Limbourides with a faint air of apology but otherwise unabashed, 'just finished work. You can't stay in this flea pit. Dress and come over to my house and stay with us.'

'What now?'

'But yes, of course, now! This, my innocent boy, is a place for prostitutes and pimps – not a hotel – a right, thieves den! You should have rung me from Piraeus and I'd have come to fetch you. Any friend of Reggie is a friend of mine. *Elate, pame* – let's get going. I'll pay your bill while you get dressed.'

Astonished by this extraordinary reception, Andrew obediently rose and dressed, piled his few belongings back in the case, retrieved his cash now hidden beneath the pillow and went downstairs to meet Limbourides in the dingy hallway. A very annoyed hotelier was calling him names, gesticulating and cursing vociferously but to no avail. Limbourides made a rude gesture with his hand at the furious Petros and informed him that he would write about him in his newspaper and tell everyone that he had a hash joint in the cellar if he didn't shut up. This had the desired effect and the fellow retired muttering behind his counter.

'Is it really a hotel for prostitutes?' Andrew asked as he followed his new-found friend along the street.

'Well – probably! They all are,' was the breezy reply, 'unless you go to the Grand Bretagne and even then I wouldn't be too sure.'

They took a taxi, which Limbourides directed to Pangrati, and they arrived in a pleasant street with one-storey houses that looked well cared for and tidy.

Limbourides' house was quite a reasonable size with a smart glass and wrought iron front door leading off a mosaic tiled porch with railings around it. Inside it felt cool with a large and attractive hallway paved with black and white marble tiles. There were several occasional tables with vases of flowers on them. Andrew was shown to a neat, simply furnished bedroom with drawn shutters and long, lacy curtains that came to the floor; here he left his bag and coat. The room was very comfortable, the sheets clean and sweet smelling as if rose petals or some other flower had lain amongst the folds.

The rest of the furnishings in the flat looked just like those he had left in his mother's house in England. The same heavy beds, tables, chairs and sideboards. He felt sure if he peered closer he would find a label with 'Made in England' on them. As it happens, he wasn't far wrong as English furniture was the vogue just then.

'Stay here as long as you like, make yourself at home' said his host with a wave of his hand around the apartment.

Andrew was now introduced to Despina, Limbourides wife, a pretty little dark-haired woman who came out of her bedroom to greet him, putting on her dressing gown, apparently unperturbed at receiving a guest at such an unsocial hour. She smiled and nodded at him and immediately went off to fetch him coffee, a glass of water and the inevitable sweet stuff on a spoon.

'Is this *glyko kidoni*?'

'No, this is *mastiha*,' she replied, 'Why do you ask?'

'I just wondered.'

The two men sipped their coffees and Andrew told Limbourides a little about himself and how he had decided to return to Greece to find his relations.

'That's an interesting story of yours,' said Limbourides. ' Maybe I should put out an appeal for you in the newspaper, eh? What do you think of that?'

'I suppose it might be an idea. This is the only address I have to go on.'

He showed Limbourides the slip of paper with the address Ethan had given to him.

'I think this might be where my grandmother lives,' he said.

'Hmm …it's in Plaka somewhere maybe? I think so anyway. What do you think Despina?'

'Makriyianni? It's by Hadrian's Arch. One of those streets near the hill there with the grand old houses. You should find it with no trouble. Just ask anyone when you get to Amalias St.'

'I shall go along later today. But are you sure you want to keep me here? It seems a great imposition.'

'How can you say such a thing?' said Limbourides looking so offended that Andrew said no more and felt warmed by their hospitality. He stifled a yawn for he felt very tired still and his host sensing this, assured him that he should go back to bed.

'I have an article to write and then I too will sleep. I may be out when you awake but I shall see you later on in the day and we'll take in all the night-spots. You're going to see Athens, my lad!'

'I would love to see the Acropolis.'

'Bah! Everyone wants to see that pile of old rocks – the English should have taken the lot. The fuss they make about it. I mean the real Athens, the theatres, bars, restaurants and good spots. Not the dives, of course.'

'Not the hashish dens then?'

'What are you talking about? As if I would go where the *manges* hang out except to report the police raids – and even they aren't worth talking about, a daily occurrence I assure you. Since Metaxas took over in August though, things have got so much better. They are doing their best to stamp out the drugs and prostitution and a good thing too.'

He looked ready to embark on that favourite Greek pastime of discussing politics but thought better of it and withdrew at last. With a sigh of relief, Andrew lay fully clothed on the bed. Without further ado he fell fast asleep.

Chapter 7

When Andrew awoke, chinks of daylight were filtering through the slats of the shutters and the bedside lamp was still on. He had slept soundly for the first time since he had left England. He felt safe and relaxed here in this comfortable home. Rising, he looked askance at his crumpled clothes and took a few belongings out of his bag and spread them out. They would need to be washed or cleaned and he would ask Kyria Despina where he could take them.

'Ah, you slept well, my child,' she said when he went into the kitchen looking tousled and still a little bleary eyed and she smiled tenderly at him for to her he was just a lad.

She showed him the bathroom and how to work the small geyser over the bath and proceeded to fill a bowl with hot water. 'Here wash and shave in this,' she said and left him to his ablutions while she bustled elsewhere on her housewifely errands. Andrew was growing a nice little moustache and regarded his reflection in the mirror over the little basin and for the first time felt quite pleased with himself. Here in Greece his face fitted; he felt he could even like that dark visage that stared back at him and not yearn to be fair and blue-eyed like his cousin Reggie. His looks weren't that bad after all.

After a breakfast of strong coffee and some strange brittle bread that Kyria Despina called toast, he gave her his dirty clothes at her insistence.

'Here's Dimitri's dressing gown,' she said, 'take off those crumpled things and give them to me to iron. You can't go out like that as if you've slept in the streets!'

Obediently he did as he was told and felt fresher and brighter than he had in a while. It was wonderful to feel welcomed and so at home.

He went into the kitchen to find Despina on a stool fixing the electric iron into the lamp socket. He helped her to do this and she then chatted to him as she ironed his things. She asked him the usual personal questions about his age, parents and marital intentions but he no longer felt resentment over this very Greek probing. It seemed to be a part of the ritual of meeting strangers. He did his best to explain a little in his halting Greek, wondering if she understood anything he said but she paid full attention and appeared to grasp what he was trying to say without any effort. In turn she spoke to him slowly and clearly so that he in turn found her easy to understand.

'Damn this iron,' she said after a while, 'it keeps overheating,' and she had to switch it off again. These modern electrics seemed to Andrew to take as long as the old fashioned irons heated in the fire which Rose still used so skilfully back at Downlands. All the same, he was surprised to find how very modern everything was when he had been given to understand that every country outside Britain was backward and uncivilised. It seemed to him to be quite the opposite. This house could be warmly heated in winter by a calorifer and water ran from the taps and were heated by the geysers. There was a telephone and electric instead of gas lighting which still existed in many parts of Britain. It all seemed very modern, smart and up to date.

'Does the name Nina Cassimatis seem familiar?' he asked Despina.

'Tsuck!...no, I don't know anyone of that name,' she said with the funny little click of the tongue and upward jerk of the chin which was the Greek negative, 'it's not a familiar surname.'

'I mean to go and search for my grandmother today,' he said.

'It means a lot to you doesn't it?'

'It means I can find out about my father; get to know what he was really like from his own mother. Who better? I may be able to see photos of him when he was young. Above all, it means being welcomed by someone whom I know will love me.'

'You don't think your mother loves you?' said Despina looking a little surprised.

'I doubt she does. We've quarrelled bitterly. I know I don't love *her* anymore.'

'What a terrible thing to hear you say about your *Mana*!' said Despina crossing herself as if to ward off some evil eye, 'you should always love your *Manoula*!'

'Should I?' said Andrew fiercely,' when she has betrayed me, stifled me – no, I can't forgive her for what she has done.'

'*Ade kale*, parents and children are forever quarrelling but you forgive one another all the time. I always have a furious row with my mother whenever I go back to the village to see her. But I never stop loving her, the old bitch! If anyone was to harm her, I'd poke their eyes out.'

'I know, I know – of course, I do love her – but …well, I've done things to upset her, she's upset me, it will take time to heal all this. That's why I'm here, I suppose.'

He dressed carefully, polished his shoes with a handkerchief and as he went out, Despina came to see him off and tucked a clean, neatly folded white handkerchief in his pocket and surveyed him.

'You look very handsome,' she said, 'your grandmother will be so proud and delighted to see you. Good luck Andreas.'

He walked along Vassilis Georgiou towards the National Gardens. Just between the buildings he glimpsed the Acropoline Hill with the remains of the ancient temple in all its white, skeletal glory. A sense of awe came upon him as he looked at it even from this far away. He knew he had to get up there and look at it more closely, sense the past, touch the stones and try to understand and absorb that all this was his own; his very own heritage. It belonged to him. He might still feel a foreigner, act like a foreigner, look upon it all with the dazed and uncomprehending eyes of an Englishman but he *was* a Greek. This was his homeland and nobody could deny it to him anymore. It had meant a lot to his mother this place but it meant so much more to him in whom the blood of the Ancients ran.

The sun was shining, the sky so blue and vivid. The buildings appeared to him to be pristine in their splendour; the little white houses clambering up the slopes of the hills with their red tiled roofs looked so cheerful. Cypress trees interspersed the houses like dark, black columns. It was like the pictures he had seen in some of his books as a child. Was it real? He had left behind a cold, damp, grey England in October and come to this place of sunshine and blue skies. His soul grew huge in his breast and wanted to encompass the whole city, the whole land. It was almost too much to bear; tears came to his eyes and for a brief moment he felt almost faint with emotion.

He would have liked to go up and see the Acropolis right now and explore the pretty houses on the slopes but Andrew had a far greater purpose in mind and couldn't wait to find his grandmother Nina. He felt he knew her already from his mother's description in the diaries. If she was as delightful and warm-hearted as the kindly Despina, he would be more than content.

His English grandmother had all but faded from his mind; his whole life in England now seemed like a strange dream. He belonged neither there nor here in Greece as yet but that no longer troubled him for he now felt master of his own fate, embarked on a voyage of discovery that excited and exhilarated him. His eyes sparkled and several young girls that passed him by threw covert glances of appreciation at the handsome young man striding along with a lithe walk that had an animal sway of abandon in it. Never in his life had he felt such a sense of freedom and joy. It was as heady as wine.

He crossed over to the National Gardens, delighted to sit for a brief moment in the tree shaded park and smoke a cigarette while he watched the mothers and nannies walking their small children in the shade of the trees. He asked one or two of the ladies if they knew the street on his slip of paper. To his surprise, many of the nannies were German and could speak good English for which he was grateful.

One of them pointed him towards Vassilis Olgas St. and told him to ask at a kiosk for directions from there. He found a kiosk and chatted briefly to the vendor who showed him his false leg and began to tell him stories about his adventures in the Great War but Andrew hadn't the patience to listen to this just now and cut him short.

'Sorry,' he apologised, not wishing to offend the old veteran, 'but I'm in a hurry.'

After some time he found the street on his slip of paper. It was a charming tree-lined avenue with faded but beautiful old houses, large and elegant. There didn't seem to be any numbers to the houses, at least not in easy evidence. It took him some time to find the one he was looking for. His heart was beating as he approached it. Would Nina still be living here?

He wondered if he had made a mistake. It was a two-storey, terraced house of attractive proportions. Up at the top were wide, shuttered French windows leading out onto a balcony. Even as he looked, he saw someone within open one of the tall windows to let in some fresh air, flinging back the shutters. The double front doors of polished wood and glass were partly open and there was a brass plate on the wall by their side. Climbing the steps he read on it,

'Aristides High School for Girls.'

Surely this couldn't be the same house. Yet the right number was there high above the brass plate. It *was* the same. He pushed open the door and went inside and stood in the dim-lit hallway and looked around. There was no one in sight, no one on the broad flight of stairs that led to the upper rooms. The doors leading from the hallway were shut but he could hear the murmurs of voices behind them. Presumably they were classrooms full of teenage girls. It was obvious then that his grandmother had sold the house and returned to Thessaloniki to be near her daughter.

Disappointment flowed over him in huge waves.

A woman came out of one of the rooms carrying a pile of books. She was quite young and looked serious and bespectacled, her hair drawn back into a bun at the nape of her neck. Why did teachers always look like this?

'May I help you?' she said rather sharply as she regarded the young man with a suspicious air, as if wondering whether he was after one of her virginal charges.

'I'm sorry to intrude,' he said, speaking in French, as his Greek wasn't really fluent enough for what he wanted to say, 'I was looking for a lady that once lived here, a Madame Nina Cassimatis.'

The woman took his slip of paper and looked at the name and address with a puzzled expression, 'Follow me,' she said and he went with her into a room that was obviously a school office. Another older lady was in there busily typing on a huge typewriter. The first woman put the books on the table and showed her the slip of paper.

'Miss Irene, you have been here since the school was founded, do you know anything about this Madame Nina Cassimatis?'

The other woman looked at the paper and then at Andrew, 'Yes, I remember the house belonged to a lady of that name but I never met her. She died, I'm afraid. I think she must have died in 1924 or thereabouts. The house was sold to Mr. Aristides in 1925 by her relations and he founded the girl's school then.'

'She can't be dead!' Andrew burst out and the pain in his voice alarmed the ladies.

'Come, sit down! I am so sorry …she is a relative of yours?' said the older woman, bringing him a chair, 'Miss Marina, do bring the poor boy a glass of water, he looks so shocked.'

'My poor boy,' she murmured and stroked Andrew gently on the head while he wept unashamedly for a few moments.

'I'm so sorry!' he gasped at last and drank the offered water in reviving gulps.

'She was your relation?'

'Yes, my grandmother and I have never met her and now I never will!'

He struggled manfully to contain his grief. The ladies looked troubled and compassionate.

'Do you have the address of the relations who sold the house?' he asked but Miss Irene shook her head.

'No, it was a long time ago, more than ten years ago. Why would we keep their address so long? All I recall is they came from round Thessaloniki, or maybe from Kavalla …a man and a woman.'

There was nothing anyone could do. He stood up and thanked them and looked for a brief moment round the hallway of a house that might have once given him a joyful welcome; then walked out as friendless as ever.

He wandered about for some time in an aimless fashion but his joy and anticipation of the morning had evaporated. Suddenly the old monuments and piles of stones seemed meaningless, just all this stuff from the past. Limbourides was so right, so sensible. He would go out with him tonight and get drunk. It was the Now that was important. He too was clinging to the past just like his mother and grandmother. He must find the Greece of today and not the Greece of his mother's past or of the Ancient past. That was the mistake everyone made about Greece. They refused to let it grow and change. The Europeans seemed to feel the Ancients belonged to them in some way because they had preserved these great men and their teachings and philosophies in universities and classrooms. Modern Greece had no right to exist and was an anathema to such scholars. Even the Greeks themselves were trapped in their former glories, yet torn with becoming European and modern at the same time. What a confusion! No wonder the country was always torn apart; it reflected the inner dichotomy of the Greek soul.

His sadness overwhelmed him. All the same, it was important to see if any of his relations were still alive in Thessaloniki. Athens was obviously not the place to look for them. His father's people were Macedonians, part of New Greece. Perhaps his aunt still lived in Kavalla and had some children. Would she welcome him as he felt his grandmother would done? He had a strange feeling that she might not. He would have to go and find them and see what reception he was given.

That evening, Limbourides returned and he and his wife consoled Andrew over his disappointment.

'Never mind, you will be sure to find your auntie at least. And in the end, you're a Greek, Andreas, a *palikari,* so don't give in. You don't need relations. I wish I didn't have any, they're a pain in the arse, always demanding, e, Despina? We could certainly do without your mother at times. Thank God, she lives with your sister in Volos! Come on, *leventis,* let's go out on the town tonight and cheer ourselves up. I'm flush tonight so we'll go to Yiannakis Bar and get merry. Then we can go and play cards with my mates till dawn.'

The next day Andrew needed time to recover from a splitting headache induced by a mixture of wine and ouzo, a frightful drink that he had never tasted before. It was like drinking liquid aniseed balls but was decidedly potent which is what he wanted just now. He needed knocking out. Despina provided him with a lunch, which he swore he could never touch, so queasy was his stomach. She assured him that *avgolemono* soup with a little rice in it would settle his stomach and she was right.

Later on they drank coffee together and Despina showed him how to drink it almost to the dark grounds and then to turn it over in his saucer and let the grounds drain down and dry out into patterns.

'I will be your *kafetzouda* today,' she said with a laugh as she turned up the cup, 'my mother was a good one in her time and people used to come and see her from miles away. She really seemed to know the future. It was frightening sometimes. They used to say she had a spirit in her. Just like the oracle at Delphi, she was. I don't have her talent but I like to have a try.'

She looked at the cup and fell silent for a while.

'Oof …this is dark cup,' she said slowly, 'there are many roads for you and you have no idea which way to go. You are in danger on one of these dark roads but you need to be brave and follow its course for it will open up at the end and you will be crowned. A crown like a marriage but I'm not sure if it is quite that. But there *is* joy at the end. First though there is much *disaresta* …problems, pain, fights. A man awaits you but he is angry and dark. And a woman too – but she brings pain – see the cross over her? Yet in the end, you come out of it all and it is open and good. Not an easy cup, Andreas.'

'My life has never been easy,' Andrew replied bitterly, 'I wouldn't know what to do with happiness.'

'Don't say that, my boy, no, no – happiness lies ahead.'

'Ach, it's all woman's nonsense,' said Limbourides, 'men need to fight and have a little pain. That's the Greek way – we're not soft types. Women always come out with this garbage – marriages and all live happy at the end. Marriage is the start of our problems not the end of them.'

His wife playfully gave him a smack on his cheek and shook her head at him.

'Pah, you men don't know when you're well off!'

Andrew decided that he would go to Thessaloniki the next day. There was no longer anything in Athens to keep him. He had no desire now to see the sights; his quest obsessed him and drew him on like the call of a siren. Limbourides said he would give him an address to contact when he got there, one of his journalist friends. Andrew took it but privately decided that he would find his own way if he could. He wanted to be free of questioning and even of kindness if possible. Just now he felt more alone than he had ever done in his life and proudly accepted that solitude as a butterfly accepts its chrysalis. It was a necessary part of some inner transformation.

Chapter 8

The train steamed out of Athens on the way to Thessaloniki. Andrew settled in a corner near the window and watched the barren landscape flitting by. The sonorous regular rhythm of the wheels lulled him into a state of dreamy vacancy while the magpie chatter and activity of his fellow travellers formed a part of the background.

Two middle-aged men were reading newspapers and arguing together over politics, totally incomprehensible discussions to ears as yet un-tuned to the nuances of the language. Andrew caught a word here and there …'the king is a good fellow,' he heard one say, 'but do we need kings? Have we Greeks ever needed kings?' …while the reply was caught up in the shriek of the train as it entered a tunnel.

Opposite him a family spread out their picnic of boiled eggs, tomatoes, bread and a small bottle of retsina. The woman seeing him looking, smiled and offered him some food. He smiled back and took the proffered egg, feeling her open-hearted goodness and wondering at it. Would a traveller in England offer their meal or even look at one on a train journey? Would they not rather hide behind their books and papers till one had almost arrived at the destination and then suddenly begin a conversation …

'Weather's been frightfully bad today, hasn't it? Hope it won't rain tomorrow. They may have to postpone the cricket match at Sodbury on the Green …'

On the other hand an English traveller would seldom want to know all about your life, which to be frank was a blessing. There were times when such anonymity was delightful.

However this was Greece and as he expected questions soon began to fly around ... 'Where are you going? How old are you? Where are you from?' By now he was used to fending off such questions, skilful at asking them instead and turning the tables.

The scenery was dull and flat with olive groves and cotton fields. As they began to travel northwards through the Vale of Tembi it became more lush and lovely even though clad in its winter sleep. In the distance Mount Olympus could be seen rising in its majesty, its snowy summit as always wreathed in mists and vapours. The Gods remained hidden today in their lofty, glorious palaces, bored with watching tawdry human affairs down below. The weather was noticeably colder and Andrew took a woolly out of his bag and put it on beneath his jacket. He had no overcoat and rather regretted the fact now. It would have to be one of his first purchases once he had settled himself.

Eventually he fell asleep as did a good many other occupants of the carriage. At Larissa the train stopped with a screech and a jerk and Andrew awoke startled, wondering where on earth he was. They were to remain here for twenty minutes so he got out and stretched his legs a little. He bought some *koulouraki* from the vendors waiting on the platform who then clambered inside the train ready to tempt with their bread, yoghurt and sweet, sticky cakes those too idle to get out.

Now the rain began to drive down in long sleeting ribbons obscuring the view. A hush fell upon everyone in the carriage; children stopped their wailing demands, the older men ceased to argue and gesticulate, folded up their newspapers and fell asleep, snoring in rhythm to the train's great iron wheels. Everyone was glad to arrive at last at Thessaloniki and with many waves and smiles they all parted and went their ways as is the way of travellers, intimate and friendly for a brief moment, flashes of connection with other human beings whose paths now moved away and disappeared into the unknown.

Andrew took his small case and set off aimlessly. It was wet and gloomy and he longed for a hot drink. He walked some way till he found a small café and went in and seated himself down at a table near the steamed up window. Here he ordered himself a plate of *meze* and a coffee, yearning for a cup of decent tea but knowing that if he asked for *tsai* it would probably arrive in a glass with lemon sliced into it and that was a horrible way to treat tea. He was getting used to a good glass of water – one needed it after the strong Turkish coffee in tiny little cups. He had learnt now to ask for his coffee to be *metrio* and not *glyko* for he hated things too sweet.

As he sat there feeling dispirited by the rain and wondering what he would do next, he saw a smartly dressed young man seated at a nearby table watching him. When their eyes met, the young man raised a glass to him and said, '*Xenos?*'

Wearily Andrew nodded. Was he always to be foreign no matter where he went? Here he was foreign because of his accent, in England because of his looks. It seemed to be his destiny never to be accepted as one of the crowd. Perhaps his accent would improve with time and he would really be a Greek then. But for the present, his halting Greek would raise curiosity wherever he went.

The young man motioned to the patron and in a short while a waiter brought over a small glass of raki and put it on the table by Andrew.

'I didn't order this,' said Andrew, surprised.

The waiter inclined his head towards the young man on the other table and motioned with his hand that there was the source.

Andrew looked at the young man who now raised his own freshly filled glass, '*Yia!*' he said heartily and downed his drink with a swift movement of his wrist. Andrew attempted the same and nearly choked.

The young man laughed and came over to sit at his table.

'Have another,' he said, 'a little raki keeps one's blood warm in this damned weather.'

'Let me offer *you* one,' said Andrew.

'Nah …you're a stranger, strangers are guests, they don't pay. E, Giorgo – bring two more and be quick about it!'

They downed the glasses of raki and these were followed by another two. Andrew was feeling a good deal warmer and lighter headed by now. Suddenly the young man appeared to be the most amiable person on earth, his brown eyes full of kindness. A glow of goodness seemed to surround him.

'What's your name?' Andrew asked.

'Sotiris Manoglou, that's me. Sotiri the Mad they call me – and you?'

'Andreas Cassimatis.'

'So where you from, Andreas?'

'I've just come from Athens.'

'Okay – I gathered you had just arrived from the station, everyone stops here who doesn't know the city or have relations. Giorgo, here, does a roaring trade from aimless travellers. So of course you've come from Athens. But before Athens, where then, brother?'

'England. I was born there.'

'A milord, eh?'

'Hardly. What makes you say that?'

'English people are all rich, that's what they say here.'

'Where on earth did people get that idea?'

'They always seem to have money to spend, the English.'

'A lot of English people are very poor indeed. Perhaps only the wealthy ones travel. But I'm not one of them,' he added hastily.

'I wonder if the English know about poverty as we do? Here we starve if we cannot get work and getting work is pretty hard at times.'

'I assure you it's no different in England! People there are also starving and have no work.'

'What sort of world's this then? Some with all the money and all the others starving. Seems there is not much justice in that! Who made up this plot?'

'I have no idea,' said Andrew sadly, 'it's a stupid world.'

Sotiris spread open his hands, 'E, well, there are compensations – like a good drink with a pal. I like you Andreas. Where are you staying in Thessaloniki?'

'I have no idea, no real plans. I'll find a hotel somewhere, I suppose.'

'Stay with us, brother – we are poor and only have a small space to offer you but you are welcome.'

'Thank you, no, I can't accept. I'll find a hotel.' Andrew felt a real need to be alone for a while.

Sotiris looked put out but said no more and at last rose and said goodbye and left.

'I've annoyed him,' thought Andrew dully, 'and he was so welcoming and kind.'

He felt very tired and his head was not altogether clear about anything.

After paying his bill, he rose and took his bag and sallied forth into the glistening wet streets. The rain had ceased at last and darkness fallen. The area was poorly lit and he wondered if he should after all have accepted Sotiri's invitation for a night at least. He had no idea which direction was the centre of the town or where he was or where to go. However, he began to walk steadfastly along the streets and found that he was walking uphill, coming to an area that was winding and twisted with cobbled streets and derelict old wooden houses.

'This doesn't feel right,' he thought, 'I must be heading up into the old Turkish quarters that Mother wrote about in her diary. Surely all the city isn't like this? I had better go downwards again; maybe then I'll arrive at the harbour-side where the hotels are. How stupid I was not to ask for directions at the café!'

The area he was walking in had a poverty-stricken, ramshackle feel about it and a sinister silence hung upon the empty, rain-washed streets. It was now very dark and lights shone dimly from a window here and there. Voices could be heard as people passed by or called from their houses to one another.

Andrew clutched his bag and hurried along, feeling foreign, foolish and lost.

The streets became tortuous, confused, his head throbbed with *raki* and his stomach churned with hunger for he had only had a few of the customary bits and pieces with his drink.

He heard a strange, soft movement behind him. His heart beat. Looking round he saw three men had emerged from a shadowy side street and were following him. They stared at him directly and he knew they were up to no good. How had he allowed himself to fall into this nightmare situation? Why had he been so frugal and not taken a taxi to a hotel?

He quickened his pace. The men quickened theirs. They were fast catching up with him. Suddenly his arm was seized, his case wrenched from him and he spun around to confront three youngish looking men whose faces in the darkened, half lit street looked to him the very embodiment of evil. They surrounded him and laughed and jeered at him.

The pack of wolves, the herd instinct. It reminded him of prep school when he had been teased for his foreign looks, called Drew the Jew and baited like a bear. But he had always fought and his tormentors had lived to regret it. Ancient rage rose up in Andrew like some thick dark tide that entered his mouth and filled it with bile.

He caught one of the men with a right hook that would have delighted his boxing instructor at school. The fellow slumped to the ground and then again Andrew hit out and caught another of them on the side of his face, a blow that made the man reel.

'You bastards!' Andrew yelled. 'I'll kill the lot of you, I'll kill you!'

He shouted at them in English but the sound of his voice and the well aimed thud of his fist on their jawbones soon persuaded the thieves that they had a determined adversary and they took to their heels, dragging the staggering, groaning youth he had first hit and momentarily laid out.

Andrew stood in the road, his hands still in fists, his eyes flaming and fury boiling up in him so violently that he shook with it. He was amazed at his own reaction just as he had been all those years ago when the boys had surrounded him at school.

'E, *palikari*, that was something to see!' said a voice behind him.

Turning, fists up and ready to fight again, Andrew saw Sotiris running towards him.

'Put those fists away, I'm not a thief, Andreas,' said Sotiris with a laugh,' but my man, that was glorious – how you hit them! Beautiful! I was coming to your aid but you sorted them out good and proper. I love you more than ever! Look come on, you'll have to come with me. Stay with us tonight, my good man – don't be a fool.'

'I'll come. I've lost my few belongings anyway,' said Andreas bitterly.

'Well, you're a stranger and haven't any more clue than a baby where to go in this happy, little city.'

'It's a nice welcome!'

'It's the kind of welcome you'll get here amongst us *manges*. What d'you suppose? – they're all starving round here. You were fair game and an idiot to boot. You're lucky they didn't pull a knife on you but you took them by surprise. Christ and the Virgin – I admire your courage, *palikari mou*! A man after my heart. They'll have sore heads for a bit that lot.'

'They've got my things.'

'*Ade re*, a few clothes, what else did you have there? Your shaving things? We'll find you some more. Steal 'em back if we have to.'

'Did you know those men?'

'Got a fair idea,' said Sotiris. 'I'll sort them out for you, never fear. They won't rob you again. People here respect me and my brother.'

They arrived at a ramshackle house further up the hill and Sotiris banged on the big wooden door. A slightly older man peered at them through a small spy hole at the top and then opened it and let them in. Sotiris introduced Andrew to his brother, Savvas, who shook his hand and looked at him with a grave expression that was not unfriendly. He was not as tall as Sotoris and yet he was of a stronger, larger and stockier frame. Sotiris chose to be clean-shaven but Savvas had a thick waxed moustache that went out at straight angles. There was a serious, sad look in his dark eyes.

In the corner of the darkly lit room sat an old man wrapped in a blanket who appeared very deaf and frail. This, they told Andrew, was their father, Old Manoglou.

The house was indeed dilapidated and cold as well. A

beautiful old Turkish stove stood in a tiled corner but it was unlit and a small smelly paraffin heater and a tiny oil lamp were the only light and heat available. Water ran down one of the walls in a continual trickle and someone had placed a little basin at the bottom to catch the stream. The steady sound of this dripping water was most depressing. After the luxury and comfort of Limbourides home in Athens, this was a real hovel. Unused to such surroundings Andrew looked about him in some dismay. Did people really live in such places? Was there really such poverty? He realised then just how sheltered and privileged his life in England had been. Suppose his mother had stayed on here and been reduced to this and they were forced to live in such a place? It was a frightful thought.

'You like our palace, milord?' said Sotiris with some irony.

'It's a roof over one's head, I suppose,' said Andrew, 'and I'm more than grateful for your kindness in taking me in on such a nasty night.'

'Think nothing of it – you'll take me in when I come to England some day. That's how it goes!'

'If I had somewhere in England, yes, I would.'

'You have no home there? – but your suit is a good one, you look well fed enough.'

'I've – I suppose I've run away,' said Andrew.

'You must be mad then. You came here to Greece? What ever for? Greece is a dump, I tell you. We came here from our beautiful homes in Smyrna but certainly not because we wanted to join these dopey, illiterate Macedonians. We had no choice, the Turks slaughtered us; they wanted to wipe out all the Christians. According to them they should have done the job when they first created their lousy Ottoman Empire. Well, they threw us out and we threw out the Turks. In Smyrna we had money there; ask my father – we had education, businesses, a lovely house and our beloved mother.'

Tears came into the young man's eyes and he wiped them away with the back of his hand.

'What happened to your mother?'

'She died as we escaped from the burning city. She got into

the wrong boat and it sank with the weight of the fleeing population. Somehow the rest of us survived and got here to Thessaloniki – but to what? Poverty, misery, we're aliens here, they don't want us. Ah, Smyrna – our beautiful city! No more! It's burnt to ashes, the Turks have taken our land and goods and raped our women. You have no idea!'

Andrew was silent. How little he knew about Greek history and sufferings. He wished he understood better for he felt the pain in his friend's voice and it reverberated in his heart like a hammer striking.

'I don't know much about it all,' he said apologetically. 'I do know the Greeks recently lost their war in Asia Minor and that there was an exchange of population. It sounds pretty awful.'

'It was the Great Catastrophe! Torn from our homes and our ancient city where our ancestors had lived for centuries. Ach, my friend, you have no idea. We were men of substance and authority there, now we are *manges*, we are less than men here. Harassed by the police and the authorities. Luckily, the present head of police likes our kind of music and turns a blind eye to some of our little gatherings. You'll have to come along to Bald Yiango's café and listen to the *amanades*, watch us dance and get drunk and forget our cares for a while, all men together. Beautiful! I play the *santouri,* Savvas plays the fiddle and my sister, Anna, sings. She is a little *haidoni*, a nightingale. The men, they love her.'

'You have a sister?'

'Sure. She'll make us some grub – I'll call her now.'

He shouted out 'Anna!' A pair of dirty curtains hanging over a door parted and in came a young woman.

'Anna, meet this friend from England. You should see him fight! He's a regular lad, a crazy man! Make us some food, we're all starving.'

Anna looked at Andrew boldly as if weighing him up. Her eyes seemed to see through to his inner soul and he felt strangely uncomfortable. He was surprised for most of the unmarried women he had met in Greece were quite modest and shy but this young girl, surely no more than eighteen or nineteen, had a wary, adult look about her. It was hardly surprising considering the adventures she had lived through. Her face was light skinned but her hair fell in dark curling abundance well past her shoulders. She was not a beauty but her face had a charm of its own and her mouth was warm and sensual.

'Welcome, stranger,' she said quietly and returned to her kitchen.

'So you see us here, poor and destitute but not without pride, Andreas,' said Sotiris, 'we people from Smyrna are proud folk. Could people take more away from us though? They took our land, our women, our homes, our money and here in Greece, the mother country as you might suppose, we get no welcome but are pushed to the fringes of society to make shift as best we can. It's all very well calling Thessaloniki 'The Mother of the Poor'. Some mother! Is there any work? Is there hell!'

'There's even less since that damned Metaxas got in power,' growled Savvas. He offered Andrew a cigarette.

'So Colonel Metaxas is the Prime Minister now, isn't he?'

'More of a fascist dictator we say. He lays down the laws just as he likes and the King lets him do as he pleases. He's given him full powers and sits back on his arse in his palace, no bother for him.'

'I thought the King had been forced to leave after the war, when Venizelos came to power.'

'Ah, Venizelos, there was a man for you,' said Savvas with enthusiasm, 'a brilliant man, a man of the people. They were always trying to bump him off, those Royalist bastards! As for the King, we got the good-for-nothing back again, didn't we, and poor Venizelos was forced to flee. And this year he died... Venizelos, our hero. Poor Venizelos, that's all the thanks he got for saving us from the Bulgars and the Austrians. It's true that he was part of the Great Catastrophe but that wasn't his fault. It was the fault of those French and English bastards who promised to help us and then ditched us, leaving us to the tender mercies of the depraved Turks whose fun consists in torturing and maiming and slaughtering and taking a pile of heads home as trophies. That's our politics here, all madness. People don't know what's good for them. We Greeks are in a real muddle, friend, we are liberated from the Turks but we haven't yet found out just who we are and what we want as a nation. We're still split. The two halves that Plato spoke about cry to be joined up and healed and made whole.'

'So Constantine is back again?'

'His son Alexander that he left here when he scarpered last time died of a monkey bite – very fitting, if you ask me. Constantine came back but abdicated in favour of his son George, whose stooge Metaxas is now in charge.'

'But presumably the people voted for him?'

'What are you on about? Nobody voted for him. *We* don't have a voice. The ordinary people have no voice, just cries of pain – but we shall see. We shall see. You can't keep the nation down; we Greeks won't have it! Freedom or Death, that's us!'

At this point Anna came in and laid steaming plates before them as they sat at the rough wooden table.

Savvas looked at the food and swore at her. 'What's this stuff? *Fasolada* again? Haven't we anything better to offer a guest than bean soup, you stupid woman! You know I hate bean soup.'

The girl placed her hands on her hips and looked at her brother unflinchingly.

'Find some work and bring some money in the house and maybe then we could offer something more than bean soup to a guest! Don't you shout at me, I'm the only one here that does any work and brings in some cash while you two play with your *santouri* and your fiddle and get high on hashish.'

And she stalked proudly back into her little hole behind the curtains. Andrew watched her with some admiration. She was quite a fierce girl and he rather liked that.

Sotiris took some bread and broke it and offered it to Andreas. It was almost Biblical and Andrew felt a strange sense of peace amongst these men made rough by a rough life. He spooned up the thick soup of beans with delight. It tasted wonderful to him.

'Your sister's a good cook,' he said, 'this is the nicest food I've tasted here so far.'

'It's rubbish and we are ashamed that there's no meat to offer you' said Sotiris, 'but I'll get some tomorrow.'

'Don't do that for me. I'm happy eating *fasolada* every day. It seems very nourishing to me. What did Anna mean about the *santouri?*'

'We earn a bit going round the Café Aman scene. We have always had musicians in our family and our music keeps us sane. It keeps us *sane.* You'll have to come out with us tomorrow and listen to us play at Bald Yiango's place.'

'I'd like that, I'd like to hear the music.'

'It will sing to your soul, you wait and see – then we'll know if you're Greek or not.'

They laughed and clinked their glasses of retsina together.

Chapter 9

Andrew felt immensely tired. Sotiris led him up the wooden stairs at the back of the house to a small windowless room. It led off from another room with a couple of beds in it and was screened by a thick woven curtain. It appeared to once have been a large cupboard or dressing area of some sort. On the floor was a thick pallet, which apparently was to serve as his bed. The sheets were clean and it seemed more than welcoming to him. Andrew took of his clothes and folded them up on a small wooden stool beside the bed but kept on his shirt and pants. He was freezing and his pyjamas had been in the stolen bag.

He was glad now that he'd had the sense to put his papers and money in the black bag tied about his waist. What a wise precaution! The thieves had got his clothes and some books but little else. He still felt nervous about his fund of money and trusted no one, not even Sotiris or Savvas. They were all poor and the temptation of seeing his large wad of cash might prove too much for them.

Andrew didn't blame them, of course. Their life seemed so harsh and they had so little but he wasn't going to let himself be robbed and reduced to their own desperate situation. He slipped the precious black bag beneath the pillow and lay down on the bed and tried to sleep. Despite being so tired, he was now awake and felt very cold. He rubbed his arms and legs trying to warm himself up.

The room he was in was totally dark but between the drawn curtains he could see a faint glimmer in the other room from the tiny devotional oil lamp, which stood on a shelf before an ikon of St. George. He watched the hypnotic flicker of the light for some time. He could hear excitable voices murmuring in the room downstairs rising every now and then to a shout but he couldn't hear what was being said. Besides he knew by now that these passionate Greeks always bellowed and gesticulated at each other as if they were having a mighty quarrel when it was merely a normal conversation.

He fell into an uneasy sleep. Dreams chased one another across his eyes like mad scenes at the cinema. Suddenly a faint sound or movement awoke him, his heart pounding. Everything appeared pitch black at first but he was suddenly aware that the wavering chink of light had broadened between the curtains. Someone was at the curtained archway and looking in on him.

Was he to be robbed or murdered? Not if he could help it! He lay still as a mouse and waited, every nerve strung in suspense, ready to spring his own surprise.

The figure silently approached his bed and bent towards him. Andrew's arm shot out and he seized the person by the arm and dragged them down.

The intruder gave a little scream. He felt warm female flesh. Astonished he let go and sat bolt upright.

'It's me, Anna, move over, you fool!'

He moved over and the girl climbed in beside him. She was totally naked and he felt her soft breasts flop against his arm. He moved away in alarm. What on earth was going on?

'What are you doing here?'

She was silent for a moment.

'Are you being stupid?' she said at last.

'No, I'm not. I'm asking you what you're doing. Your brother will be furious with you.'

She smothered a little giggle, 'Sotiris sent me to you, you English fool!'

'He sent you to me!'

'Yes, why not? – you can have me for free, you're our guest. I'm the meat you never got at dinner.'

'For God's sake! I don't want you to sleep with me, what sort of man do you think I am?'

'Well,' mused the girl, 'I thought you were a *palikari,* Andreas or I wouldn't have come. Sotiris told me of your heroism. I like a man, a real man you know. But if you don't like me ...' she added sadly, 'then I'll go. Sotiris will be most offended though.'

'I can't make you Greeks out!' said Andreas, exasperated, 'but it isn't that I don't like you ...I think ...I think you're very beautiful, Anna.'

'You do? Then make love to me, what are you waiting for?'

Her hand slid between his legs and felt for his member. A rush of blood flooded his genitals in response, stiffening him and he trembled violently. He had never in his life been so close to a woman, never felt her naked flesh, certainly never felt a woman's hand upon his private parts. He didn't know whether to be terrified or delighted by the exquisite sensations that this little hand provoked.

'See, that's better! Now your manhood's speaking to me.'

After all, he couldn't deny himself forever. He wasn't born to be a monk. All right, it went against everything he had been taught by his English upbringing and a part of him was dismayed by the situation. But surely he could put aside all that nonsense? All that English reserve and repression. He was in Greece; he could be a man and act like a man, take a woman if he wanted her. And he wanted Anna, he really wanted Anna, wanted that little hand to go on and on stroking him into a fever pitch of ecstasy.

He ran his hand along her supine body.

'Why are you trembling so much?' she asked.

'I'm cold.'

She giggled again, 'Maybe – but this thing isn't. This thing feels *very* hot! We'll soon warm you up. Come on.'

She rolled over, pulling his shirt undone, tugging at his underwear and laughing as she did so, exclaiming, 'What are all these clothes for? Get them off, stupid!' and he found himself on top of her, feeling the warmth and softness of her flesh beneath him. He bent towards her lips and kissed them; her mouth seemed sweet as honey, melting into his own. Clumsily he tried to find her and put himself inside her but couldn't seem to get things right. For some time they tussled in silence. She rolled away and sat up beside him.

'What's up with you, Andreas? You act like you hadn't a clue.'

He lay there without speaking and felt a hot flush of shame burning his cheeks.

Suddenly she understood and laughed a low, sweet laugh.

'You've never done it before. You're a virgin – go on admit it!'

He stayed silent.

She snuggled up beside him, 'Oh, Andreas, let me show you – I've never had a virgin before! Don't be ashamed of it – it's rather sweet. You a grown man and never had a woman! I think it's sweet. You do *like* women I suppose?' she added as another thought struck her, 'it's not that you're like the Turks or those *manges* who want little boys?'

'Good God, no! Of course I like women. I like you, I like you very much, Anna.'

'No problem then, let me show you, let me make a man of you …you'll remember me forever then, Andriko,' she added with a low laugh, 'your very first lover!'

Now he let himself relax and allowed those soft hands to guide and lead him in the wavering darkness into a place that was warm, scented, languorous and dreamlike. A place once known and tasted, never to be forgotten.

When Andreas awoke the next morning, it was still dark in the room. Anna had risen a long while before and left. He found himself covered with care by a tender hand and the scent of her still seemed to linger on his sheet and pillow. It was like musk, sweet but also piquant and spicy.

He was amazed at himself. He felt wonderful. It was as if he had been through an Eleusian initiation into the rites of manhood. He hadn't performed that badly in the end, had he, once he'd got the hang of it? It was all so natural and easy really. Pity she had guessed he was a virgin. He still felt foolish about that.

Well, he wasn't a virgin anymore.

It struck him then that young as she was, *she* was certainly no virgin. It seemed obvious now that she must earn her living as a prostitute – perhaps that was what she had meant by earning more than her brothers. The family lived on her earnings and her brothers were her pimps. This thought disgusted him for a moment but then he reflected that it was just as well. He wanted no entanglements. She looked a clean enough girl and she was so delicious. The memory of his pleasure made him stiffen slightly again. Men did these things all the time according to his cousin Reggie. Now he could see why Reggie was such an addict!

Rising, he dressed and went out into the other room. The two brothers were asleep and snoring in their beds and for a moment he wondered how much they had heard of what passed with Anna last night. He hoped that Anna wouldn't tell them it was his first time. He had a feeling she wouldn't.

He went into the kitchen and found Anna there giving the old father a cup of coffee.

'So you're awake, big boy!'

She laughed up at him but there was nothing malicious or mocking about her laugh. Her eyes were incredibly soft and kind and she stroked his cheek tenderly as she gave him a cup of coffee and a piece of bread.

He reached up to enfold her and kiss again those warm, sensual lips but she laughed and evaded his grasp.

'No more – don't be greedy. Later perhaps.'

'Do you have a bathroom?' asked Andrew when he had drunk his coffee and nodded a greeting at the old man who was mumbling away in the corner.

'Are you mad! In the summer we have a douche outside in the yard but in the winter we do our best over the sink. I fetched some water from the well earlier; we share it with about ten other families. So you're lucky, I heated you up some water to shave yourself. There, take this pan and fill up that basin in the sink there.'

'I haven't any shaving equipment. Those men stole it all.'

'Well, you can borrow Sotiris stuff. There look, in that cupboard over the sink.'

Andrew shaved and watched her covertly in the cracked mirror. Her movements were strong and active and determined. She was a girl he felt he could admire. An honesty and a radiance glowed through her that he liked despite her unsavoury profession. He couldn't quite come to terms with the fact that she slept with other men. He would have liked to think she was his alone, that she liked him for himself and not because her brother had asked her to go to him.

After some time, Anna went out with a small bag and told him she was going shopping at Modiano market.

'It's a joke, though,' she said, 'not much money in the house but we'll earn a bit tonight, we're playing at Bald Yiango's. And what to feed these men on? Smoking hash makes them hungry all the time. Vegetables are scarce at this time of year and what meat can I afford? You'll all have to have cabbage soup.'

Andrew yearned to give her some money but felt uncertain. Perhaps it was better not to let them know he had much money. Yet his conscience wouldn't allow him to eat their meagre supplies and not contribute.

When her back was turned he carefully took out a few drachmae and swiftly slipped the bag beneath his trousers again.

'Here, Anna, take this. It's not much but it will help with the food at least.'

'Don't be silly. You're a guest. Savvas wouldn't hear of it, take it back.'

'Please take it – payment for – for last night if you like.'

'Payment. Payment for what? Did I ask for payment – you make me sick!' and she flung the money back at him and went out in a rage, leaving him totally bewildered. Now what had he done wrong?

He heard the brothers rising and they came into the kitchen, grumbling and yawning and washed themselves at the sink in the corner.

After a good strong cup of coffee, they became a lot more human and Sotiris chuckled and rubbed his hands together and said, 'We're going to sort something out for you Andreas, you wait and see.'

'What sort of thing?' asked Andrew uneasily.

'Ah – a good thing. We're going out for a bit but you wait right here and keep the old fella a bit of company. He'll tell you a tale or two about our homeland. He talks of nothing else. I don't think he knows where he is half the time.'

'Listen, I've got to find myself a hotel to stay in. I can't stay here and eat your food and …' Andrew paused.

'And fuck our sister, eh?' laughed Sotiris with a grin and a wink, 'Did you have fun? She's a beauty, our girl. Don't look so shocked. She's worth a lot, men queue for our Anna. She's something round here. But don't talk of hotels. Of course you must stay. Stay as long as you like.'

Andrew felt shocked at first by their blatant reference to Anna but then he couldn't help but feel how natural the two brothers were about it all. They were not ashamed of their sister but proud of her talents as a singer and even as a prostitute. In some way she was like a priestess of Aphrodite in their eyes, giving herself abundantly to the stranger in the city and raising him in spirit as well as flesh. It was the sacred union of the temple prostitute and the neophyte. He felt a sense of deep gratitude towards Anna and her brothers.

'Besides,' pursued Sotiris,' you have to come to Yiango's den tonight and hear us play our music, hear our Anna sing. We'll have a little *glenti* – a party together! Brother, you'll stay with us forever then, you'll become a *rebetsa!*'

That isn't very likely, thought Andrew, but it would certainly be an experience. He no longer felt any fear of the rough elements of the city. His encounter last night made him realise he could look after himself quite well. Besides, these people had good reason to be as they were; there was little choice between destitution, dying of starvation or thievery. Who was he to judge?

'Okay, I'll come.'

Sotiris face lit up with joy and he clapped him on the back, 'Good, good! You'll love it.'

Andrew sat beside the old father who watched them all with dull eyes and tried to converse with him but it was hard to understand his accent and the poor old fellow tended to ramble and lapse into Turkish as if he thought Andrew understood him. However, Andrew nodded and smiled and tried to look attentive while his mind went to his own problems, wondering what his next moves would be. He had no intention of staying with the Manoglou family for more than this one night. He was going to find the village in the hills where his parents had met, where Eleni had once lived and make his way there. Surely someone in the village would be willing to put him up for the night for a reasonable sum.

Once that had been achieved then he would try to find some work though according to Sotiris that would not be easy.

'Thanks to the new laws this crazy government have introduced, we can't even play our music the way we used to. We're not allowed to mention drugs, sex, prisons – they want to water us down! Can you imagine? How else can we tell people our story, let them know what we have suffered and continue to suffer? Show them our pain? Bah! They want to make us all respectable and sing of moonlight and kisses. Only wealthy people can mess about talking of moonlight and kisses! This means that a whole crowd of refugees have left Piraeus and have headed for Thessaloniki where we can still get away with playing the kind of music we like. The police here don't make such a fuss; they let us alone a bit. Well now, that's all very fine as far as the music is concerned but not so good for work, you understand? There's even more folks standing by the docks now waiting for a job. Not a hope of work unless you're lucky.'

Well, I don't want to work at the docks, thought Andrew.

He could work for a newspaper maybe but hadn't enough Greek to write or typeset. He could do some sort of clerical work perhaps. For the present he had enough money to last quite some time always supposing he didn't get robbed again. All the same, it wouldn't last forever. He would have to do something to earn his living. But what?

He would trust. Something would turn up. So far he had been lucky. Besides he might find his aunt and she might help him in some way. Yes, he would trust his luck.

The old man had fallen asleep by the stove and Andrew was still contemplating his future when Sotiris returned at last.

'There!' said Sotiris triumphantly. He put Andrew's stolen case on the table. 'Told you I had something good for you.'

'That's amazing!' said Andrew jumping up and examining the case closely. It was certainly his and, apart from the broken locks, seemed intact. The contents were all of a jumble and he thought a pair of trousers and shoes were missing, but everything else was fine, the books still there. They wouldn't have been much use to anyone here as they were in English.

'Did you steal it back?' laughed Andrew

'Pah, didn't need to. I know that crowd, load of cowards! When Savvas and I turned up and looked them in the eye they handed the things over as meek as lambs. We boys have a reputation here, you know. You nearly broke their brother's jaw with that whack you gave him the other night. They won't be bothering you again in a hurry, I can tell you. Now you'll have a reputation too.'

He fetched out a bottle of *raki* from a cupboard and regarded it fondly, 'I want to toast my friend with this good stuff. Come on, bring the glasses over.'

He filled the thick little glasses and they clinked them together.

'Here's to you,' said Andrew, 'and many thanks, Sotiri, for all you have done for me.' And he didn't just mean the suitcase either.

Chapter 10

'Tonight we play, no need to look for work,' said Sotiris. He took his *santouri* out of its wrapping and laid it on his lap.

'Isn't it beautiful?' He stroked the shiny, decorated wood and gently struck a note or two with a little hammer. The reverberating sound was strange to Andrew's ears, almost a wail of distress.

Savvas in the background was preparing some *nargiles* or water pipes.

'Let's get ourselves in the mood for tonight' he said, 'time for a smoke to soothe our souls.'

'Andreas, are you going to try a little smoke?' asked Sotiris.

'No, I prefer to remain clear headed,' said Andrew, 'a cigarette will do fine.'

'Why be clear headed? It's a crazy world – why not be crazy with it?'

'Yes,' said Savvas as he unfolded the mouthpiece to his pipe, 'let go, forget, have sweet dreams …dream ourselves little lads back home in our beautiful house in Smyrna. Mamma making us our supper, Pappa well and sane, not the mess he is now, poor old fellow. Anna a sweet baby, not a whore!'

Andrew felt abashed by the passion in his voice. He knew nothing of suffering and realised that all his miseries of the past had been self-imposed. Suddenly it didn't seem so important even to find his aunt or to trace his past. What did it really matter in the scheme of things? What mattered was passion, feeling, creativity. Here were these two men with hardly any food to put on the table and their thoughts and talk were about their music. They both played their instruments for a while and

Andreas listened to the wonderful sounds they made from them, tried to understand their songs, which were often full of slang words he could not recognise. They were like Orpheus and they meant to drag Eurydice from the Underworld so that she could tell everyone what it was like down there.

The two men smoked and a look of peace enfolded them. The soft gurgling of the pipes lulled Andreas too and he felt oddly calm and quiet as if just breathing the hashish in the air affected him in some way. The effects of the dark, thin, little Balkan cigarettes knocked him out too. He couldn't quite get used to this strong tobacco. Anna returned to find them all fast asleep in uncomfortable positions, looking like a crowd of little lost boys. Only the old man was awake in his corner, nodding and talking to himself, oblivious of his sons and their friend.

'Ah, *Babaka mou*, what use are these boys of yours?' she said as she tucked another rug round the old man to keep his skinny frame a little warmer, 'they make no effort to get off their arses and find work.'

'Listen, we were all musicians, our family, we all played our instruments once,' said the old man, 'working on the docks ruins their hands, their sensitivity. Let them be, *corri mou*, let them be, daughter.'

'Let them be is all very well, but someone has to put food on the table for these great musicians,' grumbled the girl 'I suppose opening my legs for some guy every night isn't ruining my sensitivity? Oh, well, maybe someone will ask us to make a record and I'll get famous like Rosa Eshkenazi. Maybe we'll be invited over to the States where they say that they like *rebetika*. There they don't have dictators telling them what to sing about and how we mustn't upset the nice middle class ladies with our wild music.'

'*Papse, paidi mou*, walls have ears!' said the old man who wasn't as stupid as he seemed.

'Oof …prison couldn't be worse than this place. Let them hear what I think!'

She went into the kitchen and soon the smell of boiling greens began to pervade the room.

In the evening, everyone dressed up smartly. This surprised Andrew and he had to admire the fastidiousness of the two brothers as they brushed their jackets and the insides of their trouser turn-ups, put on freshly ironed shirts and did up their ties in elaborate knots then sleeked back their hair with brilliantine making sure that it was side-parted with care. They topped this ensemble with homburg style hats with wide black bands.

'You look like Chicago gangsters,' Andrew said with a laugh.

'Well, we have to fit in with the lads. Once you start to let yourself go, then things have really come to a pretty pass. We *rebetes* may be poor but we are gentlemen.'

Anna appeared in a sleek off-shoulder black dress, her hair tied back in an unruly mass of thick dark curls that fell over her creamy shoulders. Andrew found it hard to take his eyes off her.

They made their way to Bald Yiangos café, their instruments as inconspicuous as possible beneath their overcoats.

'Because these bloody police think nothing of smashing them to bits when they're in the mood to accost you,' Sotiris said with a resigned shrug.

'Just let them try and they'll get a sock on the ear they won't forget in a hurry!' snarled Savvas.

'Yes, and you'll get a prison sentence you won't forget in a hurry!'

'So what's new? I've been there already, haven't I? Life has no surprises.'

'Why do they stop you from having the music you like? It's madness,' exclaimed Andrew, 'surely everyone has to have some consolation and solace in their life? What do they think it's going to do to everyone?'

'Maybe it's because we make it sound so good to be in prison and to be stoned all the time! Maybe they think we might entice all those nice people out there, all those nice, kind people in their warm, comfortable houses to join us in our shanties and hovels,' said Savvas bitterly, 'that's how intelligent this government is. They think we're all Reds, that's the point. They're terrified of the Reds and our music stirs the peasants and the poor working people and makes them angry. And those in power are always afraid of angry people who might slit their throats and topple their regimes.'

In the tiny little Café Yiango, men were already seated on rush-bottomed chairs at small rough wooden tables, their fingers playing endlessly with amber worry beads. On the tables were their bottles of *retsina* or *ouzo*, their *mezes* and coffees. A young boy was going around carefully lighting the *nargiles* with charcoal from a brazier at the back of the bar. Those without *nargiles* were smoking the heavy Turkish cigarettes. The atmosphere was filled with smoke but no one seemed to mind.

The musicians settled themselves on a makeshift stage at the back with a thick curtain behind them. Another couple of men carrying a lute and a small drum joined them, part of the musical group.

Then Savvas began to play his violin, setting the mood for the song that was to follow with a long opening solo and the most extraordinary sound, at least to Andrew's ears, burst forth from the bits of wood and string and echoed around the room. This ancient instrument captured all the bitter harsh sweetness of Greece; its essence, wildness, heart rending pathos and sad gaiety in long waves of rolling, individualistic sound. It was heart stirring, it made the body want to move and soar into the air. Then the music became softer, sadder, delicate and full of grief.

Sotiris sang a song the words of which were not always clear to Andrew. The gist seemed to be about the sadness of life, the misery of a lost homeland and lost love. He sang the quatrains over and over again, interspersed with '*Aman, aman*'... which Sotiris had explained was an exclamation that meant 'mercy.'

'That's why the Turks called them *amanades,*' he said.

> '*I'm living in a crazy dream,*
> *Stoned the whole day through.*
> *They keep sending me to jail*

Break my heart and steal my soul,
Don't they understand at all?
Aman! Don't they understand?
I can bear the empty belly
But not the empty world.'

Anna now appeared and the men went wild at the sight of her. In the soft lights she appeared older than her years and very beautiful, a luminous goddess; yet full of deep, dark wisdom. Andrew felt a pride in the thought that he had made love to this marvellous creature but then it struck him that she might have made love to half the men in the room. Certainly many of them were leaning forward and watching her with a hungry look in their eye. For some reason this made him feel jealous and angry.

'*Aman, einai coocla!*' sighed a fellow beside him, 'God, she's a doll!'

'I'm being stupid,' Andrew thought, stifling a yearning to punch the man in the face, 'she's a prostitute. I don't own her and I wouldn't want to.'

Anna's voice rose up, thin and reedy and spine tingling.

'Look into the coffee cups and tell me what they say.
There is so much pain in me since my man went away,
They took him to the clink; they threw him around,
But he'll come back alive to me some day.'

Only you, old gypsy, must know the pain I feel.
They think they broke his spirit,
  Aman…
  …they think they broke him down
When they smashed his sweet santouri to the ground.
They smashed his sweet santouri, they tried to lose his soul
But they don't know my man, he's made of steel.

There was such yearning sadness in this music, such pain and sadness. Andrew felt it stretch like roots searching for water, deep down inside him to a place he had not even known existed in him. He felt something arise in his gut, a tidal wave of emotion that was indescribable and unendurable. He wanted to weep with grief and longing – but for what? He had no idea. It was all he could do to choke back the fierce sobs that threatened to un-man him. This unlooked for reaction shook him to his core.

As the night progressed, a man suddenly arose and began to dance in the centre and the onlookers either clapped in rhythm and shouted encouragement, '*Yia sou, manga!*' or remained very silent and absorbed. Arms outflung, fingers snapping, his head thrown back and a cigarette dangling from his lips, the dancer seemed to twist and turn about the very centre of his being like a spring that wound ever closer and closer. He appeared totally absorbed in his own movements, almost as if in a deep state of trance. Then suddenly he leapt in the air, crouched down and kicked out his legs, leapt again, twirling, clapping his foot and shouting '*opa!*' to relieve his feelings. Then he returned once more to the slow rhythm that drew him ever inwards to some deep core within. It was extraordinary to watch.

Anna had joined him at his table now and she whispered, 'It's like the earth turning on its axis.'

And it was indeed like that. Andrew was profoundly moved. He would never have thought that a man could dance like this, express his inner soul through this complete absorption. It had a religious quality as if he was in prayer. This, he felt, was the reality he had been searching for.

It was not the Old Greece that tried to shake off its oriental past and move ever closer to the European ideal as if in some way that might mean it had grown up as a nation. It was not the Greece of comfortable middle class homes like that of Limbourides, the ladies with their elegant escorts and their lovely clothes that he had seen hailing taxis outside the theatres of Athens. This was a raw, new Greece, simmering and bubbling and growing here in these dark, smoke-laden cafes amidst songs and dances of sorrow and pain. This was where new, fresh blood had been pumped into Old Greece from those ancient, ancestral places, so Turkish and oriental and yet still so very Greek. From the plains of Anatolia, the lost homelands of Smyrna and Asia Minor flowed the blood of Greeks who had been there for two thousand years and were now displaced, exiled from their roots.

Yet these people would inspire the old race, put life and soul back into it again. For the moment they were not acceptable, they were outcasts. The pain of their existence was not even about their poverty but because they were homeless, alien, Greek but not Greek. He totally identified with them.

Chapter 11

'You must never join a man when he dances the *zebekiko*,' said Anna, 'it's his moment of searching within, finding himself through the dance. He is capable of killing you if you went to join him. It's happened!'

'They seem to kill for very little here,' sighed Andrew.

'Not at all. It's a case of pride and honour. It's defending one's meeting with the inner God. People here understand that. It's only you foreigners who don't.'

You foreigners! The phrase ate at Andrew's soul. He swigged back another ouzo and grabbed the bottle for a refill, his face stormy.

Anna laughed, 'Now, I've upset you, my lad. You're a sensitive one and no mistake!'

A tall, lean handsome man approached and accosted her familiarly, running his hand across her naked shoulders and into her hair, seizing a handful of it and pulling her head back a little so that she was obliged to look up at him.

'Buzz off, Loupas, let me go, you fool!'

But she smiled up at him nevertheless with an easy smile and took the cigarette he offered her. The man lit it with his own, staring deeply into her eyes.

Andrew tried not to watch them, jealousy curling around in his gut. He had a great yearning to pull the man away and punch him in the face. It was totally irrational and he tried to calm himself down. He would never behave like this in England. Surely he would not? Perhaps it was the ouzo. He poured himself another.

The man now jerked his head in the direction of Andreas, 'Who's this *aliti*?'

'He's not a bum!' said Anna. 'He's a stranger in the city, from England. Sotiri has taken him under his wing. He needs protecting.'

'I don't think I need protecting at all,' said Andrew angrily

'Why should you?' asked Loupas with a grin, 'we're all buddies here.'

'Oh, *are* we? – that's not the impression I get.'

The older man laughed a little and blew smoke in the air.

'You're a pretty boy,' he said, 'watch it. They like pretty boys like you round here. *Yias* Anna …I'll see you soon.'

Andrew hoped that Anna might come to him in bed again that night but he was disappointed. She did not come at all and he lay in the dark wondering if he had upset her by offering her money, or simply been too callow and green for her more sophisticated sexual taste. Worse still he wondered if she had gone off with the man called Loupas. Loupas looked evil to him, handsome but evil. Yet he had sensed that these two were familiar and that Anna had some sort of feeling for him. The memory made him miserable and sad. He fell asleep at last but was woken from a deep slumber during the night. He heard a bloodcurdling yell followed by a man sobbing and waking up in alarm, rose and looked out of the curtains.

Savvas was bending over Sotiris and comforting him. The younger man was shaking and holding his head in his hands.

'It's okay, go back to sleep,' said Savvas brusquely, 'he has nightmares, that's all. He'll be fine in a minute.'

Andrew went back to his bed but found it hard to sleep again. He lay there dozing fitfully and thinking about many things till he felt it might be morning. Then he rose and slipped past the two men, by now sound asleep and snoring loudly.

In the kitchen-cum-sitting room, he found Anna already up, kneeling down beside her old father and washing him as he sat in his chair. She didn't hear Andrew enter and he stood for a moment watching the gentle and tender way that she lathered the old man's back. He was horrified by what he saw on the old man's body and couldn't help a gasp.

Anna looked round and stood up, dipping her cloth in the

hot water and wiping off the lather to reveal a back pitted with scars and fearful red blotches.

'My God, Anna – what happened to your father?'

She remained silent and looked at the old man who sat there quiet and obedient as she tended him. Andrew saw tears slowly running down her face and his heart went out to her.

He went over and put his arms about her. For a brief moment she laid her head on his shoulder and then returned to gently wiping the old man's back and helping him on with his shirt and jacket.

'Anna, oh Anna! Your life has been so horrible! Forgive me if I upset you the other day. I'm so ignorant. I want to think I'm Greek but I see that I will never be anything but English. I can't see things, feel things the way you all do.'

'Of course. You have a different history, different customs. It is what you are brought up to as a child that counts,' the girl replied as she struggled to put on the old man's jacket.

' Can I help you?' he went and gave a hand and she smiled at him.

'Well now, that shows me you are English,' she said, 'a Greek man would seldom offer to help.'

'Do you forgive me for giving you money? I'm so stupid.'

'I forgive you but curse myself for my stupid pride. It would have been useful,' she said with a sigh.

'I left it under the plate.'

'Bah! That's a lot of good. Sotiris will have changed that for hash by now. I won't see it for sure.'

'I'll give you more, give it in your keeping. '

'You need money too,' she said, 'I can't take your money.'

'I'll get you out of here one day, Anna, trust me.'

'You're no better than I am, Andreas, you have nowhere to go, so you tell us. At least I have a roof of sorts over my head even if it is a leaky one.'

'I *will* have – I like to work and I shall make myself a home here somewhere. Will you come?'

'You're a child, Andriko,' she said scornfully, 'you're just a child.'

'I'm almost nineteen. I'm hardly a child.'

'Not in years, no – but you know so little about life. I sense that you have hardly lived.'

'Well, that is true. But I am beginning to. I am learning.'

She made coffee in the *vriki* and poured it out into the little cups, handing one to her father who smiled at her and blessed her.

'Anna, what happened to your poor father?' asked Andrew in a low voice as they sat at the table together with their coffees.

'It was before the war it all began,' she said,' I wasn't born but I heard all the stories. The Turkish Pashas and the Kaiser were hand in hand, giving each other decorations and all the rest. The Germans advised the Turks to get rid of all the Christians and make Asia Minor all Moslem, all Turkish. They wanted Turkey on their side so as to have a route down to the sea. Didn't want the Greeks getting in the way! Then that Turkish devil, Mustafa Kemal, rose to power and he and his henchman were all too keen to carry this idea through. They began with the Armenians whom they slaughtered and butchered in their thousands, forcing them to go into the desert and starve or sinking them in ships, burning them in their homes. They told us it would be the turn of the Greeks next. They were jealous because we Christians had the wealth and the intelligence and made the money with our hard work and cleverness. Those lazy Turks lived on us like parasites, taxing the Christians as much as they could.'

'One day father was out of the city visiting an estate in the country and he was kidnapped by a band of Turkish soldiers. They tied him naked to a table and poured boiling oil on him. He had done nothing to any of them to deserve such a fate. They told him it was to show the Christians what they were in for when their turn came and that it was coming soon.'

'After that Father decided we should leave Smyrna, maybe go to America but then the Greek army began to win victories and Smyrna was freed for a while from those hateful Turks. All was wonderful but it wasn't to last for long. The Allies refused to keep their promises of helping the Greeks to liberate themselves; suddenly it didn't suit their purpose for the Greeks to free their people in Asia Minor though we had been there since the days of Homer and were in the majority. It was *our* homeland; the Turks were the invaders. So politically, the tide turned and the Turks swept us back. It was the Great Catastrophe.'

'I remember little of it all, Savvas was ten, Sotiris was eight and I was about four. I remember Savvas carrying me in his arms as we fled the city. I was so frightened. They had put money and some jewels in my pockets, hoping no one would search a child. Mamma was separated from us as we were herded on to the quay. Behind us the city had been set afire by the Turks, before us lay the deep ocean. I can still remember the waves crashing in the wind. People were screaming and scrambling into what boats there were. American and Italian ships were nearby but they refused to come and help us – they had been told not to. Their interests are always about oil or whatever and they didn't want to upset the Turks. The French were the only ones to join the Greek ships that were sent to help us. Sotiris tried to go to Mamma whom he saw in one of the boats but suddenly the boat sank, it was so overloaded with people, and she disappeared.'

'Is that why he has nightmares?'

'We all have nightmares, Andriko,' she replied sadly, 'those two think the hashish helps them but it makes it all worse. Sotiris will end up mad one day. I'm sure of it.'

'Don't say that!'

'I've seen it, seen them drop dead in the street from taking drugs. They go on to heroin and that's the end of them then. Sotiris is the worst with it. Savvas has always been more restrained.'

'You managed to escape in the other boats?'

'We did. We got to an island and then we came to Salonika. And here we are in our happy little hovel.'

'I make a promise to you, Anna, one day I'll take you away from all this. I'll take you to England if I have to.'

'And what would I do there?' she said with a laugh.

'You would marry me.'

'Oh, Andriko *mou* – .are you going to propose to every girl you screw from now on?'

'There won't be anyone but you.'

'Don't be ridiculous!'

He looked crestfallen and she came and kissed his neck.

'Do some growing up first,' she said with a little laugh, 'then I might consider your offer. You *are* quite sweet.'

Andrew told Sotiris and Savvas a little of his own story later on and they promised to help him.

'I want to find the village where my parents used to meet up,' said Andrew, 'My stepfather told me it was called Mistres and is up in the hills to the west somewhere. Do you suppose it's still there?'

'Of course, why not? I'll find out where it is and take you there.'

Sotiris came back later and told Andrew he had found directions to the village.

' It's a funny thing,' he said, ' maybe just a coincidence – but Yiango, who owns the café we play at now and then, comes from that village he says.'

'I wonder if he is the Yiango that used to run errands for my father? Surely it must be?'

'Maybe, but it's a pretty common name round here.'

'Could I meet him? Ask him if he knew my father?'

'Why not? It's worth a try.'

Chapter 12

They entered Bald Yiango's Café and shut the door behind them. It was still inclement weather and the rain had begun its downpour again. Freezing winds blew in huge gusts, stirring up enormous puddles in the pitted roads around the harbour side as if they were miniature oceans.

Savvas had found himself some work that morning. He had taken a big paint- brush and gone to the painter's café and sat drinking coffee with the other *bouyiajides* till someone came and employed him. Sotiris seemed disinclined to work unless he was obliged to and got off for the day by saying he had to take Andrew to see Yiango.

As they went into the café, the man called Loupas brushed past them and looked hard at Andrew as if perhaps he remembered him. He was always flashily but well-dressed and seemed quite affluent in comparison to the more shabby inhabitants of the area. Once inside the café, Andrew recognised the two young men who had attacked him in the street sitting with their coffees at a table near the window. He gave them a hard, angry stare and they shifted their gaze elsewhere rather sheepishly.

'Who is that man called Loupas?' he whispered to Sotiris.

'He's a crook,' said Sotiris, 'a regular gangster. His wife Litsa is a nice little thing to look at and he has made her the madam of a brothel down in Ladadika. He deals in drugs and all sorts of petty crime. One day they'll get him and he'll join the rest in the Yedi Kule.'

'Is it still a prison?'

'Sure. The Greeks call it Seven Towers now and it's as bad as ever it was under the Turks. But it's just right for crooks like him. He stitched up Savvas once and my brother had to serve three long years in that dump. One day, we'll get even with him, you'll see. He knows it too.'

'Is Anna …is she his girlfriend?'

'Well, he likes to think so. He likes to think he owns everyone, the bastard. But no one owns our Anna. She operates on her own and because she sings and dances so beautifully, they respect her. None of the pimps bother her. Besides they know they'd have us to deal with if they tried their tricks.'

After a while, Yiango emerged from the back of the café and came over and joined them at their table. He looked sour and middle aged but Sotiris had told Andrew that he was only just thirty years old. It was hard to believe for Yiango was now stocky in build with quite a paunch, his hair completely gone, hence his nickname. To compensate for this lack of hair, he had an enormous moustache that hung down the sides of his mouth giving him the comic look of a brigand from a Gilbert and Sullivan opera. His dark eyes however were shrewd and kindly. He regarded Andrew with some curiosity.

'So, you want to go to Mistres, Sotiri tells me. That's my village up in the hills over there. What on earth do you want to go for? There's nothing there worth seeing.'

'I want to take a look at the village and see if I can find the house that my parents used to meet in during the war. I hoped you might be the same Yiango that used to take my mother there.'

'Your mother – how would I know your mother? Who *was* she?'

'Her name was Dorothy Clarke then. She used to meet a Captain from the Greek Army, Costas Cassimatis, at a house in the village. I don't know whose house it was, nor did my mother. But she said a boy called Yiango used to meet her and act as a go between with the Captain. Do you know these people? Do you remember my mother? She was an English nurse from the hospital camp that was near your village.'

Yiango looked at Andreas in astonishment. 'You know, I thought you looked familiar in a way. Are you telling me that you are the son of this man she used to meet?'

'Yes. From what I understand, I was conceived in that house.'

'Well, in God's name! That's amazing! You are the son come back to Greece. That's amazing!'

'You remember my parents?'

'Yes, I remember the beautiful nurse. She was so beautiful. We all loved her and knew her in the village. She was friendly and even spoke a little Greek. The other nurses could be rather frightening, stern women at times. But she was gentle and sweet.'

Andrew's heart warmed at this praise of his mother.

'And my father, you remember him? '

'Well, of course. Though to be honest I always saw him in some disguise or other. He had a code name. He was a spy. We all knew that but no one there would have given him away.'

'He died in the big battle of September 1918. Do you know anything about that?'

Yiango looked at him thoughtfully. He said nothing for a few moments.

'Yes, he died in the big battle. Costas Cassimatis. He died ...' his tone changed, 'so you never saw him?'

'No, of course not. I was born in England and he died later that year.'

'You never saw him.' Yiango seemed to deliberate about something in his mind. 'So what do you want to do in Mistres? There's no grave, you know,' he added.

'I could visit Eleni's grave.'

'Who the hell's Eleni?'

'I think she was a relation of yours. She died in the war, a girl who worked for the hospital.'

'Oh, in God's name, we're going back in history! Eleni Stavropoulos. Poor girl. Yes, she was a cousin of mine. But you won't find her grave. We're not like the Jews, we Greeks disinter bodies after a while and put the bones in an ossuary. She'll be with the rest of her family now.'

'So there's no grave?' said Andrew feeling a little desperate.

'Bah, *tipota* ...nothing!'

'Then perhaps I could try to find the house my parents met in. I just want to look at it. Is it still there?'

'It's still there, ' said Yiango cautiously, 'it *was* the house of Kyria Anthoula. She was a rich widow, lots of olive groves and land; she was rich but getting old then. When she died childless she left it all to her nephew and he lives there now, on and off.'

'Would he let me see the house?'

Yiango looked a little worried.

'Better not ask – why go at all? What good will it do you? Why not leave it?'

'Leave it!' said Andrew suddenly flaring up with anger and banging his hand down on the table, 'do you realise, man, I've come all the way from England. I've left all behind there, everything, everything, to come and see this place. I *have* to see this place. Why does everyone keep denying me the right to find out something about my roots!'

'Okay, okay, keep calm,' said Yiango.

He remained silent for a little while.

'Tell me,' he said slowly, 'your parents – where they married?'

'They were engaged.'

'Ah! But not married. And your mother – has she married since?'

'Yes, she has.'

'Okay.'

He thought about it for a moment. He seemed to make up his mind.

'E, after all, you should go!' he declared. 'Maybe it's all for the best, meant to be, Kismet, e? I'll take you up in the car as far as the road goes. Then you have to walk the track up to the village. It's quite steep.'

'I don't care. But how will I get back? '

'Ask for a mule in the village. Someone will hire you one and you can leave it here. They can pick it up from me. Or you can stay in the village for a night. Ask for my mother, Kyria Toula. Say Yiango sent you. She'll put you up.'

'That's wonderful. Thank you so much. When can we go?'

'I'll be free tomorrow early in the morning. Come then and I'll take you up there. Then we shall see what happens.'

Chapter 13

After this meeting with Yiango, a meeting that fired up Andrew's spirits considerably, he decided to go off exploring the city a little. Sotiris returned home a bit put out at Andrew's insistence that he be left alone for a while, a state of being that seemed peculiar to the extravert Greek mentality. Andrew, however, yearned for some peace in which to reflect and prepare himself mentally for whatever he might see tomorrow. At times, his heart trembled. At last he was near to finding his own beginning. And what then, he wondered? What then when he had achieved this objective? What did life hold for anyone who attained their great desire, their great objective?

He walked around the now modernised and well-paved streets of the new Greek city of Thessaloniki that had arisen Phoenix like from the ashes of Judaeo-Turkish Salonika. It was a busy, highly urbanised city now and had lost all its quaint charm and elegant neo-classical buildings in the fire. Whatever was left was fast being demolished by the developers who wanted to remove all traces of Orientalism from the city and make it purely Greek, modern and European. They succeeded well enough but it also looked now like all other such modern cities, indistinguishable one from the other, featureless.

He walked about the huge Modiano market, now rebuilt and covered with a glass roof. Here stalls overflowed with produce of all kinds, the carcasses of sheep and goats hung up ready for purchase. It was a noisy place with its stall owners shouting, gesticulating and clamouring for attention, thrumming with housewives haggling over meat, fish and vegetables. Fine for those who had the cash to indulge in all this food. Unlike his poor Anna.

He sauntered along the covered Bezesteni with its smart jewellery shops and pricey goods, which reminded him of London's Burlington Arcade. Later, he took a tram along the waterfront and out to Karabournaki, trying to imagine how the scene would have looked before the fire but apart from a few older buildings that had miraculously survived, little remained.

Along Vasilis Olgas Street there were still some of the beautiful villas belonging to the wealthy Jewish families with their tennis courts and private beaches, their gardens full of palm trees and immaculately kept green lawns. Aretsou and Kalamaria were now a shanty-town full of hapless refugees with no place to live but squalid shacks and tents along the road and on the beaches. The main problem was housing all these immigrants and building work seemed to be going on everywhere he looked, huge blocks of apartments rising up all over the place. Someone was making money somewhere but it wasn't the refugees.

He made his way back later in the day to Sotiris' place in Ano Poli, the old town area where refugees had taken over the houses vacated by the Turks when they had been sent back to Turkey in the forced exchange of population. What an uprooting of people from places they had called their homes for so long! It must have been just as terrible for the Turkish people who had lived here in Salonika and loved their city, now sent to a Turkey that didn't understand them or recognise them. He reflected on the millions of lost lives, the vast, titanic scale of human misery that had occurred during these last thirty years. His mother had been right. It was as if an angry Zeus had risen on Olympus and cast his thunderbolts down amongst humanity, scattering them hither and thither like ninepins. It was truly some terrifying game of the Gods, impersonal, vast and so unfeeling. Individuality meant nothing in all this.

Yet Nietzche had once said that suffering was the only point in life, that we should welcome pain, not ask for peace and stagnation. Suffering was what fashioned and burnished us like steel thrust in the flames, hammered us into some lovely weapon.

It hadn't done Nietzche much good though, that philosophy.

When he knocked on the door of the little house, Anna Manoglou opened it. Her hands were floury and she was in the midst of cooking.

'I'm giving you a treat,' she said,' your money has come in handy! So it's *keftedes* tonight.'

She went back to fashioning long oval meatballs from the lamb's mince mixture she had prepared. Sotiris was seated by the Turkish stove, which had been lit with sweet smelling dried thyme and was casting a glow of warmth and comfort into the room. He was laughing happily and his eyes had a glazed expression as he gurgled on his nargile.

'Ah, life is great, ah, life is wonderful!' he kept saying and laughing a little crazily now and then as if some immense joke had suddenly struck him.

'Isn't life wonderful?' he asked Andrew who came and sat down beside him, regarding him askance.

'Why are you looking at me like that? You misery of a man! Here have some of this,' he offered the pipe to Andrew who shook his head.

'E! The misery – the blight on the face of the earth! *I* am happy though …so happy…'

He rambled on incoherently now.

'Don't take any notice of him,' said Anna wearily. She put the meatballs in the frying pan and a delicious sizzling aroma filled the air.

'Is he like this all the time?'

'Whenever he can get the stuff. He took the money you left the other day and blew it on best black. Now he's as high as a kite. Just let him be. At least this is a happy trip and he's laughing. That's because it's good stuff. If he gets the bad stuff, it gives him terrible nightmares. What worries me is that he's started sniffing it up as well, not just smoking it in the water pipe.'

'Where does he get it from?'

'Loupas, where d'you think?'

Andrew went into the tiny kitchenette and put a sympathetic and slightly possessive arm about Anna. She shook him off impatiently.

'Can't you see I'm cooking, you idiot? Go away!'

'Make love to me tonight, Anna,' he whispered in her ear.

She looked at him.

'And what if I'm not in the mood?'

He looked downcast. She smiled and added, 'Oh well, we shall see.'

'I want you to come because you want to, no other reason,' he said diffidently.

Anna went out later on some mysterious errand and Andrew dared not asked her what it was. He played backgammon with the other two and they put the old man to bed on the divan in the sitting room before turning in early. Savvas was exhausted by his long day's work and Sotiris was now beginning to sink into the depression that always follows euphoria.

'It's like Icarus,' said Savvas, looking at his brother sadly, 'you fly high then you tumble right back down to the depths again. You don't just hit the ground, you sink to the bottom of the sea.'

He helped his brother, who was now sobbing and shaking uncontrollably, into bed. Still Anna was not home and Andrew, dejected in his own turn, went to his little pallet.

Before long the other two men were snoring away. After a while, he heard the front door softly open and close. Anna's room was next to this one and he wondered if he dared creep in to see her. He waited a little but heard only faint sounds downstairs.

Rising he went out of the open door of the bedroom. Sotiris had to keep the door open as he felt claustrophobic. The light from the ikon wavered gently in the little draught that came from some chink somewhere in the tumbledown house. Anna was not yet in her bedroom, which was in the front room overhanging the street, so softly and silently, Andrew crept barefoot down the stairs. He saw her over by the sink, stripped to her waist, washing herself down. It was the first time he had actually seen her naked body for their lovemaking had taken place in almost utter darkness. He caught his breath and a deep sigh of longing issued from him like a cry of pain.

She looked round, alarmed for a moment, but then laughed a little and continued with her ablutions while he watched entranced by her delicacy and daintiness as she lathered breasts, neck and face, treating her body with feminine, loving care. Then taking a towel she began to dry herself. He stepped over and in silence he helped her. The old man slept soundly on his bed in the corner. The men upstairs snored on. Outside the wind howled and whistled down the streets and the rain pattered down. For once even this hovel seemed warm and cosy, the glimmer of the oil lamp softening the harshness and grime and broken down furniture.

His hands wandered over her breasts, her shoulders, her back, delighting in the exquisite firm feeling of a woman's soft, healthy flesh. She did not try to stop him but yielded up her nakedness to him. He buried his head in her hair, kissing the nape of her neck. Taking her hand he led her upstairs to her room and he lay there with her in her bed. He no longer felt clumsy or shy. It all was so natural, so simple. They fell asleep at last in each other's arms.

The next morning, when Andrew woke, he found Anna had risen early to get ready the old father.

'He doesn't like to be seen washing by strangers, especially when I wash his private bits,' she whispered.

She gave Andrew a coffee and they sat down to drink it together. There was such a sweet sense of intimacy between them now, an ease that came from having explored one another with extreme thoroughness.

'So today you go to see the village where your parents used to meet? How romantic a story! What a shame your poor father died and they never met again. I think that is so sad.'

'So do I. I would be living here in Thessaloniki if they had married and would be a real Greek. I would know who I was.'

'Is our race and our country who we are? Who am I then? Am I a Greek? I've lived here most of my life but I don't feel I am a Greek, not these Greeks anyway. I am from Smyrna, far more ancient, better educated, purer than this lot. As for you

Andrew, you are English through and through in everything you say and do. I don't think you will ever be a Greek.'

'But why not?' he asked disappointed.

'It's how you have been brought up. You don't react quite like our men here do. The language has nothing to do with it – you're doing pretty well with that. You already talk our *rebetes* slang. Better not use those words outside this place. The police might arrest you! I'm joking, it's all right. You'll soon lose it when you leave here. But what I am saying is that you react like an Englishman, you are too considerate, even when you make love. You'd think I was a piece of china. Yes, I'm used to being thrown around a good deal more! And though no one can question your manliness, you are so soft in some ways. Too polite, maybe. Not Greek anyway.'

'So who the hell am I?' said Andrew, stung by her reference to his lovemaking.

'You silly man, you are Andreas – you are yourself. You don't have to belong to a country to be yourself. Just be who you are, content with who you are and forget all this other stuff. Go and see this village, get it off your chest. Then forget the whole thing and get a job and make your own life. Or in the end go back to England. Enjoy being who you are. You may never fit in anywhere; I know how that feels! But in the end it's quite a blessing. You are unique, special. Not just one of the crowd. The people here treat me differently, Andreas and do you know why? Because I truly believe I am someone special.'

'You are special, Anna, there's no one like you. I'm so in love with you, Anna.'

'Oh, don't start all that again! You hardly know me, Andreas. You don't yet know what love's about. I'm the first woman you've really known, you said so yourself. You'll love another, wait and see.'

He remained silent, caught up in grief at what she said.

'Do you love this Loupas?'

She looked at him in disgust. 'Mind your own business! Anyway, no I don't. One day I shall sort that man out. I'm working on it. He's going to see the inside of a prison and pay for what he did to my Savvas. Him and his little bitch of a wife!'

By now the other two men had arisen and the conversation ended much to Andrew's regret. He would have loved to spend all day talking and all night making love to Anna.

Yiango drove Andrew up the made-up road, the now neglected remnant of the British army's road-laying efforts in the war. They eventually arrived at a flat grassy area where the proper road ended abruptly. A little further up the hill a rough, fairly wide track carried on into the distance. It was very muddy underfoot but Andrew had bought himself some strong boots and a good coat for it was very cold high up in these hills.

'There's the road to the village. This is where the hospital camp used to be. Your mother worked here.'

It was all deserted and empty now. No white tents, no laboratories, no mess tents or medical huts. The grass grew in little patches and the wild had reclaimed the site back again now that the tramp of army boots and the churning up of lorries and ambulances no longer marred its once virgin ground. Andrew stood and looked about him in silence, moved to his soul. He tried to picture it as his mother had described it and almost imagined he heard the noise of planes passing overhead to the French airfield, the bleating of animals, the chatter of people or more poignantly, the sound of sick soldiers groaning in pain as they were hastily transferred from overloaded ambulances to stretchers, taken to huts to be washed and have their wounds dressed.

He imagined his mother in her long blue dress, her apron with its Red Cross becoming stained with blood and pus, her delicate white hands moving compassionately over these wounded, sickly bodies, helping to relieve their sufferings. A sudden feeling of shame for his treatment of her arose in him. What a terrible a son he was, not even to say goodbye to her when he left when she had shown him that *she* had forgiven him and wanted to speak to him. She didn't deserve that. She had sacrificed herself and risked her life for others. He had done nothing at all.

Yiango looked around too.

'Well, all that's over,' he remarked,' they've all gone now. It's like a dream. Were these things really here?'

Like a dream. Yes, it was like a dream. It was all over now.

'I'll carry on up the hill then' said Andrew, 'thank you for bringing me.'

'Just a word of caution,' said Yiango, 'if the nephew is at home at Kyria Anthoula's – and he might not be as he has business that takes him to Athens sometimes or other places – if he is, be careful what you say as his wife is a funny, jealous woman. Got quite a temper I hear. He's only been married a few years so I don't really know her. But that's what they say. She might not like the idea that your mother and father fucked there. Get me?'

'I'll be careful.'

'Okay, well, good luck.'

And Yiango climbed back into his little, rattling car and set off down the road back to the city that sprawled below them. Andrew turned and began the uphill climb to Mistres.

Chapter 14

The village had not changed much, he felt sure of that. The roadway was still a smelly open gutter and a look of poverty pervaded everything, The little mossy red tiles on the roofs of the houses looked as they had looked for hundreds of years, the shutters mainly painted green, some fresh, some cracked and peeling. The doors usually wide open in summer were now shut tight against the inhospitable winter winds. It felt even colder up here, exposed to all the elements, than it had down in the city. Andrew was glad he'd had the foresight to wrap himself up well.

Fierce barking greeted him as he walked carefully along the side of the muddy main street but thankfully most of the dogs were chained up in their yards and merely strained at their leashes like mad things at the sight of a stranger in their midst. One or two of these, left free, but half wild creatures came bounding up to him, flinging their muddy paws against his chest and snarling angrily. He liked dogs and had no fear of them. He spoke to them in such a way that they dropped down again and merely sniffed him over with care and then bored, turned and slunk back to their haunts. Seeing these fierce creatures made Andrew think of his mother's diaries. The dogs had never really frightened her either. She had been willing to risk an encounter with them for the sake of her all-consuming love.

Those diaries had become as much a part of his life as they had been his mother's. It was almost as if the events she described had happened to him and the memories had become implanted in his own brain by some mystical osmosis.

Sometimes he felt he had no life of his own, that his being was sucked up in the events and past happenings of his mother. If he was to find himself, he had to find where she had been, what she had done, retrace those steps to his own beginning. Perhaps then and only then he might be freed to be himself.

As he skirted the muddy road, he savoured the memory that his mother had walked up these very streets. She had made her way to the house of Kyria Anthoula and there met his father secretly and made passionate love. It was in that house that she had conceived him, Andrew, from this defiant, splendid passion. Defiant because it flouted the horrors of war and death, had brought new life into the world, flown in the face of convention.

How many people knew the exact moment of their conception? He not only knew it but was also aware that it had been a moment of glory for his mother. Most children were conceived without love, without much enthusiasm, often unwanted. It is true that his mother's pregnancy had made her unhappy at first but given the circumstances, he didn't blame her for that. She had certainly been happy to bear him in the end and had showered him with love when he was a small child. He could only hope that the man who now lived in that house might ask him in and let him look around just a little. Naturally he couldn't tell the man that his parents had once met there as lovers. Only he himself would know and take a secret delight in the fact.

This little tumbledown village was where he had come to being. Nothing much to look at, a place like this, yet for him it had an air of magical, romantic fascination. For the first time since he had come to Greece, Andrew felt himself close to his mother again. He thought of her and how she had looked in those days, so gentle, so very beautiful with her deep auburn hair and vivid blue eyes ringed with black around the irises. If he had only known her then, he felt sure he too would have fallen in love with her.

A man walked by with a donkey loaded up with wood bound for the bakers oven and a couple of young girls with white kerchiefs on their head came out of a house and smiled at him shyly as they passed.

'Are you after someone, stranger?' asked an old man who was standing outside a café, smoking a pipe, 'come in for a coffee and tell us about yourself.' The other men in the *taverna* ceased their game of backgammon and looked out at Andrew with interest.

Andrew smiled but carried on quickly, looking for the house that Yiangos had described as his mother's. It had a blue door, he had said, the only house with a blue door and bright blue shutters.

Andrew found the house that fitted this description and knocked at the door.

A middle-aged woman, her hair already grey, appeared, wiping her hands on her apron. She looked at him questioningly.

'What do you want?'

'Are you Kyria Toula?'

'So what if I am?'

'I'm a friend of Yiango's. He told me to come to you for advice.'

At this her suspicious features relaxed and she immediately invited him into her house. In the corner sat an old lady dressed in a plain brown dress, a black scarf tied about her head, her stockinged feet thrust into black backless slippers. She was busy with some sewing and looked up at him and waved a hand in greeting.

'A friend of Yiango's, *Yia-yia*' said Toula in reply to the old lady's babble of questions.

'E, a friend of Yiango's, a city friend! *Kalosorizate, paidi mou,* sit over there and welcome. You look a smart young fella,' said the old lady in her shrill voice, 'where are you from then?'

Andrew took a wooden chair by the table and did his best to explain.

'Can't understand a word he's saying,' grumbled the old lady, 'these foreigners.'

'Don't be so rude, *Yia-yia*. The young man speaks very good Greek. It's you, you're going deaf.'

'Rubbish, daughter, I'm not going deaf at all!' screeched the old lady crossly.

Kyria Toula shrugged and went off to fetch some of her best preserves and a coffee for Andrew.

'I am looking for a house that belonged to a Kyria Anthoula,' he said when she at last sat down beside him, having ensured his comfort.

'Well, it's not her house any more, she died years ago,' squawked the old lady who had heard that all right.

'That's right. It belongs to her nephew, Kyrio Ioannides now,' said Toula with a nod.

'I wonder if you would mind showing me where the house is? I just want to speak to Mr. Ioannides for a few moments.'

'But what's a foreigner like you want with him? Is it business? He has a lot of business deals going on they say. He's always away.'

'Yes, it's business of some kind,' Andrew said, mindful of Yiango's warning not to speak too much about his past.

'Those women gossip like the dickens,' he had told Andrew, 'whatever you say will be all over the village in five minutes. Mother will be round to her friends before you take your next breath. So watch it.'

'And you from England,' said the old lady, 'they say everyone is rich over there, they eat from silver spoons. That Ioannides must be doing well to have business with the English. He's always been a funny fellow and no mistake and as for that wife of his – painted woman that's what she is!'

'For goodness sakes, old woman, do shush,' said her daughter crossly, ' Kyria Marika is a modern woman, a city woman, she's bound to be smart and wear make up. It doesn't mean to say she's godless. She goes to church regularly enough when she's staying here.'

'Is she here now?' asked Andrew.

'I'm not sure. She doesn't often come over in the wintertime. They have a house in the city, on the smart East side. They usually come in the summertime to be a bit cooler. But he comes quite a lot, winter and summer.'

'To get away from *her*, she's a noisy bitch,' said the old lady, smacking her lips with satisfaction,' ach, you can hear them yelling some days so it's a wonder the roof doesn't fly off, there's plates smashing and heaven knows what! These modern women won't do as they're told. I'd never have dreamt of disobeying my Giorgo when he was alive. He was boss in the house and used to beat me when I answered him back. That's how it should be. Reckon that Ioannides doesn't know how to deal with the woman. She needs a good beating.'

'Beating didn't do much for *your* tongue! Poor Ioannides, after all he's been through,' said Kyria Toula, 'well, shush now mother. The young man doesn't want to hear all this.'

Andrew smiled and made no further comment and Kyria Toula at last arose and said she would show him the way.

'You know,' she said, looking at him closely as they walked along, 'you remind me of someone. Not sure who – but your face is familiar. Are you related to anyone in this village?'

'I don't think so.'

'Hmm – well, anyway, you remind me of someone but the name slips my tongue.'

Andrew wondered privately if she had met his father in the past, perhaps in one of his many disguises. However he dared not ask her, mindful of Yiango's warning.

'Stay for lunch,' Toula urged him, 'I have some *makaronada* in the baker's oven. Come back when you've settled your business.'

'It's kind of you, but I won't stay. I shall probably return to the city if I can get a mule.'

'Petro Hadjistavros has one, you'll find him in the *tavernitsa*, see over there? He's always in there playing *tavli* and knocking back the ouzo. His poor wife! Don't know how she manages with that good for nothing.'

They approached the house that his mother had described in her diary and Andrew thanked Kyria Toula but she looked as if she meant to hang around and discover what was going on. They were so infernally curious these people.

The door was opened by an elderly woman in a black dress with a black headscarf wound about her head. She started violently at the sight of Andrew and a look almost of fear crossed her face.

'Is Mr. Ioannides at home?' Andrew asked, surprised at her reaction. What on earth was the matter with these people?

'He's a friend of my Yiango,' said Kyria Toula proudly indicating Andrew. The other woman looked unimpressed.

'Yes he is at home. Come on in.'

And she shut the door after Andrew, firmly excluding the nosey Kyria Toula who had a foot raised ready to follow him in.

'Who shall I say it is?' asked the woman

'Andreas Cassimatis.'

'*Po, po, po!*' she exclaimed.

She peered at him closely, crossed herself and shook her head, muttering to herself. Andrew drew back a little in alarm. Was she simple? These village women were decidedly odd.

However, she returned after a few moments and led him into a pleasant little sitting room and then disappeared to her own regions. The room he now stood in was simply furnished with the usual necessities. There were very old fashioned framed photos of a married couple on the wall, an aspidistra on a tall stand in a corner, hand-woven rugs on the bare floorboards and a stout desk against an opened window at which Mr. Ioannides was seated, busily writing.

He turned as the servant brought Andrew in and arose stiffly. He was a tall and rather stout man. One of his legs was dragging and he appeared very lame. A livid scar disfigured one side of his face and his hair was thinning. The strong, humourless features were aristocratic and refined, his eyes dark and hard and strangely familiar.

The two men looked at one another for a long while. The older man also looked at him as if he had seen an apparition.

'Who are you? Xanthi said you call yourself Andreas Cassimatis.'

'Yes, that's right. My father was Costas Cassimatis. I am trying to trace some relations of his. He died in the war …my father. But I know he was a friend of the lady who lived here at that time …a Kyria Anthoula? I wondered if you might know anything about him.'

'Anthoula was my aunt and yes, she lived here during the war. She died soon afterwards,' Ioannides paused and looked hard again at Andrew as if fascinated, as if he had never seen such a specimen before. Andrew shifted uncomfortably.

'And you are from England?'

'Yes. I was born there.'

'And how did your father manage to have a son who was born in England?'

Mr. Ioannides, shut the door of the room and spoke softly as if not wishing to be overheard.

Andrew hesitated. How much should he say? How much could this man help him? He always felt the truth was the best thing. The jealous wife was nowhere in sight so it should be safe to speak.

'He was engaged to an English nurse that he met. They loved one another; *she* was my mother.'

The man's face altered and he put a hand on his heart. The hand was also disfigured by scars and Andrew's eyes narrowed at the sight. What had happened to this poor man? He looked as if he had been in a fire, maybe the Salonika fire his mother had described so vividly, or perhaps he too was a war veteran. Maybe he even knew his father from Army days.

With hope in his heart, Andrew went on, 'My mother worked in the nearby hospital camp. Did you ever meet her?'

'Is your mother still alive?'

'Yes, she is, she's very well. She has two other children now.'

'She married then – after your father – *died*?'

'Yes,' said Andrew, wondering why he was so interested in his mother, 'Mr. Ioannides, I hoped you might know my father perhaps – Costas Cassimatis?'

'I knew him for sure, I knew him very well.'

'You did!' the young man was elated and joy shone in his eyes, 'you knew him. Tell me about him, Mr. Ioannides, please tell me about him.'

'I see him in front of me, I see him in you – you are the image of him when he was young. My God, that I should live to see this!'

The older man was totally overcome and put his arms about Andrew and to the young man's surprise and embarrassment began to weep on his shoulder.

'Andreas Cassimatis, Andreas Cassimatis!' he kept saying over and over again.

Gently Andrew disengaged himself and looked with astonishment at the older man.

But the man who called himself Ioannides still held fast to his arms and said, 'You are my son, Andreas. I am Costas Cassimatis. I am your father.'

Costas poured out a stiff whisky and handed it to Andrew.

'It's a shock for us both,' he said, 'but worse for you as you thought me dead. I knew you were healthy and lived somewhere safe and it was my consolation that you were in a comfortable home and happy with your mother. I guessed she would marry. Who did she marry?'

'Ethan Willoughby.'

'I am glad. He is a great man, a good man. I felt he would win her in the end,' said Costas with a sigh, 'ach, he was always my rival. A determined man.'

'But, father ...' Andrew paused and looked again at the man seated before him, shaking his head in wonder. *This* was his father, the man he had longed to know? Still alive? Not a glorious war hero after all but a comfortable, ageing business man. It was all so strange and he felt a peculiar wave of anger as if in some odd way he had been cheated by finding him alive after all these years of loss and deprivation.

'Andreas, my son, my dearest boy,' said Costas looking at him with pride, 'you are the only child I ever had. I thought for sure I would never see you but you and your mother have always been in my mind, somewhere, just in the background, always haunting me, filling my dreams. I have never forgotten your mother – but she didn't want *me*, did she? I knew once she was home in her own country with her people, she would forget our love affair and marry Ethan.'

'But she did want you. She went crazy when she heard you

were supposed to be dead. How could you not let her know that you were still alive? How could you do that to her!'

Andreas was really angry now. What sort of man was this?

Costas looked troubled, 'But I wrote to her twice, I wrote to her home address called …what was it …Dunland?'

'Downlands. You wrote to her there? As far as I know, she never received any letters at all, only the one from Ethan telling her you were missing in action.'

'So Dorothy still thinks I am dead?' Costas looked dismayed. 'What happened then to my letters? I told her what had happened, how I managed to escape my fate and asked her to come over to me as soon as she could. I can only suppose the letters went missing somehow. That is bitter, my son, bitter! You say she would have come? My mother wrote too. This is too terrible!'

And Costas sunk his head in his hands for a moment as if in a paroxysm of despair.

Andrew was shocked to his core. What was he to believe? This man who was a stranger yet told him he was his father whom he had believed dead for so long? His mother who assumed that Costas was dead all these years? Perhaps she too been play-acting, pretending, but he couldn't believe that of her. Her character was not that devious. Nor could he disbelieve his father if he stated that he had indeed written; he could see that his grief was genuine. Somehow, somewhere the letters had gone missing or had been apprehended – he dared not think that Ethan or his grandmother might have been the culprits. Yet who else? They both had good reason to keep Dorothy in the dark and prevent her returning to Greece.

It was indeed terrible. The truth seemed far worse than his fond fantasies and imaginings. It seemed to make a mockery of all his thoughts, ideals, plans and hopes. It flashed across his mind that he would have preferred to find his father dead and still a war hero.

The thought as it came to his mind shocked him. He felt downcast, disgusted with himself. He should feel nothing but joy at finding his father at last. Instead he felt a strange emptiness.

'My love for Dorothy was not meant to be,' said Costas sadly, 'her letter came too late telling me she was going home to England. I took the train from Athens to Salonika to find her and take her back with me. We would have married and lived in my mother's house. It seems the Gods were against us, Andrew. But *you* are here,' he roused himself from his sadness and smiled and took his son's hand. His smile was crooked when it ran into the scar and Andrew couldn't help but stare at it.

'Ah, yes, the scars of battle,' said his father touching his cheek and nodding.

'What happened, father? How did you get away from the battle?'

'It's a long story, son, let us eat first and I will tell you over a bottle of wine, ' he rose and opening the door called out, ' E, Xanthi – come!'

The old woman came out slowly and Costas drew her into the room, excitedly.

'You know what, Xanthi? This is my son, my dear son, come to find me. God has restored my son to me! He has come all the way from England.'

Xanthi looked at Andrew with the same close scrutiny she had given him before but said not a word just nodded a little.

'Don't mind her, she never shows any feeling,' said Costas pinching the woman's cheek fondly. She smiled up at him.

'It's good Kyr Costas …good you have found your son,' she said with another little nod.

'What do you have for dinner, Xanthi?' said Costas, patting Andrew on the arm and gazing at him as if he couldn't take his eyes off him.

'A chicken, oven potatoes, stuffed peppers, *bamies* – plenty of food for an army.'

'Then bring it, woman, bring it and open our best bottle of Demestica and we'll drink and shout for joy! Come on, come on, get on with it!'

Chapter 15

'To this day, I am not really sure just how I got out of that hell-hole. I was with the Serres Division and together with our 3rd Regiment we had done well. We had broken through the front line and captured some Bulgarian defences. However, the British had lost so many men attempting the high ridges that they were forced to withdraw and without any back up we had to do the same, we had to return to our point of assembly. But we had our blood up and were ready to charge into the inferno again and again and get those bastards whatever the cost. The British felt the same. This was a day of unsung heroes and bravery such as I have seldom seen.'

'After many sallies, we saw that the British were charging up the hill and I took my men after them. There was a huge dust cloud raised by all the movement and shelling. Machine guns and shells were exploding all around and it was worse than hell and yet we struggled up that steep hill, determined to get to the top as fast as we could. We reached some gaps in the wire and lay there for a while ready to go on but suddenly the dust cloud cleared away and there we were …a sitting target for the enemy.'

'I recall this. One of my men suddenly pushed me and I fell to the ground, cursing, while a shell burst directly upon us and I was buried beneath two men who fell dead on top of me. I passed out with pain for the shell had caught me too but my poor men protected me so I wasn't killed. They tried to save me, Andreas!' Here Costas stopped and struggled for a moment or so before he could carry on and Andrew felt immensely moved.

'I was out for a good while. I can only think that anyone searching for the wounded didn't find me, buried as I was. I'm not even sure if anyone was able to venture up that far. I revived later when it was almost nightfall to find myself alive, covered in blood, beneath the stiffening bodies of my comrades. One really thinks of nothing in those moments except the battle momentum and the desire to get back to it. It was now silent overhead and for the present the guns had ceased. Struggling out from the dead men around me, I began to crawl very slowly and carefully down the hill away from it all, anxious to reach the ravine, find my company and get back into action. I wanted to kill those bastards who had killed my good friends. I couldn't wait! It was a crazy notion as my ankle was broken badly, my leg gashed and most of my left side wounded and bleeding. I didn't know that then and oddly felt little pain, just this determination to get back to my men. Little did I know that they were all dead. Death was everywhere.'

'The silence was eerie and I almost wondered if I was dead after all and this was how it was to be in Hell, forever moving around in a dark limbo, not knowing where one was. I crawled over the bodies, there were bodies strewn in heaps along the mountainside. These had been brave men. What was this pitiful ending, this waste of human life? They had sacrificed themselves, they were all heroes and I truly believe are all in God's arms ...' again Costas stopped and his eyes filled with tears.

'Father,' said Andrew gently, 'don't tell me any more about it if it upsets you like this. There's no need.'

'Why son,' said Costas, shaking his head and wiping his eyes, 'do you think me ashamed to weep for these glorious men? I am proud to have been with them, wish I had died with them. You know, I have wanted to tell you this story all these years and thought you would never ever know the truth about your own father. So let me tell it all.'

'I thought I *would* die out there in the chill of the night and I was desperate for water. I cursed my fate that I hadn't had a swift end like my fellows and was going to die a slow, lingering death or be torn to pieces by wild dogs. While I rummaged for a water bottle amongst the corpses, I heard faint sounds and spotted a couple of shepherds a little way off, quietly turning over the dead to see what they could find. You may look like that, Andriko, but I don't blame them, what good are these things to the dead?'

'I knew a good many of the shepherds, they had helped me many times in the course of my intelligence work. They're rough and wild and untamed but not such bad fellows. When they are your friends, they'll see you through thick and thin. I called to them and they came running up and carried me between them some way to the safety of a cave they knew. They said their village was a long way off and one ran on ahead and came back with a mule. They put me on it and took me to their mother' house. The women of the village tended me but I was very ill, hovering between life and death. It was a couple of months before I recovered enough to get back to join the Army. By then the war was over. Naturally, I was invalided out of the Army ...I'm lame and no use to them any more so my life as a soldier has ended.'

Costas now fell silent and Andrew bowed his head. These men had suffered so much. Could he, Andrew, ever be brave like this? Giving his all? He wondered if he and his generation would ever be tested as his parents had been tested and if they would have the same courage. He rather doubted it. There had been a debate at Oxford a short while ago and the young undergraduates had all voted not to go to war for King and Country. People weren't the same as they had been then; people were different now.

After they had eaten and drunk a great deal of wine and were both feeling very expansive, Costas asked, 'So, where are you staying my son? Tell me your own adventures and how you got here. I admire your resolve – you are certainly your mother's son. She was a brave girl, your mother. Sometimes, you know, you have her look about your eyes. Her expression when she used to give me a quizzical look ...yes, just like that!'

Andrew laughed and recounted his own adventures since he had arrived in Greece.

'So you fell amongst the *rebetes*, the *koutsavathikes*? Well, they are an unhappy people. I pity them. Many are well-educated men now reduced to rags and poverty. Can you imagine how galling that must be?' said Costas sympathetically.

'The people I met have been good to me and helped me,' said Andrew, 'I hope one day I may be able to help them in return. Talking of that, I suppose I'd better be going back to the city as it's beginning to get dark.'

'Are you mad? I'm not letting you go back there. It might be your luck you met some decent people but there's a lot of thieves and gangsters in that area and you aren't going there alone at night. Besides, this is your home. You are my son – you're not a stranger.'

'Father, I can't suddenly descend on you like this, I can't trouble you. You're married now . . .'

'What are you talking about, of course you can. My God, but you are such an Englishman now! Well, it's no surprise. After all, you were born and educated there. You have your mother's ways too. Ach, Andrew, how you bring back memories for me. Such memories!'

'I hope it doesn't make you unhappy, father.'

'Well, it does, of course, for now I know that Dorothy might have come to me. I curse the unkind fate that separated us; she was the only woman, the love of my life. But it's too late now. What's past is past.'

Andrew also felt regret. How different his life would have been if his mother had returned. But then again, who was to say that she might not have been unhappy and gone back to England after a while, perhaps never settling to the Greek way of life? Life was a haphazard game of chance, a series of possibilities; the dice fell where they would.

'You stay here with me, Andriko, and let us get to know one another. We meet as adults. You are not a child, but a young man. I want you to fill in all the gaps for me and I for you.'

'Thank you, father, I'll stay with pleasure. I shall have to go and collect my things in the morning and say goodbye to my good friends, of course. But, I gather you too have married. Your wife – is she up here in the village with you – will she mind?'

His father's face darkened a little, 'Yes, Andriko, I actually fell in love again though, you understand, it was nothing of the feeling I had for your mother but it seemed as if your mother didn't want me. A man must have some consolation and I like women's company. Marika is a young widow I met in Athens and she is a regular beauty, there's no doubt about that. She seemed keen about me despite the fact that I must be a regular monster with all these scars. But the lame leg doesn't stop me from performing, I'm okay that way!' he added with a wink and a laugh.

'All the same,' he said sadly,' I shouldn't be surprised if she married me for my money. She had a little house in Athens but hardly any other dowry. I didn't want a dowry – I didn't need it. I wanted her, she's a beauty and proud and lusty. But she's not an easy woman, you know, very jealous. She has no reason to be so. What other woman would want an old war veteran like myself? Sometimes I look in the mirror and wonder, what on earth does she want with this old wreck?'

'Do you have any other children?'

'No. Marika has a couple of children from her first marriage but she's not the motherly type, she didn't want any more. The kids live in Piraeus with their grandmother. She visits them occasionally. Marika likes city life, she likes the theatres and nice clothes and good society.'

'Do you?'

'I used to in the old days. Ah, I was a different man then, Andriko, a different man! Sometimes I felt glad your mother couldn't see me as I am now, glad her memories of me are when I was younger and more dashing. Now, I like to come here to Aunt Anthoula's old house. I like to sit with my memories, my studies, smoke a pipe and enjoy some quiet time. I'm getting to be a bit of an old recluse. I have a little antique business going so I have plenty to keep me busy in the city. But I do like to be alone now and then, just now and then.'

Andrew looked about the room and wondered what memories did his father keep recalling? It seemed as if, like Dorothy, he too was locked up in the past, in some fleeting moment of joy that both had known and could never forget.

'We used to meet here, your mother and I? Did you know that?'

'I did know that. She never knew whose house it was, though, did she? You never told her it was your auntie's.'

'Didn't I? Oh, well, I was always being secretive in those days. It was the nature of my work at the time. Some day I'll tell you some of the stories of those times. What adventures we all had!'

He rose stiff and weary now and called to Xanthi to fetch them some coffee. Andrew looked at him and with the Bacchanalian glow of the wine felt mellower, more caring about the man he should call his father. Costas was a rather pitiful sight. The fire seemed to have gone, that fiery passion Dorothy had once admired so much. Would she have still cared for him, seeing his scars and disfigurements? Knowing Dorothy, he felt yes, she would still have loved him despite everything.

He wondered what to do. Should he let her know Costas was still alive? It might free her from the past or it might unsettle her life forever. It was hard to say. Yet he knew he had to tell her sometime.

Eventually he hit on the idea of writing to Ethan Willoughby at his club and letting him know first. Then leave it to Ethan to break the news in his own time, if at all. Andrew felt relief at shifting such a frightful responsibility to another. Better that way.

Costas showed him to a room and said it was his for as long as he wanted to stay.

'We shall go back to our house in the city in a few days,' he said, 'and then you can meet my wife, Marika. She'll have a bit of a shock, of course, my suddenly turning up a son like this!'

'Did she know about my mother?'

Costas rubbed his chin and said, 'Hmm – not really. She won't take very kindly to that. But too bad. She'll have to accept it. You're my son, that's all there is to it. Xanthi, let Andreas have my own room, go get ready the best room for my dear son!'

That night Andreas lay in the large wooden bed that Xanthi had specially prepared for him with snow-white sheets that smelt of delicious herbs and flowers. He looked around at the tidy, simple little room. An ikon sat upon a shelf on high and a small oil lamp burned before it. The mottled pattern illumined the walls through little holes in the lamp and in its wavering light he saw a large trunk by the wall, hand-woven rugs on the floor. Could this be the very bed he had been conceived in? How strange a thought! He had at last made the full circle and come back to his very own beginning.

Chapter 16

Costas was reluctant to part from Andrew the next day.

'You really need to go and see these people? You don't owe them anything, you know. It was just normal Greek hospitality they showed you.'

'I know but I left my things there.'

'We can buy you new things. I want to take you to the shops and fit you out. You can have anything you want.'

'Thank you. It's very generous of you but I really would like to see my friends again. I'd like to thank them – after all, it is due to them and Yiango that I was able to find you. It seems only polite.'

Costas smiled, 'This is what I love about the English,' he said, 'they are so polite about everything.'

'Am I so very English?'

'Oh, yes, the way you dress, talk, walk and act. You *are* an Englishmen, dear son. But we'll make a Greek of you yet.'

After all, why shouldn't I be proud that I am an Englishman, thought Andrew? Why want to be different? The idea of being a Greek was beginning to seem less appealing to him now that he was here. So many things about England struck him as so much fairer, easier and more civilised than they were in Greece with its complex political situations and the ferocity with which its people maintained the prevailing situation and retaliated against those who disagreed with it. English politics were far from perfect but they did seem to be conducted in a less violent manner. Life there seemed an oasis of calm and normality in comparison to life in Greece.

Would anything ever make him feel he truly belonged to

either country? Was it not true that he belonged to both places and at the same time, he belonged nowhere? As Anna had said so wisely, in this lay a strange sense of freedom, a chance to remain unattached and free from partisanship or patriotism. He could be a citizen of the world instead, or even of the universe. Belong to something far greater than the small circles of family, country or race.

Musing thus, he made his way up the cobbled streets till he reached Anna's house. For of course it was Anna he wanted to see above all, find if she had missed him, even a little.

Anna opened the door to him and with a gesture invited him in.

'We guessed you'd have to stay overnight,' she said, kissing him tenderly on the cheek.

'Did you miss me?'

'Bah! Not a bit ...' she relented when she saw his face fall, 'silly boy – I missed you. A little.'

'Better than nothing, I suppose.'

She got him a coffee and returned to her work at the sewing machine. She was busy cutting up some old trousers.

'What are you going to do with those?' asked Andrew.

'Cutting them into four panels to make myself a skirt,' she replied, 'we girls are clever at such things. How else to look smart when you haven't got a bean?'

'Leave it just for now. Come and listen to my news!'

'All right.'

She put her sewing aside and came and sat at the table, 'So how did it go? Did you find the house you were looking for?'

'I found the house and more, much more. Anna – the amazing has happened. I found my father! I found him alive and well.' Andreas told her the story as they both sat at the old wooden table enjoying a cup of coffee and a large glass of water each.

She looked at him with real delight, her eyes shining with pleasure as she listened, elbows on the table, chin in her hands.

'Do you hear that, Papa?' she shouted to the old man, 'Andreas has found his father alive and well! Isn't that the most wonderful story?'

'Wonderful, wonderful!' said the old man, clapping his hands like a child.

'I am so glad for you,' she said, 'but tell me, why is your father now called Ioannnides?'

'Father told me he had to change to his mother's maiden name because of the political situation. He was always a follower of Venizelos and things have been up and down with the Liberals for a long while and as an ex-army officer he will always be suspect.'

'Ah yes, there was this attempted coup amongst the Venizelist officers last year, ' said Anna, 'was he mixed up in that? Many officers were executed or cashiered and Venizelos went into exile.'

'That's what father said, but no, he wasn't involved in that one. All the same he was evidently involved in something earlier in 1933 and felt it best to lie low for a while. Now Venizelos is dead anyway and Metaxas and his dictatorial, right-wing government are in and the atmosphere isn't healthy for the old Venizelists. So Father's been calling himself Ioannides for some time now. The village people all know him by that name anyway as he used it before when working undercover there. He's quite a character, my father,' added Andrew chuckling a little. 'My mother used to call him the master of disguise.'

Anna smiled, 'It is so amazing you found him.'

'It was a terrible shock as well. I supposed him dead all these years. So you can imagine! He's married now and I have to meet his wife later today. I feel a bit nervous about that. I hope she'll like me.'

'Why shouldn't she? She will love your accent as we do. She will find you charming as one always finds foreign people. They always seem different and therefore more attractive.'

'You think so? I only care if *you* find me attractive,' said Andrew, then added happily, 'oh, Anna – maybe my father can help your brothers to find some permanent work. He says he is running an antique business and has promised to let me work for him. I want to earn some cash and take care of myself. Maybe he can help your brothers too. I shall ask him for you.'

'Don't rush the poor man. Let him get to know you. Andrew,

you really don't understand though do you? He is a man of upper class, he won't want us *manges* working for him. It would be the same in your own country. You wouldn't trust us at all. Don't you see that people see us as thieves and vagabonds?'

'But you are my friends,' said Andrew stubbornly, 'he will surely trust those who have helped me so much. I am determined to ask …though I agree, yes, I'll wait a little.'

'You are kind, Andreas, very kind. But anyway, I wouldn't recommend Sotiri to anyone, he has no sense of discipline or time or anything like that. Savva though, he's different and serious, always has been. Maybe your father could help him a little, that *would* be good. He'd be grateful. I hate to see him come back from working as a navvy or a painter. It's exhausting work carting stuff about like that all the time. And they get hardly any money for doing the work of ten men. They exploit our labour because we're refugees and desperate. What can we do when greedy capitalists still run the ports? Even the Jews aren't allowed to work there any more but I can't see that the new bosses are much better.'

'I will ask father as soon as it feels right to do so. I want to help you all so much.'

'Do you Andreas?' She smiled at him, 'You're such a good soul. We've done nothing to deserve it, only the laws of hospitality that bid us care for a stranger.'

'And was it just your 'hospitality' that made you come to me Anna? Was it nothing more than that?'

He took her hands and held them in his own and she allowed him to chafe and stroke them tenderly. Anna kept her eyes cast down and made no reply.

'Anna, you know I love you. Do you not feel anything for me? Do I really seem so young and inexperienced to you?'

'I care for you very, very much,' she said at last raising her eyes to his. Her deep, intense look went through him, right to his heart and for a long while they stared at one another as if transfixed.

He grasped her hands more tightly, 'Then come with me. I'll work for my father and make enough to buy us a little house somewhere. Come, my darling! We can marry and you can leave all this behind you.'

'I can't leave father and Sotiris.'

'They can come too. We'll care for them all.'

Anna gave a little smile and shook her head at him,' You are so impulsive. Well, we shall see. Look, get to know your father better. See what sort of man he is first before making all these promises.'

'He's a generous man, I know he is and he will be glad to make me happy. And *you* will make me happy, Anna, no one else. I know you are the only woman I have ever known as a lover. Isn't that so much the better? Better to have nobody to remember or compare you to? Isn't that far better? To have known and loved only you. I know that I shall never care and never *want* to love anyone but you.'

'I like your passion,' she smiled. 'You are such a *palikari,* but I'm not sure if I truly love you enough. I like my independence too much. I like to be free, my own person.'

'Well, so you shall be, I'm not a Greek man. I won't expect you to walk three paces behind me or order you about as the men order the women about here. And some day I'll take you to England to meet my mother. She will like you, I know.'

'Slow down, Andreas. Let us agree to wait, shall we? It's not that easy, there are problems …' her voice trailed off.

Andreas felt his ardour squashed by her smile and calm reply. It was almost as if he was now playing his father's role and heard his mother's careful replies in return. Like a re-telling of an ancient drama. A sudden fear gripped his heart.

'Anna, don't wait too long,' he said, 'my mother wanted to wait and then events overtook her. I am afraid in case the same thing happens to us.'

'What events? What can happen? Be patient. That's all I'm saying. It will all come about in time. But let me have some time to decide in.' She paused reflectively, 'I know I am mad; Savvas and Sotiris would say I was mad. I should be on my knees gladly accepting your good offer of marriage to a whore like me. But I have a lot of pride, you see. I can't help it.'

'I love your pride. I admire it. Besides, you aren't a whore – don't say such a thing. You are a wonderful woman, a *haitera* like Thais. That's different. That's not a whore but a woman of independence who chooses her men and isn't chosen by them.'

'You know so much,' she said in admiration,' and I like that very much. I like the idea of being a Thais! Just give me time. Who knows? Maybe I'll come round.'

He rose and hugged her ecstatically and the old man chuckled and laughed in his corner and seemed happy to see them embracing.

'That's right, my children, that's right!' he said gleefully.

Anna looked at her father and smiled. For his sake she should accept this marriage offer if nothing else. But the very idea of marriage made her want to hide away, run a mile. She wanted time to think about it all, to be sure that she could trust this young man who had suddenly burst upon her life and seemed so besotted with her. He was still so young, so very young and at times she felt as if she was a very old woman.

Andrew had agreed to meet his father at Sintrivani Square. He took a tram and walked to the square and waited near the enormous old Turkish fountain made of intricately carved marble that still stood there, watching the baggy-trousered Cretan gendarme conducting traffic from his little platform in the square. Feeling thirsty Andrew took one of the brass cups that dangled on a chain and took a drink from its gushing waters. The busy life of Thessaloniki swirled about him. How things must have changed from the days when his mother used to visit the city! Gone was the '*macedoine*' of nationalities that had bartered, bought, fought round here. The population was now predominantly Greek, though the Jewish section was still quite large, wealthy and influential and ran many major banks and businesses just as they had done before the war.

His father arrived in a smart black car and told him to hop in.

'Your friends are well?'

'I only saw Anna, the brothers were out.'

'Ah, there is a girl too! I guessed as much.'

'I'm going to marry her sometime.'

Costas looked at his son and smiled broadly, 'You're as crazy as I was at your age. Falling in love at first sight.'

'You and mother fell in love at first sight, didn't you?'

'We did. I never thought it was possible, thought it the sort of thing romantic, silly women did. Then I saw your mother, looked into those beautiful blue eyes of hers, and I was head over heels, as they say. Is she still as beautiful, Andreas?'

'She is, father, she is still beautiful.'

'Ah ...' Costas sighed deeply and fell silent. As they drew nearer the house, he said, 'best not to speak of your mother in front of Marika. You understand don't you? It is not a slight to your mother, but respect to my wife.'

'Don't worry, I understand exactly. I shall be dumb as an ox.'

A maid came to open the door to them and took their coats and hats. They entered the parquet-floored hallway of a beautiful house situated in a pleasant side street. It was furnished with sumptuous elegance. Everything was highly tasteful and European apart from certain objects such as a beautiful Russian samovar standing in a corner, or a high backed chair or wooden settle with the Byzantine double eagle carved upon the back. One might have been in a Parisian salon or a chic flat in Knightsbridge. Chandeliers hung glittering from the ceilings, beautiful rugs adorned the floors and the sofas were plush and delightful.

'How beautiful!' said Andrew in admiration.

'It's all Marika's choice. She has very good taste and I always ask her opinion before buying anything of importance,' said Costas with pride.

A woman now appeared from the salon and came towards them.

'I've spoken to her already so she knows who you are,' murmured Costas.

She was a tall, well-made woman, her fashionable clothing as exquisite as the furnishings about her; what the French would call *bien soignee*. She wore a stylish suit of pale grey that complemented the thick, ebony-black hair, which she wore in a bun at the nape of her neck. Her features were quite heavy but regular, her eyebrows thick and dark, eyes large and a very deep brown. Andrew was surprised to find her so much younger than he had imagined. She did not look more than thirty-four or five. It was always hard to tell with these Greek women whose dark colouring often made them look older than their age. She might perhaps have been even younger than that.

Marika was a woman of commanding presence. Junoesque was the word for her. She was not beautiful exactly but there was something about her, a certain glamour or staginess as if she had been an actress and knew how to sweep upon the scene and demand everyone's attention. Andrew couldn't take his eyes off her.

'This is my son, Andreas, Maroula,' said Costas, looking fondly on Andrew and putting an arm about the young man's shoulders, 'I want you to welcome my only son.'

Marika came towards Andrew and he couldn't help but think that her look was scarcely welcoming. Her eyes were remote despite the smile she had arranged about her mouth. She gave him an ice-cold hand and he, unsure of the correct procedure, kissed it gallantly. This seemed to win some approval and she smiled a little more sincerely.

'Welcome Andreas,' she said in a voice that was soft and deep, yet clear as a bell, 'come and sit down.'

She rang for the maid and sent her to fetch some drinks and preserves.

'Your father tells me you have just arrived from England,' she said as she seated herself beside Andrew on the sofa and turned her full gaze upon him.

She seemed to be studying him intently and he felt as if he was under the stare of a basilisk. A certain malignity lay behind those beautiful, long lashed eyes.

'Yes, I arrived a week ago.'

Had he really been here so short a time? It felt as if he had been here all his life. England felt a million miles away.

'I would like to visit England,' said Marika, 'they say it is a very delightful country. London, especially is what I would like to see…Oxford Street, Regent Street, the Royal Opera House in Covent Garden.'

Andrew was surprised at her knowledge of London. She smiled as she handed him a long, tall crystal glass with some strange liqueur in it.

'You see, I have studied it all. I have been to Paris, of course; that is the most wonderful city, the shops, the boulevards, the theatres! Do you like the theatre, Andreas?'

Andreas found it easy to understand her, easier even than Anna and her brothers with their strong Smyrnaika accent. Marika spoke all the time in *katherevousa*, a rather stilted and high-faluting form of the language, closer to Ancient Greek. As he knew Ancient Greek a good deal better than the modern, demotic language, this was actually easier for him to follow.

'Marika loves all that is modern and European,' said Costas, looking fondly at his wife.

Andreas watched his father respond and react with Marika. It was obvious that he cared a good deal for this woman. He cared for his wife but had never really forgotten Dorothy. Dorothy would always be the gentle, half-forgotten ideal, the great love of his life; the memory of his younger days, a reminder of lost strength, virility and passion. In just the same way, his mother cared for Ethan but had never forgotten the love she had once had for Costas. At times it was as if he had walked into a mirror image of his life in England. He felt slightly excluded from their lives; his sense of being an outsider not one whit different. But where it had bothered him with his mother and Ethan who felt far more real to him, it didn't really trouble him watching Costas and Marika. They still felt like strangers and he could observe them with total detachment, amused rather than upset.

An hour passed by in interesting exchange. Marika was a well-educated, well-read woman. She had the knack of conversation and was quite obviously a woman of good breeding. Yet, Andrew sensed something lurked beneath the layers of elegance, education and fine fashion. There was a certain sensuality, even a coarseness. He couldn't put his finger upon it.

There was anger in her too and he felt sure that he was the unwitting cause of it.

'Yiota will show you your room,' said Marika at last, 'you must feel welcome, of course. Do you mean to stay long in Thessaloniki?'

'Well, yes, I mean to stay and live here if I can. Not in your house; naturally I don't mean that. I hope to work for father or anywhere else I can find work and perhaps rent a house or apartment somewhere.'

'You're staying here in this house, son,' said his father firmly, 'you may work for me, of course, if you want to. I shall be delighted. The business will be yours some day.'

Marika could scarcely conceal a look of utter dislike as she glanced at Andreas.

'Oh, dear,' he thought, 'she didn't like that one bit!'

He remembered his father wondering if Marika had married him for his money. There seemed no doubt that, he, Andrew, was far from welcome in this lady's life, an interloper who might take from her what she deemed rightfully her own.

He settled himself in the comfortable room allotted to him, had a bath in his very own bathroom and shaved. Yet, he thought, lovely as this house is, I prefer the simple, uncluttered village home of Aunt Anthoula. He understood now why his father liked to be alone there with old Xanthi to take care of him and cook him delicious, simple peasant food. He felt sure the meal here would be as elegant as everything else but nothing like as tasty and wholesome. There was something almost overpowering in the opulent surroundings Marika had created for herself. Exquisite, yet oddly stifling. No air, no way of breathing in this cultured, hot-house atmosphere.

Chapter 17

'In a few days we shall celebrate your name day, Andriko,' said Costas, clapping his son on his back one morning.

'My name day?'

'But of course, Agios Andreas! Here in Greece we celebrate the name day of one's particular saint. That way you get two feast days – birthday and name day. We're very fond of feast days, you know. Any excuse not to work.'

They both laughed and Costas beamed upon his son and said, 'I think I shall take you into the city today and show you all the flea markets where you can pick up bargains. We can do a round of the villages some other time. I collect stuff in a warehouse near the docks and then have them taken to my shop in Athens where I sell them for extortionate prices to foreigners and snooty Athenians.'

'What sort of things do you collect?'

'Anything that is old and interesting – bedsteads, books, lamps, jewellery and of course, ikons if one can get them. They sell very well, old ikons, crosses and items like that, especially to the Germans and the French. They seem to have a penchant for religious items. I hate to think what they do with them. But ikons can be miraculous objects, or so they say. Who knows? Maybe they transform their cold, greedy hearts in some way.'

'Isn't it a shame to let foreigners have these old artefacts that belong to the Greek nation? It would be like selling bits of the Parthenon.'

'And don't think people don't do that, or at least pretend to,' said Costas cynically, 'the Greeks would sell their grandmothers if anyone wanted them. We are people who have learnt to survive by trading, selling, commerce. On the whole, we are not that sentimental. Survival has overcome sentiment, I'm afraid.'

The two men spent a pleasant day wandering about the old markets and various little back streets picking up bargains and arranging to pick up larger items later on. They then found a café down by the seafront and ordered *kebabs* and *imam bayildi* and sat drinking *ouzo* amicably. It was a beautifully sunny day and though the wind was cold and fresh, the sea shone before them, blue and beautiful, lifting the spirits. Andrew felt an immense wave of happiness that came as if from nowhere. It just felt good to be alive.

'This is the way, eh, Andriko?' said his father lifting his glass in greeting and knocking it back before refilling it once more. 'We Greeks know how to enjoy ourselves. A little work, a little play and thus life goes by pleasantly enough.'

'But I *want* to work, father, work hard and earn myself enough to get a place of my own. I don't want you to think I am here to live on you. I want to make my own way.'

'Well, you're English aren't you! That race isn't happy without a burden on their backs. They work too hard, take life too seriously and then when they do let up they go mad with it. The English can't enjoy themselves unless they are being stupid, like children. They don't enjoy themselves like men should. They just can't hold their liquor. I remember the officers in the war and how they all acted like boys at school when they went to the shows at the Tour Blanche. They used to drop bottles on each other from the boxes, climb up and down them, shout to each other and throw paper missiles. It was like a crowd of rowdy children.' Costas chuckled as he recalled it, 'But they were loveable just the same. Just like children.'

Andrew recalled similar scenes at his school when it was a half-day holiday and he had to smile. He had always stood back in contempt from such juvenile behaviour, considering himself vastly superior and adult. He refused to participate in japes and nonsense and other student activities. They were a bunch of idiots! Now he wondered if he'd missed out on some of life's playfulness. He had never really been a boy at all. Life had made him an adult too fast, too soon. And the strange thing was that because of this, he knew he was actually so undeveloped deep down inside, as if a part of himself had never been allowed to live.

He had never understood this before, but meeting Anna made him realise it. She made him feel immature and young. There was something about the girl, though she was the same age as himself that was strangely archaic and deeply wise like some ancient goddess. He sighed a little and wished he could see her. He really missed her and was in a constant state of jealousy, wondering if she was sleeping with Loupas or any other man. The thought was so abhorrent.

They finished their food and drove home together along the Kalamaria Road, skirting the coast and gazing out over the choppy but beautiful blue waters. Costas talked a good deal about the recent politics as they drove home.

'I don't talk politics in the tavernas,' he said, 'you never know who might be listening, reporting, spying. I learnt all my life to keep my opinions to myself and never air them like other fools who now rot in Seven Towers or on some foul island prison because of a wrong word in the wrong place. Our politics are so unstable and you never know who is going to be on top next. So it's best to shut up and keep your opinions to yourself.'

'You admired Venizelos, didn't you?'

'Of course! There was a man of the world, a real statesman. He had vision. I don't say he wasn't cunning, an opportunist. You need some crafty qualities to survive in this mad world. He wanted to bring Greece into the Western world, bring it out of its Oriental Ottoman backwaters. But naturally, I say nothing about all this now. Colonel Metaxas and I are old enemies, so I lie low. Few people know of me now. Maybe they assume I died as you did. Who would recognise me now?' he added with a sigh, 'I'm not the old Costas. I don't have the spirit for it all anyway; don't get involved nowadays. As you get older, you get more philosophical.'

'People keep thinking there might be another war with Germany. Do you think so, Father?'

Costas looked serious, 'God forbid! I tell you I don't like the sound of that Hitler. He's a crazy man, evil and too one-sided, worse than the Kaiser, and he was a bastard. How *can* one make a perfect race? There's no such thing. We're all a mixture and a muddle. The present lot of Greeks aren't much better, wanting to go back to old Hellenic ideals, language and all the rest. It's like Lot's wife, always looking backwards and frozen on the spot. How can you move if you are always looking over your shoulder? You know what that dope Metaxas calls this era he has instigated? The Third Hellenic Age! The vanity of the fellow. Who does he think he is?'

Costas looked angry and kept taking his hands off the wheel and gesticulating so much that Andrew felt nervous that they would never make it back home but end up in the sea.

'Well,' continued Costas, 'we played into *his* hands all right. Him and his National Socialist Regime! The problem is that the rise of the Communist party here is what swung the balance. There were a few strikes and the King panicked and brought Metaxas back into the picture, letting him do what he damned well likes – no vote, no question of asking the people what they wanted. Well, the people here in Thessaloniki never take things lying down I can tell you. We rely on the tobacco industry up here and the general slump in world trade really hit the market this year and the tobacco workers went out on strike. So it was all going to lead to a really big thing, a National Strike that the Reds were working on. Poor fools, that just played into the hands of a would-be dictator like Metaxas and his stooge the King. Gave him an excuse, didn't it, to declare a national emergency? He swooped down on that lot like an avenging angel. Thus he began his Regime of the Fourth of August as he likes to call it. Now all our rights are curtailed, censorship in the Press, strikes forbidden and all the rest of it – no freedom for self-expression anymore. We Greeks hate that kind of thing.'

'They say Metaxas is almost a Fascist.'

'As far as I'm concerned he is one. But Fascism won't take hold here, we love to express ourselves too much; we love Freedom now that we have tasted it. It's like a heady wine. Too long were we squashed beneath those Turks, rot them! I certainly don't like fascism. But then I'm not particularly keen on the Communists either. We Liberals always prefer to take a more neutral, middle stance. However, if it comes to a choice, I'll go with the Reds.'

Costas paused briefly and then added, 'When you get old, you think about these things. The old think they own the world, that's the problem. They feel they have fought and formed it as it is and so they should be in charge, their views are the only ones that are right and nothing should change. Then along come all you young whipper-snappers, hardly out of your nappies, telling us we've got it all wrong, knowing all the big words to use, the words we taught you! The young in their turn think *they* own the world. As far as they are concerned we oldies are stuck, we should be on our way out.'

They both fell silent for a while as Costas pondered within himself.

'So, if you ask me,' he went on after a while, ' all the conflicts and wars and problems are due to the clashes and tensions between the old and the young, forever at loggerheads, forever making waves. It's the grit that's crept into the oyster, never giving the poor thing any peace, painful, uncomfortable. But in the end, the grit gets a coating from the old oyster and makes something good of it.'

'This country still seems so divided,' said Andrew, 'it has had so much turmoil and heartbreaks, so much pain. Will the wounds ever heal do you think? '

'I wonder ...' said his father, looking at him briefly as he steered the car into the road where they lived. 'You have a wise head on your shoulders. What's your opinion, son?'

'I've never been interested in politics here or in England,' said Andrew, 'I consider myself a philosopher and prefer to remain aloof from it all. It seems to me that the various parties represent polar extremes and like the North Pole and the South Pole, they are joined together by an axis. They are absolutely no different in the end. They all have the same goals in different disguises. They all use the same evil tactics to gain their ends and refuse to use logic and conciliate their ideas. Political parties spring from emotions not from cool, wise logic'

'An answer worthy of Aristotle!' said his father with a big grin. 'Bravo son, what wisdom for one so young.'

'You say you take the middle view, which would be just, but it seems to me that you are just as one-sided, father, forgive me for saying so. You have your viewpoint and hate Metaxas because he was the enemy of the man you so admired. But only history will tell whether he is as awful as you say. It seems to me that he is bringing some discipline and order into Greece and sometimes that can only be achieved by being severe. Freedom can be abused too and might need to be withdrawn for a little till people sober up from the heady wine they have been drinking. Time alone will tell if he has been good for Greece or not. We shall have to see. I don't know. I don't really understand the Greek mentality, I realise that now. Maybe I'm talking rubbish. Just looking on it all as an outsider.'

'Well, no, not rubbish. You speak well, son. I admire what you say. I like your courage in speaking to me so. Again you remind me of your mother. She was not like most women, she was truthful and sincere and wise. You are certainly her son.'

'Am I?' said Andrew. He was pleased about this, felt glad that he was like his mother. Distance had rendered her beautiful again and he thought of her for some time as they sat down to dinner. He wished now with all his heart that he had not wounded her so badly. For the first time he began to see things from her point of view and felt ashamed of his behaviour and his sacrilege in looking through her private papers. How *could* he have done that! He would have hated it if someone did that to him. It made him shiver to remember what a callow person he had been. His past self seemed incredibly cruel and stupid. He would write to Ethan that very evening and send his news and let them know that all was well.

After dinner, they withdrew to the *saloni* and drank coffee and liqueurs. Marika liked to have things just so and brought out her best crystal glasses. She looked very beautiful that day in a dress of spinach-green watered silk that showed off her ample curves. His father certainly had a good eye for women. She was nothing like his mother in any way. Her beauty was of the rather florid, hothouse variety like some astonishing jungle plant with huge, colourful blossoms. His mother was like a delicate, wild flower, tiny but exquisite in her delicacy.

Marika's attitude to him was decidedly cool and hostile. She scarcely spoke to him through dinner, addressing most of her remarks to his father. It was obvious that she regarded him as an interloper and resented his presence, resented the delight that Costas had in his son's company. Andrew felt most uncomfortable. It made him all the more determined to get out of the house as soon as he was able. The atmosphere and strange tensions between his father and Marika were almost tangible in the air thought they said nothing untoward and were always immensely polite to one another. But something crackled and sizzled underneath like electricity gathering in clouds and heralding a storm.

After a while, Andrew decided to go upstairs and write his letter, leave the couple alone a little out of courtesy. He sat for some time, fountain pen in hand, chewing the top until inspiration came and he wrote a brief account of his adventures, told Ethan about Anna, then how he had so amazingly come across his father alive and well and married.

'I leave you to tell my mother if you think this is a good idea. At any rate, tell her I hope she has forgiven me for my misdemeanours and that she accepts my sincere apology for having hurt her so much.'

He sealed the letter and went downstairs to find a servant who might stamp and post it for him. Having dispatched this missive he was just beginning to go back upstairs when he heard raised and angry voices from the salon and the sudden crashing of glass. He moved a little closer and heard Marika's loud and angry voice.

'So you're changing your will and that bastard son of yours is going to inherit the lot! I suppose that's your idea!'

'Pipe down, woman! I didn't say the lot – just the business and some capital.'

'You *say* that. But that boy has come here to get all he can. He'll work on you as he is already working on you, you besotted fool. He will disinherit me and my children. We shall starve to death and all because of him!'

'Marika, stop being stupid,' Costas said calmly. 'I shall leave the houses and most of my estate to you and the children. I've already told you so. You are just being greedy. He is my son, after all. He deserves something, doesn't he? Do I ever say evil things about your children? No, I'm like a father to them.'

'*I'm* being greedy! I simply ask for my rights. I've had to put up with you for six years, you think that's easy? You think you're an angel to live with? Bah! How do we even know he *is* your son and not some crafty impostor?'

'You are a complete idiot, woman!' Costas shouted, really angry now, 'Andriko is the image of me, the image of his mother too. Of course he is my son.'

'Andriko this, Andriko that! You make me sick, And his mother? An English nurse. What's that then? Some low class Englishwoman, his mother? And he a bastard. She has no aristocratic blood like mine in her. What were you doing with such a woman anyway? Oh, yes, making her pregnant. Had you no shame?'

'What shame? I loved that woman. She is worth a thousand of you and your so-called aristocratic Byzantine forebears. You are a snob and a greedy, disgusting woman. Don't you see how it has revived my spirits to find my son? Life was hardly important to me anymore, hardly worth living, but he has fired my heart, my *joie de vivre* again. He is my boy, my only child. All these years, I have thought of him on his birthday and wondered how he was, how he was growing, who he looked like. I thought I would never ever see him but I never forgot him.'

'You have never forgotten *her*, either. I know you have a photo in your desk. I've seen it.'

'You prying, jealous harpy! What were you doing, peering in my desk, looking where you shouldn't?'

The crack of a slap across a face sounded and Marika screamed and flung another priceless crystal wineglass across the room. It splintered into hundreds of tiny shards against the wall and the dark red wine stains, tricked down like blood. Marika ran out of the room, clutching her face where she had been smacked, and bumped into the listening Andrew who drew back quickly. The two confronted one another like two fierce animals. For a long while her deep, intense eyes bored into him full of fury and hate. Andrew stood his ground and stared back, his own eyes, dark, hard and unrelenting.

'So! You creep, you pry, you want to listen at doors,' the woman sneered, '*Na, se hesso!*' and she made a gesture at him that could scarcely be called polite.

'And you insulted my mother and myself,' hissed Andrew.

'How can one insult what is low, what creeps on the floor? You can't deny you are a bastard. I hate you. Why did you come here to disturb everything, why did you enter my life?'

Andrew felt his old dark fury rise up in him.

'Did my parents ask if I *wanted* to come into this life?' he snapped back, 'Does anyone ask if not knowing my father all these years has disturbed *me*? I don't care tuppence about your life. I haven't come here to have anything to do with you, Marika. I didn't even know you or my father existed here at all. But I found him and it has made us both happy. You don't love my father, don't give a damn about him or you would understand his feelings. I *am* his only child, as he said just now and that's really important to him. Don't you care for him at all? He said you'd married him for his money. Now he knows that's the truth. Well don't worry, I shall get out of here right now. I have no desire to come between you. I have my own life to lead.'

He went upstairs and began to throw things into a bag and when he had finished looked around with a sense of regret. He had only just found his father and this crazy woman was going to come between them. Well, it couldn't be helped.

Costas caught him at the top of the stairs as he was came hastening out of his room.

'Where are you going?'

'I'm leaving. I'm not staying here to be insulted by your wife or anyone else. I'm sorry, father, but I didn't mean to come between you both. I don't want that sort of trouble. I can manage for myself.'

His father wrested the case from him, 'No, no my son,' he said, 'don't go. Please don't go! You don't know what it means to me, finding you like this. You have come into my life. You make me want to live again. Don't go son.'

The pain in his father's voice and face made Andrew pause. He felt trapped. He really wanted to go, hated the atmosphere in this house. Yet he also felt deeply for his father and his pain.

'Wait here, don't move for a minute, I'll make things right!' his father said and disappeared into his bedroom. From here he brought forth Marika who had by now changed out of her day dress and was in her peignoir ready to give herself a shower before dolling up for the evening and a visit to the Opera. She had loosened her long, dark hair around her shoulders and Costas had seized her by it, twisting the locks around his wrist and dragging her forth, screaming and cursing. He had in his other hand his old sword. He then shoved the wretched woman onto her knees before Andrew, pushing her face forward, hair tumbling and her white neck exposed. It almost looked as if he meant to decapitate her and Andrew drew back in horror.

'Apologise to my son!' snarled Costas.

Her peignoir had come undone and her heavy naked breasts swung out as he pushed her forward and down. Andrew felt his maleness respond by a stiffening in the groin and felt ashamed and sick. Hastily he turned his eyes away from the humiliating scene.

'Father, there's no need for this. Please, let her go. It's all right – she was just angry. I don't blame her now. Let her go.'

'Let me go!' screamed Marika, twisting and clawing wildly.

Costas released her, dropped his sword and seized her by the arms.

'Apologise, or you'll get beaten black and blue!'

'I apologise! I apologise!'

He relaxed and pulled her peignoir about her shoulders

again. The sight of his wife's naked breasts had inflamed him too and he swiftly steered a not unwilling Marika back to their bedroom and closed the door behind them.

Andreas stood and stared at the closed door. He had always thought he understood human nature but now he really wondered if he had the faintest clue about what made women tick. Maybe the old adage of 'the dog, woman and walnut tree, the more you beat them the better they be' was right. But he knew he could never act in this manner with a woman.

Here was a side of his father he had never imagined. Yet his mother had said that she saw a sensuous cruelty in Costas that had half alarmed, half fascinated her. For the first time, he began to think that Fate had perhaps done well to part her from her would be Greek husband. Costas might be treating his mother like this now and he, Andrew, the unwilling and horrified observer. It didn't bear thinking about.

Chapter 18

This latest incident was deeply unpleasant to Andrew. But he was to discover that it was anything but rare. Every now and then the tension between Costas and Marika would build up to fever pitch, they would have an almighty and often physically violent row, then fall into one another's arms like crazy beings. It was all beyond him. He told himself that this was not his way and never would be.

He wondered at times if his mother would have been any different. Would Costas have roused her to the furies and passions that Marika seemed to experience? He doubted it. Dorothy and Ethan never seemed to quarrel about anything. Ethan doted on her but he was firm when he needed to be and his mother never argued about his decisions. She was by no means a doormat but they worked things out between themselves logically and reasonably. Andrew had never witnessed such scenes of brutality and frenzy before and, while they horrified him, they also held a strange attraction.

Marika, it had to be said, appeared to undergo an extraordinary change of heart towards Andrew. Her attitude was far more civil, even charming and mildly flirtatious. She began to call him her son and would pat his arm affectionately at times or give him a peck on his cheek. She asked him about England and what his life had been like there. She was a good listener and helped him to correct his faulty Greek with patience without making him feel foolish.

At first, Andrew was astonished, even a little suspicious. As time went by, he began to be grateful for the warmth she now gave him, yearning for someone who might show some affection. He saw Anna whenever he could but she was always worried and pre-occupied and they had not made love again. At least that seemed to be the case but he sometimes wondered if she simply didn't want him anymore. In fact, he wondered if she had ever really wanted him at all. His heart was still rent with jealousy and despair at the thought that she was sleeping with men in order to make money to live. He felt sure it was not really in her nature to be a prostitute; she had simply been driven to that profession in order to survive.

He gave her money as often as he could. She accepted it now without demur though when he asked her not to sleep with other men she made no proper answer, no denial.

'Do you still see that Loupas?' he asked one day as he pushed a roll of notes in her hand.

'Of course I see him, he's always in the *tekedes* – what do you think? He supplies most of their hash. And he likes to come and hear me sing.'

'You know what I mean, are you sleeping with him?'

'You still trying to buy me off my life of sin?' she asked mockingly, 'Listen you don't own me, take your money back if that's your big idea. You don't own me, neither does Loupas. But if he offers me a big wad and gives Sotiris free dope, then – well!'

Andrew seized her by the arm and for a moment felt his old, black fury flare up in him, 'Don't sleep with that Loupas, Anna – don't torment me like this!'

'So what are you going to do about it?' she said with a laugh, her body leaning seductively towards him.

He pulled her into the little kitchen, behind the curtain and kissed her fiercely, his hands roaming over her body feeling her firm female flesh with pleasure and longing.

'Anna, Anna! You're so cruel to me!' he said at last. It was in this moment as he held her tightly against him and felt her warm breath on his cheek, looked into her angry, mocking eyes that he knew he wanted to crush her, strike her, force her to be obedient. He was horrified at himself. He was no better than his father after all, the same fierce, lustful blood stirred in him also. He let her go and buried his face in his hands.

'Now what's the matter?'

'I'm sorry. I didn't mean to hurt you, Anna.'

She settled her rumpled blouse and made a face, 'You couldn't, if you tried, Andriko, you're too much an English gentleman. Now a Greek would have had me up against the wall and be into my pants by now.'

'Perhaps, you'd prefer that!' said Andrew bitterly.' But I couldn't behave like an animal. If you don't like me the way I am, then you will never like me. So be it.'

She smiled a little, 'Poor Andriko! You are a Greek at heart but you have been made an Englishman. And you have no idea which man you want to be, or who you really are. I pity you.'

'I don't want any damned pity. I want you to love me – truly love me.'

'Forgive me, Andro. I'm not sure I know how to love anymore,' she said with a deep sigh. 'Life has made me wary of all men. My heart stays closed, maybe forever.'

'I'll open your heart again, make you love me, Anna. I'm a very determined man.'

She looked at him quite tenderly and stroked his cheek, 'You are. I do admire that in you. But I don't think your gamble will come off. I'm a hopeless case.'

Andrew was fast running out of the cash that Ethan had given him. He had just given Anna a large amount and now had only a few guineas of English money left. He saw no way of getting any more. His father didn't seem at all anxious for him to find work and provided bed and board and insisted on paying for anything whenever they were out together. Of course, he knew that he had only to ask and Costas would give him money liberally. This state of dependency irritated Andrew for he felt his father treated him as if he was a child in some ways, afraid to let him find his own way in case he should leave him. This would not do. Andrew was equally as independent by nature as Anna and he did understand this trait in her, much as he also despaired of it.

However, he had no idea what sort of work he could do. He was not sure he could manage such hard physical work as Savvas and Sotiris did. Also he knew his father would have a fit if he suggested it. Plus he knew he would have to have papers and identity cards and other formalities to sort out. He decided to broach the subject the next time the two of them went to the *Hamam*.

So one evening, when Costas proposed that they visit the baths, Andrew was determined to speak about his decision.

They had their steam bath and then the cold plunge afterwards and were lying in the sitting room being massaged and pummelled into shape.

'Father, what sort of work can I do? I'm doing nothing to earn my keep. And I don't like it.'

His father groaned as the masseur hit a particularly tender muscle.

'What do you want to work for? We have enough money between us. What I have is all yours; you have only to ask. Don't take any notice of that woman of mine. It will be *all* yours. You can decide if you want to help her or not. It should have been your mother's after all. *She* was going to be my wife.'

'But she isn't your wife, Marika is. And frankly if I was her I'd be just as upset and angry about my disruptive arrival in her life. No, father, I don't want you to do this to her or me. I want to keep myself, don't you understand…Greek *philotimo* and English honour both insist that I am not kept by my father.'

At this, Costas sat up and pushed the masseur away from him.

'All right, I understand. I've produced a good man from my loins. I'm proud of you son. Can you add up properly?'

'Of course I can. I'm very good at mathematics.'

'I'll find you a bit of a job with one of my Jewish friends. His uncle Yussuf was a friend of mine.'

'Yussuf! Is that the father of Ishabel?'

'Your mother told you about Ishabel, eh?' said his father with a chuckle. An attendant now brought them some coffees and little baskets with delicious chicken and other titbits and the two men sampled it all hungrily.

'I think she was always jealous of Ishabel, 'grinned Costas.

'What happened to them, father?'

'Yussuf died about ten or eleven years ago. Ishabel stayed in Athens after the fire and met a wealthy Jew from the States. They went over there a long time ago and are doing very well from what I hear. Last time she wrote, she told me that she had a couple of children. I was fond of Ishabel. A good, clever girl.'

'Maybe it's just as well she's out of Europe the way things are going.'

'I think you're right. Even here in Thessaloniki, there's a lot of anti-Semitic feeling. There never used to be in the old days but all this German propaganda is working on people everywhere. Yes, Ishabel is free and happy in the States. What a wonderful and ideal country that must be – no class structures, no king, no poverty.'

'There's plenty of poverty in the cities in America, all big cities are the same. And the Depression hasn't helped much.'

'All the same they're free citizens; democracy as it should be. We Greeks invented democracy and look at the sort of mess we're in now with a dictator. The old tyrants are back again.'

This was his father's favourite hobby-horse so Andrew led him off the subject. Costas, though a reasonable man in many ways, was utterly implacable about his politics. Andrew personally felt that many of the ideals that the present Prime Minister, Ioannis Metaxas, espoused, such as a return to the strict but honourable disciplines of Ancient Sparta were not that bad. The Greeks had become so divided and split politically, what with one army coup after another that someone strong had to try and impose some order on them for a while. Plus things *were* beginning to improve; the economy was far more stable, unemployment decreasing, many industrial and social reforms taking place. He knew too that Marika was for Metaxas and that this was another of the reasons why she and Costas argued.

'How come I keep marrying women who want Kings?' he would yell furiously, 'what use are Kings to us Greeks – we've always hated them.'

'You're just an anarchist at heart,' she would shout back, 'but at the same time you want your money and your comforts, don't you? I don't see you helping the scruffy Commies either. Yet you're so keen on social reform, At least I'm not a hypocrite.'

When Andrew heard the conversation turning round to these themes he would leave the room and leave the pair of them to battle it out all the way up to the bedroom.

His father was as good as his word and found him a part time job doing some accounts for his friend Isaac who had a jewellers shop in the Bezesteni arcade. It wasn't a high position but it was paid work and Andrew was delighted. His Greek was now improving considerably and he was determined to do well. His first wages made him beam with delight and he hastened round to see Anna and give her some money.

Sotiris was there and delighted to see his friend.

'Andriko! My old mate. Come and have an ouzo at Yiango's.'

Sotiris knew nothing about the money that Andrew slipped into Anna's hand. They both knew it was better that he didn't. She was touched to know he had brought some of his first wages.

'You're a good provider, you're my little husband,' she whispered with a laugh.

'Yes, I am and I *will* be your husband.'

'Who knows, who knows,' she murmured in her usual enigmatic manner, giving him one of those sidelong looks that always inflamed him. He longed to make love to her again. He wanted to have her to himself but not here with the old father downstairs and the brothers snoring in the other room. Maybe someday he might persuade her to come up to Anthoula's house at Mistres. It would be a strange thing to make love in the bed his parents had once used. The idea appealed to him in a Freudian kind of way.

Christmas came and passed quietly enough. Andrew was initiated into the rites and festivals of the Orthodox Church, taught how to make the sign of the cross properly and not in the Catholic manner... 'or you'll be in right trouble with all the old women!' his father laughed. He found it strange that men and women were still segregated to opposite sides of the church and that women were never allowed behind the altar screen. He was not a particularly religious person and it didn't bother him where he worshipped. He could have just as happily entered a synagogue or a mosque. It was the same God they all worshipped, wasn't it, and what did it matter if he was Allah, Jehovah or Jesus Christ? Did God care what name He was called or what clothes one wore or how one praised Him? God was something higher and nobler that one had to find within oneself and not in some human place of worship.

New Year was amusing with the children coming round to the doors bearing models of Agia Sofia lit up with little candles. They sang songs lustily outside the door, just like the carol singers back at Downlands, and scampered away with goodies or cash depending on the wealth of the household. Presents were given out and good food was spread on the table. Like the Scots, the Greeks made far more of New Year, the pagan festival when two headed Janus shuts one door and opens the next. Christmas here was a quiet and religious time of reflection.

Slowly the days slipped towards spring and the hills began to be covered with the glorious wild flowers that Dorothy had so loved. Andrew could see why his mother loved this place now that the bitter Vardar winds had subsided and the sunshine came forth more strongly with the dark winter clouds chased away. Mount Olympus was a majestic sight and it had to be viewed from the hills to be truly appreciated. Andrew and his father spent some time up in the mountains that spring. It was good to be away from the poisoned atmosphere that surrounded him and Marika in their city house.

It was here in the hills, in these barren yet splendid mountain ranges that the Allied soldiers had lived and died. It was here, near the old village of Mistres that his mother had given her all, fighting her own battles alongside Ethan and others to save the men who had been wounded or fallen prey to the foul air of the marshes. These had now been greatly cleared away with the help of American funding. Malaria had ceased to be such a problem. Now the fields were used for tobacco and other crops. Some good had come from it after all.

As for Salonika, the old Ottoman and Jewish city was no more. The fire had cleansed and purified it from the ancient dirt, squalor and ethnic confusion. Little remained of it except the squalid areas of the Old City, which had become the haunt of refugees like his Smyrnaika friends, the Manoglou family.

Thessaloniki was now a very new and modern town with smart paved streets set in tree shaded avenues, art-deco buildings with elegant exteriors, grand shops and evidence of great comfort and prosperity as well as the deep-set squalid poverty that always seems to run alongside wealth in any city. Dear old Ottoman Salonika would never exist again; the fire and the war had seen to that. Better his mother didn't return here but remembered it as it once was. Memories should be left where they belonged, shimmering elusively in the past, always more beautiful and warm and enticing than the present.

Chapter 19

A letter arrived from England one morning and Andrew's father looked at the envelope with interest before handing it over to Andrew.

'I recognise the writing,' he said. 'It's Ethan Willoughby, isn't it?'

Andrew nodded, his heart oddly stirred with delight and joy. He tore it open immediately.

'You have no idea how relieved I was to get your letter, dear boy. Your mother has been deeply troubled and upset since you left and I long to tell her that you are safe and well as it would so cheer her spirits. The thing is I haven't felt ready to tell her that you have found your father. I don't think her nerves are up to it just yet. But I shall tell her in due time and am very grateful you left this decision to me. Unfortunately though, this means I can't tell her you are safe, as naturally, she will want to see the letter. Please do write to her yourself and make your apologies. Reassure her that her son is alive and well. You must both let bygones be bygones. Life is too short for all this dramatic stuff.

However, I hope your father is in good health and ask you to give him my regards. It is amazing that he managed to come out of that fearful battle alive and I hope to hear the story sometime. I'm sure he has many a tale to tell. The children and your Grandma Clarke are all well. I do know that your grandmother misses you greatly. By the way, did you ever find Nina, your other grandmother? You didn't mention her in your last letter.'

Andrew was smiling to himself as he read this letter. It was so good to hear from home. It *was* home, he suddenly realised that fact. It would always be home. He saw his father watching him, his eyes anxious.

'Ethan sends his regards, father,' he said.

'He is always a gentleman,' said his father gravely. 'And your mother? Is she well?'

'She's pretty well. She misses me. And I miss her,' Andrew added with a sudden sigh.'

'It's only natural. How I wish I could see her, even for a moment. Even for a moment! But it cannot be; the seas flow between us and I know I shall never ever see her in this life again. It will always be my deep regret.'

'You could come to England, father,' said Andrew eagerly, 'just for a visit.'

Costas mused a little, 'It would be wrong. Wrong to bring back all the memories for us both, unfair to our present partners. No, the past has to be left behind. You are the link for us both and precious to us both because we love *you*. In you, dear son, Dorothy and I can love forever more.'

It was approaching the summer of 1937. Andrew had been in Greece for over seven months. England seemed very far away to him now and he began to adopt expressions, gestures and attitudes that rubbed off some of his stiff Englishness. He had always been a fairly adaptable person and a good mimic and it wasn't long before he too was gesticulating and shouting along with the rest of them. It was so catching! However, he knew in his heart of hearts that he was playing a part. It was him but it was not him. It was hard to say which side of himself he preferred. Perhaps he ought to be grateful that he could call on whichever role seemed useful or appropriate in any given moment.

People thought of him as a peacemaker due to his calmer and more rational approach.

'Here's Andriko, the Philosopher!' they would say clapping him on the back, 'he'll settle the problem. Listen to him, *vre* Giorgo – he'll sort you out!'

His wooing of Anna had certainly not improved with time. She still treated him as a brother though occasionally she would take him to her room and let him make love to her. He suggested the idea of going to the house at Mistres but she shook her head.

'You can't take me there, Andriko, you don't understand these peasants. They would tear me to bits, they wouldn't like the idea at all of you taking me to bed there and us not married or engaged. You've no idea how they gossip and criticise and make trouble.'

'I don't give a damn about their gossip! Besides, we can get engaged if that makes it better. You know that's what I want.'

'I do know that's what you want and I keep saying, not yet. I'm not ready yet.'

And he had to be content with that. It was all so frustrating and unsatisfactory. Sometimes it just drove him wild inside.

Marika, on the other hand, had decided to take Andrew under her wing and wean him away from the bad company he kept.

'Why do you want to keep seeing that girl in Toumba or wherever she is?' she would ask exasperated. 'It's a dreadful place, not for a well brought up young man like you. You'll be rich one day, you can move in the best society. You shouldn't be associated with these people, these 'yoghurt-eaters' from Smyrna! Don't you understand, they may think you are a Communist if you are seen with these shady characters? Suppose one of their places gets raided and you are taken away with the others to jail? Then we shall have a fine time trying to prove that you are just an ignorant foreigner who went there by mistake. Thankfully your father is well in with Koundourakis who is an Inspector at the police station here. But I tell you it frightens me to death whenever you go down to those harbour-side haunts of yours.'

'Well, I'm sorry, Marika, to upset you so much,' said Andrew sarcastically, 'but these people are my dear friends. They are the first kind friends I made here in Thessaloniki and I care about them. They can't help being poor and living in such seedy areas. They were flung out of homes as comfortable as this one and forced to come here where they have had little welcome or comfort. They are the unhappy victims of circumstances. Besides, I care a great deal about Anna.'

'Pah! If she lives there and is a singer in a Café Aman, then she is sure to be a prostitute. No, don't bother to deny it. I wasn't born yesterday! What on earth makes you fancy such a woman when there are plenty of pretty girls of your own age I can introduce to you? They would bring you a good dowry too.'

'I'm not interested in dowries. We don't expect dowries in England, we marry for love.'

'Nobody marries for love. We all need to make a comfortable place to bring up our children and to feel safe. We all need a companion. Love can come later.'

Andrew remained silent and she looked at him closely and thoughtfully. She really had no desire for Andrew to marry here at all. His marriage and his children would mean the end of her hopes of a rich widowhood when her husband died. And she certainly didn't want some little Smyrnaika whore in the house, lording it and bossing her about.

'Listen, Andriko,' she said purring sweetly at him, 'let me show you a better life than this. It's time to take you to some good places, the theatres, the nightclubs. You are young; you need to go to the 'Dancing' at Glyfada or Neo Faleiron. There's nothing like that here in this dismal, Turkish town. As for your father he does nothing now, he's like an old man. When he has a fit of working, he goes off looking for his antiques. But most of the time he just wants to sit at home and read and potter about. Or else he spends his time up in that scruffy village in the hills. He hasn't taken me to Athens in ages. Why don't you take some of the valuables from the warehouse down to his shop in Plaka; see what that good-for-nothing he employs down there is up to? Your father needs someone sensible to look after his business matters now. He won't admit he's past it – past caring anyway. Then, Andriko, I can accompany you. We can stay at my auntie's in Kolonaki – now there's a fine house! This is nothing in comparison. It would be wonderful to see some of my old friends. You have no idea how bored I get here in Thessaloniki. The weather is so awful, the people are heavy, ill-educated louts. I yearn for my beloved Athens!'

Andrew considered the idea. It appealed to him to go to Athens again. This time he would use the time properly, go and see the Acropolis and various other sights. Anna had been so cold to him of late and he had despaired in his heart that she would ever feel any love for him. It did seem foolish to keep trailing after her as if he was some yapping dog at her heels. No wonder she despised him. Perhaps his absence might make her heart grow a little fonder. And if not, then he would know for sure that she would never love him. Accordingly, he broached the subject with his father who seemed delighted at the idea.

'Marika has already mentioned it. Yes, you go, son, have some fun in Athens and take Marika with you. She's always grumbling about living here. Let her stay in Athens for a while. She is right, you know, you do need to see a better side of life than you will living here with me. I am getting old, Andriko, old in spirit anyway. And as you know my health's not so good anymore. Not much fun for the poor girl. You be her escort, look after her.'

Life in Athens became a whirl of parties, theatre outings and elegant dinners in clubs. They stayed with Marika's aunt and uncle who were what she called 'the better side of the family'. These relations had a lovely house in the smart area of Kolonaki below Mount Lycabettos. They were well-educated and cultured people and delighted to meet Andrew, charmed by his English ways and good looks. He was pampered, cosseted, introduced to many attractive young women and made much of. Unused to such attention, his memories of Anna began to fade just a little. It did seem pleasant to be amongst well-spoken and cultured people again, to be taken to see the sights and have them explained by knowledgeable professors or men of letters. Marika seemed to have a great many important and interesting acquaintances here in Athens.

Andrew also called upon his friends, the Limbourides. They were delighted to join him on his jaunts into Athenian high society.

'My, you've done well for yourself,' said Limbourides, as they came out of the Olympia Theatre one night after a striking performance of *Cavalleria Rusticana*, 'and what a thrill, meeting up with your father like that. You won't mind if I write up the story for my paper? They would love a tale like that. 'Son Finds Father He Thought Dead!' …I can just see the headlines.'

'Don't write about it, please, father doesn't want to be 'known' to the authorities at present.'

'Ah,' said Limbourides, rather dampened by this thought, 'yes, I see your point. He *was* a very active Venizelist. Oh, well, scoops come and go. Though I doubt that anyone would have it in for him now. He sounds as if he's not politically active anymore and surely no harm to anyone?'

'He knows a lot of people. I can never be sure he isn't up to something or other. My father is a mysterious man. I can't say I really feel I know him,' sighed Andrew.

Limbourides wife, Despina, had also joined the Athens paper now and was writing little gossip columns about the local '*snobbaria*' as she put it.

'I do enjoy it,' she said laughing. 'I'm invited all over the place because the well-to-do ladies want to read what I have to say about their clothes and their 'cultural' activities. I've even met the Queen. She's pretty ordinary though, nothing much, you know. Your stepmother is better dressed than her.'

Andrew smiled and had to agree that his stepmother was a most attractive woman. She too had blossomed out now that she was able to show off her clothes and furs and jewellery to an admiring audience. Her large, dark eyes sparkled these days and she glowed with vivacity. Andrew felt rather proud to accompany her and to see the way men's heads turned when she came in a room. She was elegant and majestic. And yet there was also an animal litheness about her that was most seductive.

This new life began to change Andrew. Ever adaptable, he now began to speak far better Greek, losing the slang he had picked up in the dockside cafes. Marika constantly laboured to improve his vocabulary and to groom him nicely. She delighted in taking him to the best tailors, fitting him out and making sure he looked the little gentleman she wanted him to be.

'You're a handsome boy,' she declared as she pulled and patted his tie into shape one afternoon. 'I feel proud of you. You're my beautiful son,' she added with a flirtatious little smile as she stroked his cheek, 'but you know, I'm not *that* much older than you. You're 19 years old now aren't you?'

'Yes,' he said, looking at her curiously. He in turn wondered how old she might be. She had never divulged her age but he guessed it must about thirty-two or three. Why had his father taken so young a wife, he wondered? Perhaps it made him feel younger in turn; after all, his father was scarcely fifty himself, hardly an old man. Of late, however, Costas had begun to look older and was less energetic, complaining of rheumatism in his lame leg. It wasn't surprising when one considered what the poor man had been through and the wounds he had sustained.

That evening, Andrew dressed himself with care for dinner. They were to meet some Minister or other who was acquainted with Marika's family.

'I have great hopes that he might be able to help you find a good position some time. It's useless waiting for your father to find you anything. I sometimes think Costas has lost his spirit. At first you seemed to help cheer him up. But lately he's been so moody, don't you think?'

'I suppose so.'

'Poof, he's so old for me nowadays. I feel stifled at times. It's so awful, you have no idea, Andriko *mou*. I'm young, I want to have fun!'

She looked at him and patted him on the cheek, 'How can you understand – you are so young, my boy, you have your whole life in front of you. Looking at you, I see how Costas was when your mother met him. Handsome, strong, virile. You are Costas as he was in the war days. I envy your mother that she knew him then. Do you know that? I envy her! I have him now as a cripple. If only I had met him then. But I would have been a child, wouldn't I? Ach, life plays strange tricks!'

Andrew wanted to say, so why did you marry him at all? But as he was well aware, it wasn't for love. Marika wanted to live the good life and one couldn't do that as a poor widow with two young children. Costas had provided the wherewithal for her escape, cripple or no cripple.

He despised Marika in many ways. She was shallow, manipulative and snobbish. Yet she was also well read, a good conversationalist and a perfect hostess. It was a delight to spend an evening with her discussing books, music and art. Her knowledge was very comprehensive and her wit superb. He could certainly see why his father had delighted in this woman. She was a very pleasing companion when in a happy and expansive mood as she was now that she was here in Athens.

'I always feel so depressed in Thessaloniki,' she explained. 'I must ask your father to buy us a house in Kolonaki and come here to live. I don't know why he stays up North, the damp air does him no good at all. He hardly ever sees his sister in Kavalla. Really, there's nothing to hold him there. Maybe you can persuade him?'

Andrew rather liked Thessaloniki himself. It had a far more oriental atmosphere despite all the efforts of the city fathers to expunge it. It was colourful and compact while Athens was sprawling and congested. It's true that in Athens the streets seemed wider and the squares more open and, of course, there was such a vivid link with the glorious past; temples, ancient theatres, the grand sight of the Parthenon on its hill where one might picnic on the night of a Full Moon. And in the distance was the sea, the beaches and the bathing at Faleiron, the smart night life and the clever, impressive, witty people he now mingled with.

Yet still he played a part. He would always play a part. He didn't belong to this life anymore than his life in England or the life of the *manges* in Thessaloniki.

Chapter 20

Andrew sat in the smart restaurant and looked about him, half listening to the discussion that flowed around him.

It was a glorious warm night with a huge yellow-orbed moon shining over the sea. A little orchestra played some sambas and people were dancing in the small space in the centre of the tables. He watched their movements, enjoying the cheerful rhythm of the music.

An elderly couple joined their table and he rose with the other gentlemen to greet them.

'Madame Litza, how good to see you. How divine you look!'

'Good evening Colonel Loustras, Madame Loustras. Welcome, please sit here.'

'Oh, darling, *who* is your dressmaker! Ikos Tsamadou! Oh, my God, no wonder…how lucky you are!'

The couple seated themselves at the table and a deep discussion about clothes began amongst the ladies while the men returned to their politics.

'Well, let's face it. We Greeks have shown ourselves quite incapable of being democratic. What do the stupid peasants in their villages know about democracy? The days of Pericles are over, long over. The peasants always think of their bellies and that's all. They are ignorant clods.'

'Indeed so, Yiannaki, they need keeping in hand. Did you hear that a law is being passed to restrict the amount of goats they own?'

'What's that in aid of?

'Isn't it obvious? Metaxas is making a brave effort to re-forest the mountains and hills, which have been stripped bare of every twig. The wretched creatures are eating every shoot in sight. How can the land become re-forested with those disgusting creatures on the loose on every mountain?'

'I like his style, I must say. He knows how to control these peasants and Lefties. He's put a stop to all that Trade Union nonsense. Otherwise there would be strikes every five minutes – if things were left to that bunch there'd be anarchy. Which is just what the KKE would love to see.'

'You are so right, my friend. The Communists are envious people, they envy those who have made something of themselves, saved a few drachmae and got something to show for their efforts. These lazy good-for-nothing *alites* want to take from those who have done well and have it all for themselves. That's their idea of equality. What's mine is mine and what's yours is mine. Well, there's been some law and order since Metaxas took over, thank God.'

'I think he feels that a war is inevitable. But will we support the Germans this time, do you suppose, Colonel?'

'I doubt it. I suspect that we shall stay with the British if they declare war. We need their fleet on our side. Anyway, the worry isn't the Germans so much as Mussolini and those damned Italians. They are making a lot of threatening noises. They're the real worry just now.'

'Metaxas may be inclined towards fascism but he isn't a Germanophile. He's a Greek first and foremost and cares about this country. And he's no fool.'

'He's no fool at all. The army is well prepared, I can assure you,' the speaker sunk his voice to a whisper, 'General Papagos is bringing the army up to date in readiness. If those damned Italians try anything funny we'll be ready for them'

More wine and food arrived now and Andrew who had been listening partially to the conversation and partially observing the dancers on the floor, began to tuck in with a will.

One of the gentlemen present turned to him and said, 'You're very quiet young man. What is your opinion of the current situation?'

'I can't pretend to have any opinion on Greek politics as yet,' answered Andreas, 'I don't understand enough about it all.'

'Ah, yes, you're the lad from England I believe?'

'Yes, sir, I was born and educated there.'

'Does the British government believe we shall have a war with Germany again?'

'I don't know. I don't believe they want to have a war, naturally. But I truly have no idea what the current situation is.'

The man looked at Andrew as if he thought him a bit of an idiot but then to Greeks, politics are their very life-blood.

'You are Marika's stepson, I believe?' he asked curiously.

'Yes, I am.'

'So your father is that old scoundrel Constantinos Cassimatis? He tries to hide up in Thessaloniki now under another name. But we know all about him.'

He looked at the other men and they laughed.

Andrew felt something of a chill at these words. Were they a joke or a hint of menace? He stared at the speaker and his dark eyes flashed with anger.

The man smiled a little, 'I mean no offence, *palikari mou*, no need to look like a fighting cock. Your father is a wolf with his teeth drawn out. No one worries about old Costas any more. His days are over.'

'He's not that old!'

'No, no, of course not. But he's out of it as far as politics go. I hear he's not that well.'

'I don't think he is too well,' admitted Andrew and a wave of sadness came over him. His poor father!

He looked around at the scene. The table groaned with food and everyone was stuffing themselves albeit daintily and with beautiful manners. Champagne and good wines flowed abundantly. The music was sweet and merry, light-hearted rumbas, foxtrots, sambas. A chanteuse sang her songs about love and Brazil and Blue Moons and all the rest of it. The dancers on the floor were flushed with their exertions and the beautiful dresses of the spinning ladies twirled about the legs of their partners in their smart evening suits. It was all very attractive, dim lit, relaxed and delightful.

Andrew looked at the singer, a platinum blonde with a wave descending over her brow a la Veronica Lake. She was lovely but she had nothing of the character of his Anna. How he wished he could hear that strange, reedy voice with all its pain and sadness once again, see her face turned up to him with those luscious, sensual lips half parted, delectable as honey. He wanted to be with Savvas, deep voiced, serious Savvas and feel his friend Sotiris slap him on the back in hearty greeting and then enfold him warmly in his arms. Wanted to hear them pick up their instruments and pluck forth the wailing, long drawn melodies that spoke to his soul.

Most of all he wanted to take all this abundance of food and wine and set it on their wooden table and have a feast with them. They were real people not like these shadowy figures about him now, *Karagiozi* cut outs dancing to the puppet master against a white screen, unreal and unfeeling.

And his father. How he had been stung by the tone of contempt and dismissal in that wretched Colonel's voice. His father who had fought and risked all for this country, sacrificed life and love. Now on the dung heap of forgotten heroes!

Perhaps Costas was right. He would have been better dead for his life was as nothing since he recovered from those wounds. Fancy going through all that, managing to survive; then writing to tell the woman he loved the good news and apparently receiving no response. How awful that must have been, how painful for him. What *had* happened there and how had those letters disappeared? What mischief-maker had been meddling with other people's lives like that? Costas had lost his son, his fiancée, his health. And gained that greedy, voluptuary Marika instead.

Marika leant towards him at that moment.

'What is it, Andriko mou,' she queried, 'why do you look so unhappy? Why aren't you eating? Don't you like the food?'

He wanted to say that the food choked him, that its very abundance nauseated him when he thought of his friend's bare table. Instead he gave her a half smile and shook his head.

'No, it's fine, fine. I'm just not that hungry.'

She looked at him with that deeply thoughtful look of hers that seemed to read his mind.

'I'll talk with you later, dear boy.' She rose and stretched out a hand to him, pulling him to his feet, 'meanwhile, shall we dance a little? I'll teach you the samba. *Ella, paidi mou, ella.* Let's dance!'

There was no denying that Marika could be utterly charming and vivacious. Pretty as were some of the girls seated at their table and eyeing him speculatively, he knew that he would rather dance with Marika than any of them. They seemed so very immature, over protected and sweet. He came to the conclusion that he preferred the sort of women who had complexity, maturity and wisdom, who were at ease with themselves; a quality that vain, silly young girls had not as yet acquired.

After they returned to Aunt Litza's house in the small hours of the morning, Andrew had a bath, put on his pyjama trousers and a dressing gown and returned to his room. To his surprise he found Marika waiting for him there. She was wearing her negligee loosely about her shoulders and smoking a cigarette. She offered him one and patted the bed beside her.

'Tell me your troubles,' she said, 'remember, I'm your mother, aren't I? I need to listen to my son's troubles.'

Andrew lit the cigarette and looked into those large dark eyes, eyes that turned up at the corners and had long lashes that swept down over them now and then so seductively. Some mother! However, her expression as she said this was faintly mocking. A corner of her negligee fell from her shoulder revealing the creamy white flesh beneath. He tried to avert his eyes but unbidden into his mind came that picture of her rich, solid breasts swinging forth when his father had dragged her from their bedroom that terrible evening. He shivered a little with a strange sense of fear. It was not Marika he feared but himself.

He did not accept her invitation to sit down but paced about smoking the cigarette.

'What's the matter, *paidi mou*, you're like a caged lion. Come, I won't bite you, come and sit down and speak to your *mana*, e? What's eating you of late?'

'Nothing really. I suppose I'm just bored. I miss father and feel it's time to go back to see him again. He'll be lonely without us.'

'What are you talking about? He isn't lonely. He loves to be on his own. He'll be in Mistres now, happy to be eating his peasant food with old Xanthi. That's the life he likes.'

'He likes a simple life. I don't blame him. I like it up in Mistres too.'

'Bah! Are you mad? That dusty, smelly place? Are you telling me you prefer it there to your life here with me in Athens? If so, you're as mad as your father!'

'Yes, I do mean that. I love the quiet, simple life of the village, love the kindly people there and the mountains in their changing moods. I can see now just why my mother loved it up there in the hills. She always thought it was beautiful, despite the evils of the war.'

'Your mother! You all think of this woman. She must have been something amazing,' said Marika in the petulant tone that meant she felt slighted and jealous, 'so you want to go back to your father?'

'Yes, maybe in a day or two I'll get the train home. I've dealt with all the business of the shop and frankly I'm tired of the good life. You stay of course. You don't need to come back.'

'It'll be boiling hot in Thessaloniki; you won't stand it for a minute.'

'It's boiling hot here.'

'Ah, yes, but we mean to go up in the hills soon. My friend, Loula, has asked us to join her in her little villa near Piraeus. It's so cool, near the sea. You can walk down to the beach every day. Think, Andriko, we could go bathing every day. You'd love it. Stay another week at least.'

'No, Marika, I won't. It will be cooler at Mistres than in the city and I feel sure that Father will be up there. I want to be with him.'

'Well, go then – go to your precious father. Ungrateful boy!'

'Don't be angry. I am very grateful for all you've done. You've given me a lovely time here. But it's not my sort of life. Even in England I wasn't used to it. Life has always been quiet for me. I'm not your society butterfly.'

'But you're born for it, you're a natural. People like you; they find you most attractive. Do you know you could do so well, if you only half tried,' said Marika, spreading her hands open as if in uncomprehending disgust at his stupidity.

'You know, my English cousin Reggie would have loved it,' said Andrew with a little smile. 'He'd have been a far more rewarding protégé. We are so different, he and I.' He paused, stubbed out his cigarette and added wistfully, 'But I think the problem is that most of all – most of all, I miss my little songbird, Anna.'

Marika's eyes narrowed and she looked furious.

'You miss that whore!' she spat. 'She has no time for you, you silly boy! I have made inquiries about that creature and she is the mistress of some gangster. And her brother is his Sultana. That's the sort you like to mix with. Queers and whores.'

'What do you mean – what brother?' gasped Andrew, shocked to the core by her vitriolic outburst.

'How do I know? – one of them. How many brothers are there? Maybe they all serve him. These hoodlums don't just want women, you know. The poofs!'

Andrew went over to her and seizing the cigarette from her lips ground it out in the ashtray. Then he pulled her to her feet and shook her violently.

'Just get out, Marika,' he said, 'I don't want to hear this nasty stuff. How dare you pry into my life and my friends lives? It's nothing to do with you whom I choose for friends. I don't care what Anna is or isn't. She has more goodness in her whole lovely body than you have in your little finger!'

'Is that so!' said Marika mockingly. Violence seemed as always to excite her and she allowed the negligee to fall further from her shoulders revealing her tempting nakedness beneath. Then reaching up she seized his head in her strong hands and pulling his face towards her, kissed him full on the lips. Heat flared up between them both and he responded for a while to this fierce insistence and passion. But just as suddenly he pushed her away from him and out of the door, which he slammed behind him, leaning on it as if terrified that she would come crashing back in on him like some ferocious and dangerous animal.

Chapter 21

Nightmare figures chased through Andrew's head. He saw himself with Marika, filled with desire and lust. Saw her mouth coming towards him as if to swallow him whole, a yawning cavern that threatened to engulf him in darkness and pain. Yet fearfully he was drawn towards her as a moth towards a flame. All he wanted was to seize her, implant himself in her, use her roughly and cruelly. The dreams were shameful and he struggled against them until at last he awoke, bathed in sweat and twisted up in his sheet like a spider's prey.

He lay exhausted in the faint light of dawn just peeping through the slats of the shutters. The windows were wide open but scarcely any air came in. It was hot, sultry and stifling even at this early hour. He heard the faint sounds of the city beginning to stir and wake itself, the distant rattle of wheels and the sound of an occasional car passing by. The little songbirds had begun their matins in the lemon tree outside his window.

Disentangling himself from the bed sheet, he looked at himself in the mirror. What a sight! Unshaven, haggard and dissipated. But then he had hardly slept, his dreams disgusting and troubling. He went quietly to the bathroom and doused himself down with cold water. The house was still and silent all the shutters closed and not even a maidservant up and about as yet. He crept back to his room and began to pack his bag. He couldn't stay here a moment longer. He was terrified both of Marika and of himself and his fierce response to her. What the hell was she playing at? My God, she was an evil woman! Better to go back to Thessaloniki and his father.

Should he tell his father of her advances? He knew in his

heart he couldn't do so. His father worshipped Marika, despite their quarrels. He was proud of his beautiful, charming young wife. Best to say nothing at all and hope Marika had got the message and wouldn't trouble him again.

Andrew let himself quietly out of the house and strode along in the bright morning sunshine, breathing the fresh air with delight and a glad sense of escape from something dark and terrifying.

As soon as he reached Thessaloniki, Andrew made his way to Bald Yiango's café. Here he felt sure he would find Sotiris playing cards or just knocking back *raki* and twiddling with his worry beads.

Yiango came to greet him and slapped him on the back heartily.

'E, Sotiri …here's Andriko the Philosopher! Welcome Andro, haven't seen you in ages!'

'I'm glad to be home, 'said Andrew, 'how's things, Yiango?'

'*Trupgubi,*' was the cheerful reply, 'full of beans! But I thought we'd never see you again once you got in amongst the toffs in Athens!' he added with a wink and a laugh, 'didn't the high society suit you?'

'Not really,' said Andrew, 'it's all too false for me, Yiango. I prefer your little smoke-filled café to the best restaurants in Athens.'

'There! Hear that boys? Did you hear what Andriko said? Bald Yiango's is the best place, better than Athens! So I don't want to listen to any more moaning about this and that.'

Sotiris came up and embraced Andrew warmly.

'Dear friend, dear brother,' he said, 'come and join me, help me finish this noble bottle of best *raki*. I must have known you were coming, e, Yiango? Fetch us some of your *meze* and that delicious *tiropitta*, man …my friend Andriko is here. Let's celebrate!'

Andrew felt his heart warmed by this joyful reception. These rough men were far more to his taste, earthy, racy, humorous and wise. You could have all your stuffed shirts and intelligentsia in Athens. These were real men.

When the *raki* had been duly demolished and the two men were merry and happy, Sotiris said, 'Come on, let's go home and see Anna. She'll be glad to see you.'

'Do you think so? Do you think she'll be glad, Sotiri?'

'But, of course, you know she cares for you. You're her brother.'

'Will she ever care for me as a husband, do you think?'

Sotiris considered the question. 'Hard to say, Andriko. She's a wild one, my sister, not a domestic animal, you understand. I wish with all my heart she would accept you as her man, what more does the silly girl want? You would be so good to her, she'd be rich, we'd all be happier, there's no denying it. But she has always been a law unto herself.'

'Tell me, Sotiris, does she still see Loupas?'

Sotiris looked at him thoughtfully, 'Well, you know she does see him. She has been with him for years. I told you that before.'

'Do you think she loves him?'

'I told you, she loves only her father and brothers. She has never ever loved any other men. As for Loupas –.no, she doesn't love him, Andro, she uses him as he uses her.'

'And you, Sotiris, were you ever …did you …you and Loupas, I mean.'

'Loupas owns our family!' said Sotiris suddenly and angrily. 'He always owned us. He began with Savvas when he was a young lad hanging about the markets looking for work. He took him as his *oglani*, his special boy, to make up the *nargiles* in the *tekedes* and that wasn't such a bad thing. It's no shame amongst us here. We *manges* like men better and even like to take our women that way. We don't like *poustres*, you understand – effeminate sorts of men. No, we despise them; we mock that sort. We like men that are virile, the more virile the better. Well, Savvas is a real man as you know, and we're a handsome family. He was pretty then, not so big and swarthy as he is now. So Loupas set his eye on him. And Loupas took care of him, that's the deal. You look after your *Sultana*, get him the best dope, good Turkish stuff from Bursa, make sure he gets work, find him a nice girl to marry and so on.'

'Andriko, we had no choice, we were starving. Father worked as hard as he could but he wasn't strong enough to do heavy work, his health was failing and there was nothing else available. When we came here we were living in someone's back yard like animals. Loupas found us this place and let us have it for a small rent. He's helped us climb out of the mess we were in. But Savvas has always been mighty proud. He hated being used like that, selling his body to keep us. He got fed up with Loupas, who is a jealous and possessive fellow, thinks he owns the world, you know, like all these tough guys. One day they had a massive quarrel and in a fit of stupidity Savvas threatened to expose the entire drug racket to the police. He's lucky he wasn't bumped off there and then. But Loupas is a wily wolf. He took his revenge, had him stitched up with some crime he didn't do and off Savvas went to jail. Then Loupas took me on board as his new boy and after that my sister as his mistress. He knew that would keep Savvas quiet, with no way of revenge when he came out. Savvas knew that Loupas was keeping us all, so what the hell could he do?'

'You didn't mind the situation with Loupas?'

'I didn't mind for myself. He was a good lover and generous. I like women, don't get me wrong. But we *koutzavathikes* don't bother to take wives as a rule. We might live with a partner but we don't like to follow the bourgeois ways; we don't like to follow their slavish and meaningless conventions. Women are free and equal amongst us, they go their own way, sleep with whom they like, they have dignity. Are they whores? Some call them so, but are those women who marry a man conventionally just so that he can keep them in comfort any different? Don't they sell themselves body and soul as well? Yet they are considered respectable.'

Andrew thought of Marika– she who thought herself so educated and high class.

'I'm not with Loupas now, I'm already too old for him, it's young cocks he likes,' Sotiris said with a sad, little smile. 'If anything, he's taken a fancy to you, young Andriko – better watch out, I think.'

Sotiris spoke half-jokingly but Andrew was horrified.

'If he dares make any such suggestion, I'll punch his face in! He'll 'eat wood' as the Greeks say.'

'You might *do* that too, you're a daredevil, I'll give you that,' said Sotiris admiringly, 'but I think it will be you who 'eats wood' if you try! He carries a nasty little knife and he'd think nothing of twisting it in your gut; a horrid, painful death. Believe me, I've seen him do it.'

'He sounds a bastard!'

'He is particularly nasty in a temper but he can be a good guy too. *Ade*, Andriko, we're none of us angels. But I know that Savvas has never forgiven him and just bides his time for his revenge. It worries me at times. Our Savvas doesn't easily forgive a slight. Me, I'm the opposite, don't bother holding a grudge, what's the point?'

'I think I'm like Savvas,' said Andrew.' I'm not sure I find it easy to forgive and forget either.'

The two men made their way to the old Turkish quarter of the town but Andrew said he had some shopping to do first and would join them all in a while. He had it in his mind to go and buy a load of food and drink and have a party with his friends. He felt the need for their easy-going, merry company after the oppressively smart and polite society he had latterly indulged in.

Some time later he arrived at their ramshackle house laden with parcels, bottles and jars and various other goodies.

'It's time for a real party!'

They were all delighted with his purchases and Anna hugged him and told him how much she had missed him. It was worth coming home after all!

Anna disappeared into the kitchen with the food and some time later issued forth with plates of *dolmades*, wrapped in their tender green vine leaves, *keftikes,* delicious meatballs looking brown and succulent and some fried chicken.

'I'd already made *makaronada!*' she said and brought that out too, huge chunks of thick, solid macaroni squares, full of eggs and cheese. Out came the glasses and the bottles of *retsina*, out came the bowls of peaches and grapes, the huge loaf of bread, the delicious, sickly-sweet Turkish *baklava* and *kadaifa* cakes dripping with honey and anything else that could be found to add to the groaning table. Everyone crowded happily around and fell to with good appetite.

'*Kali Orexi, paidia!*'

'*Bon appetit!*'

Then out came the *santouri* and the fiddle and Anna brought forth the *baglamas*, a strange tiny instrument with a bowl not much larger than a cereal dish.

'Savvas made it in prison, ' she said showing it to Andrew. 'You aren't allowed to play music there but the men make these tiny instruments out of whatever they can find – old coconuts, gourds, anything that can be hollowed out. Then a length of wood for a handle and pieces of gut for frets. It's small enough to hide under one's jacket, see? Isn't it beautiful?'

And it was indeed beautifully carved and decorated and had a strange sound, reedy and sweet.

'Making that, playing it whenever we could, was all that kept us sane in those hell holes of prisons,' grunted Savvas. 'They want to take everything away from us, reduce us to nothing in those places. But men must keep their dignity, somehow.'

Savvas and Anna played and sang and old Kyr Manoglou clapped time as best he could, smiling like a child as he sat in his seat and watched them, food dribbling a little down his chin. Anna handed him a sweet nut pastry and he chortled and was as merry as could be. Then Sotiris pulled Andrew up out of his chair and putting an arm about his shoulder showed him the *hasapako*, the butcher's dance. The steps were simple and had to be performed in unison.

Andrew soon got the hang of the slow and measured rhythm, a rhythm that played faster and faster till one was out of breath with it. He felt total delight in it all, felt that now he understood just what it was to be a Greek. The key to it lay in the music and these ritual, almost balletic dances and ancient instruments that had been played for centuries past in magical, heart-rending ways, conveying the feelings and emotions of an amazing race of people. They called to something deep within him in a way that no modern, European or South American music could ever do, charming, light and pleasing as it was. The Greeks were denying this part of themselves in their eagerness to be modern but it could not be denied for long. It was their soul they were denying in their frantic search for spirit. But soul had a funny way of reaching up its arms pleadingly, yearningly till one could no longer refuse to pluck it up from its Hades-like depths.

After the food was finished and stomachs full and content, the men brought out the *nargiles* and lit them, carefully crushing the dark brown hashish and putting it in the bowls of the water-pipes. Soon the sweet languorous fumes filled the air mingled with the mountain thyme that was burning in the old Turkish stove. Even old Manoglou took a *nargile* and puffed at it contentedly. While the three men smoked their pipes and Andrew lit up his thin black Balkan cigarette, Anna picked up the *baglamas* and began to sing a passionate song by the renowned Makros Vamvakaris, looking all the while at Andrew with eyes full of tenderness.

> '*Your caresses are driving me crazy…*
> *If I don't make you my partner, my Smyrna girl, I shall die…*'

'*Aman, coucla mou*! How beautifully you sing!' sighed Sotiris when she had finished the song, 'you stir a man's soul. That's a song for you Andriko, eh? Your cruel and lovely Smyrna girl?'

Andrew continued to look at Anna, his heart speaking, pleading in his eyes. She smiled back at him and putting her instrument down, she beckoned to him to follow her upstairs and off they went to her room, leaving the two smokers and the old man in their sweet-scented, dope-filled dream.

Chapter 22

Yiango gave Andrew a lift the next day and let him off on the footpath to Mistres.

'Give my regards to my *Mana* when you see her,' called Yiango as he reversed and set off for the city again, 'I'll be up to see her on Sunday, tell her.'

Andrew began the long, steep climb to the village, looking about him at the dry and barren summer landscape, the very same unchanged landscape that his mother had once looked upon all those years ago. He must write to his mother, he really must, seized by a sudden longing to see the dear faces, hear the well-loved voices of his English family. England seemed a calm, grey-green haven compared to this strange, dry, brown, dusty world of the Macedonian hills. It had a stark beauty here; there was no denying that. Yet sometimes he yearned for the softness of summer rain in Gloucestershire, the roar of the River Severn in full spate after a goodly shower, huge oaks and elms, the greenness of fields stretching to the horizon dotted with well-fed sheep and cows.

It was the gentleness of England that he loved so much. The people too were calm, steady and peculiarly undemanding. He loved it here in Greece as well, of course he did; loved its dramatic landscape and warm, urgent, passionate people. But he began to wonder now if he would ever truly fit in as he had hoped and longed to do. In the end, he might just have to accept that he would always be Drew the Wandering Jew.

According to the Bible, the Son of Man had no place to lay his head. What *did* that strange, profound declamation mean? Perhaps it meant just that. That he who belonged nowhere actually belonged everywhere.

His father was delighted to see him.

'You came back earlier than I expected, son,' he said, 'has Marika come back too?'

'No, she's off to stay with some friend near the seaside. I'd had enough of it all. So I came to see Anna and you. I've missed you both.'

'And I you, dear boy, 'said Costas, looking on his son fondly. The joy of his later years; that was his son. It was a miracle that he had lived to see the boy and to find in his youthful, handsome face a virtual replica of himself at that age. It was so wonderful the way we lived on through our children. Death cannot conquer those who bear children, he thought. God must have spared him from death in the war in order to see his beloved son. He would light a candle in the little church tomorrow in honour of the thought. He smiled to himself. He was turning to religion in his older years like most of them do; he, Costas Cassimatis, that cynical old atheist.

Marika wrote to Costas saying that she had gone to stay with her friend Loula, then would visit her mother and children in Piraeus and be back in the autumn. She made no mention of the fact that Andrew had simply disappeared one morning, without even thanking his kind hosts. He knew it was impolite but there was nothing else to do. He couldn't have faced the woman in the morning. Andrew dreaded her return and contemplated asking his father if he could live in the Mistres house permanently to avoid seeing her.

Andrew, good as his thought, sat and wrote a letter to his mother and told her he was very well, enjoying life and hoped she had forgiven him for his misdeeds.

'*I was young and foolish,*' he wrote, '*but I feel I have aged years in this short space of time.*'

He decided that he, rather than Ethan, should break the news about Costas to Dorothy, but maybe not yet. A slight sense of possessiveness made him feel he wanted to treasure his father to himself just a while longer. First of all, he would wait and see if she replied. He decided to give the address of Costas's house in the city for her reply; an address that she would not recognise as she would the address in Mistres.

There seemed to be a strange and growing unease in the atmosphere these days. Everyone kept talking about the war as if it was inevitable. The Germans had begun an atrocious campaign against the Jews in those countries under their sway. Whenever Andrew went into Isaac's shop in Bezesteni, he found the family reading it up in the papers and looking worried and alarmed.

'Let's hope Greece keeps out of it all this time,' said Isaac. 'I don't feel at all safe these days, not even here. Once this city was our second Jerusalem, the Pearl of Israel. But things change, Andreas, they change all the time and though half the population here is still Jewish, the Greeks have made it their city now. We cannot work on a Sunday anymore, we cannot work on the Sabbat and that means we lose two days work a week. Bad enough for my trade, but even worse for the poorer people. One feels the undercurrent of hate and threats around all the time; they've even created ghettos now for the poorer Jews. They long to get rid of us, you know. They say we take the work from their own people, but how can we? We have been here for years, created all this commerce, made this city the flourishing place it is when it was nothing before. People are always envious of those who do well, it seems to me. Once we all lived in peace under the Sultan. I don't think things have taken a good turn for us Jews. What have we done to deserve it, Lord!' he added with a wail, opening his arms and casting his eyes upwards to some harsh, unfeeling deity.

There was no real answer to this and Andrew suggested he send his family to the States to join their cousin Ishabel.

'I've been thinking that way,' said Isaac worriedly, 'yes, I think I shall send off the children at least. My wife won't leave me, God bless her. But the children should go, at least for a while till things settle down. Surely the Germans won't try another major war, they can't be that mad.'

'Who knows? Does a leopard change its spots?'

Even Andrew began to read the papers now sensing the undercurrent of anxiety that seemed to drift like a miasma around the city. He had left England just after the Mosleyites had clashed with the Jews of the East End. He had forgotten about that. So it was a real threat even there, back in quiet peaceful England. This repeating nightmare was unbelievable. He was aware too that there had been a march by starving and jobless shipyard workers all the way from Jarrow in the North to London and that soon after this the King had abdicated his throne because he was in love with some American divorcee. His quiet, unassuming brother Prince Albert was now on the throne, still looking shell-shocked by the sudden turn of events. Who would ever have dreamt that Albert with his shyness and stammer could ever become King George the Sixth of Great Britain?

Life was so uncertain and so unpredictable these days. A war had just finished when he was born and yet nobody seemed to have learned a thing from that terrible catastrophe. The Germans had bombed Guernica early that year and caused such suffering and losses. The Spanish Civil War was still raging. Why had Europe become again such a bubbling cauldron of madness like some evil witches brew? Perhaps it would never be any different. Peace could never be; it was all just a dream, a hopeful delusion that kept Mankind from going mad.

Peace after all was stagnation. And nothing ever happened in stagnation; everything just rotted away and became foul and stinking. It may be that strife and anger, and war and effort were always needed to prevent humanity from falling asleep as if in some sweet narcotic dream. Andrew saw that war was terrible on the individual human level of pain, the dislocation of masses of people, the deaths and losses of loved ones but on some greater plane, perhaps it was a necessity in order to move history on its path. Yet a path towards what? Sometimes it simply looked like a path towards extinction.

His mother had often said it was the Gods playing a game of chess with human beings as pawns. Maybe she was right.

It was towards the end of the summer that Marika returned from her visit to Athens. Reluctantly, Andrew knew he must face her and act as normal for he didn't want his father to be in any way suspicious or unhappy about his wife. Thankfully Marika also chose to forget the incident and seemed her usual self though imperceptibly cooler and more formal towards Andrew. He was grateful for that and Costas didn't appear to notice any difference in her manner. Marika seemed to be in a great state of dissatisfaction and got the servants in a ferment cleaning the city house, fetching the winter carpets out of the storeroom and beating them, laying them down while she sat and drank lemon teas and grumbled constantly about the Salonika weather.

'My nerves are all in pieces now I'm here again. How can you men live in such a filthy mess? I hate to think what that place up in Mistres looks like,' she said disparagingly as she sent the maid scurrying off on some errand or other in her usual imperious manner.

'Let your nerves take a rest. Don't trouble your head about it, *poulaki mou*. Xanthi keeps everything spick and span. It's comfortable and simple, the way I like it.'

Andrew had asked his father if he might stay on at Mistres and Costas had agreed.

'Pity that girl of yours won't marry you,' he said, 'it would be a lovely house for you and your children.'

'I don't ask for anything you have to give, father,' said Andrew, 'I don't want you to deprive Marika and her children. But I do ask if I could have that house in Mistres. That's all I want. Sentimental you might say.'

'Willingly, my son. The house is yours. I'll draw up the documents as soon as I can. Marika doesn't want it anyway. She'd probably burn it down. I still think she's jealous of your mother now she knows we met there,' Costas chuckled a little at the thought of his wife's jealousy. 'We had an almighty quarrel about it. Women!'

Andrew was delighted and went back to Mistres to survey what was now his own property. He told Xanthi and teased her, saying she would have to do what he told her now.

'Bah, we'll see about that!' was her reply but she smiled and accepted his kiss on her cheek in good grace. Andrew knew she was fond of him, almost as fond as she was of his father.

One afternoon as he was busy whitewashing the walls of the house, he was amazed to see Anna hastening up the street towards him.

He dropped the brush back in the bucket and ran towards her. She hugged him tightly despite the curious eyes but seemed unable to say a word.

'What is it, Anna…you're shaking all over! What is it, my darling? Come on in, the curious bastards are all coming out on their doorsteps now. Come in the house.'

They went inside and he took her coat from her. She collapsed in a chair and her face was ashen, her hair awry. Andrew was alarmed and poured out some neat brandy for her.

She took it and drank some, choking a little. A slight colour began to return to her cheeks.

'Andriko, we're finished! We're all finished – everything, everything has been lost!'

'What on earth – what's happened, Anna?'

'I've just brought father up here on the mule. Kyria Toula has said she'll look after him. I've given her the jewellery I had hidden all these years. Now it can pay for his keep at least. They won't touch him here, he's safe here. We're on the run, Andro – .we're all on the run! I can't stay here, myself…I'll have to go soon.'

She drank some more brandy. Her words terrified Andrew. He waited in suspense till she felt ready to speak again.

'It's Savvas,' she said after a while, 'he's done it at last. He's killed Loupas.'

'My God, Anna! How did it happen?'

'Savvas has always hated Loupas, hated him from a boy of fifteen when Loupas started to bugger him. He hated him even more after doing time paying for a crime Loupas and his gang committed. He hated his having Sotiri and me; knew we were all trapped – the family honour had to be satisfied. Loupas knew it was coming to him some time. He knew. He often joked about it with me. Said Savvas would do for him one day.'

'Savvas doesn't smoke dope as much as Sotiri, he isn't dependent like him. And he was worried that Loupas was pushing harder drugs on Sotiri and making him so ill. Sotiri has a bad chest, you know, haven't you heard him coughing at night? Anyway, he went to drag Sotiri from Manolis's *teke* the other night because he heard that there was heroin going round and he and Loupas began an almighty quarrel, swearing at each other, cursing with terrible oaths and then Savvas challenged Loupas to a fight and out came their knives. Sotiri tried to stop them but that's madness and he knows it, he knows the rules –*when* he's normal. You don't come between two men fighting for their honour. But he was stoned and didn't know what he was doing. He loved Loupas, you know. I know he did admire him but he loves Savvas even more and wanted to protect him.'

'He tried to get between them and got slashed on the arm and face for his pains and they dragged him off screaming. Loupas and Savvas fought like madmen they say. But Loupas was killed. Savvas is a tiger when he's mad. Nobody there would ever have given Savvas away but the police must have been tipped off by that *kativa* Soula who is in love with Loupas. She was hanging about outside the back of the *teke,* waiting for Loupas to come and fuck her later. Well, her day will be coming too. Someone will see to her all right! When the police arrived on the scene there was all hell let loose, loads of people arrested. Savvas though managed to get away with Sotiri and they ran home to warn me, both of them bleeding like pigs.'

Andrew clasped her to him again, his heart pounding. The demise of Loupas filled him with a strange joy. His wretched rival was finished. He wished *he'd* had the nerve to challenge him to a fight.

'Where are your brothers now?' he asked.

'They have taken to the mountains, gone to Vitsi to join the KKE. Savvas would rather die than go back to prison and Sotiris *would* die if he was there.'

'But Savvas said the Communists hate the *rebetes* as much as Metaxas? I didn't think he was a Red.'

'They do hate us, you're right, because they know we are anti-establishment. But not in the way they are. *They* want to impose another regime, another lot of idealogy and rules upon the society they profess to despise so much. We *manges* are beyond any sort of society, we are free of all that. We have our own rules, our own way of dressing and acting, our own way of talking. Pain and abuse has welded us together yet we are disorganised and confused and filled with dope. The KKE don't want ill-disciplined, individualistic people like us. Yes, they hate us too! Everyone hates people who don't fit into their nice moulds. Frankly, Savvas thinks that both sides are much of a muchness but he'd rather be with the KKE than anyone else. At least they're for the ordinary people. Besides he is far more disciplined than Sotiris.'

'Yet, he's taken Sotiris with him?'

'What else can he do? We're all unsafe now, even Papa. But Yiango said his mother Toula would care for him and the men in the village will defend him if they must. But Loupas's bitch of a wife will be after me and Sotiris if we stay around. She's always hated me and won't wait till she can have us run in or have someone kill us in revenge.'

'Perhaps the mountain life and the discipline will do Sotiris some good?' said Andrew hopefully, 'he won't be able to get dope up there.'

'No, he won't. They won't allow it. You're right, it will kill or cure him. Savvas, however, will love the life. He was always born to be an *andarte*. He loves guns and soldier's ways.'

'And you Anna – you can stay with me.'

She pushed her hair back from her eyes and looked at him wearily,

'I have to go to, Andriko, eventually they will find me here. I'm a danger to you and to Papa. I am going to the mountains too. I shall become an *andartina*, learn to fire a rifle with the best of them. No – don't say another word. Andro – try to understand. I can never settle and be a nice little housewife. It isn't in me. I'm a wild bird, an eagle's child. I am not the marrying sort. I want to fly in the mountains.'

'What sort of freedom is that going to be, you'll be an outlaw,' said Andrew bitterly.

'It may seem to you a strange freedom. The point is that freedom to me is in the choice – that's all the freedom we human beings ever have. We're the puppets of fate. But if I have two paths and I make a choice with my eyes open – well, that's freedom to me. Going blindly along a path and blundering about in the dark, that certainly isn't freedom, is it? Maybe I choose wrongly, who cares? The point is that I choose this path now and if I hate it I shall get away, they won't keep me. I thought of going to Athens and make my way there as a singer but you see, Andreas, I love my brothers. They are the only men in my life. We have always been together, us three, and no matter what happens we shall live and die together. It's a bond we cannot break, that none can ever enter into or destroy. We all killed Loupas in a way. I'm glad he's dead!'

'I am too, believe me, but Anna, can you really mean to go? You mean to leave me? Will I never see you again?'

'Only God knows that,' she said with a sigh.

Andrew was distraught with grief. He sat at her feet and sobbed bitterly. Anna looked down on him and stroked his head as if he was a little child, which at that moment he was.

'Andriko, I know I am your cruel Smyrna girl, I hate to make you unhappy. But I've made up my mind and nothing will stop me.'

He sobbed even more at the finality in her voice.

'Stay with me tonight – just tonight, here in this place?' he begged, looking wildly around.

This is an ill-fated house for lovers, he thought in his heart. But he wanted to make love for the last time to his beloved Anna in the house where he himself had been conceived. It suddenly seemed deeply important, crazy even, but important.

'Make love to me one last time!'

She caught his face in her hands and looked deeply into his eyes. A child! All men were children. As if lovemaking mattered at a time like this. God, she was tired of men and sex. They had been entering her since she was ten years old. But she did love this young boy. If he had been a few years older, tried, tested and matured by the buffets of life then, yes, he was a man she might have considered settling down with . . .perhaps. But he was just a boy; a spoilt child who wanted his way while the world and its problems could go hang. He hadn't lived yet, not even begun.

'All right,' she replied and smiled at the sudden joy that infused his whole being.

'Just tonight, at least,' he said and flew off to tell Xanthi to prepare a meal and then change the sheets on the big, deep wooden bed upon which generations of lovers had consummated their love.

Chapter 23

Immense grief overcame Andrew after he parted with Anna. Without her life seemed pointless, useless. He looked around the house at Mistres, which he had claimed from his father. He loved the house but had hoped against hope that one day Anna might join him there and they would settle down to some sort of family life. But it seemed this was to be denied to him.

'What have I done to deserve it, Lord!' he said to himself, echoing Isaac's complaint.

Staying in the house just now was too painful, too lonely. He couldn't abide it. The villagers were always kindly and helpful and sensing his grief they plied him with food or drink or good advice, depending on what they felt might cure his ills. It merely irritated him to the very core of his being. So he went back to his father's house in the city and threw himself into some work, helping out at Isaac's shop, sorting out antiques and taking journeys with Costas to the neighbouring villages to see what they could buy up from the peasants. They always managed to find some amazing old thing in a corner or in an outhouse, beautiful iron bedsteads, wrought iron lamps, strange farming implements or some other item that to the owner's mind was totally useless. As far as he or she were concerned they were being paid good money for old rubbish and if these city suckers wanted to take away their old iron, let them.

Andrew and his father felt that they were growing closer and closer in understanding, despite the vindictive spirit of Marika hovering in the background, ever anxious, jealous, interfering and trying to manipulate them both.

'You are so unhappy lately, Andriko,' said Costas one day as the two men sat together one evening after a good meal.

He had lit the beautiful, old Russian *samovar* that stood in pride of place in the sitting room. It heated up the water swiftly and stayed there bubbling and ready to make endless pots of tea. The tea-pots were kept at the ready, warming on a shelf encircling it. Costas rose and turning the spigot, deftly filled a fresh pot and brought out some glasses.

'You like your tea with milk and sugar, don't you?' he asked with a smile, adding these vital English necessities, 'not the way tea should really be drunk at all.'

'I'm used to it, I suppose,' said Andrew. He took the cup and sighed deeply.

'There you go again, like some old buffalo, sighing and sorrowing – come on son, what's the matter?'

Andrew told his father the whole story of Loupas and Savvas and their fight.

'Now Anna has left for good. I don't think I shall ever see her again. You know, the irony of it is that just before she left, she told me that she really did love me. She tells me that and then goes!'

'We're not very lucky in love, you and I,' said his father sympathetically, 'but never despair, son, who knows what the Fates have in store for us, who knows? Besides, you are very young, you'll meet and love other women. That's life. Anna has suffered too much, you too little. I don't know if it would have worked, Andriko. You are from such different backgrounds.'

'That's the trouble, father,' said Andrew with a groan, 'I am from a quite different background although I am a Greek in my heart and soul. I know I am. When I hear her sing, hear Sotiris play his *santouri*, it moves me to my depths. What can I say? I found some old *rebetika* records in a flea market the other day. You know, the real stuff, swearing, singing about jail and hashish and women. The man had them hidden away because he said they were illegal now. He had to hide them and only sell them to the Americans who paid well for them. I assured him I wasn't going to go rushing to the police with them but really loved the music and wanted to play them privately. I want to play them on our gramophone and try to dance as the *manges* dance – that strange slow dance they do. Do you know this dance?'

'You mean the *zebekiko*? The 'Son of the Eagle' they call it.'

'Yes, yes! It is such an amazing dance. Englishmen don't dance like this on their own, only ballroom dancing with a female partner. Scotsmen dance alone and even wear kilts like the Greeks. They aren't any less manly for it, though, are they? But in England it would seem ridiculous, effeminate even, for a man to dance on the floor by himself as men do here. I too would have thought so once. But now I have seen it, seen how it is when men dance together or on their own, I realise it is a very manly thing to do. It has a sense of ritual sacredness about it, a connection with the ancient and mysterious past. It seems to me to be a way of getting all this pain out of the heart.'

Costas agreed. 'It does do that. It is an expression, a very personal expression that arises from the passionate depths of a man's heart, from his soul. It draws a man closer and closer to himself. The English find it so hard to let go and be natural about their feelings. I remember how stiff they used to be when the Serbians would have a *slava* and start to dance the *kola*. The English officers were fine if they'd had enough to drink. Then they'd lose their inhibitions and absolutely love it. But if they were sober they would be embarrassed and stiff as boards.'

'How true, that is. We are always stiff unless we've had a drink or two,' said Andrew with a smile, 'but that English side of me is shifting away, thank God. '

'That's a good thing. My mother taught your mother, Dorothy ,to dance the ladies dance, the *tsifteteli*. She was a very good pupil. When she wanted to she could shed that cool English exterior with ease. She was something special, your mother. I never forget her dancing with me – that was sacred indeed! And you know, that's why we never applaud a man who rises to dance, no matter how brilliant he is, nor would anyone dare to join him on the floor. For in that moment, he is indeed in a sacred space that none may disturb.'

Costas paused and drank his tea in a gulp and then said heartily, 'So you have *rebetika* records – well, bring them down, let's play them and I'll show you some of the basic steps. Then you can improvise around them.'

Andrew brought down the records and the two men let the music and songs begin to move them. After some time of listening during which both men were deeply immersed in their own thoughts and private sense of pain, Costas got up and despite his lame leg, began to dance slowly and quietly, not a sound, not an '*opa!*' but with deep concentration, faltering a little on his feet at first as if searching to find himself within the steps and the rhythm of the music. Andrew watched him, mesmerised. He had never seen his father dance and it warmed his heart to see him, to feel the manliness, courage, and fierce pride shining out of his movements. If only he could move like that. Sinuous as a snake. And Costas had a lame leg too!

Then Costas beckoned and took Andrew through the steps.

'They used to call the *rebetes* 'dervishes' said Costas, 'because the Dervish used to have monasteries called the '*tekke*' where they lived. And this dance reminds me of the way the Whirling Dervish dance, spiralling around and going deeper and deeper within themselves. They represent the planets in the sky they say, the spinning planets around the sun. In their dance they reflect the whole mystery of creation. And spinning round and round they are totally still within, spinning on their own axis.'

'That's what Anna said. She said it was like the earth spinning on its own axis.'

'And so it is. Come, first let's dance a *hasapako* together as best we can. Remember I'm not much use at this stuff anymore.'

'Why Father, you dance so movingly.'

'E, well…I did once. Long ago.'

Later in the privacy of his own room, Andrew played the records again and rising to his feet began to dance silently. He began by moving in the traditional four square pattern about an imaginary centre, moving further and further within it, knees bent, arms outstretched, letting the music flow through him, moving his limbs as the mood took him. He felt tears streaming down his cheeks as he circled downwards towards the floor, crouching like some wounded animal upon his haunches, yearning to curl within this small space like a child returning to the womb. But an impulse of life made him begin to rise out of this small, confined, lowly place, move upwards slowly, his arms out-flung once more, fingers snapping to the rhythm, snapping at life and it's monstrous inconsistencies, snapping at danger, at the very Gods themselves who thought they had him by the scruff of his neck. He felt as if he could soar away now, an eagle like Anna.

'Son of the Eagle'! Strangely, it was through this dance that he understood her as he had never done before. He had to admit, his love had been based on youthful lust. What did he really know of her strange, dark, complex soul?

Andrew felt closer to his father after this evening, closer to understanding the uninhibited individualism of the Greek nature. His pain seemed to lift from him and he felt lighter in his spirit. Music indeed hath charms to soothe the savage breast.

As he came and sat down to breakfast one morning, Soula the maid brought him a letter on a silver dish.

Costas, glancing at it said, 'That is your mother's writing, I swear.'

'It is mother!' exclaimed Andrew and began to tear it open while Costas watched him with avid eyes.

Marika put down her coffee cup and stared at the two men. Andrew's eyes were shining with joy; Costas was unashamedly bending over, trying to read the letter sideways.

These two men and that wretched Englishwoman! It was Costas that infuriated her most because she felt that he still loved that woman whom he hadn't seen in all these years and even then had known so briefly. Hadn't *she* been his true churched wife all these six years, put up with his moods and his ailments and the fact that he was no longer the good-looking fellow of his youth? He thought he was still such a great lover too!

And now this son of his had arrived from nowhere and cheated her of her money as well. She would take him to every court in the country; there was no way he was taking her money from her. They were so wrapped up in one another of late, father and son, nobody paid her any attention at all and she was fed up about it.

At least Andrew had lost that frightful whore of his and no longer went to that hovel in the Old Town. He could have brought such trouble upon them mixing with those guttersnipes, those jailbirds from Smyrna.

She arose from the table and flung down her napkin. The men paid her no heed at all. She went out of the room, her heart dark and plotting.

It had been good to hear from his mother who assured him that she didn't blame him and apologised on her own part for having denied telling him about his father. Ethan had now told her, she said, that Takis was still alive and she had been deeply shocked for a while. But it had cleared up something for her too. She felt so much better knowing that Andrew had found his father and was happily united with him, more than happy that Takis was in good health –.she hoped he was anyway! The missing letters he had sent to Downlands were a total mystery, she preferred not to think about it and nothing could be done about it all now. Their love affair, she said, was like something out of a Thomas Hardy novel, full of missed appointments and opportunities. It was all in the past and at last she felt she was ready to let go of it.

'Thank you, my dear son, for having the courage to go on this search of yours, this amazing Odyssey to find out about your father. You have helped me make my peace with the past and feel ready to face what is left of the future. Your grandmother sends you her love and hopes you'll come back some time to visit her. She thinks she is frail and will go before you come but I assure you, she isn't, she is as tough as can be and always has been.

Ethan though is not very well these days and he does worry me. But we all take care of him and as you know, the dear man is never complaining. He is so good.

Give my love to your father and tell him that he has never been forgotten and never will be. Besides you, he was the best thing that ever happened to me.'

Costas read these words and wiped the tears from his eyes.

'My Dorothy,' he murmured, 'my beautiful angel! You too, never forgotten, *chrysi mou!'*

Chapter 24

Marika was in a bad mood all day. The two men felt the weight of her seething anger hovering in the house like some miasmic cloud and their spirits were weighed down by it. They went out in the morning and took themselves off to the warehouse to catalogue some recently acquired items that Costas intended to sell in the auction house. Then they enjoyed a peaceful ouzo and a light fish lunch together in a little *psarotaverna* by the seashore.

At dinner that evening Marika continued her heavy silence and the two men looked at one another and shrugged. Conversation flagged in this atmosphere.

'That was a lovely meal, Marika.'

Silence.

'The wine is very good. Is it the one I brought over recently from Istanbul?'

Silence.

'What is it, *poulaki mou*,' asked Costas in a mild tone, 'what's eating you today, my dear?'

'What is it, *poulaki mou*, what is it?' echoed Marika in a jeering tone, 'you know perfectly well what it is you wretched old hypocrite, you old goat! You still think of yourself as a smart, young fellow with your beloved Dorothy...that's what's wrong. Didn't I see you drooling over her letter?'

'In God's name, you stupid woman, I have a heart haven't I? Of course, seeing her letter brought back memories. Sweet memories. I can't make them disappear to please you, you heartless bitch! Do I ever ask you about the days when you weep over the photos of your first husband? Do I fly into a jealous rage or keep silent as the grave?'

'She was never your *wife*, though, was she? She was an English tart and you know it!' screamed Marika.

Andrew saw the fire rise in his father's eye and decided it was time to disappear and leave them to battle the matter out between them. As he went upstairs to his room, he heard the voices rising and falling, the insults thrown back and forth like armies lobbing shells at each other. He shook his head and wondered what on earth these two were doing together. How could they bear one another?

He put on a record to drown out the noise, which was now accompanied by the inevitable sound of splintering glass or shattering plates. It must cost these Greeks a fortune, their mania for smashing up crockery! The servants, like himself kept to their quarters when master and mistress began a row. Everybody fled the battlefield. He laughed a little, amused by the madness of it but also angry that his father was dogged by this woman's jealousy and irrationality. Still, it was his choice.

He went to his door and leant against it smoking a cigarette, listening half amused to the yelling which by now had reached an unusual pitch of fury. At this point Marika fled the dining room and ran up the stairs as if the hounds of hell were following her. She came to the landing and stopped to lean over the banisters and see if Costas was following her, as he would normally have done. But he did not. She seemed to pause irresolute and shaken.

Seeing Andrew, who was watching her coolly from his room, she turned upon him and shouted, 'And you, you filthy bastard… you love to listen, don't you? Shall I fix a window in your room so you can watch us screwing too!'

And she flung herself into her bedroom and turned the key in the lock.

'So I'm a bastard today, am I?' mused Andrew, 'yes, as far as you are concerned I am father's love child and you'll always remind me of it, won't you, dear Marika?'

All fell silent now in the house and Andrew returned to his room and began to write some letters and lay on the bed smoking and listening to his records. He heard his father come upstairs after a while and try the door of the conjugal bedroom but Marika still had it locked fast. Andrew listened, wondering if he meant to break the door down or something equally dramatic, but he heard the sound of his father's carpet slippers shuffling back downstairs again. There was not a sound from Marika. This was not quite the usual turn of events and strangely Andrew felt troubled. Their mad making up was all a part of the game as a rule but it seemed that tonight they had insulted each other more deeply than ever before.

After a while, the oppressive silence bothered him. He came forth and went downstairs. He found his father asleep on the large sofa, looking old and tired, an arm trailing on the floor. Andrew looked at him and felt for the man. He felt a wave of love for him.

Returning to his room, he found a spare blanket and went down again and covered Costas with it. Shutting the dining room door, he came slowly and quietly up the stairs. He then saw Marika in the same pose he had himself adopted earlier, standing against the door of her bedroom and smoking a cigarette. She was now in her dressing gown, her flowing black hair, loose about her shoulders. She looked at Andrew with a long, level look that disturbed him.

'So the old goat is asleep?'

'Don't insult my father, Marika. You can insult me as much as you like, but be more respectful of your husband.'

'Oh, we're the little English gentleman tonight!' she said mockingly.

They glared at each other for a few moments and then Andrew turned on his heel and went into his room. To his dismay she followed him in and shut the door behind her, leaning on it and watching him like a cat with a mouse.

'Well, my little English gentleman,' she said, 'I wonder what sort of men you are, you English – they say you are good husbands but lousy in bed. Maybe that's why your little *poustrina* decided to leave you, e? Maybe you didn't match up to her gangster in the end. Maybe your dick just wasn't good enough!'

Her coarse taunts infuriated him but he kept calm.

'Leave my room, please, Marika. I'm not my father. I don't hurl insults back. You're just not worth it.'

But she did not leave. They both stood their ground and looked at each other like two animals, watchful, twitching, angry, ready to leap at one another and rend each other to pieces.

Suddenly a seductive smile came to Marika's face. She slowly let her dressing gown fall from her, revealing her rich nakedness. Andrew felt his heart jump.

'Well, prove it then, prove that an Englishman can be as passionate and masterful as a Greek. Prove yourself! What kind of man are you – little boy! Are you little in every way?'

They advanced towards one another. Andrew tried hard to control himself. He went to seize her arm and push her out of the door as before but she laughed a delicious little laugh, evaded his grasp and circled about him, poking him with her fingers, taunting, teasing. Something snapped between them. They both came together as if pushed by a blind, uncontrollable force of lust and energy that made them both gasp with the suddenness of it. Mouths clamped together, he began to steer her towards the bed, she pulling at his shirt and buttons. They fell down together, rolled, fought, tore at each other like mad, possessed beings. Hate was in their eyes as they glared and slapped and bit and mauled. Talons ripping, beaks biting, they were eagles mating in the sky.

Forgetful of everything in this strangely ecstatic and yet demented moment, they both shouted and swore at each other in their own language. The door to the bedroom was flung open and yet blindly, heedlessly Andrew thumped into the woman below him all his anguish and pain over Anna; she, tearing at him with her nails, rent upon him all her jealous fury over Costas.

'What the hell . . .!' Costas's agonised voice rose over their cries at last and the two fell apart, panting and wild-eyed.

Andrew seemed to be looking at the world through a film of red. But suddenly it cleared and he came to his senses. His father stood stupefied as if at a scene of utter madness, which indeed it was.

446

Marika lay panting on the bed and stared back at Costas insolently. He seized her and dragged her from it. As he pulled her towards the door, he stopped, looked at his son and said in a terrible voice.

'Get out of my house! I want you out of here.'

Marika turned her head and looked at Andrew. A slow smile of unutterable triumph spread over her face.

Andrew was violently sick in the toilet. He, drank some water, washed himself of the still bleeding wounds Marika's sharp nails had inflicted upon his face and shoulders and hastily went back to his room and began to fling on his clothes. He could hear his father beating Marika from here and her screams were horrifying. He felt sick again to the depths of his being. Sick of their relationship, sick of his betrayal and above all sick that Marika had connived all this. She obviously felt a beating from her husband was worth the gain of ridding herself of Andrew.

He flung what he could into a case, took his passport and as much money as he could find, put it in his wallet and took himself off from the house.

He wandered out and along the road. It was one in the morning. People were still around and looked at him curiously. He took a taxi and went into the city as far as the harbour, then walked to Bald Yiango's. There was nowhere else to go. He had no real friends in the city now the Manoglou family were all gone. Only Yiango remained his friend.

Yiango was just shutting up the café and looked at Andreas in amazement.

'What's happened, my boy? My God, you look ill!'

'I can't explain, Yiango! Just keep me for the night –.just tonight. I'll go tomorrow.'

'Stay as long as you want. Let me fix you a tot of *ouzaki*. That'll do you good.'

Yiango asked no more questions. Gratefully Andrew went back to his flat with him, flung his case in a corner and himself on a sofa.

He couldn't sleep. It was impossible. After tossing and turning for what seemed like hours, he rose and went out onto the little balcony and stared out over the sea. The moon was rising, full and lovely and the scene looked so tranquil and peaceful. It was almost an insult to the terrible misery in his heart. God, what sort of a creature was he? He had alienated his mother and she had thrown him from *her* house. Well, she had played her own part in that and had now forgiven him. But now, now he had betrayed his father who had been so loving, so kind to him. It was not his father's fault that Marika was a scheming, disgusting bitch! Or that his only son was so unable to control his own anger and lust that he committed such a dreadful crime in his own house with his own wife.

He would never be forgiven for this and didn't want to be. He had lost everything that was precious to him, his father, Anna, his good friends and above all his honour. What sort of *palikari* was he? The Greek men would spit on him for this. They had their honour. Even Loupas had some sort of code of honour.

He was almost glad Anna had already left him. He would have hated her to know about his shame and humiliation. He shuddered to think that his own father had seen him in an act that had hardly been human, so terrible was the sense of rage and hate between himself and Marika.

Andrew looked down at the wide pavement below. It would solve it for everyone if he threw himself over this balcony and smashed himself upon the stones below. His guilt was this vast.

Eventually sleep claimed him and he awoke later in the morning to find Yiango bending over him with a coffee in his hand.

'How are you, Andriko?'

'Terrible.' Andrew gulped down the coffee and arose after a while. He shaved his lacerated face gingerly and made himself look decent. Then he drew some cash out of his wallet and offered it to Yiango for the night's stay.

'Are you trying to insult me?' said Yiango looking offended.

'Of course not. Forgive me. Many, many thanks. You're a good friend.'

Andrew wandered down to the seashore after Yiango had gone off to open the café. He was grateful that Yiango asked him no questions but simply accepted that all he wanted was some help. He stood smoking and staring vacantly at the waves as they came rolling in towards his feet. It would be good to just walk into these waves and let Neptune claim him. But he was still young, still full of life and hope. It wasn't time for Neptune to claim a victim yet.

He knew what he must do. There was nothing left for him in Greece anymore. He had proved to himself that he was not a true Greek and that somehow he could never really belong here or understand the heart of these cruel, brilliant, generous, warm, savage people. He would go home. Like his mother before him, the old, familiar places pulled him back and his heart ached for the relative sanity of England.

Chapter 25

September 1946

Andrew stood on deck and watched the harbour drawing nearer. It was nine years since he had left this city and he had thought then that it would be impossible ever to return again.

He had left in disgrace, his life apparently in ruins. Now he felt that this had been exonerated. He too had played his part in a war, another war as fierce and destructive and dramatic as the one his parents had fought, worked and loved in. He was a hero himself, or so they said, medals in his drawer to prove it.

Dorothy joined him up on the deck and they watched the land coming closer. She leant her head on her son's shoulder. He smiled and looking down at her, put an arm about her shoulder.

'How does it feel, Mum, seeing Thessalonika again?'

She looked at the horseshoe-curved sweep of the bay and shook her head sadly.

'It was so lovely then, Andrew, the coloured houses, the minarets, the church domes and cypress trees. Now it looks all white blocks of apartments and high buildings and they seem to cover the hills for miles. It's so built up even from here. It's not the same place anymore. I don't expect it to be, of course. It's almost thirty years ago since I came here and the fire destroyed so much and the Turks and Jews have all gone. I shall look on it as a tourist might; a new city.'

'It looks different even since I was here,' he agreed, 'how time changes things.'

'*We* have changed too, haven't we, Andrew?' said Dot, looking up at her son proudly, 'we've both learnt so much.'

He gave her a little hug and they fell silent for a while.

'Do you ever regret coming here? Regret what happened?' said Andrew.

'How can I regret having such a wonderful son?' Dot said fondly, 'nor do I regret my love for Costas. Life is a story woven for us by the Fates. There is nothing we can do about it except see it for what it is – a story.'

'*A tale told by an idiot, full of sound and fury?*' said Andrew with a laugh.

'Yes, something like that.'

They disembarked and when they had been through customs, hailed a taxi and asked the driver to take them to a good hotel. Dorothy looked out upon the now unfamiliar streets feeling a little sad and nostalgic. It all looked so ordinary now, just like any other big European city. It was improved, of course, cleaner, less congested, better paved and lit. Oxen with their rumbling carts had been replaced by fuel driven horse-power. It certainly didn't smell the way it used to do! Yet a pall of sadness hung over the city. Its people had been through so much during the war years. This poor city had been well nigh decimated.

Although Metaxas had been considered a fascist he was never strictly so, rather he had a repressive, authoritarian and often brutal regime. Yet it could not be denied that he was a brave man. When Mussolini demanded that his troops occupy Greece throughout the war in order to ensure Italy's safety against a British attack, Metaxas had given them his famous reply, '*Ohi!*' ...'*Non*,' he had said, he would not agree to any such occupation. The Italians then attacked but Greece had been well prepared, one of the few countries to be in readiness for the inevitable war. Metaxas himself led the smaller and weaker Greek army and routed the Italians, driving them back into Albania. There was rejoicing everywhere. But as Hitler began his terrible advance through Europe things became very dangerous and Greece was obliged to ask the Allies to send some troops to help them. Andrew had joined the RAF by then and was working as a wireless and teleprinter operator, decoding and sending messages. Along with his unit, he had returned in 1940 to Athens and during this time looked up his old friends, the Limbourides.

'I've sent Despina and the two children to Alexandria to stay with her aunt there,' Dimitris had told him. 'Everything is moving too fast. My feeling is the Germans are advancing on us swiftly. Will the British hold out do you think? '

'Hard to say. There aren't really enough troops. But we'll do our best not to let Greece down. We managed it before with just a few troops, didn't we?'

'You did, but this is quite a different war. Hitler knows what he is doing and has planned it all thoroughly; he's not a bumbler like the Kaiser,' Dimitris said, 'but all we can do is pray and be ready to fight.'

He looked sadly into his brandy glass and swirled the liquid around, 'You know, I do miss my little Despina – I *miss* her. All I can do is pray we can hold the Germans back. I mean really pray. Me that never went near a church in my life! Tell me, have you heard from your father, Andreas?'

Andrew sighed, 'Things ended rather badly there, I'm afraid. That's why I returned to England.'

'That's a shame. You found him and then lost him, eh? What was the quarrel about?'

'I can't really talk about it.'

'Okay, I can take a hint. By the way, I heard his wife had left him – she's here in Athens now really living it up. Despina says she is with another man, a younger fellow, son of some shipping magnate.'

So Marika had left Costas in the end. It was hardly a surprise. Nor was it a surprise to learn she had found someone younger and wealthier. That gold-digger! It made Andrew shudder even now to think of her. Dimitris noted his change of expression when he mentioned Marika but wisely kept his thoughts to himself.

'Have you any idea where my father is now?' Andrew asked a little diffidently.

'No, haven't heard a thing. He'll still be in Thessaloniki, I expect. As far as I know, he's still alive.'

Andrew felt sure his father would have retired to Mistres and be living in the house there. He longed to go and see him and ask his forgiveness but it was impossible in the present situation.

In September 1941 the Germans entered Thessaloniki and began their march to Athens. Andrew was in a restaurant with Dimitris Limbourides when a car arrived and told him he had to report for duty immediately. It was time to retreat to Crete. And fast.

Luckily for Andrew, his unit was evacuated swiftly at night on a Sunderland sea plane, leaving all their kit bags and belongings behind them, even their guns, in order to be able to pack as many men into the planes as possible. They were taken from Hania on Crete to Alexandria long before the Germans made their famous parachute drop on the island. Andrew spent the rest of his war years in Egypt, operating in the desert.

Dorothy had been so glad to see her son again. He had told her pretty much the whole story, though he hadn't told her how violent the rows between Costas and Marika had really been. There had been too many secrets in this family and he wanted her to know and understand the truth but felt that this information would be too much for her. Why know everything about Costas? Let her keep loving memories of the man.

Andrew had felt sure she would be disgusted by his own behaviour but instead she surprised him by taking his part.

'Poor Costas, 'she mused,' he is such an unlucky man, isn't he? But Andrew, I don't blame you. You are young and it seems to me that this woman wanted to harm your relationship with your father. It was so evil of her to seduce you.'

'I don't mean to put the whole blame on her, Mum. She is what she is; she felt threatened, I suppose. I accept my own part in it all. I feel most ashamed of myself.'

'You're a young man and got stupidly carried away. *She* knew what she was about,' said his mother and added sadly, 'but I *do* feel for poor Costas.'

'Do you think he will ever forgive me?'

'I don't know. I don't know if he is the forgiving sort, Andrew. From all I ever knew of him he strikes me as a man who is loyal in love but also capable of keeping a grudge. He was never a man for half-measures.'

Dorothy still thought about Costas a great deal but not as before. She had put the diaries away and hadn't looked at them since Andrew had confessed that he had read them. It wasn't the same anymore. Now, she was glad the boy had read them and knew her innermost heart. It felt a special bond between them. Glad too that he had had the courage to go and find his father.

She felt that Andrew, despite his painful adventures in Greece, had experienced a catharsis and was in some strange way cleansed of his own unhappiness. There was something different, clearer, more open about him; she saw that straight away, the moment he walked in the room and hugged her on his return to England. He was a man now, not a lad any more. He had found a job at once, settled himself in a little apartment nearby in London and seemed to have dropped the intense loneliness and moodiness that had eaten at his vitals before. It was as if he had at last joined the rest of humanity.

The war broke out in September 1939 and Andrew joined up at once. Much to everyone's surprise, Reggie informed all and sundry that he was a conscientious objector and utterly refused to have anything to do with the war. He wouldn't even report it in his newspaper. So strong were his feelings that he even risked going to prison or into the coal mines and only his father's frantic string-pulling managed to secure him some harmless desk job working for a business friend of theirs. Thus Reggie spent the war quite comfortably and quietly.

'That boy is a disgrace to us,' Grandma Clarke had said. 'My son fought and died to keep that madman the Kaiser out of this country. One wonders why he bothered if it is to be left to the likes of Reggie. That boy won't lift a finger to save us from that frightful man Hitler who is ten times worse than the Kaiser, if that is at all possible.'

She was so infuriated by what she saw as Reggie's lack of patriotism and courage, she decided to change her will and leave Downlands to Andrew.

'Agnes is well off enough and I won't have Downlands sold or passed on to make Reggie rich! Andrew loves the place and will preserve it. At least he's his father's son, he's fighting for us and risking his life and limb.'

She also felt that it somehow assuaged her guilt over the way she had interfered with Dorothy's life by destroying those letters from Greece. She had never confessed to her part in this and though everyone involved suspected the culprit, nobody ever challenged her. There really didn't seem to be any point. What was done was done. It was a secret that she took with her to the grave. She died in 1944 of bronchial pneumonia and Andrew found himself her sole inheritor much to his amazement and delight. Hard to believe that Downlands was his now.

As soon as the war was over, he moved in there. The house had been badly neglected and he hired a team of young men from the village to come and help him restore it all to its former elegance. Rose was still alive and stayed on to do the cooking for him and she brought her daughters to come and help around the house.

It was when Ethan fell ill just a short while after Grandma Clarke died, that Dorothy realised how much she really loved this man. She watched over him tenderly as he lay on the bed, wasting away before her eyes and felt deep sorrow. It was painful to wonder if she had really given him the love he deserved. Half of her had been elsewhere for so many years, pining for what could never be. Now she realised with something of a shock, in fact a sense of betrayal to her dream, that she wasn't sorry not to have married Costas. He had been a part of a beautiful delusion, a time of great feeling, romance and longing. It was Ethan who was her husband and who had cared for her all these years and whose children she had borne. She smiled as she remembered the first time he had arrived at Downlands, just after Andrew had been born...

...she had been wheeling Andrew about the garden in his pram, enjoying all the loveliness of the lilacs coming into bloom when she heard a car coming down the drive. It wasn't at all familiar and she had wondered if Papa had an unexpected visitor when a familiar voice called out her name.

'Dorothy!'

There stood Ethan Willoughby.

'Ethan! What on earth are you doing here?'

He smiled and took her hands, kissing her fingers and grasping her hand in his own. She was shocked to see how thin he was, his face yellow and drawn.

'Don't be alarmed, Dot,' he said, 'I've been invalided home. I'm so disgusted by it. I could have carried on but had malaria rather badly, I'm afraid, and it has knocked me up a bit. So here I am back in dear Old Blighty!'

Her parents had taken to him at once and her mother had hinted that maybe she ought to forget the Greek fellow and stick to this man instead. Ethan's feeling for her were so obvious to everyone else. But, of course, Dorothy wouldn't hear of it, not then.

Ethan had stayed the night but made no more proposals or romantic gestures. He was his usual calm, quiet self.

'I mean to go back as soon as I can, they aren't getting rid of me that easily,' he said as he prepared to depart after lunch.

'Is that wise, Ethan?'

'I was offered a posting in Alexandria. But I want to go back to Salonika, Dot. They need doctors there so desperately and a big offensive is due soon. I must go back there and help.'

'Ethan, take care!' she said, touching his cheek briefly with her hand and looking anxious.

'Dot, I want to give myself as our men are giving themselves. What greater sacrifice is there than to lay one's life down for another?'

'You are such a good man, Ethan. You make me feel so bad. Look at me, here in comfort while you mean to go back to that hell out there. I have been so rash – got myself into trouble as they say. Yet you are not shocked, you don't upbraid me.'

'Once I would have been very shocked, Dot. But being amongst all that carnage and these life and death situations gets a man's ideas in perspective. All that moralistic stuff is such nonsense. God doesn't judge us by these man made rules. He is Love Itself. You loved, Dot. You loved too well. And amidst all this death you have created new life. That is the wonder of woman. She can create life. She brings forth a new generation to replace the one that has been mown down. And canny old Mother Nature has this miraculous way of producing more male children during a war. Isn't that amazing!'

'It is amazing, dear Ethan. My thoughts and prayers will be with you.'

'Will they Dot? Thanks for that. I may not come back, nor does it much matter. I'll *lie in some corner of a foreign field that is forever England* as poor old Brooke said. '

'Ethan, stop begging for sympathy!'

He laughed, 'Wicked girl...allow me a little sentiment at least.'

'It doesn't become you.'

He smiled and climbed into his car.

'Goodbye, Dot. See you again sometime.'

Maybe it was then that she realised she loved him. Not as she loved Costas. It was a far quieter and deeper thing...

Ethan lay in his bed and looked up at Dorothy as she came and sat beside him, taking his limp hand in her own strong, firm grasp. He had loved this woman from the first day they met and he loved her still. His was not a changeful nature. Their eyes met and he managed a faint smile.

'Fraid ...my time's up. Should have been up long ago if it wasn't for you,' he whispered.

'Ethan, must you go and leave me?' Dorothy said sadly.

'I'm tired, Dot ...tired. Another war ...it makes you feel what's the point of it all?'

'The children and I – aren't we the point?'

'You are the whole point of my existence. You know that.'

He fell silent and then said with some effort, 'I want to ask you a question ...needn't answer if you don't want to . . .have you ever loved me, Dot?'

She looked at him for a long time with the utmost tenderness, her eyes full of tears.

'Ethan, I have never stopped loving you. You are the best man in the world, there's nobody like you.'

He smiled and squeezed her hand a little. Fred and May, his two children, came into the room. He looked at them as they came over to the bed. May was crying quietly. He was leaving them all and there was a great pang of regret in his heart. But something in him was strong and bright. He felt sure they would all meet again somewhere, in some other time or place.

Chapter 26

Andrew made his way along to the old and derelict district near Lahadika and soon found himself at Bald Yiango's café. He had hoped against hope that it might still be there, so many other familiar sights had disappeared from view. Thus it was with a sense of relief and nostalgia that he gazed on the familiar but now rather tattered blue and white awning that flapped in the wind.

It was hard to put one's finger on it but the city was quite different. It was true that he was bound to look upon it now with the eyes of a mature man and not a lad of nineteen to whom everything had been new and exciting. He had seen so many cities, been to so many places since then. It wasn't the streets and old customary sights that had changed as much as the atmosphere. The people here had undergone a terrible occupation, slaughtered in their hundreds by the German or Bulgarian soldiers. They had known starvation and deprivation as well as violent reprisals. Refusing to be cowed, many had gone to join the partisans in the hills but they had paid the price of that. In some places whole villages had been wiped out in retribution.

Since the war however, rather than settling to peace and some kind of unity a tremendous Civil War had broken out. That strange split in the Greek character surfaced at last and the Cain and Abel of their nation had to be played out. This time it was the Communists that were the dark and evil menace that had to be expunged from the land. Fierce fighting and atrocities on both sides did little to secure a just outcome. The European war just about over, the British intervened and did their best to help the Greek Government stamp out the threat of Communism, which so alarmed every capitalist nation at that time. Andrew, however, had by now been de-mobbed and had no more taste for warfare and fighting. He had returned to his old job in the City. His only news of what was going on in Greece came from newspaper reports and the odd letter from Limbourides.

He often wondered about Anna and her brothers and how they had fared during this terrible, violent time. Where were they now, those people from his past? He felt that he might never see them again and yet a faint hope flickered in his heart that perhaps one day he would find them.

Entering the café, Andrew looked around and felt saddened by the look of neglect and weariness that seemed to be everywhere like some insidious disease. People sat hunched up over their coffees and ouzos talking in undertones and with less gesticulation than before. Faces everywhere were painfully thin and the usual excitable Greek spirit seemed to have been diluted by their suffering and misery. Would things ever cease to be in turmoil in this unhappy city?

He sat down and after a while, a young man came out of the back regions and took his order.

'Where is Yiango these days?' Andrew asked rather tentatively for one never knew what had happened to anyone. He could have died of starvation, tuberculosis, or even been murdered by one side or other of the political regime.

'Yiango? He's fine. He and his wife Frosso are doing the cooking in the back there. You know him?'

Relieved, Andrew replied, 'Yes, I knew him many years ago. If he has a minute, ask him to step out and say hello to Andreas Cassimatis.'

The young man delivered the message and in no time at all, out came Yiango, wiping his hands on his apron. He shook Andrew's hand and greeted him gladly. He seemed as enthusiastic as ever.

Looking at him, Andrew was startled. He hardly recognised the man. Yiango was a good deal thinner, his comfortable paunch of before now a hollow bag of skin and his plump face had become skeletal, lined and furrowed with worries and fears.

'Andriko! Good to see you. You made it then, you survived the war!'

'I certainly did, they weren't getting *me* that easily. And, thank God, you too have survived Yiango.'

'E, well,' said Yiango casting an uneasy look about the café and dropping his voice, 'I just stay out of it all and do my job. I survived those damned Nazis and I'm not letting a bunch of Commie hoodlums get me now. However, let's not talk about that stuff. We're used to difficult times here. I just keep my nose clean, if I can.'

He sat at the table and sent the young lad to fetch a bottle of ouzo and then clinked glasses with Andrew.

'Here's to peace and prosperity – *one* day', he said with some irony. 'Tell me about yourself, Andriko. What happened to you after you left Greece as if the Devil himself was after you. Are you ever going to tell me what went on there? – not that I don't have my suspicions and theories. Servants always have a tale to tell.'

'Oh God! I suppose they spread all sorts of gossip around,' said Andrew with a sigh.

'*Ade re paidi mou*! That's how it is; nothing stays a secret, especially in this god-forsaken place.'

Andrew outlined a little of the old story for Yiango in order to 'get the record straight' as he put it. It seemed such a foolish story now and he wondered how he had been so green, so immature. It was a lifetime ago and he another person then. Not a person he was very proud of, but he'd been young and stupid. One had to forgive oneself sometime.

Yiango looked thoughtful when the story was finished and said, 'My mother was always taken with Kyria Marika because she was a smart 'townee'. She was impressed by her clothes and educated, superior ways. But that sort of crap never fooled the old Grandma. She always thought she was a regular *kativa*, a bitch!'

'Is your *yiayia* still around, and Old Manoglou?'

'God, no. The old ones couldn't survive; there was no food for the children, let alone them. Old Manoglou had tuberculosis anyway and went in no time. Poor man, probably just as well. Grandma was a tough old thing but she soon pegged out, too. Mother is fine and my brothers and sisters managed to keep going. They sold just about everything they had; it was the only way to keep going.'

'I heard that the Nazis imported all the Greek wheat and produce for their own soldiers and left the population to starve.'

'That's the sort they were!' said Yiango bitterly. 'But, who can say they are the only evil ones? Now our own people turn against one another like wolves quarrelling over a bone. There's a truce just now but I doubt it will last. Everything is still simmering under the surface. It's a mad world!'

'It certainly is.'

'Well, we manage as best we can. I'm married now and got two little sons. How about that, eh? Yourself?'

'No', smiled Andrew, 'I've come pretty close but somehow never quite found the right girl. I'm still looking.'

Yiango looked at him and smiled a little sadly.

'Pity,' he said, 'a good wife's a real treasure. Frosso is an angel. You know, I feel for your old man at times. That Marika! What a lousy woman she turned out to be. You know she left poor old Costas, don't you? Yes, well, he still lives up in Mistres in the big house there. Are you going to go and see him?'

'I do want to go and see him. My mother is with me. She wants to see him too.'

'Your mother! The lovely English nurse. Don't give the poor old fellow a heart attack! Maybe you should send him an advance warning.'

'Yes, you're right. It might be a bit much. Besides he may not want to see either of us again.'

'I *don't* think that – I was only joking – in fact, you should go and soon, my good friend. You're in for a big surprise,' said Yiango, grinning broadly.

'What's that then?'

'Just go and see. No he'll be glad to see you, I know he will.

We men forgive each other's indiscretions, it's only women who keep up all that bad feeling and want revenge. He soon learned what a bitch that Marika was when she upped and left him. He won't hold past misdeeds against you. '

'Tell me Yiango, have you ever heard from Anna and her brothers?'

Yiango's face changed. 'Sure I did. They joined the Commies as you know and they fought bravely for the Resistance. People forget that – that the Reds, whatever their faults, helped us be free from the Nazis. Naturally they hated the Fascists. So they became a regular thorn in their flesh, blowing up bridges and all the rest of it. Anna and Sotiris were captured along with a bunch of their comrades and the Germans hanged them all in the village square as an example to the rest of us. The bastards! Savvas managed to escape and went off to Albania or somewhere. Nobody's heard of him since.'

Andrew felt his heart constrict. His beautiful Anna dead! He had half expected that it might be so but the truth was always painful and irrevocable. He sat in silence for a while. Yiango looked at him sympathetically and re-filled his glass of ouzo.

'She was a nightingale our little Anna,' he said sadly.

My first woman, thought Andrew. *No, I shall never forget her though I have had many women since and may well have many more before I settle down. But loving Anna will always be with me, just as loving Costas has always been a part of my mother.*

Yiango introduced him to his wife who was busy in the kitchen. Between them, they had now turned the old Café Aman into a regular *taverna* with the tables now covered in neat check-patterned cloths and a more wholesome and scrubbed look about the place revealed the feminine touch. The old stage with its curtained backdrop where the *rebetes* had once played their wild, sad music was now gone for good. No place for their particular sorrow anymore; the sorrow had become universal.

Yiango said if he hadn't stopped the *rebetika* music, the police would have shut the place down. Under the Metaxas regime, it became illegal to play or record anything that sounded even faintly obscene or oriental. Recording studios and equipment had been smashed up by the police and the *amanes* were heard no more in public. Now and then someone might come along and play the bouzouki and sing silly modern love songs but it wasn't the same atmosphere at all. *Rebetika* had been totally banned and flourished only in some underground or private manner waiting like seeds in a desert to sprout and flourish again when the time was right. The old *manges* had joined the partisans, died of starvation or simply become swallowed up in the new order of things. Some of the regular crooks and spivs had flourished as they had in all countries, peddling their black market goods, collaborating with the enemy for profit and surviving by sheer craftiness and entrepreneurism. Now many of them had big businesses going, taking over the huge empty spaces in commercial life left by the Jews who had been carted away in droves and fed into the maws of the gas chambers of Auschwitz.

Andrew felt sure that his old boss, Isaac and his family had all disappeared this way. It was very unlikely that they had survived. Up until lately, little had been known about the fate of the Jews but now the shocking stories were all pouring out upon a horrified world. Salonika's Jews had fared the worst, 50,000 of them taken away to the slaughter and a mere handful managing to escape or be hidden by benevolent Greeks. Ancient libraries had been despoiled, treasures stolen. The vast Jewish cemetery had been desecrated and the area was now a waste ground and Yiango said there was talk that they might hold the Trade Fair there from now on.

Dorothy was deeply shocked by it all. She too couldn't believe how much the character and population of the city had changed.

'It's not at all the place I knew and loved,' she said to herself over and over again, 'it's just not the same!'

She looked forward with some trepidation to meeting with Costas after all these years. Would he welcome her, would he find her old and changed or conversely, would she feel he was so changed as to be unrecognisable as the young and dashing captain she had once loved so passionately? Would he, like the city of Salonika, be another incarnation, another manifestation, changed and scarred by turmoils, bitterness and pain?

Despite her fears, she knew that they must meet and settle this ghostly image that still haunted them both. Whatever the result, whatever their feelings towards one another might now be, it was necessary to come full circle for their own sake as much as for that of Andrew, their son. She was prepared in her heart and soul for whatever was to be.

Chapter 27

Their arrival at Mistres caused quite a sensation. People came out of their houses to stare and call out to them. To Dorothy's surprise a few of the older villagers remembered her and shouted out affectionately,

'*Yia sas,* little English Sister!'

One woman in her late fifties came up and taking Dorothy's hand, kissed it and said, 'You saved my daughter when she was a little girl, remember? Here she is now.'

A woman of about thirty-six came up and smiled and shook hands with Dorothy.

'I have two daughters and a son of my own now,' the woman said.

Kyria Toula bustled up to them, embraced Andrew and greeted his mother shyly, 'The English nurse,' she said in wonder, 'everyone remembers about the English nurse. So good to meet you, Madame. Won't you step inside my house and have a cup of coffee?'

'Thank you, Kyria Toula, we will call later if you don't mind. We really want to go and see my father first,' explained Andrew and eventually shaking off the hands that reached out to them, the voices that greeted them, they arrived, followed by a dozen small and curious children, at the door of Costas home.

'Good grief, Mum, I didn't know you were so famous!' said Andrew with a laugh. 'They never got that excited over me.'

Dorothy was equally bemused by her reception.

The door of the house opened and Xanthi appeared, arms akimbo, attracted by the racket going on outside. She was now an ageing woman in her late sixties, looking wrinkled and skinny but still fit.

She stared at them and raised her hands and made the sign of the cross.

'*Aman, aman*! In the name of Christ and the Virgin...you are like ghosts come back!'

'Who is it, who is it, Xanthoula?' said a voice and a young girl of about eight years old appeared behind the servant, holding onto her skirts and peering round wide-eyed at the sight of strangers.

'Go to your *pappou* and call him,' said Xanthi, 'go quick!'

Andrew had never heard her so animated in his life.

She ushered them into the house and after a while the child re-appeared with Costas hastening behind her.

He stood still in the dim hallway and stared at them as if they were apparitions. The child danced round, excited and happy.

Poor Costas really did look white and shocked and Andrew wondered if it might have been kinder to have sent some warning. However, in a while his father recovered himself and asked them into the parlour.

All was as before, nothing in the furnishings had changed at all since Dorothy had first come here, not a picture moved or a rug replaced. Time had stood still in this house. In Andrew's eyes, Costas had aged considerably. Like everyone here, he was painfully thin, his hawk-like features prominent again where before he had looked plump, comfortable and prosperous. Yet to Dorothy, he looked much the same Costas she had known before for she had never seen him in that middle-aged and comfortable period of his life. Still the strong, bony face, the slender form, no longer so upright, alas!. – but still recognisable and the bright black eyes staring at her with a look of unutterable amazement.

'Is it truly you, Dorothea!' he said, 'is it truly you?'

'It's truly me, Takis.'

'But you are as beautiful as ever,' he said and took her hands in his. They gazed upon each other for a long time, the feeling between them palpable. The child, sensing something important was happening, stood still and watched them both with an intent, fascinated look. Andrew felt tears come to his eyes.

'So, you've come back at last,' murmured Costas.

'Are you glad, Takis? Glad I came?'

'How can you ask that? All these years, I've been dreaming of you. All these years your memory has been the sweetest thing in my life. It was good of Willoughby to let you come to see an old, broken man.'

'Ethan is dead now,' said Dorothy sadly.

Costas fell silent for a while.

'I am sad for you. He was a good man, a better man than myself.'

'He *was* a good man,' said Dorothy, 'but not *better* than you, Takis.'

'Have I changed very much? You see what a mess my face is, the scars on this side, see? And my leg.'

'Don't be silly. You know these things don't bother me. We've both grown older, that's all.'

'Not you – you are as ever, not a day older.'

'Why Takis, you're just being foolish. I've got grey hairs and hundreds of wrinkles.'

He laughed. 'You still are my Dorothea, still the sensible and practical one. And I the foolish dreamer!'

He turned now to Andrew who stood waiting in the background. He held out his hand and Andrew shook it and said rather diffidently, 'Do you forgive me father? '

His father shrugged his shoulders up and said arms outspread, 'What is there to forgive, for heaven's sake? You're a man now, a *palikari*! We can't keep thinking of the crazy things we've done in our youth. I wouldn't even speak of the crazy things I've done in my day, they're too ridiculous!'

Andrew opened up his own arms, forgot he was half English and gave his father a huge hug. Dorothy looked on, smiling and glad and the little girl looked up at her and took the hand of the pretty lady in her own.

Xanthi was standing in the doorway looking on the scene, smiling and crossing herself repeatedly. Costas asked her to fetch them some refreshments and she went off still shaking her head and saying, '*Aman, aman*, who'd believe it!'

'And now,' said Costas, drawing the mysterious little girl towards him, 'now you too have a surprise, Andriko *mou*. Here is Nina your daughter, your own child. This is Anna's child and yours!'

Andrew looked at the little girl in astonishment. Now he looked at her closely he could see some resemblance to her mother. Had history repeated itself so amazingly? That last night he had seen Anna and made love in the very bed where he himself had been conceived, had that act of deep and solemn feeling produced this sweet little child? His heart filled with joy and he blessed Anna for leaving him this wonderful gift.

'She came back to the village and stayed here with me till she had the child, nursed her and then went back to the *andartes*. Some girl that one! You've no idea the brave acts she performed in the war. You heard that . . you heard . . .' Costas paused.

'I heard she died.'

'A brave death, she wouldn't speak a word against her comrades though the Gestapo tortured her. Believe me, they were terrible days. And still things aren't safe. I live in terror that they will come and take little Nina away ...the communists with their *paidomazoma*, they take the youngsters, boys, girls from these villages and force them to join their ranks and turn against their own families. Just like the Turks used to do to us! She is still young but I live in fear they'll take her and was thinking of going to live in Athens where things aren't a lot safer but better than up here in the North, anyway. Still, it seems that God has protected the child, sent her father to find her. You can take her back to England with you where she'll be safe.'

'I don't want to go, *pappou*!' said the child.

'You must my child, you must, for your own sake. Besides, this is your father here. You *must* go with your father.'

Andrew held out a hand but the child looked unconvinced and clung to her grandfather tightly.

'I want you both to come with me,' said Andrew. 'We have lots of room in Downlands. Xanthi can come to, if she wants.'

His father looked at him and fell silent for a while.

'I'm not sure I can go anywhere now,' he said, 'I'm not sure

– and I'm not well enough, my son, even the idea of Athens seems a struggle. But I'd have gone for Nina's sake. And Xanthi, what would she do in your country? She won't leave. This is your house here too, remember, it belongs to you still. When all this trouble is over then you may want to come back here. Who knows? You'll find me again. You have a foot in each country and always will have, won't you, my son?'

'Yes, I always will have. God willing, things will get better and little Nina will be able to visit both countries freely one day.'

'She will, she will. Things will change as they always do.'

When the time came to leave, Dorothy told Andrew that she would remain for a little while longer to care for Costas.

'It seems my destiny to care for these two men,' she said with a sad little smile, 'first Ethan, now Costas. I loved them both in their different ways. They are both wonderful men and I feel proud to have known them. Our Fred is doing fine in the Army and May has become engaged and she's happy living in London so I have no worries about them. Rose and her daughters will help you care for little Nina. I might just as well stay here awhile. I'll persuade Costas to come to England. Don't worry, he'll come in the end. He isn't well and needs taking care of but he finds it hard to leave just now. These things aren't so easy as you grow older.'

'He doesn't look well, Mum, it's good of you to stay and care for him.'

'I suspect he has tuberculosis. Perhaps with loving care he may get better.'

'There's no one more loving than you, Mum.'

'I wish that was true. Ethan is the person who has always inspired me with his selfless devotion. I always remember his saying – what's life about if it is lived only for yourself?'

After Dorothy and Costas had seen their son and granddaughter sail away on the boat for England, they returned to Mistres and shut the door of the house behind them.

Silently they stood together in the bedroom, which was virtually unchanged since they had made love in this very bed all those years ago. Xanthi had changed the sheets that morning and the sweet scent of rose petals and herbs filled the air. Their thoughts were filled with old memories, sighs, heartaches and passion, love lost, love regained.

'I never believed we would ever meet again,' said Costas, taking Dorothy's hand and kissing it, 'the Fates play such strange tricks!'

Dorothy nodded and smiled and then from her pocket she brought out the thick gold ring that she had preserved all these years.

Costas laughed and taking it, he slipped it on her hand again as he had done all those years ago.

'We could still get married in Agios Dimitrios, you know,' he said playfully.

THE END

THE END

Acknowledgements

The quote from *The Corsair* by Lord Byron is taken from the 1862 edition *Poems* published by permission of Routledge, Warne and Routledge. (Now Taylor and Francis Grp. Plc.)

Lines from 'Tipperary' composed by Jack Judge and Harry Williams about 1912

'A Batchelor Gay' from a recording sung in 1917 by Peter Dawson.

'Smyrna Girl' written by Makros Vamvakaris from *Songs of the Greek Underworld* by Elias Petropoulos.

If you enjoyed this story, why not leave a review on Matador, Amazon or Goodreads? Just a few lines would be most welcome.

Other Matador books by this Author available in print and ebook versions.

The Crimson Bed: A character driven love story about artists set in pre-Raphaelite Victorian London

Middle Watch: A suspenseful love story set amongst the rugged coasts and the lighthouses of England.

Dying Phoenix: A sequel to The Long Shadow.

You can visit and contact Loretta Proctor at her website: http://www.lorettaproctor.com